THIS IS
HOW IT
ENDS

THIS IS HOW IT ENDS

EVA DOLAN

RAVEN BOOKS
LONDON · OXFORD · NEW YORK · NEW DELHI · SYDNEY

Raven Books
An imprint of Bloomsbury Publishing Plc

50 Bedford Square   1385 Broadway
London   New York
WC1B 3DP   NY 10018
UK   USA

www.bloomsbury.com

BLOOMSBURY and the Diana logo are trademarks of Bloomsbury Publishing Plc

First published in Great Britain 2018

© Eva Dolan, 2018

Eva Dolan has asserted her right under the Copyright, Designs and
Patents Act, 1988, to be identified as author of this work.

British Library Cataloguing-in-Publication Data
A catalogue record for this book is available from the British Library.

ISBN: HB: 978-1-4088-8664-9
        TPB: 978-1-4088-8665-6
        ePub: 978-1-4088-8662-5

2 4 6 8 10 9 7 5 3 1

Typeset by Integra Software Services Pvt. Ltd.
Printed and bound in Great Britain by CPI Group (UK) Ltd, Croydon CR0 4YY

MIX
Paper from
responsible sources
FSC® C020471

To find out more about our authors and books visit www.bloomsbury.com. Here you
will find extracts, author interviews, details of forthcoming events and the option to sign
up for our newsletters.

THIS IS HOW IT BEGINS

Ella

Now – 6th March

This had been a happy home once.

You could see it in the scatter of light patches on the walls where photographs of a large and loving family had hung. In the placement of the his-and-hers armchairs, positioned close enough that they could reach out and hold hands as they watched television. They'd done that for over forty years. A whole lifetime together passed in relative contentment.

But all Ella could remember were the final weeks of acrimony, the fights she'd witnessed, unwillingly and uncomfortably. Him wanting to take the money and run. Her insisting they stay until the bitter end, even if it ruined them, looking to Ella for support because she was the authority they had all been deferring to for months. Despite her youth and the fact that they hardly knew her.

There she'd sat, at the small melamine table underneath the broad, condensated window that overlooked the Thames, a not-so-neutral observer as they tore chunks out of each other. She'd decided to play the peacekeeper, because by that point damage limitation was the best she could offer the couple.

Now they were gone, off to a new flat in a town by the sea. Rundown and dreary. Family nearby but their friends left behind. Ella hoped they were settling in. They were a nice couple. They deserved better.

In the end, they left quickly. One of them had slipped a card under the door of the second-floor flat where Ella was technically squatting. A postcard of the shiniest new landmarks, the

Shard, the London Eye, the Millennium Bridge. What the city was becoming and what they were being pushed out for.

'Thank you for trying to help us.' That was all it said. Such a brief message it felt almost sarcastic, but Ella knew they weren't those kind of people. Just taciturn, a generation who held their emotions close. She respected that. Wished sometimes that she was tougher.

Times like now.

She forced herself to stand and walk over to the window, clung on to the sill to keep herself upright. As always her gaze was drawn to the new tower, less than thirty metres away, standing so high and so close that she felt it might topple, its splayed lines made even more precarious-looking by the severity of the balconies, each one coming to an accusatory point. But that building would not topple. It would remain long after this one was gone.

Soon the second tower would start to rise, but for now the acre of cleared land was just rubble and dust, pierced by huge splinters of steel reinforcement, bent like pipe cleaners. Nothing left of the flats, which were still occupied before Christmas. The site looked like a war zone, ripped apart and churned up. The only thing missing, its dead.

Ella shoved the window open and let the night breeze chill the flushed skin across her cheeks. The Thames was a dark slash, smeared with lights from the parade of new developments to east and west, the reflections so long in places that they almost reached the opposite bank, linking the old money of the north to this new money south.

She closed her eyes, hearing the sounds of the party she'd left behind dropping from the roof, traffic noise thrumming reassuringly and then a sudden, ill-natured shout going up from the Embankment path below. When a siren blared she opened her eyes again, saw the strobing blue of a police car speeding across Vauxhall Bridge, heading this way. She slammed the window shut and turned her back on the city.

The party noise kept coming, muffled, through the ceiling. A hundred guests. Her friends and supporters, all drinking and

2

talking and laughing. Her Kickstarter project was fully funded. The book would happen, the voices of London's lost would be heard.

Cheering and toasts, smiling faces and Prosecco in paper cups. She'd made a speech she couldn't now remember, even though she'd spent hours writing and rewriting it, polishing and memorising, knowing it would be quoted across every social-media platform, picked apart and attacked.

Now she didn't care what she'd said.

Ella looked away from the man's dead body. Dead, she thought, but didn't know, because she couldn't bring herself to touch his skin again. She could feel the places where he'd touched her. Knew they would be bruises tomorrow, perfect impressions of his fingerprints.

Overhead the music was getting louder and soon someone would realise she was gone and come looking for her. It was her night. She couldn't just disappear. Not for this long.

But there were dozens of empty flats she could be in and, in the distant, still logical part of her brain, she knew that the odds were in her favour for a while longer. This door locked, at least. Hadn't been kicked in like so many others.

Every few minutes her phone vibrated in her pocket, like a series of aftershocks, as another notification came through.

A gentle fist tapped at the door.

'It's me.' No more than a whisper.

Ella crossed the room shakily, feeling like each footstep was an impossibility until she made it, like the whole building was tilting and skewed around her. She pressed her eye to the spyhole, needing to be sure the person she heard was the one she was expecting, and with a sigh of relief that relieved almost nothing, she fumbled back the security chain and hauled Molly in, closing the door quickly behind her.

Molly looked worse for wear, bottle-black hair mussed around her face, kohl sweaty and smudged into the deep creases under her eyes. Was it a mistake to call her? Was she in any fit state to help?

3

Ella watched with trepidation as Molly walked over to the man, footsteps heavy in her biker boots, no hesitation in her stride. This wasn't the first person she'd encountered laid out in a room he had no place being, Ella thought. Except this would usually be an accidental overdose or a kicking from a debt collector gone too far.

There was an explanation on Ella's tongue, but she swallowed it. Gulped it down hard, her throat dry and closing up again as the anxiety reasserted itself.

'Who is he?' Molly asked, in a toneless voice which suggested that no answer could possibly faze her.

'I don't know,' Ella said, the last word barely audible as she felt the fear curl a fist around her windpipe.

She stumbled across the room, catching hold of the arm of a chair in time to stop herself falling. Molly was with her in a moment, easing her down. Dry, strong palms on her cheeks, eyes boring into her own, reassuring in their intensity.

'Just breathe,' she said, in her forty-a-day voice. 'You're going to be fine, sweetheart. It's not real, it's just fear. It can't kill you.'

The room blurred. Ella put her head between her knees, while Molly stroked her shoulders, talking her down the way she had so many times before. She didn't listen to the words, only the rhythm and pitch of them, until her breathing calmed again and the pattern on the sun-faded carpet between her feet resolved into sharper lines.

'It was an accident,' she said finally, forcing herself to look at him.

Ella

Then – 6th March – evening

'Ella, hi.' The man stuck his hand out for her to shake and when he didn't get an immediate response took it as an invitation to drag her into a hug. 'It's so good to see you again.'

She stiffened as his arm went around her shoulder, and patted him on the ribs. He was six inches taller than her, dressed in jeans and a plaid shirt, smelling of a long day's work not fully covered by a potent spritz of body spray.

He caught on at last and dropped his arm, stared at her with a horrified expression.

'Shit, you don't remember me, do you?' His face crumpled and he looked towards the small group of people he'd just peeled away from, as if they would vouch for him, but they were deep in conversation around the trestle table where the Prosecco was being poured.

Ella didn't recognise them either. Backers, she guessed, definitely not residents, not members of any of the local action groups either. Bloggers or press, maybe; she'd sent dozens of invites out to people she barely knew, hoping to stoke up some more buzz, spread the word.

'Manchester...' His hand turned in the air, encouraging her to finish the sentence.

'Of course, yeah,' she said, smiling a duchess smile. 'Lovely to see you again. I just have to go and check on someone, but let's chat later. Have another drink. Food's ready soon.' She pointed towards a couple of guys in black aprons sweating over a grill on the other side of the roof, the smell of burgers and falafels wafting over. 'And thanks for coming out and showing your support. It means a lot to us all.'

He started to speak again but she was already moving, heading for a circle of old milk crates they'd found in the basement this morning and carried up to the roof, the best they could do for seating on the limited budget. Molly was sitting there swaddled in a red fake-fur coat, a woman about her age but much older-looking, rolling a joint next to her. Carol was one of Molly's friends from way back. Ella had met her at a vigil last year. Afterwards, Ella took them both to the pub and listened as they shared their war stories: Greenham Common and Reclaim the Streets, road protests where they'd chained themselves to diggers, incursions into animal-testing labs.

Since then Ella had attended sit-ins and marches with Carol, drunk with her, been to her house, been taken into her trust and lost it again, and still she couldn't decide if Carol cared about everything or nothing. If protest was just a way of life she'd fallen into and now had nothing to replace it with. She was fifty-seven and had been doing this since the mid-eighties. No partner or children, just like Molly, but a network of people she considered family. And one man, in particular, she regarded as a son.

He was the reason Ella hadn't expected to see her here, why she'd not invited her.

Evidently Molly had decided to play the diplomat, take this opportunity to encourage two of her closest friends to make peace. Judging by the sour expression on Carol's face, she wasn't in a forgiving mood.

As Ella approached them, Carol lit her joint, took a quick drag and held it out to her, giving her a challenging look. Daring her to reject the deliberately inappropriate olive branch.

'You know Ella doesn't.' Molly plucked the joint from between Carol's fingers. 'She's a good girl, aren't you, sweetheart?'

'It makes me paranoid.' She drew up a crate. 'And I'm already nervous as hell about giving this speech.'

'Just tell them what you think they want to hear,' Carol said. 'That's worked out well for you lately.'

Ella glanced at Molly, who gave her an apologetic shrug then tucked her chin down into the collar of her coat. 'How many are you expecting?'

'We've got fifty people who took the patron option – they're the only ones who paid enough for an invite.' Ella warily eyed Carol, who was staring at the guests with open contempt. 'Then we sent out another eighty invites to locals and some of the other people who'll be involved in the book, but you know how it is, not everyone who says they're coming comes.'

'People are so unreliable these days,' Carol said coldly.

Ella scanned the crowd, perhaps sixty strong now and mingling well. She spotted Derek from 309 talking to a young reporter from the local paper. No sign of the other remaining residents she'd invited but it was still early. They were the people she needed to be here. Human stories commanded column inches and, while Derek would happily talk even the most patient reporter's ear off, one man wasn't enough.

She recognised a couple from the local residents' association, waved at the man when she caught his eye. They'd cornered a freelance journalist and were, no doubt, explaining how the homeless shelter they both volunteered at was currently fighting closure. They'd get their coverage, Ella thought. They were young, photogenic and fiercely committed, just the kind of people she'd wanted involved. He was doing a series of shorts for the book, putting regulars at the shelter to the Proust questionnaire. She was contributing a piece about the shutting down of historical gay bars in the area.

'What's all this lot cost?' Carol asked.

'We managed most of it with volunteers and donations,' Ella said, knowing why Carol disapproved. 'Nothing's come out of the main fund.'

She could have asked who paid to get Carol to Sizewell B all those years ago, who bought her bolt croppers and the fabric for her banners, but she wanted tonight to go well so she changed the subject.

'How are things going with your community centre?' she asked.

Carol grunted. 'Developers are saying they "no longer have the requisite funds" to build it. It's a hundred and fifty grand, for fuck's sake. They think we're idiots. It was a condition of their planning permission and the council are doing nothing to force them to comply.'

Ella nodded, half listening as Molly started questioning Carol on the details, avenues she might go down and people who could help.

Two guys came over and sat on the crates opposite her, started tucking into their burgers and talking animatedly about an exhibition they'd just come from at the Damien Hirst gallery on Newport Street. No sense of irony, Ella thought. Happy to spend an evening going from one site of gentrification to an event trying to help the very people pushed out by the process. Still, they'd have a copy of the book when it was finished, could put it on their coffee table next to the gallery catalogues they'd collected and enjoy the playful juxtaposition.

Behind them the Rise 1 tower thrust arrogantly into the night sky and she noticed a lone figure on one of the balconies, watching this party. It must look like a sad gathering from so high up, a celebration for a non-victory, because this building would come down and a bigger, shinier one would go up in its place. They were causing the owners only minimal disruption with their refusal to take the offers that kept coming in, upped by a couple of thousand pounds a time. While the real estate itself increased at a much faster rate. Even in this economic climate.

The words of her speech, which she was running through in her head once again, sounded hollow and naïve. This crowd would cheer, they would raise their glasses in drunken defiance, but tomorrow morning the same choice would be facing Molly and others: go now or go later.

She looked at Molly, bent double with laughter, and knew she must realise that too. Every fight she'd taken on had been lost – roads got built, power went nuclear and women were no safer on the streets – because the system was too huge to fight and it had stopped allowing the little people their small victories, because even the stingiest concessions led them to believe they deserved better and that belief was too dangerous to be tolerated.

'If you give them an inch, they'll take a mile.' One of her father's favourite sayings, now seemingly a global policy.

Ella shook her head, told herself not to think like that.

People were still fighting and, one thing she knew for certain, fought all the harder when their backs were against the wall.

More guests had arrived during the last half hour and, without her noticing, the background chatter had become a babble. She saw the man who had approached her earlier talking to a young woman who exhaled her e-cigarette vapour into his face, watched him wave it away, refusing to read the signal she was giving. The man went to fetch two bottles of beer and by the time he turned back to her the woman had joined another group, obviously friends because they circled her protectively.

Molly elbowed Ella, holding out a bottle of bourbon she'd brought from her flat. 'For your nerves.'

'Do I look that scared?' she asked, trying to make a joke of it.

'Only because I know you.'

Ella took a small mouthful and forced herself to swallow. She wasn't a big drinker, especially neat spirits. But it started some warmth spreading through her chest and into her belly and the second go wasn't quite as unpleasant.

'We'll corrupt you yet,' Carol said humourlessly.

They passed the bottle around between them and Carol rolled another joint, the smoke diesel-smelling and heady when she blew it out. Ella was sure she was aiming it in her direction on purpose, as if she could get her high like that. They thought she was a puritan and Ella wouldn't correct them. They didn't need to know how much she'd smoked at university, how she'd bought weed rather than food during most of her first year, blasted through it alone, because nobody seemed to want to be around her at Trinity, not her housemates, or her classmates; not even the couple of other girls who'd come from her old school,

9

bringing the childish barbs and gossip and the nicknames along with them.

If they could see her now, she thought, watching the crowd begin to coalesce at the centre of the roof between the drinks and food, as if they knew the evening was reaching its purpose.

The alcohol had silenced the negative voice at the back of her head, the one that had been dogging her all day, reminding her how bad she was at public speaking. She would not forget her lines. She'd been through the speech two dozen times; it was seared on her brain. This was important, it was the right thing, it was what people wanted from Ella Riordan.

'Now?' she asked Molly.

'If you're ready.'

'I am.'

Molly and Carol shoved a few crates together, placed one on top to create a platform.

A police helicopter passed overhead and Carol paused to shout at it, raising her fist with the joint between her fingers. A few other people followed her example and a bottle went sailing over the edge of the roof, missing the helicopter by thirty metres or more, but it got a cheer and something shifted in the air, a new edge of menace creeping through the crowd, a chaotic ripple that momentarily stopped her from taking the makeshift stage.

The small, scared voice inside her wondered if they might turn on her next.

'Come on, sweetheart,' Molly whispered, holding her by the elbow. 'You've worked hard for this, enjoy your moment.'

The crates wobbled slightly as she stepped up on to them, but she kept her footing.

'Everyone!' Molly shouted. 'Your attention, please.'

Molly

Now – 6th March

I can't stop staring at him, there on the floor, his legs bent like he's flying, arms thrown out at his sides. And his head. His head tilted at a bad angle on the ugly marble-effect hearth, eyes open, mouth slack, staring right back at me.

If I keep looking, he's going to blink and groan and roll on to his side and this problem will go away.

Ella is mumbling to herself, her face in her hands, and I think she might be praying. These are the situations where even the staunchest atheists turn to God.

There's almost no blood on the green-veined tiles. Whatever happened, happened quick. I can see him falling, off balance, his skull striking the fireplace with a single hard crack; dead in an instant. Like those street fights that go from a scuffle to murder in a moment.

'It was an accident,' Ella says from behind her hands.

She keeps saying it.

'I know.'

I don't know. All I have are the bald facts of him and her in this room and the dizzying feeling of being shunted into someone else's bad night.

'Maybe he's okay.' Ella blinks above her fingertips, bloodshot eyes so hopeful I feel my heart clench. 'He might just be unconscious.'

'Haven't you checked?'

'I couldn't.' She shakes her head. 'I'm sorry.'

I'm sobering up by the second, adrenaline clearing my head, but I'm shaking as I walk across the room and I feel my stomach lurch when I squat next to him. I brace my arm against the fireplace and ride out a sudden swell of nausea that sends bile rushing up into my throat.

He's going to flinch when I touch him. He's going to snap to life and ask what the hell I think I'm doing.

Slowly, I reach out and press my fingertips into his neck. His skin is cool and rough with stubble as I look for a pulse I know I won't find. I hold my breath and hear my own pulse beating in my ears, waiting for him to come ticking along with me.

And now I'm praying too, silently but fervently.

A weak flutter will do, faint as a moth's wings.

'Come on,' I whisper.

I can smell the detergent from his clothes, mingling with the metallic scent of his blood. It's matted in the weave of his grey beanie, drying already, and I wonder how long Ella has been in here with him. I wonder why she called me instead of an ambulance, but some part of me is glad that she did. I'm the first person she thought of, the one she trusts to get her through this.

'He's dead, isn't he?' she asks timidly.

I nod and she starts to cry, small sobs, becoming fuller.

'Oh, God. What have I done?' She covers her face with her hands and lets out a soft howl which cuts through me. 'Oh, God, I'm sorry. I'm so sorry.'

My legs refuse to straighten but I reach for her hand as I sit awkwardly on the low hearth and she grabs it like a drowning woman thrown a rope. She squeezes my fingers so hard that my rings dig into my bones. I can feel her pulse beating too fast, how cold she is and how her skin slowly warms to the same temperature as mine as we sit there. Minutes pass and I try to say soothing things, but I don't think she hears me.

She keeps apologising – to me or him, I'm not sure.

She keeps saying it was an accident, like that will stop it being real.

Like it will make it true.

I push the unwelcome thought aside. Of course it was an accident. Ella is a peaceful girl, too small and too smart for violence.

He'll have had a fit or a stroke, the result of some obscure hidden condition, the kind that occasionally cuts down the young without warning. Or he'll have taken something that got the better of his system.

Either way, a stumble, an unlucky fall against the tiles. An accident, just like Ella says.

'Have you called anyone?' I ask finally.

'You,' she says.

'An ambulance?' I suggest. 'The police?'

'No, not yet.' Her fingers relax around mine slightly. 'I needed a few minutes to calm down before I did that.'

It's been more than a few minutes. Maybe fifteen since she called me. And a while before that too, judging by the lack of heat in his skin and the drying of his blood. I'm hardly an expert, but even I can see this scene isn't exactly fresh. Why has she waited all this time? It could just be shock but if she didn't know whether he was dead or alive why didn't she call an ambulance? Come back up to the roof and shout for a doctor or someone with first-aid experience?

Why did she do nothing to save him?

Unease creeps up my spine.

'Do you know who he is, Ella?'

'I've never seen him before.'

'Was he at the party?'

'I don't know. I don't think so.' She bites her lip. 'Maybe he came with someone else. Did you see him up there?'

He looks like half a dozen different men I've spoken to tonight and I find it difficult to believe that he wasn't one of them. We've had every kind of weirdo in the building since it began to empty out, the opportunists and the oddballs. But he doesn't look that sort. His clothes are new and clean, and even with the heavy beard hiding much of his face, I can see he isn't going hungry. I doubt he's sleeping rough either.

13

He looks like a man who'll be expected home tonight or at work tomorrow.

Right now his friends on the roof might be wondering where he's got to. If he's pulled.

'What were you two doing in here?' I ask.

Ella looks at me, stunned, like she's forgotten I'm in the room.

'He dragged me in here.' She drops her gaze. 'He was in the stairwell. I don't know if he was waiting for me or if I was just the first person who came down.'

'The first woman,' I say, anger starting to beat through my bones. 'Is that what you mean?'

Ella pushes her sleeve up to her elbow, showing me the marks his broad hands have left on her pale skin. 'It all happened so fast.'

The room seems to shift around me as I reappraise his posture on the floor and her cowed body language. I read violence in the loose curl of his outflung fist and intent laced into his heavy leather boots.

I test my gut for softer feelings and find no sympathy for him there. Not any more.

Above us the sounds of the party continue. Almost midnight now and it will be winding down soon for all but the hardcore. Most of them need to be at work tomorrow morning. Early starts, demanding bosses, grinding commutes across and under the river. Tonight they can raise their fists in defiance but only for so long before the gravity of real life drops them.

Ella's phone vibrates again and she ignores it.

People will be wondering where she is, too. Soon someone will come looking for her.

Suddenly I feel very exposed. I ease my hand from Ella's grasp and go to draw the thin, unlined curtains that graze the flaking sill. I pause, looking at the windows of the new building, trying to work out if they can see into here as easily as I can see into there. The lit ones aren't the problem. It's the darkened ones that scare me … anyone could be watching; they would have a prime view of this messy drama.

Why would you turn your attention towards this crumbling eyesore, though, when the totalitarian bulk of Battersea Power Station glowers to the west and Millbank's sparkling distractions draw you east? A party boat glides by, heading towards the glittering span of Chelsea Bridge, the people on deck small shimmering figures, the white of tuxedos standing out among all the little black dresses. That's the London our neighbours are paying £1,500 per square foot to survey from their open-plan living areas, not this version.

But I still feel observed as I pull the curtains closed.

Ella has stopped crying and she sits with her head in her hands, an occasional tremor rocking her body.

A plan is forming at the back of my mind. I'm not sure if it's the sober and logical part or the bit that's still drunk and slightly stoned.

Good idea or bad idea?

Nobody could tell the difference at a time like this.

I'll only know when it's done. And not even then, because the *thing* is only the beginning. What comes afterwards will decide whether I'm right or not and I'm not sure of anything but the need to save us both. That I need to do something because Ella is falling apart and I'm not far behind her, just a few precious minutes that might make all the difference, but I'm squandering them in doubting myself. I can see her becoming smaller, giving up, and I know what she'll want to do and that she's wrong even if I'm wrong too, wanting to do the opposite.

The fear is surging along my spine now. It's pooling at the point where bone joins brain so that my head sits disconnected and I'm looking at Ella and the dead man and weighing her life and mine against his unchangeable death.

'What am I going to do?' she asks.

'What do you want to do?'

'I should call the police.'

She doesn't move for her phone.

'What are you going to tell them?'

'That he attacked me, obviously.'

15

'You don't look like you were attacked. Few bruises on your arms. Anyone could have done that.' Anger flashes behind her eyes and I press on, knowing I'm antagonising her, but she needs to understand how the police will treat her. 'You get your arm pinched, he gets his head bashed in. You're the aggressor here. The murderer.'

'It was an accident, I told you,' Ella says, her voice rising. Tears prick the corners of her eyes and she squeezes them shut. 'All I did was defend myself.'

'So, you'll be charged with manslaughter rather than murder,' I tell her, not mentioning how she's already contradicted herself. 'That's five to eight years in prison rather than ten to life. Assuming the police and the CPS believe you acted in self-defence.'

'Why wouldn't they?' she demands. 'Do you think I'm lying?'

I sit down on the arm of the chair and hug her to my side. 'All I care about right now is keeping you out of prison.'

Ella gives another low wail and stifles it with her fist.

'I'll explain,' she says, but there's no force to her words.

'They won't care.'

'It wasn't my fault.'

'Since when did that matter?' I ask, allowing myself a bitter moment's drift back into memory as I brush her shoulder with my thumb. 'He attacked you, Ella. A man like that isn't worth ruining your life over.'

Something is scratching behind the wall, furious and desperate-sounding: rats scenting fresh meat. I imagine their sharp little claws and yellow eyes, trying to break through into this room. If we leave him here, how long before he's discovered? How much of him will be left by then?

'There's a reason you called me and not the police.' Ella's shoulders stiffen and she pulls away from me, but we're face to face now and I can see my own fear reflected back at me, along with a determination that gives me hope. 'You know what needs to be done.'

She presses her mouth into a firm line, as if she's holding in a response she isn't sure of yet, and I know she's going through the same process I did. Wondering if she can be that person, if she already is.

Almost nobody comes up to this floor now. Only one flat's occupied and it's at the far end of the landing. It could be weeks or months until the smell permeates through the rest of the building and, even then, it will just be another rank odour, to go with the damp and the mould and the reek of bathrooms left uncleaned when their owners left, the kitchens where food is slowly rotting in cupboards.

He might never be found.

Not until the breakers move in and begin the methodical work of dismantling this place room by room, level by level. And I doubt the developers will let it slow their progress. His body will be quietly disappeared. Just a homeless man, they'll decide. Not worth the hassle of involving the police.

'We can't,' Ella says finally, bowing her head.

I take her chin in my hand and turn her face up into mine.

'We have to.'

Ella

Then – 6th March

'How many people left now?' Sinclair asked.

'Six,' Ella said, looking up at Castle Rise just as the reporter was doing, at all the empty windows, some whitewashed, some bare, boarded over by Callum – their handyman of last resort – with whatever he could scavenge off the building site that now separated the flats from the river. Work was beginning on the second apartment block, only footings at the moment, but Ella knew how quickly it would climb.

Sinclair took out a packet of Greek cigarettes and lit up, cupping his hands against the stiff wind blowing off the water. 'Six people, Ella; that's no kind of fighting force.'

'Are you regretting getting involved now?'

'Molly has a way of dragging people into things,' he said, with a faint smile. 'But I'm happy to help, you know that.' He took another pull of his cigarette. 'Are *you* regretting getting involved now?'

'Of course not,' Ella said. 'I'm proud of what we've made. The book's going to be brilliant and we've raised twenty thousand pounds for a homeless shelter. How can I regret that?'

He gave her a searching look. 'Did you think you were going to stop the demolition with it?'

'No. God, do you think I'm stupid?'

'That's the last thing I think you are.'

Ella felt her cheeks flush with the compliment and was glad he wasn't looking at her any more, his attention turned towards the building now.

'You might have got somewhere if it had some architectural merit,' he said. 'Not quite brutalist, not quite modernist. It's no Balfron Tower.'

Way of the world, she thought. Only the beautiful get defended. And Castle Rise was, unquestionably, ugly. Low and long and squat, built in rough, reddish-brown bricks that reminded her of public toilets in dodgy parks and shopping centres in dying cities. Flat-roofed and four storeys high, it was a toad of a building, vaguely malevolent-looking with its deep recesses and blunt turrets at the corners.

But it was the inside that mattered, she reminded herself.

People made places.

Briefly she thought of the village where she grew up, all chocolate-box cottages and Britain in Bloom plaques, an immaculate, sterile enclave.

'How was Athens?' she asked, pushing the thought aside.

'Still smouldering,' Sinclair said. 'But no one's much interested now. If the riots start again, then yeah, they'll want coverage. Otherwise … who gives a shit if the hospitals have run out of penicillin and the suicide rate's sky-rocketing? That's not sexy.'

She flicked an eyebrow up at him. 'Unlike this story.'

'You know what my editor's like – she'll print anything with a photo of a pretty girl to head it up.'

Ella gritted her teeth. He was joking because he knew it annoyed her how so much of the press had been focused on her youth and her looks. Which were nothing special but, since politics was showbusiness for ugly people, anyone even slightly more attractive than average counted as 'hot'.

Although, according to the trolls who targeted her day and night, she was 'too gross to get raped'.

No doubt Sinclair's editor had them in mind when she green-lit the profile, knowing her haters outweighed her supporters two to one and in the cut-throat world of online journalism all clicks counted as equal.

A few spots of rain hit her face.

'Shall we go up?'

They headed for the main doors and Ella punched a code into the electric keypad. As they entered, an elderly man togged up in a bright orange padded jacket was coming out.

'Hey, Derek, going to the shops?'

'Jenny fancies cream cakes. I have my orders.' He nodded towards Sinclair. 'Who's this young man? Your fella?'

'This is Martin; he's writing a piece about Castle Rise.'

'Good to meet you, sir.' Sinclair held out a hand and Derek shook it briskly. 'How long have you lived here?'

'Me and Jenny were the first couple to move in. Nineteen sixty-eight. Had our picture in the local paper getting the keys.' Wistfully he stared beyond them, to the green space in front of the building, where the grass was now churned up and the trees were reduced to stumps.

The developers had torn up the communal garden within weeks of buying the land, reminding the residents that they no longer controlled their environment.

'They'll not force us out,' Derek said, his voice low and hard. 'No matter what dirty tricks they try. We were first in, we'll be last out, even if it's in boxes.'

Sinclair was watching him intently, seeing what she had seen in the old man herself, she guessed. A strength at odds with his soft face, the kind of hard-won toughness he'd earned during a life-time driving cabs around the parts of the city where not getting tipped was the least of your worries.

'You come up and talk to us,' he said, jabbing a finger at Sinclair. 'Three-oh-nine. There's plenty we can tell you about what's gone on here.'

Derek walked away, out through the doors and into the grim morning.

'He seems determined,' Sinclair said.

'Derek's a good guy, stubborn as hell.' Ella led Sinclair into the stairwell. 'His wife's the same. She had a massive stroke about six months ago and somehow the developers got wind of it, bumped the offer by five per cent and promised them accommodation in an assisted-living facility out in Romford. They should have taken it really, I told them no one would think any less of them if they went. Given the circumstances.'

'But they're still here.'

'She wouldn't go. She could hardly speak but she made it abundantly clear she wanted to come home. She's made a bit of a recovery but the state the building's in … it's not helping.' Above them a door slammed against the wall as it was flung open. 'Thing is, her whole life's been here. She had two kids here, lost both of them. She's convinced some part of her boys is still in the flat. How could you leave thinking that?'

Ella nodded to a young woman coming quickly down the stairs, saw her eyes flick, predictably, towards Sinclair as she said hello. Ella knew the kind of smile he'd be giving the girl. He liked them young and smart enough to recognise his influence.

'She'll be at the party later, if you're hanging around,' Ella said.

'Oxford Union tonight.' He winced. 'Sorry. Don't know how I got double-booked but—'

'It's fine,' she said, hoping her disappointment didn't show. 'Way more important that you get to our future overlords than keep preaching to the choir here.'

Up to the fourth floor. Sinclair was dragging his feet as they went to the far end of the hallway, past doors kicked in, standing open on rooms that exuded the smell of mould and rot, dust hanging in the air, dead flies peppering the carpets. Some had been stripped bare, others vandalised by exiting tenants in fits of rage; a few had been left as if their owners were due to return at any moment. Those were the ones that unnerved Ella. So easy to imagine somebody coming out of the kitchen with a cup of tea, or water gushing suddenly in the bathroom, a tuneless whistle rising above it.

Ella unlocked the door of the Moores' old flat with the key she'd found after they moved.

Everything in the flat was as they'd left it, except for the photographs missing from the walls and the surfaces stripped of trinkets. They hadn't owned much. Were savers rather than consumers. Had a thirty-year-old three-piece suite, unfashionable shelves and coffee table, pot lamps with cardboard shades scorch-marked from the dusty bulbs inside.

Ella couldn't work out why they'd left so much behind. Was it simply a matter of speed, or were there too many painful memories bound up in the items? Would it be easier to start again without being reminded of this place?

She hoped they'd bought nice new things for their old age. Allowed themselves to recapture the thrill of decorating a new home they must have felt the first time around.

'It's like the *Mary Celeste*,' Sinclair said, going through into the kitchen.

'You're better than that cliché,' Ella called after him. She sat down in one of the armchairs next to the electric fire, reached to turn it on, wanting to chase the chill out of the room, and stopped herself, remembering that the power was off.

Sinclair came back, nodded towards the sofa where her sleeping bag was unfurled. 'Are you living here now?'

'I've just been here for a couple of nights. There's been a lot to do and,' she sighed, 'the developers stepped up the pressure on another tenant. I wanted to be here to help her deal with it.'

He turned the other armchair to face her. 'You wanted to stop her caving to the pressure, you mean.'

Ella felt her face harden, seeing the amusement in his eyes, hating the insinuation. Had it been a mistake to trust him? He'd promised a sympathetic profile and some positive coverage of the residents' fight, but he was a hack all the same.

Molly said never to trust the mainstream media. They were just the propaganda arm of the establishment, but that was another cliché and one Ella wouldn't live by.

The key was picking friendly journalists, watching your words, saying nothing off the record you wouldn't say on it. And, crucially, giving them nothing to pique their interest beyond the bounds of the story you were selling. Most didn't have time to go into full investigative mode. Not now. Not like back in Molly's day.

Even Martin Sinclair, with his big, sexy expense account and his non-fiction bestsellers, was working to tighter deadlines and narrower margins. He would save his splurges for stories much bigger than her and Castle Rise.

'It's been a hard winter,' she said. 'That takes the fight out of people. Do you think this was a pleasant place to spend Christmas?'

Sinclair nodded his understanding as he reached into his waxed-cotton messenger bag to take out his recording equipment. Primary and back-up, two small devices.

'What about you? Did you go home for Christmas?'

'Shall I wait until we're running to answer that?'

He shrugged, leaning towards her, placing the recorders on the arm of her chair. 'Up to you.'

'You want to hear me say it?' she asked.

A rueful look creased Sinclair's brow. 'Ella, I know what it's like to disappoint a father. Believe me. The only way my old man would think this is honest work is if I filed my copy from the bottom of a coal mine.'

'Dad doesn't talk about his work and I don't talk about mine,' she said, the lie slipping out with ease, because it wasn't entirely a lie. They didn't talk, they argued. 'We have enough in common – hiking, rugby league, craft beers – we can spend hours together without mentioning our jobs.'

'He must be proud of what you're achieving,' Sinclair said. 'Even if he doesn't agree with your politics.'

'I'm not doing this to get anyone's approval. Least of all his.'

Another semi-truth and she heard the fierceness in her voice as she delivered it, knew it made her sound defensive. Sinclair could draw whatever conclusion he liked, probably the one every journalist had. That this crusade, as they generally described it, was a rebellion against her upbringing. As if she was solely defined by her father's career in the police force.

'All I've ever wanted to do is help people,' she said. 'That's what this Kickstarter project is about. Helping people who are being forced out of their homes and economically penalised for simply living on land which now has a frankly obscene market value.'

She kept going, telling him the figures – that these flats were compulsorily purchased at prices decades behind the booming London market; £150,000 for the flat they were sitting in, and the one that would be built in its place would sell for four times as much.

'These aren't going to be new homes for London's keyworkers. They're safety deposit boxes for overseas buyers, bought with money nobody bothers to check the source of.' Ella moved forward in her chair. 'People like the Moores, and Derek and Jenny Kerr, are being economically cleansed from their homes in order to create shiny new money-laundering opportunities.'

'Can you prove that?' Sinclair asked. 'It's a strong accusation.'

'I'll send you the research,' Ella said. 'Thirty per cent of new homes in London are bought with money held in complex shell schemes where the actual buyer can't be identified.'

Sinclair put his hand up. 'But this development. Can you prove it's happening *here*?'

'I didn't say it's happening here, I said it's a city-wide problem.'

She got up and beckoned him to follow her. Led him out through the sliding doors on to a balcony.

The wind was more insistent on the fourth floor than it had been on the ground, carrying the sounds of the building site in front of them, engine thrum and radios playing, voices shouting. Heavy lorries had been coming and going all morning, working on removing a pile of rubble two storeys high; all that remained of the building that had stood there before Christmas.

'See that,' Ella pointed to the top of the new apartment block to their right, its vaguely Scandinavian cladding, the gleaming steel and acres of glass. 'The penthouse sold for one point five million over a year ago. Off-plan. The buyer never even saw it. Nobody lives there.'

'That's pretty standard,' Sinclair said, leaning against the edge of the balcony, close enough to her that their arms were pressed together. 'It doesn't mean I should put you in print accusing the developers of facilitating fraud.' He gave her one of his paternalistic looks. 'I'm just trying to keep you out of trouble, Ella.'

'Trouble's good for the cause,' she said, smiling slightly.

Sinclair didn't smile back. He turned and braced his hand against the balcony, almost enveloping her, and she thought of the last time they'd been this close. A bar in Hoxton, a mutual friend's birthday, kitschy cocktails and a klezmer band playing R&B covers on the roof terrace and then they were going downstairs, silently, him trailing her to the basement and the sudden hush of the ladies' loo where they fucked urgently in a cubicle while other women came and went and pretended they heard nothing.

'I saw that piece you wrote,' he said. 'About the death threats.'

'It's the cost of being a woman in public, right?'

'But you're okay?' he asked tentatively, his thumb brushing across her wrist. 'It's not escalated?'

'Escalated beyond the decapitation and rape threats?' A deep sigh rose up in her chest. 'None of them are brave enough to act.'

'You can't know that.'

'I'm still here, aren't I?'

She squinted into the wind, looking for the part of herself that refused to be scared, the part that had brought her this far and would see her through to the end. Some days it was there and some days it wasn't and then she had to fake it like she faked so much else. Today she felt thin and brittle, so insubstantial that a strong gust might knock her down. But she couldn't let Sinclair see that.

She straightened her spine.

'Nobody's going to silence me.'

Molly

Now – 7th March

You're supposed to wake up innocent.

When you've done something bad you're supposed to get a few seconds' grace, where the morning feels new and clean, before reality rears up and slaps you around the face.

I've never been so lucky. No morning serenity for me. Probably because I never seem to dream, not in any coherent way. It's always just been colours and sensations; I blame the acid I did. And the mushrooms and the weed and the Ecstasy I was too old for by then that I took anyway. All of that stuff and the prescription pills I'm on now, because no woman hits sixty complication-free.

This morning there's a shadow hanging over me when I come around in the fast-starting fashion I've begun every weekday with for the last five years. Ever since the builders moved in. Eight a.m. on the dot. The drilling starts. The boring. Piles being driven into the sludgy Thames-side earth because if you built anything on here without ramming in a hundred feet of reinforced concrete first, it'd fall over.

They say.

Funny, this place wasn't so carefully constructed and it's still standing after six decades. The same as me. Crumbling through ill-use and neglect but, miraculously, both of us remain.

The piling shakes the whole site. I'm sure it's the reason the fissure in the ceiling over my bed is getting wider, dusting my sheets with plaster. Before the builders rolled on to the site it was a hairline crack; now I could fit my fingers in there and wiggle them around in the void. The whole building is shifting and sliding, destabilised by the vibrations.

One day the front of the place is going to collapse. Leaving us all exposed in our flats like the world's grimmest doll's house. Most rooms abandoned and sad and the little figures inside so forlorn. We've been played with too much. We're almost broken.

Six of us left. Almost three hundred gone.

And one more resident this morning than there was last night. Lying at the bottom of the lift shaft.

Poor Ella.

She probably hates me this morning. I don't feel so great about myself, but the right thing is never the easy thing. It would have been easy to call the police and sit there, watching him cool and stiffen as we waited for them to arrive. They wouldn't have believed us. The scene was too neat, no signs of a struggle. Even if we'd staged it better, if I'd punched Ella in the face and smeared her blood on his fist, they would have concocted a narrative to make it her fault.

Because Ella Riordan is a scalp too big for any copper to lose.

It's not vanity to say I'd be a nice bonus for them as well.

When I sit up a muscle in my shoulder screams and I collapse again, waiting for the pain to ease. It feels like a tear. I've shredded something moving that huge, dead weight.

He was bigger than he looked. Solid in the way some apparently slim men are, all the muscle lean and hard rather than bulky. He must have been twelve stone, easily, maybe thirteen, and cumbersome as we manoeuvred him along the corridor towards the lift.

Ella took his legs; I didn't want her to hold his head, thought that such close proximity to the wound might tip her over the edge. She was hardly breathing as we struggled along with him. All the colour drained from her face, her eyes wide and bulging, but she kept moving and I'd never been prouder of her than I was at that moment.

Now it all feels sick and unreal to me. How we approached his body like an awkward sofa to be twisted and turned through a slightly too narrow doorway, dealt with him as if he was nothing more than a logistical challenge. I know we needed to behave that way – self-preservation, I suppose, emotional insulation against the fundamental horror of what we were doing. You have to make your enemy less than human.

You have to call him enemy rather than victim.

And at the time I had no problem doing that. He attacked Ella; he got what he deserved. And I had – still have – no qualms about helping her hide his body.

Maybe the guilt will come later.

This morning I have the fear instead. Percolating through my bloodstream, carrying the gnawing dread into every atom of my being, making me feel sick beyond my stomach, driving the sensation into my face and fingertips and sending it crawling across my scalp. I am wrapped in fear now, wearing it like a second skin.

Because he's going to be discovered, sooner or later. Even in the dead of winter in a draughty building where the condensation ices over on the inside of the windows, he'll eventually begin to smell. But there's no reason for anyone to think it was murder.

I need to keep telling myself that.

I need to construct a narrative that I believe or I'm not going to be able to function, and if I can't function then who's going to pick Ella up?

Just an accident. Another drunk, stumbling into a lift shaft in a badly lit corridor. Blame the neglect of the council or the developers, who didn't come and attend to the lift doors that were stuck half open or change the dead bulbs in the caged strip lights.

Isn't that the most perfectly credible explanation?

We'll need a story for the time Ella was away from the party, but that can wait. Today's going to be tough enough on her. I'll let her work through the worst of the shock before I bring it up. Work through it myself, too, because I'm no good to her like this, shivering under my duvet and grinding my teeth, the tension on a time delay.

How we managed to return to the party after that I'll never know. Adrenaline, I guess, and necessity. You can make your body do amazing things with that combination, they say. We smiled and laughed and made small talk with people and every now and again – too often, probably – we made eye contact with each other, wordlessly checking, desperate for reassurance that we were doing okay, and I remember how manic she looked and I must have looked the same. But the only person who might have noticed was Carol and she'd already left. Most of Ella's friends were drunk or a little high and I don't think they realised how edgy she was under the hyper attitude she'd struck to cover it up.

It bodes well for when the police come. I'm trying to take some comfort from that, because her composure is by no means a given and so much is riding on how we both react to those first tentative enquiries. I'm an old hand, of course, and Ella's been on the receiving end of their attention before. Nothing as serious as this, but she's learned the drill.

The photograph hangs on the gallery wall in my living room. Only my best shots go up there, the ones that would be called iconic; miners' wives breaching the gates at Orgreave, women linking arms around the perimeter of RAF Greenham Common, burning cars overturned during the Brixton Rising, bloodstained banners and felled police.

And Ella.

May 2016, student and faculty members out on the streets of Camden to protest against the introduction of zero-hours contracts for lecturers. After UCL and Exeter, it was one peaceful protest too far for the police, who decided to make an example of this group, stamp down hard in the hope of staving off another summer riot season. Those kids weren't going to smash up shops and nick trainers, anyone could see that. They were soft, naïve, allowed themselves to be kettled, because at heart they still believed the police existed to protect people like them.

Afterwards the Met branded Ella a ringleader, but she wasn't.

She would become one, later.

Their doing.

And mine.

I wasn't going to go along. I'd done the others, got some decent shots, sold a couple for a pittance. There was no real drama at the earlier ones and no reason to think the St Luke's sit-in would be any different. Two hours into the kettling I got a call from a lecturer I knew from way back, stuck at the centre of the sweating, increasingly agitated group, saying things were about to kick off.

Fifteen minutes after I arrived, they did. But it was no mass push. Just one young woman, small and pale with a shock of peroxide-white hair.

Ella said it was a panic attack that propelled her towards the cordon of riot shields and masked faces. That she didn't remember making her move, still didn't understand how she forced her way through them.

Mobile-phone footage surfaced after the event, showing her scrambling over the shoulders of the police, fear making her nimble. Her hand braced against a helmet, her foot came down hard on some big bastard's shoulder, and she was out. Cheers went up, one of the riot police broke formation and went after her and that was when I made my own move.

My first shot caught the moment his baton struck the back of her knee. I saw her crumple. The sunlight flashing off his shield. I kept moving closer as she lay there, too new to this to even curl up into a protective ball. She possessed just enough survival instinct to throw her arm up as he went in for another blow and I captured the instant it landed, heard the crack of bone and the howl that broke out of her.

That was what made the image compelling enough to go viral – the freezing of the precise second that Ella Riordan lost her innocence.

I saw her through that and I'll see her through this.

Gingerly I lift my throbbing shoulder from the mattress and it complains but not so much that I need to lie down again. I pull a navy fleece dressing gown on over my pyjamas, slip my feet into fur-lined boots as quickly as I can, before the cold floor can leach out any more of my body heat.

30

In the kitchen, I make a cup of coffee, think about taking it back to bed and talk myself out of it. It's too easy to hide and hope things fix themselves. They never do and time doesn't heal, it just degrades and festers and complicates. If I act like everything's normal I might be able to fool myself that it is. At the very least I can fool other people. Witnesses. Because that's what my friends and neighbours have become overnight. Witnesses to my behaviour after the fact.

And I don't think I could fool them, not today. I'm not ready yet to put on a brave and innocent face.

Maybe I could go back to bed again.

No. I go to my desk and check my emails while my coffee cools, like a normal person. A former student inviting me to a gallery show in Whitechapel next month – I RSVP, knowing I might be in no position to attend once the time comes, but he's a talented young man and I want him to feel he still has my support. There's an offer of some supply work at UEA, maternity cover, very last minute, and I turn it down even though I need the money.

Money's something I try not to think about too often, even though it's a constant and pressing need, worse now than ever before, and I was never affluent, not even during the brief double-income period of my marriage. He had his vices just like I had mine and they clashed in the most destructive way. While he wanted to buy himself happy, I wanted to give my money away and we both believed that behaviour signalled a deep-seated lack of self-esteem in the other. Once you've seen how your life partner tries to stave off their own sense of worthlessness there's no going back. Because if they don't value themselves, how can you value them?

If I'd stayed on track after the divorce, worked five days a week and all those long evenings of marking and lesson planning like my old friends did, I'd probably be comfortably off now. Mortgage-free and embracing approaching retirement, maybe with a little place in France or a long-anticipated world tour booked.

But that was never me.

31

It only took one long, rainy night around the fire at Greenham Common to make me realise how little I cared about financial security, how small and selfish an aim it was in a world with so much going wrong in it. Returning home afterwards, dirty and tired but invigorated, only to find him purring over a new lawn mower he'd bought while I was away, that was the final break. I couldn't be with a man like that.

Instead I've had thirty years of supply teaching and cover jobs, which has allowed me to focus on more important ends and has left me with a virtually worthless pension. My only income beyond that are the ever-decreasing monthly payments from the photo agency who pimp me out, and dwindling royalties from my earlier career. It was the right choice. I've never doubted that for a moment.

And I hate that he's snuck up on me right now. That old life I rejected. *Him.* Who I never think about from one year to the next, coming at me because I'm so scared that any memory is safer to linger in than the ones from last night.

I need to get out of this flat.

Stand up, move, resist the fear.

I dress in jeans and a heavy black jumper and my tatty parka, put on flat boots and fingerless gloves: camouflage-wear. Some days it feels good to be noticed but not when I'm working. Before I leave the flat I stow my laptop under a pile of old magazines, drag a box of even older books in front of it.

Since the flats started to empty out, the break-ins have increased. Opportunists too stupid to realise none of us have anything worth stealing, junkies looking for somewhere to lay low, kids who just want to smash shit up.

Every time I leave I expect to come home to devastation.

It nearly broke the Moores. By the end they weren't leaving at all. Holed up protecting their family photos and the collection of china she inherited from her mother, made paranoid by the noises this place produces at night, the sound of the wind coming through the broken windows and the doors sucked at and slammed. The voices. The laughter. The footsteps in the hallways.

He was probably one of them. The man Ella killed.

As I approach the lift, my feet slow and I find I can't walk past it.

All of the lift doors are permanently shut now, except for on the top floor. The car itself is stuck halfway between ground level and first and that's where he is, on the roof of it, lying across whatever bulky mechanisms make the thing rise and fall.

At the stairwell, I go up rather than down, to the top floor where only one resident remains and he's always out at this time of morning, taking his daily run along the river. Ella has been sleeping in another flat up here, but she went home with a friend last night.

There's nobody around to see me creep towards the open door of the lift.

The gap is less than three feet wide and I remember how we struggled with his unwieldy bulk. Ella pushed his legs through first while I took the full force of his weight. And then we shimmied him through the rest of the way, one arm each, our knees pushing into his shoulders until finally he fell.

I lean against the door and immediately step back, seeing the mess of handprints which must be ours. With the cuff of my jumper I wipe them away in circles, top to bottom, over and again. Because I know our fingerprints, if they were lifted, would contain minuscule traces of his blood.

Part of me is that logical still.

The rest, when I tentatively put my head through the gap, is not so composed.

I peer down into the darkness and think I can see his light-coloured combats. When I switch my phone to the torch app and direct it down towards his body I can't make out his face but he doesn't seem as shattered as I expected. His limbs aren't weirdly twisted; his neck appears to be straight still.

Something clangs down there and I step back swiftly. There's the sudden clenching sensation of being caught looking at something you're not supposed to see. Like shame. My cheeks flush with it.

33

I hurry back to my flat and lock the door behind me, aware that I'm breathing heavily, the torch still lit in my hand, shining on the wall of photographs, picking out the one of Ella, on her back, trying to save herself from another blow.

She can't know about this. If she finds out there's even a tiny chance he's still alive down there, she'll want to call the fire brigade and ambulance.

I kick off my boots and leave my parka where it drops on the floor, crawl into my still-warm bed and pull the covers up over my face, turning and curling into a ball.

It won't have been the light from my phone that made him stir.

There isn't enough of him left in there to think I'd come to save him.

There can't be.

Ella

Then – 1st March

There it was, predictably, a few seconds after she slipped into an empty seat near the window. The feeling of eyes on her.

Ella hated using public transport. Always had but even more so now that she'd graduated from generic female to be stared at just because to a specific, occasionally recognisable female to be photographed and tweeted/instagrammed/whatever while she sat on the bus or stood on the Tube.

She fought the urge to hunch down lower in the hard seat, not wanting to give whoever was watching her the satisfaction of knowing she felt uncomfortable.

It didn't make her feel any safer, though. So far she'd been lucky and the hate she'd faced had been contained online, aside from the odd aggressive heckler at an event. And at those there would always be someone nearby to shield her if they crossed the line from throwing insults to physical intimidation. But Ella knew it was only a matter of time before one of her critics cornered her.

And then what would she do?

Her father had raised her to stand up for herself, trained her to find an opponent's softest spots, hammer their weakness until they were laid out flat at her feet. Because he knew better than anyone how dangerous the world was for girls and he wouldn't send her into it ill-equipped.

You couldn't do that, though, not in her position. Better to be the bloodied and defiant victim than defend yourself and let your enemies paint you as the aggressor. Even if it went against all her instincts and principles.

Ella shook herself out of the thought. This was happening more often lately: she'd convince herself she was being followed or bugged or that the person trying to be her new best friend had some dark, ulterior motive. It was natural, she knew that. She'd been warned how this business twisted your perceptions and that some of the time you were actually right so it was always best to assume the worst.

You couldn't publicly slam the police without picking up more attention from them. You couldn't attack major developers and their corrupt friends in local government and expect them not to retaliate. Surveillance was a given, she'd been told. Accept it and ignore it. Unless you're meeting someone you need to protect.

Like today.

The Tube would be pulling into Tottenham Court Road station within the minute. She needed to know if she was being followed. Start to work out how best to lose them.

Ella dragged her rucksack on to her shoulder and stood up, making a quick sweep of the carriage as she started towards the doors. Four people. An elderly couple in matching trench coats. A suited young woman engrossed in a paperback and, next to her, a man in a leather bomber jacket and wool hat, hiding behind a paper. Not reading it, actively hiding behind it.

The couple gathered up their bags and umbrellas, the woman steadier on her feet than her husband, who she held under the arm, supporting him as they shuffled out of their seats. They were blocking Ella's view of the man, but they were shielding her too, and when the train stopped and the doors opened she bolted for the escalator, weaving through the sparse post-commuter crowd, running up the steps until she was stopped by a family laden down with luggage, two small boys attached to their father's wrist by springy leads, the mother with a baby in a sling across her chest.

Turning to check behind her, she saw no sign of the man and relaxed a little. She smiled at one of the boys, who looked blankly at her and began to chew on the bright orange lead that tethered him to his father.

A fine rain hit her face as she emerged on to the street and she pulled the hood of her parka over her head, rounded her shoulders and started down Charing Cross Road. She skirted slow-moving shoppers and tourists, ducking under their umbrellas to stay hidden, until she slipped into Foyles and quickly made her way to the glass lift, feeling, as the doors slid shut, that she was finally free of her unseen, possibly unreal, pursuer.

The cafe was bustling as usual. Waiting for her drink she studied the customers, wondering if the person she was expecting was here yet. She didn't know what the woman looked like and wouldn't usually go into a meeting with so little information, but Molly had introduced her and Ella trusted her ability to weed out all but the most reliable sources.

'You were here last month,' the guy behind the counter said, as he placed Ella's green tea on the tray. 'The Martin Sinclair event, right?'

She nodded. 'Are you a fan of his?'

'I don't think he goes far enough.'

Ella found a table and sat down facing the stairs, checked on her Kickstarter page for the third time today. It was getting to be a nervous tic, worse than waiting for a message from a lover, more desperate and more thrilling when she saw that someone had taken the last £200 sponsorship – the most expensive package, strictly limited to twenty donors.

They were less than £300 short now, with a week to go, and she was sure they would hit the target before the deadline. A piece she'd written about online harassment was running tomorrow and that was bound to bring a few more people out in support, even if it was only the £10 e-books.

She tried not to think about all the work still to do and the rate it was piling up at. Copy to chase, more to edit, her own introduction stubbornly refusing to sparkle on the page.

'Is anyone sitting here?'

'I'm waiting for—' She looked up and immediately scowled at the face smiling down at her. 'I'm meeting a friend.'

Dylan pulled out the seat opposite. 'I've only got an espresso; I'll be gone in a minute.'

He snatched his hat off and ran his fingers through his greying hair, straightening it into some better shape; vain as ever. She should have recognised him on the Tube, but there was no reason for him to be there, except that he was following her and why would he do that?

Suddenly the neighbouring tables felt very close and she was sure the conversations had dimmed, the people angling their bodies to listen to what would be said here. Because it must be obvious, the thrum between them, the strings tying them together, knotted tighter than she could stand.

Ella sipped her tea, eyeing him across the rim of the cup, but he was concentrating on sugaring his coffee, looking around the cafe, like any normal person awkwardly sharing a table with a stranger.

Her contact was already running late, could be here any moment. Ella refused to let Dylan encroach on that. Knew exactly how he would behave, the charm bordering on obsequiousness he always pulled out for women. Women other than her.

'You've been ignoring me,' he said finally, leaning across the table in a pose that would look like fascination from a distance, until you got close enough to see the anger in his eyes and the hardness around his mouth.

'I've been busy.' She glanced up from her phone. 'You can't expect me to come running whenever it suits you.'

'I understand how important your "work" is, Ella.' Under the table his knee struck hers and she drew back sharply. 'But it's no excuse for leaving me hanging around waiting for you when you've got no intention of showing up.'

'Pretty sure I texted you,' she said, trying to lighten her tone.

'Who are you meeting?' Dylan asked, fingers steepled around his cup. Those fingers, which had twisted her hair and stroked her throat, dipped inside her and teased and kneaded and come out glistening to smear the taste of her across her open mouth.

He grinned at her, like he'd seen the images in her eyes. He was too good at this, could always read her.

'Just a friend,' she said.

'A "friend"?' His brows went up. 'A work friend or a personal friend?'

She knew where this was going.

'Work.'

'Well, you'd better call them and cancel.' He threw back his espresso, swiped his mobile off the table as he stood up and gave her the barest nod before he walked away, cutting confidently through the tables, moving aside with a smile to let a woman pass with a precariously loaded tray.

Ella watched him until he disappeared, knowing how perkily he would go down the stairs, how obscenely satisfied he must be with himself right now. She took a deep breath and blew it out slowly, aiming for some small pool of calm. Then she saw it, peeking out from under his cup and saucer.

A slip of paper folded around a plastic keycard, a room number written on it. She saw the name of the hotel on the card and recognised it as one he'd taken her to before. A place he reserved for the times he sensed her dedication wavering. Last summer: an afternoon of sweltering sex and cooling showers and circular conversation, which turned into an argument, then a full-blown fight.

If she could have ended it that day she would have.

There was no walking away from him, though.

Ella tapped out a quick apology as she left Foyles, certain she would be able to draw the woman back into conversation. She hadn't seemed particularly skittish, not like some of the people Ella dealt with, and Ella's excuse had been a good one. If there was one thing she'd learned from Dylan, it was the art of lying to women.

She felt exposed as she turned on to Moor Street; too many people hanging around, eyeing everything, smokers outside the pubs and cafes, a taxi idling in front of the hotel's discreet black entrance. More people in the courtyard when she went in, a man drinking a smoothie under the canopy, a woman vaping with her face turned to the sky, staring up at the glass walkways and wood cladding and all of that polished steel.

The room was on the second floor and Ella ran quickly up the spiral staircase, her fingers gliding through the raindrops beading the handrail, feeling her anger already becoming arousal and then anger again, at herself, for letting him manipulate her like this.

He was naked when she opened the door, didn't even flinch, and she knew what he was doing, making this about sex so she wouldn't challenge his behaviour. She resolved not to fall for it this time, even if her body was already reacting.

'That was an important meeting you just wrecked,' she said.

'Another journalist?' he asked. 'Keeping your profile up?'

Ella glared at him. 'Actually she's a librarian.'

Dylan turned away from her, opened the bottle of water on the table and drank from it long enough to signal his complete disinterest in what she was saying.

'She's organising a direct action against the company who won the contract for her borough. The library staff are all being laid off, so she's looking to do something pretty serious,' Ella said, the colour rising in her cheeks as he kept his back to her. Disinterest beginning to feel more like disdain and she couldn't stop herself explaining, hearing the excitement infecting her voice, wanting him to feel it too. 'She's been heavily involved in animal rights for years, so she's capable of anything. This could be big.'

'Big enough to justify ignoring me?' His voice remained even, but she saw the tension tightening his shoulders and the way he planted his feet wide on the blackwood floor. There was something more going on, though, she thought. A slight moue, a twitchiness about him that she rarely saw.

Was this what it looked like when Dylan's feelings were bruised?

Ella knew she'd been neglecting him but she thought they'd reached an agreement. A tacit understanding that things were different now and he couldn't just click his fingers and have her snap to attention for him.

'Is that why you were following me?' she asked, more curious than angry. 'Because I've been ignoring you?'

'I wasn't following you.' He shrugged, a faint hint of embarrassment on his face. 'You were leaving the house as I got there and I decided to see how long it'd take you to spot me.'

'I spotted you on the Tube.'

He smiled slightly. 'No, I don't think you did.'

'I could feel you watching me.'

'And it felt good?' he asked, the smile becoming deeper and dirtier.

'Creepy, actually.'

'I always know when you're lying, Ella.' He crossed the tiny room in two steps and slipped her coat off her shoulders. 'Don't pretend you didn't like it.'

Ella could feel the heat coming off him, sensed the desperation too. It had been a month or more since she'd seen him last. The longest they'd gone without meeting and she realised she was desperate as well. There had been other men in between, but not like him.

'You know what I was thinking, while I was looking at you?' He unbuttoned her denim shirtdress and Ella watched his fingers working, wanting to bite them. 'I was thinking about everything I was going to do to you once I'd got you here.'

'And what are you going to do?'

Dylan described it all as he slowly stripped her, and Ella let go of the anger she'd walked in with and the old annoyances that had kept her away from him for so long.

She stumbled as he tried to unroll her thick, black tights, fell backwards on to the bed and he was on her instantly, pulling them the rest of the way down, laughing at the size of her sensible knickers and batting away her offer to leave if they weren't sexy enough for him. Then he flipped her over and there was no more laughter.

He pinned her down and slipped into her, but not all the way before he pulled out, while she shouted at him to just fuck her. Deeper and slower and he pulled out again, as she gripped the pillows and arched her back where his mouth grazed her skin.

Five times, six, and she was raging and aching, wanting to get on top and finish this, but she couldn't move from under him. She pressed her face into the mattress, cursing him and moaning, as he whispered in her ear, telling her no other man could make her feel like he did, no one would ever fuck her like this. Would they? Would they, Ella?

'Nobody knows you like I do.'

She came, bucking and gasping, and for a few seconds there was nothing but the white noise of her orgasm and the starched cotton rough under her open mouth as her breath slowed again. He slapped her thigh and climbed off her, headed straight for the shower.

Ella snagged his T-shirt from the floor and dried herself with it. The self-loathing a distant note but already humming as she listened to the shower running and a vacuum cleaner going in the next room. He hadn't paid for this, she realised, probably just bunged the receptionist a few quid so they could slip in between the previous night's guest and housekeeping. He had fucked her on sheets that hadn't been changed yet.

Ella pulled her clothes on quickly, stamped her feet into her Chelsea boots.

'You're not going already?' Dylan asked, emerging from the shower with a towel around his waist and his wet hair slicked back.

'I've got stuff to do,' she said, rebuttoning her dress.

He started drying his back, the muscles in his arms flexing as he reached behind him, watching her all the while as if he was waiting for the moment when she would change her mind, decide that the rest of her day was better spent here with him. As if neither of them had other responsibilities.

'Why were you coming to the flat?' Ella asked. 'You never come to mine.'

'You weren't taking my calls, so you didn't leave me much option.'

She knew what he was doing: making her wait, wanting her to ask. Beg him, if he could get her to. But he'd come this far to tell her and Ella forced herself to stay silent.

'I wanted to tell you in person,' he said, as she was zipping up her parka. 'It's about Quinn...'

Ella froze.

The white room, the code words, the smell of kerosene and burning wires and charred confetti raining down on a predawn street.

'What about him?'

Dylan tossed the towel on to the bed. 'He's wangled an early release, apparently. He'll be out next week.'

Ella fell back against the door, saw his mouth moving, his serious expression, but she couldn't hear what he was saying. Blood was rushing in her ears, a sound like fire raging out of control, the sound she would always associate with Quinn.

Molly

Now – 10th March

It's too cold to sit out on the balcony but I'm getting sick of the inside of my flat. This is the longest I've ever spent holed up in here. Coming up on three days; even when I had the flu last winter I still managed a walk down to the river and a medicinal brandy in the Rose. The brandy didn't shift the flu and the evening air isn't fixing my mood.

I've always been claustrophobic. Not in the sense of panicking in confined spaces or freaking out on the Tube, but in knowing I'm trapped in a situation.

That's what brought me to London in the first place, the unbearable strictures of dinner at half-six precisely and the same meal on each night of the week, month after month, year after year. The same radio programme playing while the dishes were cleaned, the same soap opera recycling its stories and the same process of filling out football pools and washing the car on Sunday and a clean shirt on Monday to be worn until Friday. Restricted conversations, restricted thought patterns. It made me feel like I was locked in a box that I needed to kick my way out of.

As a child I got through it by promising myself that once I was old enough I would never stay in a situation I hated. Whatever the consequences I wouldn't let myself be trapped.

I did, of course. Got married too quickly and far too young to a man I'd met at college and liked, but not that much. Not until he followed me into teacher-training school and hotly promised

44

he'd keep following me anywhere I wanted to go. I thought that was deeply romantic. That's how young I was.

Would I have found it so touching if I'd known his 'anywhere' included driving five hours through the night to the Greenham Common Peace Camp? That he needed me so much he would try to physically haul me away from the protest?

He learned what I was really made of that day.

And so did I.

I take another mouthful of whisky. Some cheap blended stuff I don't even remember buying. It barely tastes like whisky, no peat or fire to it.

From my spot, tucked back under the shadow of the balcony, I can see into the new tower. At night it seems more glass than not, long expanses of it exposing sleek black kitchens and living rooms with huge sofas and factory-painted abstract expressionism, bedrooms too pristine for anyone to ever fuck in. They are shrines to pressed white shirts and red-soled shoes and the greedily acquired symbols of urban affluence bought by people who probably grew up like me. Out in satellite towns dreaming of different versions of themselves, dressing them up like dolls, mentally testing them out in new stage sets.

I wonder how the reality is holding up.

I should feel hatred towards them, I suppose, but I can't. I see the hours they work and how their heads hang as they strip off their suits in the burnished light of the bedrooms before they trudge towards their rainforest showers. I know they're killing themselves for that eight hundred square feet of high-spec living.

They would reject my pity, but they have it all the same.

The most intriguing windows are the ones that light up and go dark on timers, revealing unfurnished rooms that feel pregnant with bad possibilities. I wonder how long a murder victim could lie on one of those polished concrete floors before they were discovered.

This is the way my mind has been turning for the last three days. I can't shake myself out of it. Half of me knows he must be dead but the other half credits every odd noise the building

45

makes to his escape attempt. Last night I dreamed he was climbing the rusting cable in the lift shaft, broken fingers sticking out at unnatural angles as he slowly dragged himself up, hand over hand, past the second floor, past the third, heading for the light above him and the gap in the doors.

Without thinking, I pick up my phone and check the display to see if Ella has called me back. She hasn't, and the clock tells me it's only fifteen minutes since I last looked.

It seemed like a good idea to give her space to process what happened but after the first ignored phone call I started to worry and now, with still no word from her, I wonder what kind of state she's in. Her social-media feeds are still ticking along, but I know that stuff can be scheduled in advance.

Is she at home in bed, unable to crawl out from under the covers?

Shit.

Has she gone to the police and confessed?

The world lurches under me as I imagine her in a holding cell, knowing she'll be handled as harshly as the law allows, because she's Ella Riordan and her stance on the police is well publicised.

No.

This is just my overactive imagination talking.

If she'd done something stupid I'd know about it by now, wouldn't I? If she'd dropped off the map her friends would call me first. I'm her London next of kin, the nearest thing she has to a mother here. And maybe in general, judging by how little she's ever spoken about her mum.

No chance of taking this dilemma back to Durham and the Riordan residence to thrash out a coping strategy. Her parents would probably perform a citizen's arrest if they knew what she'd done. Self-defence be damned.

She'll be scared, that's all.

And haven't I been just as bad? Hiding in here, and listening for corpses coming along the corridor, sleeping in fitful jags and scanning every news outlet I can for reports of a man going missing.

A fist batters my door and I start so strongly I spill some of my drink. Shaking my hand dry, I go to answer and I've had this dream already, looking through the spyhole and seeing *him*. Standing frozen as his broken fingers turn the handle, so slowly, the dirt in the mechanism screeching, the lock non-existent, and then...

I open up to find Callum holding a four-pack of Beck's and a Domino's box.

'You're still alive then, hey,' he says, coming straight in and heading for the coffee table, which is covered in paperwork and photographs, my laptop open but powered down. 'Where am I putting this? My arm's getting greasy.'

'On the balcony?'

'Is it not a bit cold for that?'

'I thought you Highlanders didn't feel the cold,' I say, going out again.

'Aye, but I've been down London so long now I'm a proper soft southern bastard when it comes to the weather.' His accent drifts as he says it, an attempt at cockney he's never quite got the drop of. 'That why I've seen hide nor hair of you – winter getting into your old bones?'

He smiles, cheekily, and it charms me as usual.

How was he a soldier, I wonder. Not for the first time. I hate soldiers. It's a visceral thing. I hate everything they do and everything they stand for, their obedience and psychopathy and squeaky-clean brand of filth.

And yet I like Callum.

He insists he was in the catering corps, but I'm sure that's a lie. No army chef ever admits it. They were all special forces or some dumb macho shit. Only the proper hard cases want you to think they did something so innocent. The ones with the wrong kind of blood on their hands.

Cooks don't wake up screaming in the middle of the night either, clenched and sweating, with tears running down their cheeks.

'Face on you,' he says, handing me a beer and pushing the pizza box closer. 'What's up?'

'Nothing's up. I've just been busy.' I take a slice of pizza, surprised at how hungry I am suddenly. 'Ella's party the other night made me realise how close to the deadline for the book we are. I've got hundreds – thousands – of photos to go through, select the best ones, edit them. We agreed not to do too much to the images because it should be real. We want to see the real faces of the people this is affecting. But even doing the minimum takes time.'

Callum shifts in his seat, turns away from me for a few seconds, looking out towards the river, but I know he doesn't see it. His eyes are bad and he hasn't replaced the glasses he smashed a few months ago, insisting he can get by just fine without them.

He doesn't believe me.

I don't blame him.

The second slice of pizza doesn't go down as easily but I need to eat and it's a distraction I hope makes me look more at ease than I feel.

'I ... uh, is Ella alright?' he asks finally, chin tucked into his chest.

The last mouthful sticks in my throat and I wash it down with a swig of gassy beer. 'Far as I know, yeah. Why?'

'I heard her arguing with some bloke the other night. Reckon it was her. They were outside my place.' Callum grimaces. 'I thought about going out and seeing what was up, but I didn't think she'd thank me for that.'

'When was this?'

But I already know.

'When she had her party,' he says.

'Are you sure it was Ella?' I ask, trying to sound calm even though my heart is hammering. 'She never said anything to me about getting into a fight.'

He passes a hand over his skull. It needs shaving again, grey stubble coming through, long enough already to see where he's receding.

'I dunno.'

'They all sound the same, don't they? All Home Counties playing at street.' I force a smile. 'Some girl from the party having a set-to with her boyfriend, was it?'

'Aye, probably.' The tension goes out of his face. 'That's what it sounded like. She was giving the poor bastard a right earbashing.'

'Won't have been Ella, then.'

Quickly I change the subject, ask him if he managed to find another bathroom sink to replace Derek in 309's broken one. He tells me he's tried a dozen empty flats today and found the whiteware irrevocably damaged in every one of them. Something that would have made a lot of noise if it was done for sport, but he heard nothing and suspects it's the developer's handiwork. Putting the flats out of commission to deter squatters. Or, more likely, to stop us repurposing the items left behind.

I've stopped listening. I'm just nodding and sipping my beer and trying to keep my eyes fixed on him as my thoughts slip away, back to Ella and that man she was arguing with outside Callum's flat.

Callum is too sharp-eared to have mistaken her distinctive Durham accent when it's only a thin wall away from him. Which means something more went on and she was too scared to tell me about it at the time and so scared she hasn't been able to talk about it since, either.

Is this why I've not heard from her?

I've been selfish, wallowing here just when Ella needed me the most. Telling myself I've been giving her space because I've not been ready to face the fallout from what we've done.

No more hiding.

Ella needs me.

Ella

Then – 15th February

Ella hugged her folded towel to her chest and tried to tune out the sound of her flatmate's boyfriend singing in the shower. She'd been waiting in the hallway for pushing fifteen minutes and the longer it went on the more tempted she was to go back to her room and have a quick wash in the kitchen sink.

At this rate all the hot water would be gone anyway.

He had a good voice, to be fair to him, but she'd heard enough of it last night, when he'd drunkenly serenaded his girlfriend from the street.

Ella had spent her Valentine's night curled up under a blanket, watching *Roman Holiday*, thinking about how it reinforced shitty gender stereotypes and promulgated the lie of *noblesse oblige*, as she wished she was riding down winding Italian streets on the back of a scooter with some tall, dark smartarse.

She'd received one card, from her mother, who still sent them every year to her and her brother, just as she had since they were teenagers. It had annoyed Ella back then, but now it made her smile, especially since it came in a care package with good espresso and the marmalade she couldn't afford to buy herself, plus a Tupperware container of homemade cinnamon biscuits.

Sometimes she did miss being at home.

Finally the shower shut off and the bathroom door opened, her neighbour's boyfriend coming out in her polka-dot dressing gown, his skin scalded red, hair plastered to his skull.

'Sorry, didn't know you were waiting,' he mumbled.

Ella told him it was fine through gritted teeth, and went in to find the floor wet and the air steamy. She switched on the extractor fan and brushed her teeth while it wheezed and clattered, slowly clearing the fug, washed her face and decided her hair would be fine for another day. When she stepped into the shower she found the water lukewarm and cursed her inconsiderate flat-mates and the cheapskate landlord who had made it clear that he knew the boiler wasn't powerful enough for a three-storey house carved into seven studios but would be doing absolutely nothing about it.

Not unless they were prepared to accept a significant rent rise.

Prices were going up here just like everywhere and Ella was sure the landlord would love to get them out, turn the building back into a single house he could sell for seven figures to a family who would appreciate the high ceilings and sash windows.

She dried off in her room and dressed in jeans and a chunky jumper, ate a slice of toast smeared with butter that was starting to go rancid, the news playing on her laptop until she closed it and slipped it in her bag.

The British Library Reading Room was waiting for her, but before that she was supposed to meet Dylan. Her PhD pulled her in one direction and him in the other, the work she was doing at Castle Rise pushing everything else to the sidelines, leaving no room to breathe.

In her quieter moments she could admit to herself that she wasn't up to this. The nights she was too tired to sleep were becoming more frequent, plans and actions chasing each other around as she lost a grip on which conversations she'd actually had and which she'd only imagined. When she finally dropped off she would dream of empty flats and endless corridors lined with doors that opened impossibly on to rooms in other build-ings: her parents' kitchen, where the range would be ticking away, welcoming her back, reminding her she didn't have to live this life; classrooms she had sat in, always at the front, always the first to put her hand up; hotel bedrooms in disarray and half-remembered offices and the police interview room she kept returning to, her arm in a cast, her mouth sealed shut, staring at her reflection in the two-way mirror and seeing a face she didn't recognise.

Maybe Dylan was right, maybe all this was becoming too much for her.

He'd told her not to get involved. Right from the start he pegged Castle Rise as a lost cause and she'd agreed with him privately, but his attitude rankled, how fiercely he'd told her not to waste her time on 'those people', as if they were worthless.

And when she tried to explain that she was doing it for Molly, because she'd been good to her and she didn't want Molly to lose her home and have to leave London and all her friends, he said, 'You don't need Molly.'

If he'd never said that, Ella might have walked away. But now she would stick with it until the last resident was forcibly removed, just to make him understand that he couldn't dictate to her.

Not always.

Not on this.

She *did* need Molly and if he couldn't understand that, or at least pretend to respect it, then maybe he wasn't the right man for her.

Outside it was one of those crisp winter mornings that felt almost like spring: cloudless, chilly and so bright that she regretted leaving her sunglasses inside. Mornings like this made Ella long for the countryside. She found she was thinking of home more often lately and wasn't sure why. Was it just that she'd been away for so long? Did the place where you were born really tug at you? She'd never believed that, but she felt something, an impulse to escape she immediately stamped on.

Ella rearranged her bag, setting it straighter across her body, and started towards the canal, passing the chaotic roar of morning break time at Our Lady's, which was swiftly drowned out by the sound of brickwork being cut through inside a house caged by scaffolding and shrouded in opaque plastic from roof to basement. At the pub on the corner she saw just how dusty the house must have been inside, three men powdered white sitting outside on a wooden bench with pints of lager, just their mouths wet.

She wondered if her landlord owned the house they were working on. He was an old Greek guy, started buying around here in the early sixties when everywhere was cheap but here even more so, liking the proximity to the Orthodox church and his own house at the top of the street. He kept a close eye on his properties, she'd been told by an elderly neighbour who had known him for decades and who seemed to believe he was a real gentleman. He kept the area 'nice'. He didn't allow 'undesirables'.

The woman complained that her own children couldn't afford to rent, let alone buy here, but she didn't seem to understand how her hero was creating the problem.

All the wealth, trickling up into the hands of the old, Ella thought. Not even trickling any more. Rushing. Her parents had given her brother and his wife a deposit to buy their first home – she wasn't supposed to know about that, but he'd let it slip after too many beers, suggesting she try to get them to do the same for her. 'Best getting it now, Ella. We'll be clobbered on the inheritance tax otherwise.'

Maybe he was right but it was a sick and ghoulish thing to say all the same, she thought.

Then again, he had his own home now and she had nothing.

She crossed Regent's Canal at St Pancras Way and cut down on to the towpath.

Dylan had said half past ten, but she wasn't going to jump because he clicked his fingers. Almost eleven now and she knew he'd be getting impatient, already thinking about whatever he would be busy with this afternoon once she left again.

It was coming to an end.

They both knew that, but neither was quite ready to make the break.

A shrill bell sounded behind her and Ella glanced over her shoulder as a woman on a Brompton bike approached, riding perilously close to the water's edge as she passed, putting her hand up in thanks, although Ella didn't know what for. Maybe just because she hadn't got in her way. There were a couple of joggers running two abreast ahead of her and they parted reluctantly at the third sound of the woman's bell, shouted after her in voices too hard for the sunny morning and calm water.

Her mobile rang as she was going under a bridge, the screen pulsing with an unknown number she almost rejected out of habit but didn't, because she gave her own out so freely now it might be important.

'Ella?'

The reception was crackling.

'Hold on, give me a second.' She hurried through the tunnel and out into the sunshine again. 'Who's this?'

'That Ella?'

A man's voice, thick with cold.

'Yes, hi. Who's this?'

'You can't tell?' He sniffed hard and she heard the mucus roll into the back of his throat. 'Be this cold I've got. Bad living conditions, you know?'

She knew.

Knew exactly who it was now. Instinctively she turned, feeling like he was watching her even though she knew it was impossible. Dozens of blank windows looked down on her, but he wasn't behind any of them.

The only windows Quinn looked out of lately were high up, reinforced and barred.

'What do you want?' she asked, starting up the brick steps.

'I just wanted you to know I've not forgotten about you.'

Ella stopped midway up the stairs, gripped the handrail tighter, feeling the corroded metal against her skin and the paint flakes sticking to her palm. She told herself to tough this out. Don't show weakness or guilt because it would only encourage him.

'Are you seriously going to do this?' she asked, making her voice hard and contemptuous. 'You're pathetic, you know that, right?'

He laughed, half-grunt half-snort. 'Me? You're the one who ran off like a little bitch.'

'Keep telling yourself that's what happened,' Ella said, feeling her pulse thudding where she held on to the rail, blood rushing into her ears so loud she was sure he must be able to hear it too. 'You're a fantasist.'

'Oh, no, Ella. If anyone here's a fraud, it's you.'

She closed her eyes. 'Is that it?'

'Nobody can see what you are—'

'And what am I?'

'You're a careerist. You don't believe in anything, you just get off on the adulation.'

Ella laughed, tipped her head back to the sky. 'Wow, you are the first person ever to say that to me. How very original of you. I'm not told that like fifty times a day online at all.'

'I'm going to expose you,' he snarled.

The laughter caught in her throat. It was as if he was there in front of her, face contorted with rage, body blown up and pumped for the fight.

'I know what you did, Ella.'

A man ran up the stairs, clipping her shoulder as he passed but she hardly noticed.

'And I know how you did it,' Quinn said.

Molly

Now – 11th March

It's a grim morning, cold and blustery, the city cowering under a sky like end times, tumbling boulders of granite-grey cloud sitting so low it feels like they might crush us all. For once it's a relief to ride the escalator underground into the tail end of the morning rush with all the wet raincoats and dripping umbrellas, the contorted skeletons of folding bikes, which make me think of the broken body I've left behind in the lift shaft of Castle Rise.

He's never far from my mind.

I managed a few hours of mercifully dreamless sleep last night, brought on by beer and whisky and the exhaustive efforts of screwing a younger man. I might have slept longer if Callum hadn't woken up shouting around three a.m. He left then, even though I stroked his shoulders and kissed his hair and told him everything was fine. Maybe if I'd told him I didn't want to be alone he would have stayed, but we both carry our shame close to the surface and take our time in exposing our wounds to one another for salving.

Suddenly the weight of all that earth above me begins to feel like a hammer poised to fall on my skull and I realise I need to get above ground.

At Warren Street I'm spat back out on to Euston's dank topside, the traffic at a standstill, pumping exhaust fumes into the heavy air, and I see my bus turning the corner away from me as the driving rain fills my eyes. I shelter briefly in an alleyway near the stop until the next 29 arrives.

There's a seat halfway down and I'm grateful to have it, even if the big guy in the window smells like he's carrying rotting meat inside his distressed-leather jacket. Not an artfully distressed one, but the kind that has been slept in and on and under, which might have put out fires and soaked up puddles of indeterminate fluids.

At Mornington Crescent a frail elderly woman with chestnut-brown hair beautifully curled under a plastic headscarf gets on and I see the panic on her face when she sees she will have to stand, how tightly she grips the handrail. I get up and help her into my seat and it's only once I'm close to her that I realise we are probably the same age.

I'm going to keep fighting. Even if I feel like shit right now, tired and scared and besieged, I won't allow myself to fold.

I get off the bus at Camden High Street, go straight into Poundland and buy an umbrella, which probably won't last all the way home, but I only need it to keep me dry the half-mile to Ella's place. Thinking of her holed up there for days, knowing she won't be eating, I make a quick circuit of the nearest supermarket: basic supplies, tea and sugary things.

By the time I reach the front step of the chopped-up Edwardian townhouse she lives in, the umbrella has buckled against the wind, two spokes broken and its skin flapping with each new gust. I hold down the buzzer until the door is answered. The boy doesn't ask who I'm visiting, barely looks up from his phone and immediately heads back into his own room.

The house is full of muffled noises as I go up to the second floor, the sound of music playing and feet moving over creaking, clacking floorboards. Silence from inside Ella's room. I knock and wait and when she doesn't answer, knock harder, pushing away images of her overdosed in bed, choked on vomit, already long gone.

I'm readying to bang harder when she finally opens up. She isn't surprised to see me. She isn't anything, standing there in crumpled joggers and a jumper with frayed cuffs pulled down over her hands. Her eyes are puffy, lips cracked dry, her hair lying flat and greasy.

'I was going to call you today,' she says in a hoarse voice, and walks away. 'I think I've got a virus or something. I don't feel good.'

Her room smells sickly: stale breaths and her unwashed body, the bin, which needs emptying, and takeaway cartons mouldering on the counter. This isn't like her. She's usually fastidious about her little flat, insists she needs to be because it's the only way to live healthily in one cramped room where your bed is only ten feet away from your kitchen sink.

She's crawled back under the duvet. There are books on the floor to her side, her laptop half covered with papers. It looks like she's tried to do some work but I guess the distraction wasn't good enough.

There's no hiding from what we've done. I could have told her that if she'd answered the phone when I've called her.

'Are you hungry?' I ask, trying to sound upbeat.

'I can't eat anything.'

'You need to try. I've brought pastries and some sandwiches and stuff.'

Ella rolls over in bed, turns her back to me.

I start to clean up. This doesn't come naturally but it needs to be done. I clear all the debris into a bin liner, knot it and leave it out in the hallway for later, fill the sink and put her dirty cutlery and bowls into it, wipe down the small square of counter while the kettle boils, then make a pot of coffee.

There's a dinky cafe table and two folding chairs set up in front of the only window and I spread out the food there, pour our coffees, feeling absurd as I do it, acting like everything is normal when inside my head I'm raging at her, wanting to drag her out of bed by her arms, shout at her to pull it together.

'Come on, Ella. Just eat a croissant or something, then you can go back to bed.'

She hauls herself up, drags a knitted blanket off the bed and wraps it around her shoulders before she sits down opposite me. She picks up a Danish pastry and takes a single bite out of it, her eyes drifting away towards the window. The long garden out there is untended, wildly tangled with glossy creepers and the barbed whips of last year's blackberry crawlers laid like tripwires across the weed-choked grass. At the bottom is a rickety black shed with a bush growing through its collapsed roof. Not a view worth looking at.

'Have they found him?' Ella asks finally.

'Not yet.'

'They're going to.' She takes another mean bite of her Danish. 'I keep thinking about the sound he made...'

That dull crunch, the clang of bone hitting metal.

'It doesn't matter now,' I tell her. 'All that matters is what we do next.'

She snorts. 'Wait to get caught – that's what we're doing, isn't it?'

Whatever I expected, this is worse. I knew she'd be guilt-stricken but I didn't think she'd be so defeatist. She's spent the last eighteen months fighting battles for other people, often thankless and unwinnable ones, but now, when it matters most, when her liberty and mine is hanging in the balance, she gives up?

This isn't the Ella I know.

She's been alone too long. Four days here, talking herself into this state. I should have come sooner. I should have known her conscience would get the better of her. She's still her father's daughter.

'Ella, lovey, I know you're scared. I've been going crazy with this too.' She gives me a sceptical look. 'But we need to hold steady, okay?'

'Okay,' she says, too easily, and throws her chin up. 'We're both calm and collected now, having coffee, eating pastries. What do we do next?'

This is why I never wanted children. They dig themselves into holes and when you pull them out they blame you for making them muddy.

'We need to keep acting like normal,' I say firmly. 'You have to get back to your life. We can pass off a few days in bed as a bug, but much longer and it's going to start to look like you've got something to hide.'

Her fingers are shredding the rest of the Danish pastry on to a plate, slowly, violently tearing it into tiny pieces, her face flushing.

I keep talking.

'When he does get found – and he will, you're right, probably soon – it's really important nobody can point back to now and say, "Ella was acting weird." You understand that, right? You need to look innocent.'

'But I'm not,' she snaps.

Here's the anger she kept buried right after it happened, bubbling up hot and directionless. I try not to take it personally; stay calm, because one of us has to. Just like that night, it's on me to be the cool head and a small part of me resents it even as I feel for her.

Ella buries her face in her hands. 'I killed him.'

'In self-defence.' I unpeel her fingers from her face, making her look at me. 'Ella, you can't get consumed by guilt. You have *nothing* to feel guilty about. He attacked you. He made the decision to put himself in danger the second he did that. You were entirely within your rights to fight back.'

'Then why did we dump his body?' she asks. 'If I was within my rights, why didn't we call the police?'

I wonder how clear her recollection of that night is. Between the fear and the drink and the shock at what she'd done, how aware was she of the conversation we had and the agreement we came to?

'We went through this already,' I say wearily. 'Where do you think you'd be right now if we called the police? You'd be on remand somewhere. Or out on bail, at best, waiting to go to trial. Ella, for God's sake, is that what you want? Do you want to go to prison? Do you have any idea what it's like to be locked up?'

She looks away from me. 'Maybe it's what I deserve.'

The quietness and the low pitch of her voice set my nerves jangling.

'Please tell me you're not thinking about confessing.'

Ella starts to bite her thumbnail; the skin there is already red and cracked from being incessantly worried at.

'Confession isn't good for the soul,' I tell her. 'You won't feel even a tiny bit better if you go to the police. All you'll do is add more fear and stress and danger to the situation you're already in.' I'm not even sure she's listening to me, but I can't give up on her. 'Sweetheart, I understand that you feel guilty. But you being in prison isn't going to bring him back to life and it isn't going to make the guilt fade any faster. It doesn't work like that.'

'It's not up to us, is it?' she asks, her voice dull, all drained of anger. 'This isn't a question of confess and go to prison or keep it in and stay free. We could get caught for this, Molly. We committed a crime and it's going to be investigated. Aren't you scared?'

'I've never been more terrified in my life.'

For a few minutes neither of us speaks. The rain lashing the window turns to tiny hailstones, which come at the glass in waves, peppering it like shot. I can feel thin draughts trickling in around the wooden sash, finding my exposed neck, a sensation like a blade pressed to my skin.

'We were so stupid,' she says quietly, staring at the blank wall in front of her. 'He's down there covered in our DNA.'

'If he was at the party he'll have come to congratulate you, hugged you, whatever. There's bound to be a perfectly innocent reason for your DNA to be on him.'

Ella looks at me. 'What about yours?'

I force a smile. 'Well, you know how I get around younger men.'

She laughs and it's just as fake as my smile but it feels like the ice melting.

Ella picks up a chicken wrap, tears the packaging off it and takes a big bite. I let her eat, top up my coffee and pass her a bottle of orange juice. I want to smoke but I can't open the window because of the rain, so I just hold my cigarette for comfort.

'What's important now is that we use this time to work out our story,' I say.

A stiff gust of wind rattles the window.

'And working out a good story starts with the truth.'

61

'I told you what happened,' she says, concentrating on picking pieces of chicken out of her wrap. It's not real meat. It's the kind they blow off the bone with water jets and stick together with glue; uniform and too white, its texture all wrong.

'Callum heard you arguing with him.' I want her to look up but she doesn't. 'He said it sounded like you knew each other.'

She stares out of the window, where the hail has stopped but the rain keeps coming.

'When I told you I didn't know him, that was the truth. I didn't really *know* him.' She picks the blanket back up and draws it around her shoulders. 'I met him last year after some *Guardian* masterclass, I can't even remember which one now. A load of us went for drinks, and him and me got talking. We went back to his. We had some completely mediocre sex. I didn't come. He didn't care. I left straight after.'

The blanket is up around her jaw and she's sinking into it, ashamed even though she has no reason to be.

'Then what?'

'Then,' her face tightens into a bitter smile. 'Then he started emailing me. He wanted to see me again, when was I around for coffee or lunch or something? He thought there'd been a spark. Didn't I feel it? Was I too stuck up to date someone like him? Wasn't he useful enough to me? Who the fuck did I think I was?' She spiels it out in a monotone, like this isn't the only man she could tell this story about. 'I ignored him. He went quiet. Then he started again, tried to be more polite. Told me he had a contact I should talk to at Lambeth Council about some dodgy dealing with a Chinese development firm. I thought it stank and even if I believed it I wouldn't have wanted anything from him.' She bit her lip. 'Maybe I should have shot him right down then, but I just kept ignoring him and eventually he seemed to get the hint. I thought he'd moved on to someone else.'

'And then he turned up at your party?'

She nods. 'I didn't see him, though, that's the weird thing. He must have been there because he followed me down the stairs, but he didn't come up to me when we were there.'

'Probably realised it wasn't a good place to start a scene. Not if he was planning on...'

'Raping me,' she says, in a small but forceful voice. 'That's what he was going to do, Molly.'

'I know, sweetheart.' I reach across the table and rub her arm, proud of her for facing up to the reality instead of making the emotionally easier retreat. 'But he didn't get the chance. Did he?'

'No.' She wipes her nose on the back of her hand and for a split second I see something pass behind her eyes which looks a new kind of terrible and I don't want to press her on it but I have to.

'Ella, if he did, you need to tell me. I'm sorry, but the DNA, we might need to do something more about him.'

My mind begins to whirr through the options. Fire? Bleach? Bleach then fire, pour whatever we need to down the lift shaft and throw a match on top of it, let him burn.

'We don't need to worry about that.' A single, fast tear runs down her cheek. 'You know, I always wondered how I'd react in that situation. I thought I'd freeze up and just ... let it be done to me.'

The expression on her face brings tears to my eyes. It stirs memories I don't want to examine but can't avoid; the feel of Dralon under my bare skin and a fist hovering over my face and a smile so wide I saw a missing tooth right at the back.

I dry my face and Ella apologises even though she doesn't know why.

'Why didn't you tell me about him before?' I ask. 'If you'd told me while he was emailing you, maybe we could have done something.'

'I didn't think he was going to go this far,' she says.

'Have you got his emails still?'

She shakes her head. 'I deleted them as they came in.'

'There's going to be a paper trail to you.' I roll the unlit cigarette between my fingers. 'But he fell into the lift shaft by accident, right?' She nods. 'When the time comes we stick to that. We believe it one hundred per cent. He came to your party, he had some drinks, he wandered off into the building and he fell. That's all we know.'

Again she nods, slightly firmer this time, and I see a little of the fear leave her face. We've had days of this, both of us, running through worst-case scenarios and all the ways we might get caught and all the ways this could have been avoided, and I want to ask her why she didn't just bang on Callum's door when this man was harassing her, but she's calm now and I know it will sound like I'm blaming her for what happened, which I shouldn't. I understand the desire to fight your own battles. I respect it.

But that pride of hers has brought us to this. Two frightened women in a bedsit, putting on brave faces for each other, while we contemplate our precarious futures.

Ella

Then – 26th January

The pre-theatre crowd were out in force when Ella turned on to Bateman Street. The pavement outside the Dog and Duck was thick with bodies, the frosty air full of easy chatter and laughter that billowed white. A hard-faced young woman in a matted fake-fur capelet was moving between them, cradling a single copy of the *Big Issue* wrapped in plastic, asking for any spare change. She'd timed it well; the crowd was softened up, made generous by drink and the prospect of a good evening and the guilt that they could afford to drop so much money for two hours' entertainment.

Ella heard her pitch as she passed by.

'I've got a place in a hostel, but they charge.'

And a woman with a broad West Country accent saying it was shameful that she was expected to pay for a safe bed at night, while she opened her purse.

Ella wondered if the story was true. Knew there was a fair chance that somewhere, maybe nearby, a man she considered her boyfriend was waiting to take the money, spend it on whatever he needed to get him through till morning.

She hoped the girl would keep back enough to save her from sleeping out tonight.

Inside the tiny Victorian pub bodies were rammed wall to wall, people leaving the bar slowly, inching their way through with drinks held high, light from the chandeliers bouncing off bottles and wine glasses. She loved this place. It reminded her of the old Ealing films she'd watched on Sunday afternoons with her dad. And the first time she'd read *Hangover Square*, a gift from a boyfriend who thought she needed to expand her literary horizons.

It was like this, she thought, wood-panelled and Minton-tiled, small round tables loaded with empties, golden light smeared across faces touched by alcohol and anticipation, the blurriness of half-formed ideas and just-remembered gossip. The phones ruined the fantasy, but there were fewer out than in most pubs, and ones she saw were turned towards the building's antique flourishes, people wanting to capture this, as if they knew it might not last.

Maybe it wasn't quite like this back then, she realised. What was missing was cigarette smoke, thick and blue, and the sense of incipient danger bubbling up behind the bonhomie.

Quickly she found herself pressed against the bar. She ordered a half pint of St Austell, eyeing the other real ales they had on offer while the guy pulled hers. The thought that her father would love this place prompted a smile, which didn't last long because she knew she would never be able to bring him here.

When she turned away from the bar she saw Martin Sinclair waving at her from a table down the back. The bench either side of him was taken up by a crush of people lost in their own spirited parties, but he grabbed a stray stool as she made her way to him and set it down.

'You did well to get a seat,' Ella said as she went in for a brief, polite hug.

'I've been here since three,' he told her, with a smile that hitched higher on the left than the right, a souvenir from an old injury he claimed to have picked up when he was covering the riots back in 2011. 'I've been busting for a slash for an hour.'

She slipped into his spot while he went to the gents and looked over the notes he'd been working on. They were written in some incomprehensible journalist's shorthand she supposed he was old enough to have learned when he started out. Underneath was a proof copy of a book on the history of the protest movement in the twentieth century. Sinclair was putting together something similar himself, she knew, and she guessed he had it to study his competition. When she flicked through it she saw sections under-lined and notes scribbled in the margins, questioning the author's analysis and the reliability of their sources.

Ella stopped when she saw Molly's name.

> Molly Fader – an art teacher turned professional agitator and photographic chronicler of the Greenham Common protests – was strongly suspected of involvement in the attack, which left PC Gareth Kelman in a coma, but no charges were ever brought.

On the opposite page the young PC stared out at Ella. He was fine-boned and pale-skinned; highly breakable, Ella thought, despite the hard stare and the short back-and-sides of near-military severity.

The author had found an old image of Molly, and Ella was surprised how little she'd changed. Her long, poker-straight hair and blunt fringe were the same, although that crow's-wing black came out of a bottle now. Same deep-set eyes and sharp, high cheekbones, but without the softening of the last thirty years she had a bandit vibe about her. The photograph looked like one taken by police monitors, a line of women with banners and signs thrust up in the air, faces wild and raging. Molly held a loud-hailer, her mouth wide and her fist pumping the sky as the shutter snapped.

Ella had heard about the protest camp there before, but Molly always claimed she'd gone along as a photographer, never did anything more than take supplies and help get the word out.

Why had she lied about that? It seemed like something she would be proud of if she was guilty, and furious about if she was innocent. Either way Ella thought it was a subject she'd be likely to have discussed with her. The fact that she hadn't made her uneasy.

Was this something too big for Molly to trust her with it?

As she was about to turn the page Sinclair came back carrying two more drinks. She cleared the books away to make space for them, moving aside the empties he'd accumulated during his afternoon stint.

'I thought I'd best take advantage of the lull.' He nodded at the book. 'Load of old bollocks, that is. You can't go into those groups off the back of freelancing right-wing think pieces and expect people to talk to you. Eighty per cent of that book's come direct from the police. Unfiltered. Unexamined.' He went for his pint. 'Bloke might as well be auditioning for a press officer's position at the Met.'

Ella showed him the page she was looking at. 'What's this about?'

Sinclair wiped the beer off his top lip. 'Molly not told you about it? I thought you were her amanuensis.'

'No Geordie should ever say that word.' Ella smiled. 'I'm surprised you even know it.'

'You Durhamites don't have the monopoly on pretension,' he said, grinning back at her. 'She should write her memoirs, though. It'd blow this shite out of the water.'

Ella sipped her beer, seeing how he swayed slightly on his stool. He'd been here three hours already and it was showing on him. She wondered if he was up to the event they were due at soon, whether she should be drinking, in case he took more chairing than she'd prepared for.

'So, what's the truth?' she asked. 'Did Molly attack that copper?'

Sinclair took a theatrically deep breath. 'Young PC Kelman was a piece of shit. That's the truth. I've interviewed dozens of women who were at the camp and they all say the same thing – Kelman was a predator. Wasn't shy about using force when force wasn't required. You know the type.'

'Don't I just,' Ella said, glancing automatically at her right arm, even though the scar was hidden under her jumper.

'Kelman didn't keep it in the field, though. He assaulted a woman who'd been arrested. Right there in the station, while she was down in the cells.'

'Did she press charges?'

'It was a different time,' Sinclair said. 'Look at how hard it is to get charges to stick even now. We're talking thirty years ago. The general population still trusted the police back then. The woman didn't even report him.' He took another long mouthful of beer. 'And that didn't look good for any of them, because it looked like the protestors were waiting to take their own revenge.'

That didn't sound like Molly, but some of the women she'd introduced Ella to … yes, she could believe it of them.

'One night Kelman's on his way home, stops off at his bookie's. And when he comes out someone's waiting in the bushes for him. They jump out and smack him across the back of the head with a hammer, leave it right where he dropped.'

'A copper coming out of a bookie's?' Ella asked. 'Surely there would have been loads more likely suspects than Molly and her friends?'

'That was the thinking until he came out of the coma a few weeks later. Kelman said it was definitely a woman. Said he smelled her.'

A waiter shouted out an order and Sinclair called him over, took a bowl of thick-cut chips off him and a basket of fat, battered scampi, passed back a few empties to clear some space.

'He smelled her?' Ella said, putting a molten-hot chip in her mouth. 'That's hardly compelling evidence.'

'This is coming from the police, remember. There's absolutely *no* evidence to back it up.' Sinclair shook salt over the chips. 'It was most likely a smear campaign.'

'You don't think she did it, then?'

'You know her better than I do. What do you reckon?'

'I can't see her doing something like that. In self-defence maybe, but not in a premeditated way.' She snagged a piece of scampi, ate it while she tried to picture Molly crouched down in some bushes with hammer in hand, watching and waiting; pictured her springing up and striking a man across the head without a moment's hesitation.

No, she couldn't believe it.

More likely Molly was the one the police picked to smear because she was vocal and influential, the woman who'd drawn most attention to herself and become a target because of it.

'What happened to Kelman?'

'He survived. Did very well for himself, as a matter of fact. Served with distinction in the Battle of Orgreave.' Sinclair shot her a tight and humourless smile. 'Wound up as a chief superintendent. Currently insisting he had nothing to do with covering up abuse at a Cumbrian boys' home.' He took a few chips, spoke again with his mouth full. 'Shame Molly didn't hit that rotten apple a bit harder, hey?'

Sinclair's voice seemed very loud suddenly, the bark of laughter that followed almost obscene. At the next table one couple were leaving, gathering shopping bags and coats, while another pair waited to take their seats, as Sinclair launched into a well-worn diatribe about the miners' strike. Ella knew she was expected to give the right encouragement in the right places, knew also how easily he could spin this subject along a road she didn't want to go.

'Time for another quick one?' she asked.

He drained his glass, slammed it down. 'Yes. Good woman.'

Ella took out her phone at the bar and made a note to check up on the case of PC Kelman once she got home tonight. She suspected there would be little about it online, but she wasn't prepared to ask Molly what had happened without knowing more than Sinclair had told her.

She wasn't sure she even wanted to know. If Molly confessed to it, what then?

If it was a mistake or a slur, it seemed strange she'd not mentioned it. Wouldn't Molly have loved one more story about how corrupt the police were?

Ella slipped her phone away. Maybe it was best not talked about. Or not yet, anyway. Molly was so fixated on the campaign to keep Castle Rise occupied that there didn't seem to be room for anything else in her mind. They'd lost another family today: a mum and three kids all packed up and gone off to grandparents in Slough, one spare bedroom and a four-berth caravan to house the lot of them.

Another five flats would empty out over the coming weeks, all owned by the same buy-to-let landlord who had been holding out for the very best price. While her tenants scrambled around for alternative accommodation, finding no help from the council and with the local housing charities all stretched beyond breaking.

At least one couple were going to end up on the street, Ella knew, unless something miraculous happened. Molly was calling shelters for them, churches and hostels, writing letters to their MP.

Back at the table, Sinclair had moved into her seat and was slipping his books into his messenger bag.

'I had an interesting call about you,' he said as she placed his beer in front of him. 'Ta.'

Ella sat, took the last chip in the bowl. 'I hate sentences that start like that.'

'I was contacted by a guy in Wandsworth nick. He's trying to sell a story about you. Wants to send me a visiting order, get an interview set up. Tell all, he's saying. Career-ending.'

Quinn.

Ella tried to keep her face blank.

'You know who it is?' he asked.

'I have an idea, yeah.'

'Is it true what he's claiming?' Sinclair seemed to have sobered up instantly, no more matey chatter, back into investigative-reporter mode.

'If it's the same crap he was claiming when he was arrested, then no, it isn't.' Ella held his gaze, saw the faint trace of interest evaporate. 'Ryan Quinn has had it in for me for a long time. He thinks I'm a fake, basically. In it for the glamour.'

Sinclair smiled. 'I figured it was bollocks; you wouldn't be stupid enough to get involved with anything like that.'

'Quinn made an idiotic move and it achieved nothing but getting him locked up and making the rest of us – who protest peacefully – look like animals.' Ella heard the anger in her voice

71

and felt it in her chest, forced herself to speak calmly. 'He's doing the police's job for them. The thing is, I don't even think he realises that. He thinks he's a hero. A martyr for the cause.'

'He's not the first bloke to do more damage than good like that,' Sinclair said. He checked his watch and reached for his pint. 'Drink up, we'd best be getting off.'

Outside, the theatre-goers had migrated to their plush seats, the young beggar moved on to fresh and busier patches. Sinclair was talking about the event, checking whether she was prepped, asking her how she wanted to structure it then telling her how he wanted to do it. Ella answered distractedly, kept walking when he stopped to light a cigarette, and only realised she'd lost him when she turned towards the empty pavement. He caught up with her, laughing about her inability to hold her beer and how you could apparently take the Durham out of the girl once you'd taken the girl out of Durham.

Ella laughed along, acting on autopilot. She followed him through the front door of Foyles, where his face was plastered large and lightly photoshopped in the windows and on boards near the staircase he ran up ahead of her.

Pull it together, she told herself. People are watching you.

By the time they reached the top floor, she found him already talking to the events manager, warmly shaking his hand. She played her part, trailed them into the green room, answering more questions and turning down a drink then requesting a jasmine tea if it wouldn't be too much trouble, listening as Sinclair asked about the size of the audience and then rang his PR, who was stuck in an Uber with a driver whose satnav was broken.

'That's what you get for not supporting the cabbies, Imogen.'

He looked at Ella and she smiled like she meant it but even as they emerged on to the small stage, into the polite applause and the lights, she was thinking about Quinn and what would happen to her if the next journalist he tried actually bought his story.

It would be the end of this.

The end of everything.

Molly

Now – 11th March

I didn't ask his name.

It only strikes me as I'm walking across Vauxhall Bridge, needing the breeze that blows up off the river to sweep the sickroom smell of Ella's bedsit out of my head. Maybe it's best I don't know. It will make the inevitable lying that bit easier.

I look down into the water. There's a grizzled, grey-haired man walking along the bank, eyes fixed on the mud, prodding at it occasionally with his toe. This isn't the right place for mudlarking, the bank too narrow, the water too high, but what do I know, anyway?

On the bus home I kept thinking about the people at Ella's party that night; witnesses, all of them, all carrying their surveillance devices. There will be photographs strewn across social media and blogs already and he'll be in some of them, if only in the background, in profile. When he's found and the police realise he's too well-groomed to have been homeless they'll start trawling the party footage.

They'll realise too that he should have been carrying a wallet and phone, but Ella took those before we dumped him and I suppose she disposed of them wisely. I tried to take them, but she accused me of treating her like a child and time was passing so I let her have her way.

Maybe the police will buy it as a robbery gone wrong. No reason to look at either of us if that's the story.

They have enough reports on file for undesirables at Castle Rise that another one slipping inside under cover of the party is credible. Ella's friends looked like easy pickings, even to me.

This is what we needed to talk about this afternoon. We should have been working through narratives we could have nudged the police towards. Instead we bitched and sniped at each other. At least she's getting her head together, though. I need her to be solid.

The old man on the muddy bank drops into a crouch, holding on to his stick with one hand as he digs into the ground with a small trowel. I want desperately to know what he's found. It's almost a physical longing in me as I watch him straighten up, wipe the thing clean and examine it, before tucking it away in his pocket.

The urge to go down there sweeps over me. I want to know this man's life, what draws him to the river and forces his hands into the silt. I want to know what he finds there and where he spirits his treasures home to. An irrational part of me wants him to wipe me clean and tuck me safely away.

I step back into the foot flow and follow the southbound bodies across the bridge.

Ahead of me the grotesque ziggurats of St George Wharf fist the sky and I feel a little stab of nostalgia for Camden, with its rows of dignified townhouses and old corner boozers, an area that still looks like people actually live in it, eat and drink and buy ordinary, everyday things. This is real estate as unreal as plots of land on the moon, square footage most owners will never walk across.

It's earlier than it feels, the end of lunch hour, but the bars and restaurants along the river path are busy, full of people who aren't tied to their desks with a homemade salad. I don't see a single suit among them and it makes me think how much easier it was to tell the ruling class from the rest of us when they all wore Savile Row. Now the entry-level nobody wears the suit and the billionaire dresses like a student and it's impossible to stake your claim for individuality with anything as basic as your attire.

Everything is harder for this generation.

At the entrance to Castle Rise the very black tarmac is covered in clods of mud and smeared tracks from whatever heavy machinery has been in and out today. Two hefty men in full body suits, high-viz jackets, hard hats and safety glasses are shovelling the dirt into wheelbarrows. I wonder what they need so much protecting from, out there on the open road, before I catch myself. Better they're safe, I think, remembering the man my dad worked with, who lost his hand because the piece of machinery he operated didn't have a guard on it. One second's inattention, that was all it took. No more evenings at the snooker hall or digging his allotment.

Something's different on-site. There are workers swarming the place, more than usual it seems, and as I get further in, closer to the newest block, I realise they're tidying the place up, brushing down pathways, clearing away swathes of opaque plastic and lengths of rope, and all the rubbish the wind blows in.

They must be due a visit from the bosses tomorrow. That or someone they consider a very serious buyer, the kind who acquires property by the tower, rather than in mere blocks of two or three.

It would be a good time for us to mount an action.

A call to arms tonight might gather a few dozen supporters. Enough for coverage in the local press, and if we could provoke someone into a rash reaction – one of the executives or the drivers or site security – we might get useful video.

My heart isn't in it, though.

And the last thing we should be doing right now is drawing attention to ourselves.

Callum is coming out of the main door as I approach, holding a clutch of plastic carrier bags, the cheap, thin kind you can see right through, and I know what's in them by the greyish-brown bulk. More rats.

He holds them up. 'Big as fucking cats. Four of them.'

I wrinkle my nose.

'Do you want to see them?' he asks.

'You sick bastard.'

'I thought you were an artist. Aren't you creative types into death and decay and that sort of thing?' He lifts the lid of one of the big bins and drops the dead animals inside, wipes his hands on the back of his jeans. 'Must be the time of year, they're coming in from the cold.' He looks up at the empty sky, like he can read the air. 'Do you want me to put some traps down in your place?'

'Have you got enough?'

'Four more than I had this morning, aye.' He opens the door for me and we go into the lobby. 'Or I've got poison. But you don't want poison really, because they take themselves off to die and then you never know where they're going to wind up. Might find one rotting round the back of your fridge or something. Reckon I've got one in my place. Reeks in there.'

My heartbeat stutters and skips at the thought of Ella's nameless dead man rotting in the lift shaft. I slip my arm through Callum's for support and resolutely avoid looking at the pair of lifts as we pass them. He's in the one on the left and I'm sure I can smell him now too, even though I noticed nothing this morning when I went out. The power of suggestion is working on me and I hate it. This is what happens when you're tired and scared. The fear takes a stronger hold on you.

Is he beginning to ooze? Are his fluids pooling under him, spreading out and spilling into the grooves of the lift's ceiling, looking for places to settle, little cracks and holes to drip through?

How long before his death becomes something audible?

'We need to find the nest,' Callum says, taking the stairs slowly, at what he thinks is my pace.

Callum searching the building is the last thing I want.

'You won't stop them coming,' I tell him, finding my voice again at last. 'Rats are part of city living. Don't waste your time. Let's just try and keep them out of our flats, okay? They can have the rest of the building if they want it.'

On the half-landing he stops, his face showing concern. 'You're giving up.'

I grip the handrail. I don't want to argue with him, don't even want to talk to him right now, I just want to go into my flat and close the door and sit in silence for a while.

'Cal, there are probably hundreds of rats in here. You could wipe them all out today and a bunch more would come in tomorrow. This isn't worth you messing about with.'

'You won't say that when you wake up with one on your bed.' He's getting agitated, his left leg beginning to jiggle, and I've seen this before, know he's on the cusp of going into one of his odd moods. I don't have the energy to deal with this on top of everything else.

'Okay, look, can you come up later on and put some traps down for me?'

'You need to keep them out,' he says, eyes bulging.

'Will you bring the traps up?' I ask, trying to get him to focus.

He nods. 'Yeah, yeah, I better go and do the ones for Derek and Jenny first. He caught one yesterday, you know, found it in the bathroom when he got up for a slash. He goes four or five times a night, the poor old fucker, prostate, he keeps sayin' I should get mine checked, but ahm no' old enough far tha'.'

He's slipping back into the accent he's largely lost, his posture changing in front of my eyes, becoming slouched and sly, his head tilting at a new and wrong angle.

I can't deal with him as well.

'I'm going to have a kip,' I say, pushing past him up the stairs. 'Give me a couple of hours, yeah? I'm knackered.'

Gratefully I shut the door and lean back against it for a moment, close my eyes, wishing I was somewhere else, far from here. I don't need a five-star hotel or a sandy beach, just a bolthole would do, any place beyond human contact, freed from worrying about other people, the living and the dead.

But that isn't how it works.

I retrieve my laptop from its hiding place, switch it on and make a cup of strong coffee loaded with sugar. As tired as I feel, sleep won't help.

I start with Twitter, find plenty of photographs from the party sent to Ella and a few to me as well, selfies I don't remember agreeing to but I look drunk enough to have agreed to anything, beaming into high-held phones and mercifully filtered afterwards.

It's the backgrounds and group shots I'm interested in, though. I blow up each photograph, work methodically, moving and zooming, looking for him among the crowd. I search for his profile, the knit of his hat, the shape of his beard, that army green flak jacket, which wasn't heavy enough for the cold weather.

Picture after picture of laughter and smiles and frozen conversations, beer bottles poised an inch from parted lips and heads tipped back to empty plastic wine glasses, the odd blue dots of e-cigarettes floating.

There he is.

There *they* are.

Ella and her dead man standing close together.

She's lied to me again.

Ella

Then – Christmas Eve

Ella's mother was waiting for her at Durham station, overdressed as usual, in a camel coat and leather gloves, her ash-blonde hair whipped up into a chignon simultaneously too old and too young for her. She was tapping out a message on her phone, probably checking Ella's father was up to speed with the list of last-minute Christmas prep she would inevitably have given him.

The Riordan household began bracing itself for festivities the day after Bonfire Night, when her parents presided over a party attended by half of the village, with a fire that took a week to build and a guy fashioned after whoever her father deemed most worthy of burning. It had been Jeremy Corbyn this year, her father had gleefully informed her, sending half a dozen photos of their badly formed proxy perishing in the flames while the fat Rotarians and members of the golf club toasted him with mulled wine.

Christmas would, hopefully, be less political. All the friends and professional acquaintances should have been and gone already and Ella only had to survive her family.

The other passengers off the 10.30 from King's Cross progressed slowly through the ticket barriers, struggling with bags and looking for tickets which should have already been in their hands. Ella's mother finally placed her phone back inside her handbag and waved in her reserved fashion as Ella made her way through the crowds.

Ella swung her holdall off her shoulder and hugged her, smelling hairspray and vanilla perfume, underneath it a slight trace of the cigarettes her mother occasionally smoked with less stealth than she realised.

'You look tired, Ellie darling. Late night?'

'Early start,' she said, ignoring what might have been a barb. 'It's so good to be home.'

'It's so good to have you home.' They linked arms and walked out towards the car park, carol singers collecting for charity on the pavement, filling the air with bells and song and the rattle of coins. 'I was down your way last week but I didn't want to bother you. You're always so busy.'

'You should have told me you were coming,' Ella said. 'We could have gone for lunch.'

'Oh, no, I didn't want to put you out. It was all rather last minute. Christmas shopping.' She thumbed her key fob and the lights flashed on a black Range Rover just ahead of them. 'And I know you don't enjoy shopping as much as I do.'

'This is new,' Ella said, as she placed her bag in the back.

'Your father insisted.' A little shrug of delighted resignation. 'The other one was getting troublesome.'

On the drive home Ella let her mother do most of the talking and listened with half an ear to the updates on which neighbours were ill or downsizing or having affairs, which of her old school-friends had done very well since she was there last Christmas and who the less said about the better – a phrase that always heralded a far lengthier and more involved story than it suggested.

The countryside blurred by the window, her mother driving in the reckless way she always did on rural roads. There was something about being in a tank, Ella supposed: you didn't have to respect any oncoming vehicle smaller than a combine harvester and those were long packed up in their sheds now. The familiar woods were greener than she thought they should have been at this time of year; she was sure she remembered them barren and skeletal in previous winters.

Now, as her mother slowed behind a man on a horse at the edge of the village, Ella noticed daffodils in bud around a blind-bend sign, could already see the tips turning yellow.

They passed the pub, thick with the lunchtime crowd, the car park crammed, smoke billowing out of the chimney. Nothing changed here. The same people would be inside, having the same conversations they'd been sharing for twenty years or more, and Ella found it didn't oppress her like it once had. Now she didn't have to be here she found it oddly comforting. In London you'd go down a street you hadn't walked along for a couple of months and a building would be gone, razed to the ground and the site boarded ready for work to begin, and she would find she didn't remember what had been there before. Here a front door being painted a new colour would be noticed by everyone, a side garden becoming a building plot could be blocked for years, fought to the highest level and then seethed about for evermore.

Her parents' house stood separated from the village green by the narrowest of roads. A stone and thatch cottage five hundred years old, long and low and resolutely solid. It had been a bakehouse once, derelict when they bought it soon after their marriage, but carefully restored before she was born, her mother only a couple of years older than she was now. Ella struggled to imagine living a life that sensible and settled at such a young age. But she knew her mother couldn't understand the choices she'd made either.

The gates were open and they pulled along the gravel driveway up to the open barn at the back of the house, where her father's bashed-up Defender was parked, alongside the peppermint-green Alvis he'd started to restore when he retired. He didn't seem to be making any progress on it and Ella wondered if he'd got bored, or distracted by other things. Her mother had let slip that he was doing consultancy work now, but wouldn't go into details, insisting it was hellishly tedious and she never listened when he talked about it.

Ella was convinced her mother just didn't trust her to know what he was working on or who for.

Ever since the last arrest Ella had noticed she didn't ask what she was doing any more. Not when she phoned or emailed, not even during the half-hour car journey from the station. Ella decided she wouldn't mention anything herself, see how her mother managed to avoid the subject for three days.

It would be nice to ignore it herself for a while, too. She'd hoped her release without charge would be an end to the speculation, but it hadn't slowed down the gossip or convinced people who thought she was involved that she hadn't been. Never mind that she had an alibi and absolutely no reason to get tangled up in something so senselessly destructive as arson.

Regardless of how hard she protested, it fitted certain people's idea of who Ella Riordan was, added a layer of 'dangerous allure'. Someone had said that, right to her face. A man, naturally.

So, if her mother wanted to talk about other things, that was fine.

In the house Ella dropped her bag and went straight to the postbox-red range, more from habit than a need for warmth. The kitchen was fully decked for Christmas, garlands of pine cones hanging from the beams, smelling of cinnamon and the orange peel her mother would have dried herself at the beginning of the month. In the far corner a short but dense tree was strung with the same old red and white decorations, lights twinkling in the foliage.

Ella gasped, remembering how thoughtlessly she'd thrown her bag down, and rushed over to find the package she'd brought, pulling out clothes and books and the other presents she'd carefully wrapped back in her flat. She stopped when she found the small purple box and handed it to her mother.

'I hope it's not broken.'

'Ooh, Liberty.' She opened the box and lifted out the mercifully intact bauble, a warm smile spreading across her face. 'It's perfect, Ellie. Beautiful. Thank you so much. Do you want to put it on the tree?'

Ella took the delicate red-and-white candy-striped decoration and found a space for it at the front of the tree, between a gingerbread man and a felt stag.

'Coffee?' her mother asked, as she hung up her overcoat in the boot room. 'Or would you like one of my special hot chocolates?'

'Have you got marshmallows?'

'I'm insulted you need to ask.' She started on their drinks while Ella sat down at the long oak table and they talked about the charity work her mother had been doing, making up hampers to give out at a food bank in Newcastle. 'Nobody should have to have a sad Christmas.'

That jolted Ella back to Castle Rise, the nine families still remaining, who would be enduring rather than enjoying their break, knowing that the trees they'd put up would not see another year in the same place, that the orders to quit might arrive before Twelfth Night.

Ella had bought them each gifts, only small things, but it seemed important to do so; biscuits in pretty tins and coffee liqueur, hot-water bottles with knitted covers and Lego kits for the kids. She stopped off there yesterday evening, late, so they wouldn't feel pressured into reciprocating.

Molly had already bought her something. Or, rather, not bought, Ella realised when she opened the package to find a signed first edition of *Nights at the Circus*, well-thumbed and a little battered around the edges, but worth a stupid amount, Ella suspected. Not that she'd ever sell it.

'I can't accept this,' she'd said. 'It's too much.'

Molly had waved away her half-hearted protest. 'Please, who else am I going to leave it to?'

It wasn't until she was on the Tube home that the strangeness of Molly's words struck her. Was there something wrong with her? It would explain the expression on Molly's face when Ella told her she was going home for the holidays, a look of piercing disappointment. Molly had told her before that she was welcome to come over for a couple of days if she was on her own in London, tossed it out casually even though it clearly wasn't. Christmas was tough when you had no one, Ella thought, but Molly didn't seem the type to be bothered by that ordinarily and she would have Callum with her; two lost souls, improbably clinging to one another.

But what if he was going to his family?

The idea of Molly alone in the flat was heartbreaking. The absolute, crushing sadness of it. Ella prayed that Callum wasn't going away. She wanted him to surprise Molly with an extravagant breakfast on the day or turn up with a tree on Christmas Eve and coax her into decorating it with him. That they'd do something to alleviate the recent grim monotony of life at Castle Rise.

Ella finished the last of her hot chocolate, realising how heavily her mother had spiked it with amaretto. Her face felt flushed and she smiled.

'That was *extra* special, wasn't it, Mum?'

She shrugged, innocent-looking. 'Well, it is Christmas.'

'I think I need a lie-down after that.'

'Go on, I'll wake you for supper.'

Ella started towards her bag, its contents strewn on the flagstones around it.

'I'll take care of your things,' her mother said. 'You go up, darling.'

Opening the door to her childhood bedroom provoked a moment of sharp dislocation. Only now did she remember the conversation about redecorating. Everything would be carefully put away in the attic, her mother had reassured her, and Ella didn't doubt it was all up there, but this gilt and mahogany boutique-hotel interior was going to take a little getting used to.

The bed was more comfortable than her old one, though, and she fell asleep within a few minutes, lulled by the familiar sound of the back boiler heating the house.

When she woke up again the curtains had been drawn and a woollen throw placed over her and she could hear voices downstairs she recognised as her brother and his wife. Ella groaned into the lavender-scented pillow. She'd hoped to avoid them until lunch tomorrow but of course they were here now, ready for the short walk across the green to midnight mass. Another Riordan family tradition she could have done without.

She delayed the inevitable for a little longer, took a shower and washed her hair, seeing under the en suite's brilliant lighting how tired she looked. That was more than one night's bad sleep and an early morning, it was everything – her PhD and her campaigning, all the worry and responsibility, the clutching fear that kept her awake into the early hours – all of that piling up on her. Ella swept tinted moisturiser on to her damp skin, added a quick flick of liquid liner, and she looked almost ready to face her family.

As she was getting dressed she heard a mobile phone ring in the next room, her father answering – 'It's Christmas Eve, can this not wait?' And apparently it could because by the time she was in the hallway, he'd fallen silent again.

The door to his study was half open and she saw him sitting at his old captain's desk under the window, a brass lamp casting the only light in the oxblood room, throwing his shadow across the wall where his photo gallery hung. She had stood here a thousand times, waiting to go in, and the scene hadn't changed since she was small; her dad, straight-backed and broad-shouldered, although she'd swear his steel-grey hair had thinned a little more at the crown since the last time she saw him. He'd come to Edinburgh during the festival and taken her to lunch at a restaurant near the station, which he'd seen favourably reviewed in the *Telegraph*. She'd called him from her hotel room in a panic that morning and he'd caught the next train, calmed her down, talked the sense she needed to hear even though she didn't want him to be right.

'Don't stand on ceremony, Ellie love.'

He spun away from his desk and Ella walked into an enveloping hug. He smelled of woodsmoke and old wool, reassuringly unchanged, as he kissed the top of her head. When she stepped back he looked her over and nodded.

'Yes, there's my little firebrand.'

'Dad, please...'

He chuckled and went over to the space on his crowded bookshelf where he kept a few bottles of Scotch, poured two measures, while she curled up in his leather wing chair. There was a book splayed on the arm, a dry-looking exploration of Middle Eastern geopolitics. He picked it up when he handed over her drink and went to close the study door before returning to his seat at the desk. She'd hoped this might wait until Boxing Day but her father wasn't the kind of man to put things off. And, she supposed, he was worried too.

Ella sipped the Scotch, knew it was a good one but not why; they all tasted the same to her.

'I'm fine,' she said, before he could ask. 'It all got sorted.'

'And that's an end to it?'

'I hope so.'

'You don't sound very certain,' he said. 'And you don't look confident. I'm your father: you can't hide from me.'

She looked away from him, towards the photographs on his wall where he posed with local politicians and councillors in his dress uniform, all smiles and friendly handshakes. In this light you couldn't see how strained some of the expressions were – sometimes his, sometimes theirs, depending on what had happened in the run-up to the photo opportunity. The only one where he looked like her dad rather than ACC Alec Riordan was taken with some old Newcastle United player at a charity golf match.

'You're treading a dangerous line, Ellie.'

She glared at him. 'I know what I'm doing. I'm not a child.'

'You're my child, no matter how old you are and how clever you are. And I'm fully entitled to worry about what you're doing with your life.'

There it was.

'I'm not going to stop just because you disapprove,' she said. 'I'm sorry, Dad, I know this isn't what you wanted me to do with my life but it's important work. And,' – she threw her hands up – 'most people don't care. They wouldn't want to do it, but somebody has to.'

'It doesn't have to be you.'

'I'm good at this.' She hated the desperation in her voice right then; a little girl wanting Daddy's approval. 'Dad, I'm making so much progress.'

'At what cost?' he asked quietly, looking down into his drink. 'Would you have gone to prison for this?'

'It didn't come to that.'

'Because you were lucky.' He nodded at her. 'This time, you got lucky. But what about next time?'

'I'm not going to do anything stupid,' Ella told him, deflated by the conversation, wishing he could have just told her how proud he was, that even if he didn't agree he could appreciate how hard she was working.

He drained his drink. 'You know we'll always be here for you, don't you? If things start to go too far, you only have to call me.'

And then where would she be? Reputation shot, friends scattered, she'd be exactly what her detractors always thought she was: a copper's daughter playing at rebellion to make a point.

No, she'd worked too hard for that. Nothing would ever induce her to use his connections.

But it was Christmas and he'd had his say and there was no reason to argue with him.

'I appreciate that, Dad,' she said, reaching to squeeze his hand. 'Thank you.'

Molly

Now – 13th March

I haven't slept.

Not even a brief nap last night and now I'm having palpitations at my desk while I bury myself in denial, working through the last couple of weeks' photographs, deciding which ones are good enough to put up on the image banks that keep me in pappy white bread and instant coffee and these dodgy Marlboro I buy under the counter, dirt cheap and tax free.

Ella *knew* him.

OK, she told me that – her tepid one-night stand; she was entitled to lie about it, I suppose – but she said she hadn't seen him at the party. Why lie about *that*?

I get up from my desk and pace around the living room, taking deep, sandpapery drags, blowing the smoke out slowly. Back and forth, ash flaking on to the garish carpet I'd always meant to get rid of but gradually came to love for its clashing colours and the pattern so hideous it was almost beautiful.

Doesn't Ella trust me?

Is that it?

Once again I switch to the tab where the incriminating photograph is blown up as large as its resolution will allow. Ella's back is to the camera, her shoulders straight with tension, but this is a millisecond captured and frozen and I know better than to read her entire mood into what might have been a quick shrug.

He's leaning towards her in the photo. Most of his face infuriatingly hidden from the lens. I have enough to know it's definitely him but not enough to judge his mood or behaviour. This is the only image I can find and it tells me nothing.

I get rid of the picture, bring up something sedate to work on for a while. A Georgian front door, weathered and scuffed, its paint faded, ironwork rusted. These photos sell well. Doorways and alleyways, old staircases and stone steps. People can't resist them, the allure of secrets hidden and opportunities waiting.

People get killed in alleyways, that's what I know. Beaten or raped. Nothing good ever happened to anyone behind a door that looks like that.

And Ella doesn't trust me.

It's a physical pain like my ribs are closing in around my heart and lungs. She made me her accomplice, knowing I'd help her even at the risk of my own freedom. She knows how deep my loyalty runs. This isn't the first time I've shown her that.

I want things to be as they were a week ago, when we were sisters in arms, fighting the good fight. Ella accomplishing things I don't have the youth or energy to get done, taking my advice, learning from my mistakes. Half the contacts she's built her reputation on are mine. I've vouched for her to people who wouldn't have trusted her with their surnames, let alone anything more. A copper's daughter. An assistant chief constable's daughter, for Christ's sake.

Is she keeping things from me because she's planning on going to him for help?

The less I know the more difficult for me to contradict whatever story he cooks up to get her off the hook...

But I can't see that happening. Not knowing what I know about their relationship. Going to her father now would confirm every bad thing he believes about her. It would put her at his mercy. She's run this far from his iron grip, betraying everything he stands for along the way, dragging his profession through the dirt; I can't see her running back to him.

I take a deep breath, my hand pressed to my heart, feeling every beat hit my palm. Try to calm down, try to think.

My eye catches on the ugly steel rat trap Callum brought up yesterday evening. It's behind the sofa, laid along the skirting board. That's where you catch them, Callum says. They burrow into the upholstery, tear clumps out to take back to their nests, and they run along the wall, straight into the traps.

Rats are smarter than that, though, I'm sure.

He's baited it with half a chocolate Pop-Tart but it's still a trap and rats haven't survived this long with the whole of human ingenuity railed against them by falling for such cheap tricks.

I grab my mobile and call Ella.

It goes straight through to voicemail but I don't leave a message. Her Twitter account shows no activity beyond a few links to news items and petitions she's encouraging her followers to sign; one to boycott the raising of a statue dedicated to an Edwardian philanthropist and espouser of eugenics, another calling for the support of a local library being threatened with closure.

I send her a text. Telling her I need her opinion on the latest batch of photos for her book.

She'll realise it's a lie, but you never know who else will see these messages.

I check on the other traps Callum has laid, one behind the fridge and another behind the toilet, the last hidden in the airing cupboard, where the rats have been rootling around, leaving scratch marks on the chipboard and gnawing at the lagging on the pipes. That's where he'll catch one if he's going to.

Thinking of snapped bones and sprayed blood, I remove the clothes hanging from the lowest shelf, a lambswool jumper I bought from Help the Aged and a vintage silk blouse I've had since the seventies, printed with tiny tulips, and put them on the radiator. Two generations I've owned that blouse and I can still remember the song that was playing in the changing room when I tried it on – Roxy Music, 'Both Ends Burning'.

Time isn't supposed to move this fast.

I go back to my desk, stick my earphones in and turn the volume up on an instrumental playlist heavy on the Afro-Cuban funk, forcing myself to concentrate on the photographs that still need editing.

At my back the photographs I took in my prime watch over me, and when I'm doing this kind of work I feel judged by them. Protestors and club kids, gangsters and rent boys and musicians long gone to obscurity. People whose personalities burned so hot through the lens they could have singed my eyelashes.

I keep going.

A Victorian soap advert painted high on the gable wall of a condemned mansion block. I'd noticed it across a building site, hidden there since its neighbour went up in the sixties and only revealed now because an office block has been demolished. A bulldozer was pulling on-site as I walked away, ready to obliterate that building too. This might be the only photograph of the sign in existence.

I pause for a bite of the sandwich I made hours ago and forgot. Bread and jam, just like when I was a kid and we didn't have anything else in the house to eat because payday wasn't until Friday. Jam or salt-and-pepper sandwiches, that was your choice. When I got out, got money, I'd think it was a total nostalgia trip to sprinkle cracked black pepper and kosher salt on a slice of fresh-cut sourdough bread, spread thick with white butter. Like I was reclaiming those years of poverty.

But here I am again, the snotty-nosed girl with the falling-down socks and the darned jumpers, living on nothing.

I start on the next picture, select the best shot, crop and tweak and save, and then there's another in front of me and another and my back is aching in the swivel chair and my eyes are furring over, flakes of the mascara I didn't take off last night gritty under my lower lids. The playlist has been running on repeat and I've lost track of time, grown cold and stiff-fingered.

My phone rings but I don't hear it, only feel the vibration shake the desk.

Ella.

I whip out my earbuds and snatch up the phone.

'What's wrong?' she asks, before I can say a word. 'Is this it?'

'No, Ella. Calm down.'

Through the sliding door I see how late it has got. Dark out now and the room reflected over the glass is small and messy, so

91

stuffy I can almost see the staleness on the air. I switch the light off and open the door, letting the night breeze in.

'Can't you talk right now?' Ella asks.

'I can talk.' I brace my hand against the door's metal frame. 'Ella, there's a picture of you with him on Twitter.'

'Who?'

'Who do you think?'

'There can't be,' she says. 'I didn't see him. Are you sure that's who it is? You're always saying everyone looks alike to you now.'

'I'm not likely to forget his face, am I?'

I shudder as I remember his dead eyes staring up at me, staring right through me as we carried him along the corridor towards the lift shaft.

'I'm sure I didn't see him.' She sounds genuinely perplexed. 'I'd remember. Wouldn't I? No, this is stupid. I didn't see him at the party, Molly.'

I stay silent.

'You and Carol kept giving me drink,' Ella says, her voice dropping. 'That's the problem, I can hardly remember anything after I sat down with you two. That weed she was smoking – she kept blowing it into my face. You know how sensitive I am to it.' A growl. 'God. I didn't think I was that out of it.'

Ella *had* been drunk, more than I'd ever seen her. I remember how she stumbled as she climbed on to the platform we built for her from milk crates. She got through her speech well enough but, now I think about it, it wasn't the usual polished Ella talking; she'd rambled a little and beaten her chest, showing a more raw and inspiring version of herself. Until her foot slipped and we caught her to cheers from the partygoers, raised her up like Jesus.

'Send me the picture,' she says.

'It's probably best you just look at it.' I tell her the username of the person who posted it and wait for her to find the image, knowing she has by the way she swears, softly, almost regretfully.

'Molly, I honestly don't remember this. Please, believe me.'

It sounds like the truth. I close my eyes, listening to the sound of her breathing, the traffic noise and music floating up from a bar on the river, the inevitable sirens, very close. Too close. I step out on to the balcony and see blue lights flashing across the front of the building as a patrol car pulls up. Derek and Callum are down there already, waiting.

Ella has heard the sirens too.

'What's happening?' The panic is tight in her voice.

I want to shout down to Callum but it's too late; the police are out of their car and Derek is moving towards them. He looks shaken and Callum is tense, holding back, arms wrapped around his middle. As if he feels my eyes on him, he looks up to the balcony and looks away again.

Did he see me?

Does he know?

Callum leads the PCs inside and I know where they're going, which floor they will stop climbing at, exactly what they are going to see. My stomach lurches and I bolt through the living room to the bathroom, where I drop to my knees so heavily I set off the rat trap behind the toilet. I throw up bile and coffee, my eyes stinging.

I spit out what little is left in me and sit back against the bath, hearing Ella's voice, a dim and distant version of her which, for a second, I think I'm hallucinating, until I realise my phone is still in my hand, the call live.

'Molly?' she asks desperately, almost shouting. 'Are you okay?'

'They're here,' I say. 'The police. They've found him.'

Ella

Then – 26th November

A mobile phone trilled into the quiet of the Reading Room and Ella looked up in annoyance, along with two-thirds of the people there, towards a young man several desks over who fumbled to get the phone out of his pocket. He apologised, his face flushing, the ringing continuing, echoing around the cavernous space and bouncing off the glass that protected the collection of books and manuscripts. Finally, just as he brought the phone out, it stopped ringing.

There were huffs and sighs and a woman with a cut-glass accent muttered, 'About bloody time.'

Ella was the only one still looking at the guy and she gave him a reassuring smile, because she'd done the same thing herself the first time she came into the British Library's holy of holies. Was sure she'd switched her phone to silent, only to have it blast out a plunging, polyphonic ringtone at full volume a couple of minutes after she sat down.

Quickly the room settled back into its habitual near-silence.

This was what she needed. Somewhere to sit quietly for a few hours, no laptop, her phone definitely off, just a pen and paper and the latest draft of her thesis to read through. Except she couldn't hold more than a few words in her head before she found her mind drifting.

This morning she'd woken to a text message from Ryan Quinn.

'They're coming for you, bitch.'

Dylan was still asleep next to her, radiating more body heat than any man she'd ever slept with, like he somehow generated his own microclimate. She was glad he hadn't seen the message or her reaction. She had no intention of enduring another lecture from him. Somehow she'd managed to get out from under his proprietorial arm, dressed quickly while he slept, and left the flat, heard him call her name as she closed the door.

She stuck the pen in her mouth, bit down on the plastic and felt it begin to give between her back teeth, stopped before it shattered.

'Ella Riordan?'

A woman stood behind her, dark-suited and severe-faced with her blonde hair scraped into a ponytail. Nearby stood a young man who might have been an estate agent if not for his stillness and attention and the other half-dozen small tells that said 'copper'.

'Am I under arrest?' Ella asked.

At the surrounding desks all work had ceased.

'We'd like you to come with us, Ms Riordan.' The woman spoke in a monotone. 'We can arrest you if you're not prepared to come along voluntarily.'

'I have a right to know why I'm being hounded.'

The woman leaned in. 'We're not bit players in your publicity campaign, Ella. Collect your things and stand up.'

Ella was aware of the room's attention on them as she packed her papers into her satchel. 'This is what happens to people who peacefully protest in Britain now, is it?' she asked. 'You come to where we're studying and drag us out like criminals.'

'Save it for your blog,' the young guy muttered.

They escorted her out of the Reading Room and Ella held her head up high. As they passed through the main doors, into the grim morning, the woman took hold of her elbow and turned her on to Ossulston Street, where a car was waiting for them.

It was an unobtrusive gunmetal saloon with another man driving, old and bald, and he didn't move as the woman palmed the top of Ella's head and shoved her in the back, came around and got in next to her. It suddenly occurred to Ella that they might not be police at all. How many people had she pissed off? How much money had she cost developers with her stunts? All those accusations she'd made about bribes and corruption and money laundering – was this how they would come for her? No, she told herself, as she felt her breath growing short.

No, she knew exactly what this was about. Quinn had been kind enough to warn her with his message this morning.

Woolwich: that was why they'd come for her and where they were heading.

It was an ugly 1960s police station in need of overhauling, the reception area battered, the reinforced glass protecting the desk sergeant peppered and crazed like it had taken a shotgun blast. She was walked to a claustrophobic lift and then up through white corridors that smelled faintly of damp and singed wiring and gave on to a row of interview rooms.

A bolt of remembered discomfort hit Ella's stomach as she was taken inside and told to sit down. It looked just the same as the one she'd been taken to after the Camden demonstration, her first time being cautioned.

Now she was expecting the caution and she waited until the policewoman, DS Conway, had finished before she said, 'I'd like my solicitor to be present. I won't speak without him here.'

Conway sighed. 'If you want legal counsel you'll have to go down to the cells and wait for him to arrive. He might be tied up in court all day. You don't want to spend the night here, do you, Ella?' She attempted a concerned face, wholly unconvincing. 'We've only got a few questions.'

'Patrick Milton,' Ella said, then recited the number she'd memorised almost two years ago, when Molly gave her it, saying he was one of the good ones. 'I'm perfectly happy to wait.'

In the custody suite they stripped her of her belongings and put her in a cell where the padded bench was still warm from its previous occupant, and she did what everyone said you shouldn't in this situation, laid down with her back to the door and tried to have a nap.

Coppers put out the line that only a guilty person could sleep in a cell because the last thing they wanted was to question you fresh and rested. Her father had told her that. Chuckled when he said it.

Last night she'd discussed this with Dylan. Spilled everything she could about Quinn and what he'd done and they worked out the best way to handle it. He was furious with her, disappointed and hurt that she'd not trusted him until she was so terrified she had to tell someone. But he calmed down eventually, after she'd stroked and placated him and explained that he was the only person who was smart enough to help her through this.

'You haven't done anything, Ella,' he'd said. 'That's all that matters here. Whatever they accuse you of, whatever they threaten you with, just hold on to that and they can't touch you.'

She closed her eyes and drifted off, the sounds of the people in the other cells always at the edge of her consciousness, calling out for bathroom breaks and food, a woman crying as they locked her up. Gradually those noises faded and she slept properly, dreaming for the first time in months of riot shields and angry eyes distorted by helmets, of the crush of the crowd and freedom beyond the cordon and how for a moment it had felt like she was flying, before her legs were taken from under her and the ground came racing up to her face.

The cell door opened with a clang and she started awake, turning over to see the woman who'd brought her down.

'Solicitor's here.'

Patrick Milton was waiting for her in the interview room with a bottle of mineral water and a chocolate bar ready on the table. Ella smiled at his dishevelled brown suit and the knitted tie hanging askew over a mismatched checked shirt.

'Do we need a few minutes?' he asked Ella.

She was aware of DS Conway waiting for the answer too, ready to draw her own conclusions from it.

'I don't even know why I'm here,' she told him.

'Let's see what they have to say for themselves, then.' Patrick pulled out a chair for her, ever the old gent, then sat down with his hands clasped loosely on the table. Ella noticed a slight tremble running through them, saw Conway notice it too and hoped it would make the woman underestimate him.

Conway watched Ella in silence as her constable set up the tapes and Ella forced herself to hold the woman's gaze, noting every line around her unusually blue eyes and how red her lower lids were, as if she had allergies. It would be easy to write her off, scruffy and dull-looking as she was, but she knew that these were the most dangerous coppers, the kind you never saw coming.

Conway opened a file and removed a series of photographs, lying them out methodically in front of Ella, her face in a disapproving pout.

They showed a line of protestors outside an estate agent's office in Woolwich, its interior new, pristine white, and several figures in dark suits looking out angrily at the people keeping their customers from the door on their first day of trading. Ella was among them, alongside Carol, whose face was half hidden by a scarf and sunglasses. Many of the others had covered up too but Ella knew their names, remembered the police cordon and the officer filming from behind them.

'Can you tell us what was going on here?' Conway asked.

'Your people were there,' Ella said. 'I'm sure you know what we were doing.'

'You were protesting against the opening of this business.'

'Peacefully protesting, yes. As we have every right to.'

'It didn't remain peaceful very long.' Conway cocked her head. 'Did it?'

'We weren't the ones who instigated the escalation,' Ella told her, throwing her chin up in defiance, back there in the moment. 'Have you charged any of the people responsible yet?'

'I can't comment on that. It's a separate investigation,' Conway said. 'How do you feel about what happened there?'

'It's a separate investigation.' Ella gave her the merest hint of a smile. 'I shouldn't comment.'

Conway glanced at her constable, a brief eye-roll. 'Oh, but they intersect, Ms Riordan. How long had you been campaigning against the opening of that estate agent's office?'

'Since the summer, when they forced out the charity that was based in the building. They were using the upper floor; we wanted the owners to allow them to stay on while they rented out the ground floor to Brighams.'

'The owners have a right to do what they want with their property, surely?' Conway shrugged. 'Who are you to tell them otherwise?'

'We didn't tell them, we asked them to consider the option.'

'And when they decided against it, you tried to block the legitimate business occupying the building.' Conway shook her head. 'Those are the tactics of a protection racket.'

Ella turned to the constable, who had said nothing more since he'd set the recording equipment up.

'Do you live here in Woolwich?' she asked.

'That's none of your business,' he said.

'I'm going to hazard a guess that you can't afford to live where you work. Unless you're renting a room in a shared house. Forget renting somewhere by yourself, forget buying.' Ella's voice rose slightly. 'Brighams are why hundreds of thousands of people like you and me will never be able to own our own homes. They move into an area, inflate prices, aggressively pursue buy-to-let landlords and socially cleanse entire boroughs.' Ella stabbed the table with her finger. 'That's what we were protesting.'

The constable gave her a dead-eyed look. 'But you didn't stop them, did you?'

'Not that day, they didn't,' Conway said.

Ella stiffened in her seat as another photograph came out of the file: Quinn's mugshot.

He looked proud of himself as he stood in front of the height marker and stared down the camera lens, amusement and contempt shaping his features. Ella had stood there herself and she'd felt fear, despite her anger and indignation. Quinn looked as if this was the culmination of a life's ambition.

'Do you know this man?' Conway asked.

'Yes, that's Ryan Quinn.'

'And how do you know him?'

'Quinn's an anti-gentrification activist,' Ella said, letting some of her disgust for him come through. 'I've run into him at events.'

'He's an ally of yours, then.'

'I don't think either of us would say that. Quinn believes I'm a fraud because I refuse to engage in direct action and prefer to use peaceful forms of protest and try, wherever I can, to foster dialogue and open lines of negotiation.'

Conway made no comment, only rearranged the photos so the one of the protest lay on top. 'Is Quinn in these photos?'

'I'm not sure,' Ella said, looking at the images for a moment. 'He was there that day. I remember him trying to stir things up. He was spoiling for a fight.' She reached for the bottle of water. 'Ironically, when it did kick off, he was nowhere to be seen.'

'Did you speak to him after the protest?'

'No.'

It was a lie and Ella saw that Conway suspected as much, but doubted she could prove it. Her only contact with Quinn from that point had been via a ghost phone she'd since dumped in Regent's Canal and she knew Quinn would have been even more careful with communications at his end. He'd boasted of how his computer system was programmed to self-destruct unless he keyed in a code twice a day, putting it beyond the reach of the Met's tech department.

Ella took a drink of water, watching Conway tidy the photos away, saw there were still more of them.

'Can you tell us your whereabouts between midnight on November twenty-third and five a.m. November twenty-fourth?'

'I was at my friend Molly's flat in Nine Elms,' Ella said. 'I went around in the evening to talk about a book we're working on and stayed the night on her sofa.'

'We need her details.'

Ella gave them, knowing the first thing they would do was check Molly's record. It would make for a fun read.

'Assuming you were in Nine Elms all night,' Conway said, 'can you explain how we have an eyewitness who places you on Powis Street, Woolwich, at that time?'

'Eyewitnesses are notoriously unreliable, as you well know, Sergeant Conway,' Milton said in a kindly tone. 'Perhaps if you were to offer up CCTV footage...'

'This eyewitness is very reliable,' she said smugly. 'He was inside Brighams' offices with you, Ms Riordan.'

'I've never been inside Brighams,' Ella told her, making her voice firm enough to brook no argument. 'Not since they took over, anyway.'

The last few photographs came out of the file. The previously pristine office interior burned black, its plate-glass window blown out, everything drenched with fire-stained water, which was running out of the shattered front door on to the pavement, carrying scraps of charred paper into the gutter. The Perspex desks had buckled and melted and the computers sitting on them had sunk into their surfaces.

Ella looked at Conway, hoping the detective didn't see the unexpected mix of satisfaction and fear she felt. She touched her tongue to the roof of her mouth, making her face hard before she dared speak.

'You think Quinn did this?'

'Quinn and you,' Conway said.

'This had nothing to do with me.' Ella placed her fingertips on the nearest photo. 'I'm a campaigner, not an arsonist. This kind of action damages the work I do. I've always been very clear that peaceful protest is the way forward.'

Conway smirked at her. 'I'm sure you do say that, publicly. But we know you were there, Ella. This attack was your idea. You conceived it after your "peaceful protest" failed and you recruited Quinn to help you make it happen.'

'Do you have any evidence to support this claim, Sergeant Conway?' Milton asked, picking a photograph up to squint at it through his wire-rimmed glasses.

'Your accomplice has given you up,' she said, ignoring his question.

'Ryan Quinn is not my anything,' Ella told her. 'He loathes me and now he's using you to try and damage my reputation.'

'I believe you've already charged two people for this crime,' Milton said.

'You've been following the case?' Conway nodded to herself. 'Almost as if you expected your client to be brought in.'

'Does your second suspect place my client at the scene?'

Ella saw annoyance darken Conway's face.

'He won't protect you for ever, Ella,' she said.

'You haven't managed to induce him to collude in this lie, you mean?'

Conway straightened in her chair, colour rising in her pale and sunken cheeks. 'You should be very careful where you say things like that. Accusing the police of corruption is a very serious business.'

'I'm well aware of how you operate,' Ella said fiercely. 'I've had first-hand experience of your tactics. As I'm sure you already know. And I won't be bullied by you now.'

Next to Conway her constable blew out a slow breath, like he was bracing himself for her to erupt. She seemed the type to throw her weight around, Ella thought. She'd seen enough of these people to spot the worst of them.

'You don't appear to have any valid reason to charge Ms Riordan,' Milton said.

Conway conceded that with the barest inclination of her head. 'But I think we'll keep Ms Riordan here until we've had a chance to check her alibi.'

Molly

Now – 14th March

We can't leave our flats now. Not until the body has been removed.

The lobby is cordoned off, the hallway on the first floor around the lift as well. Both stairwell doors are covered with sheets of white plastic so none of us can see what they're doing down there. It's going to be an awkward and messy job, I guess. The lift is stuck halfway between the floors and they won't get him out easily.

Ella wanted me to go down and see what they were doing but that would have been madness. By the time I managed to pick myself up off the bathroom floor, the stairwells were already sealed anyway.

She's panicking.

I'm not. Not any more. Strangely, it feels like a weight has lifted off my shoulders and I realise it was the uncertainty that was paralysing me, keeping me trapped in here for the past few days like a spooked animal.

Now he's been found the real trouble begins, but I'm ready for what comes next, because now I have something to work with. We'll be questioned tomorrow and when the police have gone we'll get together as neighbours and discuss what was said, because that's what happens at times like this. And from that I'll find out how seriously his death is going to be taken by the police.

'I can't believe it,' Callum says, again.

His eyes are wide like he's still there in front of the lift doors he'd levered open, following Derek's directions. The pair of them were convinced the smell was the source of our rat infestation, or at least an attractive site to them, which could be cleaned up.

'It's hardly the first dead body you've seen.' I slip another cigarette out of the packet and light it with the butt of its predecessor. 'You must have seen them in a far worse state, too.'

He looks at me sharply and I almost choke on my cigarette. Remembering that I haven't been down there. I didn't know what was happening until he knocked on my door and told me. Callum's chin drops and he focuses on turning his mug around on the kitchen table by its chipped handle.

'I was just a cook,' he says softly.

It's easy to forget where he's from and what he's seen and I feel bad for belittling his lingering trauma. I reach out and hold his hand across the table, feeling the power in his fingers as they close around mine, gentle as he always is with me. But his softness is another man's demonstration of force and I sometimes wonder how strong he really is. What he'd be capable of if pushed in the wrong direction.

We both jump at a snap in the next room.

'One of the traps,' Callum says, but doesn't move.

If it isn't a clean break the rat will likely hang on for a few minutes. I don't like to think of it suffering, perhaps trying to pull itself away from the steel teeth and spring-loaded bar, but I can't ask him to do something about it. Not when he's in this state.

'Do you fancy some food?' he asks abruptly. 'I could do us cheese on toast?'

'That'd be good,' I say, even though I don't want anything. 'I think there's bread left.'

'Aye, good stuff. That's what we need. Bit of comfort food.'

While he cleans off the grilling tray I go out on to the balcony with my cigarettes, wrapping my heavy wool cardigan tight around my body against the frost that stings my nose. It's late. Gone two and the streets are at their quietest. That's how you know this area has achieved respectability: expensive homes mean big mortgages mean early starts. Nobody's tearing it up tonight, except me and Callum and our visitors downstairs.

Across the site the lit windows of the unoccupied flats draw my eye as they always do, but not for long. Below me the police vehicles are parked haphazardly on the paved area in front of the building, watched over by two uniformed officers. A third comes out of the building to join them, dressed in a white coverall now thrown back off his face. He bums a cigarette and gets a light, walks a few yards away to make a phone call. His gaze is turned up towards the neighbouring tower and I wonder if he envies them, what kind of place he'll eventually go home to when he's done here tonight. If he's thinking about knocking on those doors for witness statements.

Will he be the one who questions us all tomorrow? The one Callum has briefly spoken to, given him the story he's already given me. Does the detective believe him or has he pegged Callum as trouble? He probably looks the sort, to a copper's eye. We all will. Hanging on in here in a way only the mad or dangerous would. Decent people, honest people, wouldn't fight the developers. We'd make way for our betters in a quiet and dignified fashion.

Another plastic-clad figure comes out and opens up the back of a vehicle shaped like an ambulance but marked differently. A moment later I hear the sound of wheels moving slowly across the tarmac and swearing as they catch.

I lean over the balcony, holding my breath, not wanting to draw any attention to myself. I can see a black body bag strapped down on to a trolley, a person at the head end, another by the feet. I watch them load it into the vehicle, slam the door shut on him. They strip off their protective clothing and climb in the front, drive him away from here.

They will take his fingerprints and swab him for DNA. They're going to find traces of me and Ella on him. I've already thrown out the clothes I was wearing that night. And luckily I have other black jeans and grey jumpers that will pass for those I'm wearing in the photographs. If it comes to that.

When it comes to that.

'Food's up,' Callum calls.

Back inside he's put the radio on, a classic rock station turned down low. He has very old-fashioned taste sometimes. The kitchen smells of toasted bread and hot fat and I realise I am actually hungry. We eat in silence, an occasional slamming door or shout coming up from outside. There's the brief whoop of a siren as a car pulls away, off to answer a call where something might still be done. They have as much as they want or everything they can get and I take encouragement from the fact that they've only been here a few hours.

This won't be a priority crime. It can't be.

'Who d'you think he was?' Callum asks, wiping grease off his chin with the cuff of his sweatshirt. The question sounds casual but I'm not sure it is.

'I don't know. Homeless guy, maybe.' I shake my head. 'You'd have to be pretty out of it to end up walking into an empty lift shaft, wouldn't you? Maybe a junkie.'

'He wasn't dressed like a junkie.'

'There's lots of kinds of junkies, Cal.'

'Not round here there's not. This boy looked clean.' He props his elbows on the table, one big fist curled into his palm. 'Looked to me like he was maybe one of the lads from Ella's party.'

My face feels like a mask, cold and stiff, the flesh too tight across my bones. Callum is not stupid. He knows me. He knows where I've been and the things I've done. Some of them. The ones it felt safe to trust him with in a warm bed, in a dark room, in the early hours of mornings when he's woken screaming and needing reassurance that he isn't the only person who wishes they could erase parts of themselves.

'I think we'd have heard by now if one of Ella's friends went missing,' I say slowly, so it sounds like the truth. 'They're not the type of people who just drop off the face of the earth without anyone noticing.'

For a long moment he stares at me and I don't know what he's thinking but the hard look in his eyes is so disconcerting that when he pushes back from the table I flinch.

Immediately his expression switches to concern and I smile at him. 'I've had way too much coffee today, my nerves are shredded.'

'Go and see what's on TV; I'll make you some warm milk.'

I force a laugh. 'You're making me feel like your elderly mother here.'

'It's been a long, strange night, hen.' He comes around the table and settles his hands on my shoulders, quickly kisses the top of my head. 'We could both use something to help us sleep.'

But I don't sleep. We drink warm milk spiked with bourbon and lie together on the sofa, with the dead rat in the trap behind us leaking an ammonia smell like spilt nail-polish remover. The television is playing, showing a film I've seen before and don't like, but it's one of Callum's favourites. He drifts off before the second ad break and I stay there for a while, my head on his chest, hearing the slow pump of his heart and a rattle in his lungs that sounds like something he should see a doctor about.

When I'm sure he's deeply asleep I carefully get up and go out into the corridor. I head for the fourth floor. Another bulb has died since I was last up here. There's only one left now at the far end and its light barely reaches where I stand. The shadows feel alive around me, the rooms haunted by their absconded tenants, the sheer weight of all that empty space pressing in as I bring out my phone and turn on the torch.

The light is sudden and stark and I yelp as it hits a rat sitting in the centre of the floor, flashing across its eyes before it darts away into a gap in the wall.

I steel myself and turn the torchlight on to the doors of the lift shaft. A dulled reflection stands in front of me, as blurred and insubstantial as I feel. A ghost of me, the me that was here that night, and I wish I could communicate with her and tell her not to get involved.

But it's too late for that and I suspect I wouldn't listen to me if I was her anyway.

Tonight the doors look different. The torchlight picks out patches of near-black where fingerprints have been lifted, but that's the only sign of police activity.

Tentatively, I make my way to the far end of the corridor, to the flat where it happened, and find the door still locked, as I left it. The key is on the other side. I wish now that I'd kept it instead of pushing it under like a departing homeowner might have done. I desperately want to go in and look the place over one last time, check that I've cleaned the blood off the fireplace as carefully as I thought I had, that there's no lingering smell of bleach.

It might be days before the police decide to check the flat. If they bother at all. They have no more reason to look in that one than in any of the others and will they waste resources searching each of the sixty flats in the building?

Not unless someone tips them off to its importance.

Back downstairs I find Callum has migrated from the uncomfortable sofa to my bed. He's snoring as I tug off my fur-lined boots and unpeel my leggings but he murmurs when I lift the cover and climb on top of him. I work him with my hand until he's hard and he smiles a sleepy smile and takes hold of my hips, pulling me down on to his cock. Neither of us speaks; there's only the creak of the bed and our quickening breaths and the sound of skin on skin and, briefly, everything else falls away and I'm spared my fears and suspicions and the clockwork whirring of planning how to get free from what we've done.

'Sorry,' Callum gasps, a second before he comes.

The room spins back into focus.

He starts to move down the bed.

'It's fine,' I say. 'You can owe me one.'

He gives me a questioning look, because it isn't how this usually works; I've trained him better than that. I kiss him then burrow into his chest so he can't see my face any more.

As I'm drifting off, my phone rings and I want to let the call go unanswered, but I shouldn't. Callum barely stirs when I slip away from him, grabbing my dressing gown from the back of the door, closing it behind me as I take the call.

'Did I wake you?' Ella asks, her voice slow and slurring around the words. 'It's too late, isn't it, Molly?'

I feel a stone drop in my stomach. 'Too late for what?'

'Talking.'

'Ella, sweetheart, have you taken something?' I ask, trying to sound calm.

'Just vodka,' she says. 'Don't worry, I'm not going to do anything stupid. Nothing else stupid, anyway. Though, who's to say if it wouldn't *actually* be a very smart thing to do?' She lets out a long sigh and then I hear her go for another drink. 'I was always the smart one, you know?'

'You still are,' I tell her, curling up on the sofa, imagining her alone, drinking in bed, exhausted from the crying I can hear a residue of in her voice. 'You're smart enough to get through this, Ella. You just need to hold it together and stay calm. You can do this.'

'I can't.' It's a whisper, wet and loaded with despair. Then she starts babbling. 'I'm going to crack, Molly. When they talk to me they're going to see I'm guilty and I'll see that they see it and then I'm going to come clean. I won't be able to stop myself. I can *feel* it, it's like I'm getting guiltier the longer I don't tell anyone.'

'You told me,' I say desperately. 'You've come clean, you don't need to tell anyone else.'

Quickly I go and double-check the bedroom door is closed. Callum is snoring but I can't risk him hearing this conversation. Even my side alone is damning and I feel sure we're not through the worst of it yet from the way she's whispering to herself, caught in a loop of recrimination and self-loathing between long swigs of vodka.

More than anything I want to grab that bottle off her, but she's there and I'm here and all I have is my phone and as long as it takes to talk her through this.

'I should go,' Ella moans. 'This all ends if I disappear. I can get some cash out and I'll just take the Eurostar and disappear. You can tell people I went to meet up with some group or other. The police won't even expect to find me then. Martin knows loads of people in Greece. He'll know someone I can go and stay with. He says it's pretty much lawless over there now; who's going to come for me in that mess?'

There's a worrying edge to her voice, a reckless determination similar to when she told me about Ryan Quinn's plan for her. She knew that was stupid and she knows this is too, but she's well capable of going through with it regardless.

'If you run now you'll be admitting your guilt,' I say. 'The police will definitely go looking for you and, given who your dad is, Ella, they're going to be sure they bring you back. Don't you think he'll be worried about you? Don't you think he'll pull every string he can to make sure you're brought home safe? Shit, he'll probably trek across Europe looking for you himself.'

'My dad...'

She speaks the words so softly I can't get anything from the tone.

'What about your dad?' I ask tremulously, thinking this is it, she's already told him. We're done. Or she's going to tell him and we'll be done then. 'Ella, honey, what about your dad?'

Another big, jagged sigh. 'It'll kill him if he ever finds out.'

'He won't find out,' I tell her, as firmly as I can. 'Not if you stay here and keep calm.'

'All I ever wanted was for him to be proud of me.' The sound of a cover rustling and a small sniffle. 'I've messed everything up, Molly.'

Quietly she begins to sob and I feel a tug in my chest, wishing she'd come to me rather than working herself up into this state.

'You haven't messed everything up,' I say. 'You've been unlucky, that's all. There's a way through this, Ella, believe me.' I force a smile I hope she can hear down the phone. 'You are such a clever girl. You're strong and resourceful and you are going to get through this. *We* are going to get through this together.'

Ella laughs. It's almost a gasp, like a last breath before drowning.

'I'm doing important work, aren't I?'

'Too important to give up on, yes.'

'I don't want to waste my life,' she says, so desperately that I feel tears coming. 'I want to do so much more than this.'

'You can.'

'I want to change things.'

'You will,' I tell her and even as I hope it's true, I fear it isn't. That she can't get beyond this, that I can't bring her through it in one piece.

That neither of us are quite good enough.

Ella

Then – 24th November

Suddenly it all very felt real.

Sitting on the floor of the back room of an empty house a minute away from their target, a single, heavily shaded lamp lighting the faces of the men sitting opposite her, all of them waiting for it to get late enough for the streets to empty so they could make their move.

'We'll give it another half hour,' Quinn said, but he kept fidgeting, toying with the laces of his trainers and the zips on his black combat trousers.

Next to him the younger man Ella knew only as Lewis was perfectly still. He looked almost like he was meditating, with his legs crossed and his hands on his knees, palms turned up. But his eyes were open and by the lamplight she could see the agitation stirring there. He was all angles, long-legged and rangy, too big for stealth, she thought, but he was Quinn's friend and she couldn't stop him coming.

Three of them to do this; it was madness.

One person could accomplish the task easily enough, two was better so they'd have a lookout, but Quinn insisted they all go. That this was a group effort and everyone should share in the triumphant final act.

Lewis had scoped the place out, made several passes, day and night, and picked between three and four a.m. as the ideal time. He'd suggested the best route to evade the network of CCTV cameras and the windows of the flats that overlooked their target. When Ella had made her own survey of the site she realised there was no clean way in. Dozens of windows gave on to the single viable entry point and they only needed one insomniac busybody to blow this.

That was when she started to get nervous.

Walking along the side street on a blustery afternoon last week, with a scarf pulled up over her nose and a hat tugged down to her eyebrows, she'd tucked every strand of hair carefully up under it so she couldn't be identified when the footage was later checked. A good copper would go to those lengths, know that they should look for anyone reconnoitring the spot in the days preceding an attack.

She'd gone to the supermarket across the road and bought a few things so she'd have a shopping bag and an excuse, then walked a circuit of the block the building stood on, checking for escape routes and hiding places she felt confident of reaching if things went south.

She didn't trust these men.

Part of her suspected this was a set-up; Quinn wanting to get dirt on her. He didn't seem to appreciate that she would be getting the same on him.

Lewis … Lewis she couldn't figure out at all.

They'd met twice before and he'd said very little, was precise and controlled and didn't appear particularly impressed by Quinn. If Lewis had deferred to him that would make more sense – another acolyte devoted to the cause. There were hundreds of them on the fringes, and they all made damn sure you knew how dedicated they were.

But there was something not quite right about Lewis and that was setting her nerves on edge. His stillness, the way he looked at her now, with a slight smile, then looked away again.

Quinn stood up and started out of the room.

'Where are you going?' Ella snapped.

'For a shit,' he said. 'That alright with you?'

He stomped out into the hallway and up a set of uncarpeted stairs, unbothered by making noise in what should be an empty house. Another nerve frayed.

Ella knew she should get out now, before she'd done anything illegal. Leave these idiots to it. There was too much she could lose and no certainty of gaining anything beyond an already hollow sense of satisfaction.

No, she reminded herself, there was more at stake than that and if she wanted to fulfil her true potential she needed to push through the nervousness and silence the timid voice that always wanted to retreat, stay safe, be sensible.

Sensible people never make history, she thought.

'Ryan's just nervous,' Lewis said, in a soft West Country accent completely out of place in this stripped and mouldering room. 'He's not done as much of this kind of thing as he likes to make out.'

'What about you?' Ella asked.

'Bits and pieces back home when I was a kid.' He shrugged, gave her a sly, self-deprecating look. 'But we need to fight them where they live, don't we? Too late by the time they're down my way buying their second or third fucking holiday cottage.'

Ella wasn't sure how he thought tonight's action would stop that.

'How long have you been in London, then?' she asked, feeling absurd making this small talk.

'Two years. I got into UCL; history.' He twisted to face her full on, beaming now. 'I was at the Camden protest. I saw you break the cordon. That was – shit – it was superhero stuff.'

'It was stupid,' Ella said, her fingertips going to her arm, feeling the bone through her skin. 'I'm lucky all I got was a broken arm.'

'Scum,' he spat. 'Did you ever go after him?'

Ella's toes curled away from the end of her boots, all the recoil she could allow herself.

'No, I never found out who he was.'

Lewis nodded. 'Took his numbers off, yeah?'

'Yeah.'

'Shame. We could do something now. Two years on, nobody'd connect it to you. Fuck knows how many people he's laid into since then. Plenty of other suspects to take the fall.' He took a sip

113

of coffee from the lid of his Thermos. 'Your old man was one of them, right?'

She nodded. 'He was, yeah. We don't get on.'

'No, I bet you don't.' Lewis grinned and lifted his cup in a toast. 'Sticking it to the man.'

Ella wrapped her arms around her shins, rested her chin on her knees. She felt anxiety bubbling in the pit of her stomach. She hadn't eaten all day, too nervous to swallow even a bite of toast, and now she regretted that. She felt vague and woozy from low blood sugar, unsure of herself.

'Was it his idea for you to go into the police?' Lewis asked.

It had been a long time since anyone had mentioned that and Ella thought the conversation was long done with. But Lewis didn't know her and she could understand why he needed to hear it from her mouth. Especially now, when he was trusting her just like she was trusting him.

'Dad didn't give me much option,' she said. 'He forced my brother to sign up – morally blackmailed him, basically – and he's not made for the job. He wanted to be a chef, but Dad was having none of that. Then he did the same thing to me.'

'What did you want to be?'

'A teacher,' Ella said. 'I wanted to help people. Dad told me the police help people more than teachers. He thinks they're all Trots.'

Lewis snorted. 'The country wouldn't be in the mess it is if they were.'

'My history teacher was one. Really hardcore; she got in shit every year because she wore a white poppy for Remembrance Sunday. She told me to stand up to Dad and do what I wanted, but it's not that easy, is it?'

'You got out, though,' he said. 'Eventually.'

'Three months at Garton.' She bit her lip. 'You wouldn't believe what that place is like.'

'My cousin's at Deepcut,' Lewis said. 'I know what kind of shitholes those places are. She hates it, but she can't get out. You know what happens to the women.'

Ella nodded and he looked away. He knew what she knew. That was on record as well; the official investigation and her own writing about it. Lewis had been thorough, checked her out ahead of time, and Ella found it reassuring that he'd done the research.

Perhaps he was someone she could work with again, if tonight went off without a hitch. Shut out Quinn, bring Lewis in closer.

She pointed to the line of ink just visible under the pushed-back cuff of his black jumper.

'What's that say?'

He shoved it further back and held his forearm out to her. Ella took his wrist and leaned in, turning it gently into the light.

'"You are responsible for the predictable consequences of your actions,"' she read. 'Chomsky. Nice.'

'It's to remind me not to do anything reckless,' he said, with a wry smile. 'Have you got any?'

'They're not as easily accessible as yours,' Ella said, sitting back.

'Another time then.'

'Maybe.'

Quinn came back into the room, gloved up now, jacket zipped to the chin. The weather was cold enough to justify it but all three of them, done up like that ... if they were seen it would be obvious they weren't just passing through on their way home after a heavy night out.

He clapped his hands.

'Time to go, boy and girl.'

The streets were deserted, disconcertingly quiet, but in the distance Ella heard sirens and she flinched, sure that somehow they knew and were heading in this direction. She reminded herself of all the bad things that happened in the early hours of the morning, all the other dramas playing out around the borough that were bigger and more immediate than this.

Barnard Close seemed wider and more exposed than it had last time she'd walked down it, and she hung back a few paces behind Quinn and Lewis, giving herself space to run if she needed to. Out the corner of her eye she saw a mangy fox slinking into the shadows, only for it to disappear through a gap in a wall and into a high-sided yard, setting off the security lights with an audible snap.

Her breaths were beginning to shorten and she told herself to focus, get through this, move beyond it. She had her exit strategy; she was safe as long as she stayed alert.

They went down a narrow alleyway narrowed further by a line of stinking bins and leaking bags and into a dead space behind a run of buildings, all in darkness, a cafe and some offices, none of them with any visible form of security. The upper windows were covered and maybe the rooms were occupied, but surely not by anyone who would call the police, Ella hoped.

The back of Brighams was walled and solidly gated and there was the security camera Lewis had reported, ringed with a spiked collar. He went on ahead and sprayed out its lens.

He boosted Quinn up over the wall and Ella heard him land on the other side. Lewis held out his cupped palms towards her and she hesitated for a second.

'I've got you,' he whispered. 'Come on.'

She planted her foot on his hands and he lifted her up like she weighed nothing. Ella grabbed the top of the wall and hauled herself over. A couple of seconds later Lewis was next to her and she realised how unprepared Quinn was, standing waiting at the bottom of the fire escape they'd decided was the weak point, jiggling from foot to foot, making the contents of his backpack rattle.

Lewis went up the metal stairs, light-footed, but in the silence every step rang out. He took a crowbar from his bag and began working at the door, near the lock, prying and levering. The sound of the wood splintering seemed deafening.

Quinn grabbed Ella by the shoulder and pushed her up the stairs ahead of him.

Lewis was already through the hallway, empty offices opening up on their left, a stale-smelling, disused kitchen on the right. The charity previously housed here had been cleared out with little warning and no ceremony, taking only what they absolutely needed, leaving desks and chairs and battered filing cabinets behind.

Ella heard a series of beeps coming from downstairs and got there in time to see Lewis punching a final string of numbers into the alarm's keypad. Engineers' codes he'd got from some security forum, allowing him to disable the system and reset it.

Then he was moving again. Spraying out another camera, this one placed to watch over Brighams' employees and customers rather than intruders.

Even by the weak light filtering through the security shutters Ella could see how in control he was, like someone who'd done this many times before. He reached into his bag and tossed her a can of spray paint.

'Five minutes.'

She felt a thrill run through her as she started blanking out the Brighams signage on the very white walls, the smell of it catching in her nostrils. She glanced at Lewis, who'd taken off his black gloves, revealing a pair of thin surgical ones underneath, and saw him plug the USB stick containing the virus into the machine.

They could have done it remotely but the message was as important as the action – we've broken you from the inside. It was spectacle more than disruption and damage.

Gradually Ella became aware of another smell. Not spray paint. Lewis turned away from the desk just as she turned to look for Quinn.

'Where is he?' Lewis asked.

Ella looked down the corridor leading back from the office, couldn't see Quinn.

Lewis was on his feet. 'That's kerosene.'

Quinn came in, a bottle in each hand, pouring out two lines of pungent liquid along the floor, flicking it up the walls. He was singing under his breath as he did it and the weight of this miscalculation hit Ella square in the middle of the chest. She dropped the spray can she was holding, the room blurring in front of her.

'This wasn't the plan,' Lewis said, striding across the room. He shoved Quinn against the wall. 'We agreed. No violence.'

'It's not violence in an empty building, you pussy.'

Quinn pushed him away. Liquid splashed across their feet and Ella started backing towards the door, slipping on the kerosene. Quinn doused more of it over the desks, the padded white swivel chairs and the display stands filled with properties.

'There could be people in the other buildings,' Lewis said angrily. 'Are you happy to risk that?'

Quinn kept moving. 'This won't blow the place up. It's just for effect.'

A siren blared outside, blue lights spiking through the gaps in the shutters, the vehicle going past at high speed.

'We should leave,' Ella said, her voice trembling, fear knotting her stomach. 'We've made our point. This is what they *want* us to do.'

'They don't want this, believe me.' Quinn threw the empty bottles down, took a lighter out of his pocket. 'No one cares about your sit-ins and your petitions and your stupid banners. They don't give a fuck. Nothing changes until you start attacking property.'

'The police are in the area,' Lewis said, gesturing beyond the shutters. 'How the fuck do you think we'll get away if they're parked up round the corner?'

Quinn was smiling behind his balaclava, eyes crinkling with pleasure. 'You scared, big man?'

'I'm sane,' Lewis said wildly. 'I thought you were.'

Quinn struck the lighter.

'Ryan, just think about this for a minute.' Ella watched the flame jump and snap, mesmerised by it and the power it contained and the pressure on her now to stop it. 'We won't get away with this. We already have a track record with Brighams; if it goes up we'll be the first people arrested.'

'They don't know about me or Lewis.' He smiled viciously. '*You* might get a visit but it's all part of your learning curve.'

Ella licked her lips. 'What about Carol? They know about her. She's going to be their prime suspect.'

'She wants this done,' he said, but there was a flicker of doubt in his voice.

'Does she want to get arrested for it?'

'She's got an alibi,' he said. 'She's working a night shift.'

The moment of doubt had passed, Ella realised, seeing him draw up straighter and nod, as if satisfying himself that all the angles had been covered.

'There are people in the flats next door,' she said desperately.

'The place'll have fire alarms; they'll be fine.' Quinn shrugged. 'See, Ella, this is the problem with you. You've got no fucking commitment. I've said it all along. I said you were a tourist and look at you now.' He gestured towards her with the lighter, the flame licking his thumb. 'You're just another wannabe.'

Lewis shoved a chair aside and started towards Quinn.

'I'm not going to let you do this, Ryan.'

'You're not going to stop me.'

Ella grabbed Lewis's arm. 'Come on, let's get out of here.'

'If you're not up to it, then both of you go,' Quinn said. 'You don't deserve to be part of this.'

Lewis took Ella's shoulders and walked her back into the hall-way, his eyes fixed on hers as she protested, talking over her.

'You have to run,' he said. 'Hide. You were never here.'

'For God's sake, Lewis, don't let him take you down with him.' She tried to drag him along but he shrugged her off and turned away and for a second she stood in the stinking corridor, hearing Lewis try a new placating tone, then Quinn laughed.

And she ran.

Molly

Now – 15th March

It's barely light when I wake up. Callum is gone, his side of the bed still holding a trace of body heat. He's always up at six on the dot, conditioned by his army days, but he usually wakes me before he goes and I don't want to think about why he didn't do that this morning.

In the kitchen I tune the radio to a local station, listen to their middle-of-the-road playlist as I make a cup of tea and shove the last slices of bread into the toaster. When the news comes on I turn the sound up, waiting to hear the report of a body found in a Nine Elms flat. But there's nothing. Maybe it's too soon for a press release or just not important enough to warrant one.

How many dead bodies surface every day in London? Heart attacks on parkland paths, late-night, drunken tumbles into the rivers and canals, hit and runs that might be murder and the endless assorted and boring ways we find to hurt ourselves and each other.

This death is nothing remarkable.

I doubt the detective I saw last night has woken up with the scent of the chase in his nostrils. Careers are not made like this.

I'm not expecting some genius to turn up here, but I still need to be careful. Look respectable, give them no reason to start delving. They'll profile every single one of us. I need them to look at me and see an inoffensive sixty-year-old woman too physically frail to move the corpse of a full-grown man. The copper who comes will be young, I think; they all are now. I'm probably the same age as his grandmother; he'll see me as a fossil tragically clinging to youth with my black-dye job and tattoos.

Until they check my record.

Or maybe even that will take on an inoffensive cast with the benefit of age. Will they look with condescension at my protests and battles, all stripped of energy and heat by the intervening years? Will they even be able to see the youthful me underneath this face and conceive of a time when I was unashamedly fierce?

In the bathroom I pull my hair into a loose ponytail, pin back my fringe, exposing my wrinkled forehead, the softness at my jaw and the hollows at my temples, decide to forgo the black kohl liner I put on every day, even if I'm staying in on my own. My face looks wan and unstructured without it, my eyes tired and sad; this is the woman I would have become if I'd stayed in Bedford. This is my mother's perpetually disappointed face staring back at me from the mirror.

From the bottom of my wardrobe I dig out a pair of black leggings. I decide against a bra, pulling on a Sex Pistols T-shirt and a baggy cardigan three sizes too big.

'What do you look like?' I ask myself.

An old woman who can't let go of the seventies. And like all the best disguises it works because there's an element of truth in it.

The flat is a mess but the wrong kind of mess. Too many books strewn around, and they're the wrong kind too.

I pile up the most damning ones on a shelf, spines facing inwards, clear all my paperwork away into the desk drawers, along with the tin where I keep my small stash of resin, leaving a pad of innocuous doodles next to the keyboard. My camera is sitting there too, expensive-looking, professional. I open up my latest batch of photographs so it appears that I'm working away untroubled: a row of pretty Georgian townhouses, front doors freshly painted, window boxes planted with winter flowers and ivy.

The other photographs in the room aren't quite as inoffensive. Some are going to damn me if the copper looks at them.

121

The punks and club kids are fine, the drag queens and diamond geezers might even raise a smile. The Brixton riots, though, Greenham Common Women's Peace Camp, the police rampaging at Orgreave, their descendants itching to do the same at Occupy St Paul's ... those are the images that give me away, bristling with furious energy, clenched fists and clenched jaws, bloodstained shields and rigidly locked arms.

Out on the balcony I smoke a cigarette, thinking back to the peace camp at Greenham, looking at the ragged scar on the inside of my ring finger, thin now and paled. I can still remember the sharp taste of blood as I licked the wound and how quickly someone else took the bolt croppers off me to continue cutting the fence.

I hear them coming. Two sets of feet in the hallway, storm-trooper heavy, wanting to inspire fear behind every door they pass, even the ones they don't plan to visit. It's what they call high-visibility policing.

The knock is brisk, businesslike. I take my time answering, pausing to turn the sound down on the TV, and when I open the door I find two plainclothes officers looking at me. A lumbering young man with ginger hair and a spray of psoriasis wrapped around his neck above his stiff white collar, and a petite woman in a hijab and pinstripe suit who smiles warmly at me as she holds up her identification in fingers tipped with glossy purple nails.

'Good morning, madam.' Her voice is high and lightened by the particular inflection reserved for the elderly. 'I'm DC Wazir, this is DC Gull, I wonder if we could ask you a few questions?'

'Sure, fire away.' I lean against the doorframe, hands tucked into my pockets. 'This is about the bloke who fell down the lift, is it?'

'Can we come in?' Wazir inclines her head and starts towards me before I've agreed.

I would stop her. The woman I need them to think I am steps back and lets them into the flat, asks if either of them would like a cup of tea.

'I'm out of milk but I might have some powdered.'

Old people always have powdered milk. Young people never want it.

'We're fine, thanks,' Wazir says. She makes a beeline for the gallery wall while Gull goes to sit down on the sofa, behind which the rat is still in its trap and I notice Gull's nose wrinkle as he takes out his notepad. 'These are really good. Did you take them?'

'Thank you, yes I did.'

She moves along the wall, leaning in to see the detail. 'It's funny, nowadays everyone's got a camera on their phone and we take pictures all the time but there's a mile of difference between what a real photographer sees and what the rest of us do, isn't there?'

I need to watch this one.

'A lot of it's about knowing which images to discard,' I say.

Wazir nods. 'My cousin's a photographer – not like you are, he's not an artist, he just does weddings and stuff, but he's shown me some of the ones that don't make it into the albums. He catches these moments and these looks that nobody wants putting down for posterity.' Another smile, this one quicker and sly, an invitation to conspire. 'I think they're probably the more honest records of the day, though.'

'It sounds like he's got an artist's eye.' I fire the same smile back at her. 'A lot of people wouldn't spot that stuff at all.'

On the sofa Gull is getting impatient when he'd do better to watch his partner and learn from her. I suspect she's taken in everything in this room already, made her calculations and adjusted her approach accordingly. She'll probably be his boss soon and he won't even understand why.

'Is this the Camden sit-in?' she asks, pointing at the photograph of Ella, with the baton coming down on her.

I nod. 'Were you there?'

'We both were.'

Wazir offers no further comment and I don't follow it up, suspecting she'd like me to. She goes to the sofa and sits down next to Gull, who clicks his pen in readiness. I take a seat opposite them, cross my legs and fold my hands in my lap.

'You're Molly Fader?' she asks. 'Is that right?'

123

'Yes.'

'Is it okay if I call you Molly?'

Fuck no. I don't even want you in my home.

'Sure.'

'You've heard about the body?'

'My friends found him,' I say.

'Do you have a lot of trouble here?' Wazir asks.

'Surprisingly little, considering. When people first started moving out there were a lot of break-ins, burglars looking to see if anything had been left behind. But I guess they've finally worked out none of us have got anything worth pinching.'

'You've got some nice kit, though.' Wazir glances towards my desk, the camera and the laptop.

'I hide my computer when I go out. Or I take it with me. And I never leave the flat without my camera.'

'Because that would be the day you'd miss the perfect shot?'

'Sod's law, right?'

'Did you take it up to the roof party on the sixth?'

There it is. What she really came here to talk about.

'No, I didn't bother.'

'So you do leave it here occasionally?'

'It was a party. I was pretty sure I wouldn't be in a fit state to take good photographs.' I shrug, give her a faintly embarrassed look.

'What was the party in aid of?' she asks.

I'm certain she already knows; Callum and Derek were both there at various points in the evening; they will have told her. But I tell her as well, watching her closely, seeing what precisely spikes her interest. Not a flicker when I mention Ella.

'Was there any trouble at the party?'

'It wasn't that kind of crowd,' I say.

'Trouble can come from unexpected quarters.' She opens her hands up, almost as if she's suggesting that quarter might be her. 'Were you involved in the organising of the party?'

'A bit, at this end. I got a couple of the boys here to help set things up. Bought a few crates of beer and wine.'

'That was very generous of you.'

'It's a good cause,' I tell her. 'The book's proceeds are going to a local housing charity. God knows the council aren't doing much to help.'

Wazir nods thoughtfully. Gull writes a few lines on his pad.

'Do you have a guest list we could take a copy of?' she asks.

'Sorry, no. I just had a rough idea of numbers to make sure there'd be enough booze.'

'Who would have one?'

'Do you think the dead man might have been at the party?' I ask, leaning forward like it's a shock.

'We need to check that out,' she says in a perfectly neutral tone. 'So, who would be best for us to ask?'

'Ella, I suppose. Ella Riordan. She organised the Kickstarter, so she sent out the invites.'

Wazir asks for her details and I give her them, address and mobile number, feeling like it's an act of betrayal, but what option do I have? If we're innocent we'd both want to help.

'How long have you known one another?' It sounds conversational but this is not a conversation, it's an interrogation without the benefit of legal advice or the protection of recording equipment.

'About two years,' I say.

'Are you close?'

'We're friends, yes. She's been very helpful in spreading the word about the evictions here and providing support to the residents. It's important to try and raise awareness of what's happening but it's not easy if you don't have press contacts. Ella has lots of them.'

It was supposed to come out casually, but my fear makes it sound like a warning, an overcompensation.

Wazir stands and Gull follows her lead, tucking his notepad away into his jacket pocket, giving me a flash of ugly petrol-blue lining and a dry-cleaning ticket. Again he sniffs and I smile this time, thinking of him wondering all day whether there's something wrong with him. That ammonia and rotting-meat smell is going to linger in his nostrils for hours.

I walk to the door and open it; he goes out first. Done with me. I wish he'd come alone.

'Thank you for your help, Molly.' Wazir hands me a card. 'If you do think of anything that might be useful, please don't hesitate to call.'

'Of course.'

I close the door and wait until their footsteps have receded along the corridor before I allow myself to heave a deep sigh of relief.

For a few minutes I pace around the flat, light a cigarette I forget to smoke. I go out on to the balcony and see their car is still here.

I call Ella. There's music playing loudly at her end and she apologises, tells me to hang on a second while she turns it down.

'The police have just been here,' I say quickly. 'They'll be coming to you soon. They want a guest list for the party.'

'This is bad.'

'It's normal,' I tell her, trying to use a soothing tone, wary of infecting her with my nerves. 'You need to tread carefully, though. The woman – Wazir – she's smart, she's going to try and draw you out. You need to give her enough that she thinks she's got your measure, okay? Don't clam up, don't get combative, but don't be too passive either. They know what you are, Ella. They'll be expecting resistance.'

'Okay.'

Is she taking this advice in?

'Ella?'

'I'm good, Molly. Really. I'm ready.' A knock at the door her end but it can't be them, not yet. 'Look, I have to go. I'll report back later.'

She ends the call.

I don't like this. Twelve hours ago she was crying her eyes out down the phone, talking about running, taking her passport and hopping the Eurostar into Paris, disappearing off the face of the earth.

Somewhere between then and now she's calmed down and I can't help but think the only person who could reassure her to this degree is her father.

Has she put aside her fears about how he will react to finding out she's killed someone? Has she realised he'll do anything for his little girl?

Is that who was at her door?

Three hours from Durham to King's Cross. If she called him last night and he took the first train, he'd be arriving around now, sweeping in to use his reputation.

Or, more worryingly, help her formulate a story that he knows his fellow officers would buy.

Because nobody knows how to get away with a crime like a copper. They've heard all the lies and excuses, they've watched bravura performances by men who've killed their wives and wept through half a dozen press conferences, they've seen people confess to crimes they didn't commit and deny ones where the blood is dry and cracked on their hands.

I look at the photograph of Greenham Common: a woman being dragged away from the fence by three men twice her size. One has her hair twisted around his fist, the other two hold her legs. In the foreground a toddler in a padded snowsuit looks on crying. The image is black and white, but I remember the suit was a grubby red and the little boy's nose always snotty. The boy had been sleeping in his mother's arms when the police came for her. They picked the boy up and sat him on the floor, dumped him there like a bag of rubbish. No thought for who would pick him up with his mother arrested.

That's the kind of man Ella's father is.

If he wants to get her away from us all, show her the error of her ways, extract her contrition, he'll cut through as many of us as necessary to achieve that.

I go into the bathroom and find the softest, chunkiest kohl pencil in the cabinet, slowly ring my eyes with it, smudging it up over my lids with my thumb, then pull my hair free from the ponytail and roughly shake my head until I look like me again.

But I don't feel like me.

Ella

Then – 11th November

'Burn, Brighams, burn!'

The rallying call rang out across the high street, fifty voices now, up from the twenty they started with just before nine o'clock, striking up their chant as the manager arrived. He'd braked when bodies spilled off the pavement and blocked the road in front of the estate agent's, swung the car into reverse and took another road in. Luckily for him, the shop had a rear entrance and he'd got inside.

But they wouldn't be doing any business today.

Ella could feel him glowering at them through the plate-glass window. There were two other men with him and a woman who'd got off a bus at the stop across the road and visibly steeled herself, patting her fat, high bun and straightening her quilted handbag on her shoulder, before she marched up to the front door and forced her way through the protest.

They made it easy for her. Had no option with a dozen uniformed police officers looking on. But Ella knew it would have been a different matter if one of the men had tried it.

'You should be out here with us, sister,' Carol had said, as the woman reached for the door.

'I made fifty grand last year, I'm not your fucking sister.'

Carol had grabbed the door handle, stopping her momentarily. 'To paraphrase your darling Maggie – a woman who, beyond the age of twenty-six, finds herself on a bus can count herself a failure.'

Ella had laughed and Carol winked at her, went back to chanting with renewed vigour.

Now, three hours later, she was looking less inclined towards throwing quotes and more ready for throwing rocks, pumped up on Red Bull and adrenaline, snarling at the police officers who had arrived mere minutes after the protest started but who had, so far, failed to live down to her expectations of them.

That wouldn't last, Ella thought.

When the crowd was mostly women and reedy boys in glasses the police cordon had been calm, but the group had swollen throughout the morning, calls to arms on social media and private messaging bringing out the late risers. These were the kind of people coppers bent on trouble loved to see arrive. Big guys in balaclavas and kaffiyeh, women wearing Anonymous masks, all in heavy boots made for smashing things up. They kept their faces and hands hidden, no identifying marks or tattoos on display. They chanted louder and harder, stamped the ground and banged their drums, all of them at the front of the crowd, nearest the police, wanting to force them into giving territory.

A rangy guy turned away and started towards Carol. All Ella could see of him was his eyes. They were too wide, hyper-alert, and the remnants of a bruise was visible under the right one.

'You got any papers?' he asked.

Carol dug into her pocket and handed him a pack. He started to roll a skinny cigarette, looking Ella over while he did it.

'You kids met before?' Carol asked.

'I know who she is,' the man said.

'This is Quinn,' Carol told her, leaning in to whisper his name, like it was something dangerous or sacred. 'You've got a lot in common. You should get together after this.'

Subtlety was never her strong suit, Ella thought. Quinn seemed dismissive of the idea. But Ella had heard of him, that he'd come out of the anti-capitalist movement and had started getting involved with anti-gentrification protests, targeting the offices of architects working on major regeneration projects, the contractors who made them physical realities and even members of the local councils suspected of corrupting the planning processes.

Nothing concrete. No evidence that anything claimed about him had actually happened. But companies like that rarely reported break-ins or criminal damage. It tarnished their reputations, created a stink around them, which didn't sit well alongside their glossy brochures and aspirational branding strategies.

If he was serious, rather than just another loudmouth looking to play the big man, then maybe he was someone she should get to know. She knew she couldn't keep her hands clean for ever. Not if she really wanted to make a difference.

But finding people who were prepared to back up their boasts was proving more challenging than she'd expected.

Quinn unwound the scarf covering his mouth so he could smoke, but kept his back to the police, shifting slightly so the crowd would block him from their view. The plainclothes officer with the camera had spotted him, though, and was moving around to try and capture his face.

The fact that they wanted it piqued her interest even more. That and watching how he tracked the cameraman's movements reflected in the window, waiting until he was seconds away from a clear shot to hide himself again.

'Let me give you my number,' Ella said.

His eyes crinkled and she could hear the sneer in his voice. 'I can find you whenever I want to. Not like you're shunning the spotlight, is it?'

He ground the cigarette butt out against the window and tucked it into his pocket as he returned to the front of the crowd. Another good sign, she thought. Never leave anything behind that could be used to retrieve DNA or fingerprints. His caution suggested he didn't have a criminal record yet and was trying to stay out of the system. Which meant he was the kind of smart she was interested in.

Carol was talking about the officer with the camera, commenting on how his own face was covered up, but Ella was only half listening. She was still thinking about Quinn, watching him carefully now, seeing how he whipped the others up around him, but always held slightly back. If you were looking for it, you'd see his orchestration, but to a casual observer the mood was turning spontaneously.

He changed the chant and the rest of the crowd took it up immediately.

'Woolwich for workers!'

The words were calmer but the tone was darker and harder, the drumbeats thumping, whistles sounding in ear-splitting bursts. Shoppers were no longer slowing to watch and take photos; now they were crossing the road rather than stopping to ask questions and take fliers, hurrying along their curious children.

'Woolwich for workers!'

Ella looked at the faces of the people inside Brighams, saw the men had been infected by the rising rage outside. Conferring in a huddle, they stood hands on hips, stabbing fingers at the window. The woman had left at some point. Ella wondered if she'd chosen to or was sent home. They looked like the type to try and protect the little lady, even though she'd displayed more spine than any of them when she arrived.

Maybe that was why they were puffing themselves up finally.

Three hours was a long time to hang around powerlessly in your office while protestors halted the flow of money.

'Woolwich for workers!'

A masked woman with pastel-pink hair stepped up to the police cordon, raised both arms in a V, fists clenched. She kept chanting, strutting back and forth, until she stopped in front of the biggest guy there. He'd been flexing his fingers inside his gloves for the last half hour and Ella wondered if the woman had spotted that. If she wanted trouble.

He put his hand out. 'Step back, miss.'

She didn't move.

'Someone pull her back in,' Carol said.

Nobody did.

The drums slowed to an ominous tempo. One coordinated strike every five seconds. The woman was inches from the PC's face, skinny arms still raised. She barked:

'Burn, Brighams, burn.

'Burn, Brighams, burn.

'Burn, Brighams, burn.'

The drums kept striking. The silence in between punctured with the woman's voice and then others joining her, peeling away from the body of the protest, crossing the clear channel of pavement that had separated them from the police all morning.

That cordon represented peaceful protest. Now it was breached, anything might happen.

Ella felt a nervous excitement stirring in her stomach, bounced up on her toes to check where Quinn was. Saw no sign of him.

When she looked back she saw the pink-haired woman had an air horn in her hand. She raised it into the face of the nearest PC and let it off. They were on her immediately, a flurry of bodies, and within seconds she lay unmasked on the ground, still shouting as she was cuffed. Two other officers pushed back a man who was trying to get to her. He yelled that he loved her as she was led away. The rest of the group was still chanting, but they'd moved back again now their temporary leader was gone.

'Always one.' Carol shook her head.

'We need more than one, don't we?' Ella said.

'We need more than this.' Carol turned towards the estate agent's window. 'Look at them in there. Fucking raging but they don't have the arsehole to come out here. What do you think they'd like to do to us?'

The men were jeering at them. One had his wallet open now, waving a black credit card in their direction.

Carol laughed scornfully. 'Back in the day that would have been a wad of cash. Now the stupid bastard's proud to be flaunting his debt.'

She reached into her coat pocket and brought out a paint can, shook it up vigorously.

'They're probably worse off than some of the people out here.' She started to spray a metre-wide red circle on the plate glass. 'One overblown mortgage payment from the streets.'

On the other side of the window the men were shouting. They looked like caged animals, Ella thought, silverbacks preparing to assert their dominance. She wondered if Carol realised how much anger she was provoking and if it made her feel as uneasy as Ella did. She'd finished the large circle and was spraying a second one inside that, forming a bullseye that framed the biggest man's head.

He barked at them, his words dulled by the thickness of the glass, but Ella could lip-read his insults well enough as he slammed his palm against the window. The sheer intensity and immediacy of his anger forced her to take a step back.

'See that,' Carol said, putting the final dot at the centre of the target, blocking out the man's face. 'His sense of ownership's getting pricked. Some disposable suit on fifteen grand a year basic, plus commission and a shite car. But he's losing it because I've painted on his bosses' window.' She dropped the can into her pocket, nodded towards the door. 'Here it comes.'

The door flew open and the man barrelled through the crowd towards her, fifteen stone of incoherent rage bearing down on her, and Ella saw his hand curl into a fist as Carol threw her chin up at him, ready to have her say. She didn't even get a word out.

His fist crashed into her nose, so hard it snapped her head back with an audible crack, and Ella lunged to catch her under the arms. Carol yelped, blood running out of her nose, down her face and on to her T-shirt.

'The fuck d'you think you are?' the man shouted, looming over her, fist still clenched.

Carol climbed to her feet, but the police were coming, shoving people aside.

'We're going to have you,' Carol told him, in a low voice clogged with the blood running down the back of her throat. 'See how long that black card lasts when you're jobless.'

Ella didn't see the second shot coming. He caught Carol as she was stepping back, clipped the side of her head with enough force to send her into the window. This time she didn't pick Carol up. Instead she grabbed a sign that had been lying against the shopfront and stamped on it to free the wooden handle. She felt adrenaline and fury tightening her muscles, didn't think, didn't hesitate, the noise of the crowd falling away, only her own heart-beat clear and fast and strong in her ears as she moved.

The man was elbowing his way towards the police now.

'Why aren't you arresting these people?' he demanded.

Ella slowly followed him, holding the wood low by her side, focused on the path clearing ahead of him and the space he left behind. No matter what else had happened here today she would make sure this man understood that they weren't people he could push around without consequences.

She was four metres away from him and his mates were already with the police, gesturing and shouting. He would be there within seconds. It was now or never.

As he was stopped by another protestor just as big as himself she swung the piece of wood – straight into Quinn's outstretched hand. He'd stepped into her path from nowhere.

'Not this,' he said, gripping her makeshift weapon. 'Not now. Get Carol to a walk-in or something and have her nose fixed up. She'll say she's fine, but she needs looking after. Okay? Can you do that for me?'

She nodded.

A smile lifted his eyes, the only part of his face visible, as he twisted the wood out of her hand and threw it to the ground.

'I'll be in touch, Ella.'

Molly

Now – 16th March

We've lost another one.

Stacey Frears and her daughter are leaving. Young Beth, I like her. Smart girl, smarter than her mother by such an outstanding degree that I've always wondered where that brain could have come from. Not her father, apparently, who they've not seen since the night that Stacey brought baby Beth home from the hospital; he went out to buy nappies and Dairy Milk and never came back. A man so stupid even Stacey says he's as likely to have got lost than done a runner on them.

'What about your degree?' I ask Beth, who sits on the cream leather sofa toying with her phone. She's probably passing on the bad news to her mates and telling her boyfriend this doesn't have to be an end to their relationship.

'She can take the points from her first year and transfer them to another college,' Stacey says, with the confidence of someone who doesn't realise the huge gulf between the educational standards of a Russell Group university and whatever her new city has to offer. 'Clever's the same, no matter where you get your degree from.'

Beth's brow creases and she curls up tighter, lifting her phone closer to her face. She makes no comment and I've never seen her silent before. It's like the decision has rendered her mute, and I wonder how far she was consulted, if she even considered the option of staying here and making her own future.

I was younger than her when I left home and more than ready for it.

Beth's position is so much tougher, though, forced to choose between family and education, and she has the added complication of actually being close to her mother. For me the emotional bonds were already severed and the hard realities were so much softer. My generation 'stood on our own two feet' thanks to generous grants and affordable rents and no security tags hidden in the back of expensive textbooks, jobs you could pick up and leave on a whim, knowing the place across the road would be hiring. It's easy to forget how wide and well sprung our safety nets were.

Beth doesn't have the luxury of independence. Not yet. Maybe not for a very long time. She's a child of London who might never be able to find her way back here.

'What have they upped the offer to?' I ask Stacey. 'You were at one-eighty with them, weren't you?'

The same as I've been offered.

'They've not upped it,' she tells me, staring into her tea. 'They're never going to.'

'Not if you don't dig in, no.'

'Molly,' she virtually sighs my name. 'They've got us by the balls and they know it.'

The last two years have aged her. Living in this crumbling building, the uncertainty about her future and the constant low-level fear of break-ins and vandalism. She's stopped dyeing her hair and now wears it short and grey, a few strands of the black it used to be threaded through at the crown, the same colour as the eyebrows she paints in defiantly every morning. You can always afford eyebrows.

I understand her resignation, but I don't like it.

Maybe if I had a child to consider I would have made a different decision. Maybe I'd have caved at the first round of offers rather than being one of the last to leave. It's a test I'll never be put to, so it's easy to convince myself I'm better than that.

There's a knock at the door and Stacey tells Beth to get it.

It's Ella.

She looks flustered, pink-cheeked from the cold and like she hasn't had enough sleep. I wonder if the police pulled her in yesterday after they left me. She never called me to report back on what they'd asked her. Has she only just got out of custody? Is that why she's been silent?

I've been worried – just one more layer of worry painted over all the others – and I wish we weren't here in Stacey's flat, with the rest of this conversation to be had. The fight for Castle Rise is over, we all know that, and the pantomime of trying to discourage Stacey from the course of action she's already committed to is wearing on me. I'm sure Ella has no heart for it either.

'You're leaving then?' she asks, not even bothering to remove her coat or sit down.

There's a trace of exasperation in her voice, but you might take it for anger if you didn't know her and what she's going through.

'We've got to,' Stacey says, meeting Ella's gaze with admirable defiance. 'There was a murder here, for God's sake! How can I keep going out to work nights, leaving Beth here on her own, when whoever did it might come back?'

Ella's cheeks flush.

My mouth goes dry.

We don't look at each other.

'The last time was bad enough,' Stacey says. 'I wanted to pack up and leave then, but you two talked me out of it.'

'And they'd only offered you one-eighty at that point,' Ella snaps.

'It's not about the money,' I tell her softly. 'Stacey's right. She needs to think about what's best for her and Beth now. Maybe none of us are safe here any more.'

Ella drops on to the arm of the sofa, shoulders sagging.

'I'm sorry,' she says. 'Stacey, Beth, you two have been so tough. I've got so much respect for you, staying on here when everyone else bolted. Honestly.' She finds an unconvincing smile from somewhere. 'I hope they've done right by you with the money.'

Stacey doesn't tell her the figure and I decide I won't either.

'What did the police say?' Ella asks. 'Did they tell you it was a murder? I thought it was an accident.'

'"Not ruling anything out," they said.' Stacey shrugs. 'They wouldn't tell me anything else. They acted like I was being ghoulish even wanting to know what happened. I *live* here but I'm not supposed to be curious. I'm not allowed to be worried.'

'It was probably an accident,' Ella says reassuringly.

'Probably,' Stacey agrees. 'But we don't feel safe here any more. I'm sorry. I feel really bad about letting the rest of you down.'

'You've got nothing to feel bad about,' I tell her, getting to my feet. 'Just let us know if you need any help before you go, though, okay? Paperwork, legal advice, anything like that. And don't sign the contract without having someone read it through. You know they'll stiff you at the last minute if they can.'

Stacey nods and assures us she still doesn't trust them, she knows what they are.

Ella and me leave the flat together and say nothing until we reach the stairwell door. She automatically starts up towards my floor but I stop her.

'Let's go down to the Embankment. I need some fresh air.'

We walk to the river in silence and the longer it goes on the thicker the space between us becomes, filled with traffic noise and sirens and the ever-present sound of heavy plant at work; the gap feels freighted, occupied by some invisible third party.

This distance didn't exist the night it happened or in the days afterwards. Not when she cried in my arms in her bedsit like a child or when she cried again down the phone. This is new.

And it frightens me.

Last night I did some reading up on Ella's father, Assistant Chief Constable Alec Riordan, and I didn't like what I found. He's too clean. For his generation – the one caught up in the miners' strike and the Birmingham Six, Hillsborough and all those child-abuse scandals quietly covered up or discredited – clean is more suspicious than dirty. It makes me think he was just smarter than the others. He must have dirt on people. The kind that would keep Ella out of prison.

If I was naïve, I'd feel relieved at that, because if she stays out then shouldn't I stay out too? But sacrificial lambs are always handy to have around and I'm eminently expendable.

As we reach Riverside Walk, my eye is drawn to the bulk of Dolphin Square rising behind a line of bare-limbed trees on the north bank.

'Do you want a coffee?' Ella asks.

'I'm fine.'

'I'm getting one for myself.'

I can't wait any longer.

'Ella, what did the police ask you?'

She holds her hand up as she walks away from me. 'There's nothing to worry about, Mol. Just let me get a drink, okay?'

I bite my tongue. Again.

Down on the riverbank the mudlark is back. He's wearing a wide-brimmed hat, finger-stained at the rim, pulled low to shade his eyes against the morning sun bouncing up off the water, the same too-large waxed jacket and baggy cords tucked into his wellington boots. He pokes in the wet earth with a stick, posture hunched and focused. There's something bulky in one of his pockets, another unearthed treasure.

I'm not the only person intrigued by him today. A young Japanese couple stand watching from the white-painted river wall twenty feet away, the woman filming him with her phone. A curio himself, unearthed in an unexpected location, as surreal to the girl as anything she will see in this city.

The couple eventually move on, pass me as they head upriver towards Battersea Power Station, their arms linked, looking up into the bright morning sky.

Ella returns with two cups of Waitrose coffee.

'That's illegal, you know.' She gestures towards the man.

'Mudlarking isn't illegal,' I say, surprised.

'It is here. This is the only stretch of the river where you're not allowed to do it. Something to do with the MI6 building.'

I don't care.

'What did the police ask you, Ella?'

'Just about the party,' she says. 'They wanted a guest list. I suppose they're trying to work out if anyone's missing from it. I told them we had some extra walk-ins. I said we tried to keep it to donors and press only but people brought friends along and I couldn't really keep track of everyone who was there.'

'That was a good idea.'

'It's true,' she says. 'Which helps. I saw a whole bunch of people I didn't know.'

'And what about him? Are they going to find him on the list?'

Ella sips her coffee, it must be scalding hot. 'I don't know.'

'You must know his name. Come on, Ella.'

'I told you, I can't remember. He was a one-night stand.' The flush on her face creeps down her neck. 'It wasn't like I was screaming it out.'

'But what about the emails he sent you?' I ask, feeling like a detective myself, poking holes in her story. 'He must have signed them.'

'He always signed them "M", with a kiss.'

'What a fucking romantic,' I sneer. 'How about his email address?'

'It was his blog name.' Ella screws her face up, thinking. 'It was something stupid – something techie – shit, sorry Molly, I can't remember. But I think he was a Matt or a Max, maybe. Max?' She rolls the word around in her mouth a few more times, before she shakes her head. 'I don't think he was a donor, anyway. He was skint; he couldn't have afforded to drop two hundred quid to get an invite. I think he must have seen me posting about the party and decided to crash it.'

'So he shouldn't be on the list?'

'I don't think so.'

'He was skint?' I ask and she nods. 'Was he in a shared house? Are there people who might report him missing?'

'Yeah, he was renting a room. He said he didn't get on with any of his housemates because they were all stuck up. That should have been a red flag, shouldn't it?'

I nod. 'What about work?'

'Freelance something or other.'

'So he probably won't be missed in the office.'

'No. Not for a while, anyway.'

'Family?'

'We didn't talk about our families. I suppose he has one,' she says, her voice dropping, as if this is the first time she's considered the possibility, that there are people somewhere who might be missing him already.

But maybe the relationship she has with her own family is behind that mental block. She hardly ever mentions them. Only when absolutely pressed and then reluctantly, briefly and with little affection. I know she doesn't speak to her mother from one month to the next, her father even less frequently.

Has that changed, though? These are times when even the weakest family bonds can strengthen more than anyone involved would have believed possible.

She's looking increasingly uncomfortable. She won't meet my eye, but instead stares out across the river where a procession of goods barges are making slow progress, carrying some elaborate prefabricated structures. The pieces have been wrapped in plastic, but in places it has come loose and snaps in the wind, revealing elegant arcs of copper.

'The woman,' Ella says. 'Wazir – she thinks he was murdered.'

'Did she say that?'

'Not in as many words, but she was too thorough for an investigation into an accident. And she was very interested in who had access to the building either side of the party. What did I think about the remaining residents? Why hadn't you all moved?' Ella bites her lip, forehead creasing. 'They must be wondering if he was anything to do with the party at all. I don't know how precisely they can fix the time of death.'

Maybe you should ask your dad, I think, but keep it to myself.

She says, 'If they can't get a precise time of death – the party was only three hours, he could have died before or after, right? I think they're wondering if it's something more personal with one of you and him.'

I shiver inside my coat, draw it closer around myself and tuck my chin down into the funnel collar.

'If they find the flat...' Ella looks across her shoulder sharply as feet pass behind us, but the man has huge bright-red earphones

141

on, drowning in music. 'We're done for if they work out that's where it happened.'

'I cleaned up,' I tell her, remembering the smell of the bleach and the sting of the fumes rising into my eyes. 'There's nothing visible to make them look closer. They'll only know to give the place a thorough search if someone tells them it's that one.'

She nods, gaze fixed on the water once again. 'Then we're safe.'

But I don't feel safe.

Ella

Then – 29th September

'We shouldn't be doing this,' Ella said, dragging her fingertips across Dylan's bare stomach, gravitating to the scar on his hip, earned in childhood when his sister shot him with a bow and arrow.

He'd grown up in the countryside, just like her, and initially she'd thought it would bond them. Until he started talking about the isolated farmhouse, the lambs dying in snowy fields and the sheepdogs shot behind the barns when they became too old to work or too expensive to be treated by the vet. It had surprised her how easily he spoke about his unhappy early life but then, people talked to her, they trusted her. She didn't know why, but it was a gift that sometimes felt like a burden.

As her forefinger traced the line of the scar, he reached down and took her hand, brought it up to his chest and held it there in the thatch of wiry hair.

'If anyone finds out…'

'It happens all the time,' Dylan said. 'It's frowned on, sure, but as long as we don't go streaking up Camden High Street hand in hand then nobody's going to say anything.'

Ella smiled, automatically mirroring him. But not really feeling it.

'Have you done this before?'

'I didn't have you down for the jealous type.'

'I'm not,' Ella said, already picturing another woman here with him, tangled up in the sheets, which hadn't been aired thoroughly enough, another woman's head on the too-thin pillow now smudged with her lipstick. If she flipped it over would she find a smear of some gaudier hue on the other side? The image made her angrier than she expected. She barely thought about him when she wasn't with him but at moments like this she felt a possessive tug, which scared her in its intensity. 'Have you, though?'

'No.'

She didn't believe him.

Men like Dylan were magpies, always looking for the shiny new thing to play with. Even when it was expressly prohibited. *Especially* when it was. She could cost him his job. They both knew that. And there was little he could do to her in return.

She was the innocent in this inappropriate relationship, after all; the impressionable one, the vulnerable one.

Ella stretched out, pressing hard against him for a few long seconds before she relaxed again, throwing her arm across her eyes to block out the early-evening sun, which had found its way in through the dormer window of this tiny attic room. Clarinet music seeped in from the neighbouring flat. A simple melody played over and again in ever more complex variations, the musician turning it inside out with an ease Ella thought you'd have to consider virtuoso.

Times like this, when they didn't speak, she could almost convince herself that what they had was healthy and normal. Pretend one day he would take the train up to Durham with her to meet her parents. That eventually she would get to hear his sister's version of the bow-and-arrow story and they would laugh together and gradually become like sisters themselves.

'Do you want to tell me what's wrong now?' Dylan asked. 'We can keep pretending a bit longer if you prefer, but just so you're aware, you're not fooling me.'

Ella sat up, drawing the pillow to her chest without thinking, hugging it tightly.

'This,' he gestured at her. 'Tell me how you feel.'

'The same.'

'That's not an answer.'

'I'm fine,' she said, hiding her mouth behind the edge of the pillow, smelling her coconut shampoo on the polycotton. 'Stressed, obviously. Tired, obviously. The same as always.'

'Are you sleeping?'

'Five hours a night. It's enough.'

Five hours on a good night, but he didn't need to know that. What good would it do to tell him about the nights she was too anxious to even close her eyes? That sometimes she could barely even blink she was so wired, trying to keep everything straight in her head.

'I've got pills if you want them,' he said. 'But it'd be better if we worked out why you're not sleeping.'

Ella rolled her eyes. 'Are you serious? I can't sleep because I'm trying to keep up with my PhD and save the fucking world and I've got all these people on my back constantly, wanting me to help with this campaign and that campaign, and I can't turn anyone down because if I do then I'm an elitist bitch or a fraud or I'm only interested in doing stuff that builds my profile. Like I'm seriously killing myself for the sake of my blog stats.' She raked her fingers back through her hair and tugged at the ends. 'People are losing their homes and they're looking to me to make it stop. I don't know how to do that. But I can't tell them to take the money and run, can I? One of the old ladies is in such a state she's just had a stroke. A stroke! And Molly's telling her husband to hang in for a better offer because now his wife's going to need expensive extra care. I – it's stupid – it's a stupid fight to have. Why does nobody see that?'

Dylan reached out and wrapped his fingers around her ankle, a look on his face she didn't like. It went beyond basic concern. She shouldn't have said so much. But there was nobody else she could vent at. Not about the pressure she was under, not about the people who she sometimes felt were using her up and draining her dry. She had to be the most perfect version of Ella Riordan to everyone else in her life, because if she slipped, even for a moment, they might not like who she was underneath. They wanted her to be righteous and incorruptible and … pure. Nobody could be that all the time.

'You can stop,' he said gently. 'Whenever you want.'

'I don't want to stop.'

'You can't tell me you're enjoying this.'

'Because that would be a great reason to do it? Fun?' she sneered. 'I thought you'd get it.'

'I do. I can see that you're driving yourself into the ground and I think you need to start to think about putting yourself first. It's obviously fucking your health up. And what are you achieving? Really?'

She reeled from his words, suddenly light-headed, realising that in his eyes she'd already failed, that there was absolutely no point pushing on because he didn't believe she could make a difference.

Was he right?

Maybe she genuinely wasn't up to this. No longer the smartest student in class, the effortless A-grader. It was a cliché for a reason, that university is where intelligent kids find out precisely how ordinary they are, competing against their actual intellectual peers for perhaps the first time in their lives.

Is that what was happening here? Ella felt like she was coping well with her PhD. She knew she was making progress, but everything else? The campaigning, the protests; was suceeding there simply beyond her capabilities?

'Ella, we talked about this, didn't we?' He was using his quiet/ loud voice, the one she hated. She'd prefer he shouted at her. 'You need to be honest with yourself. Acknowledge when you're taking on too much and let some of it go.'

No, she wasn't ready to give up.

'This isn't going to beat me,' she said, low and hard.

'Is that how you see what's happening?' he asked. 'Like a fight?'

'It's just a saying, stop over-analysing every word out of my mouth.' She growled with frustration, wishing she'd never let the conversation go this far. 'You know what, yes, I do see it like a fight. If this isn't one, then what the hell is? I'm fighting for something important here.'

'But you feel like you're losing?'

'At Castle Rise, yes. We've already lost.'

Dylan sat up, placed his hands on her knees. 'You were always going to lose, Ella. Don't you remember what we talked about when you decided to get involved there? Do you remember what I told you?'

'You told me to focus on the big picture.' She looked away from him, the intensity in his eyes making her uncomfortable. 'But this is big-picture stuff. Castle Rise is going to get demolished, we all know that, but it's brought people together. I've met dozens of other protestors and activists because I got on board there and helped Molly when nobody else was prepared to. I can make a real difference with those people.'

'Do you feel like you're making a difference?'

'It's slow-going, but yes. I'm making good contacts and that's where it starts, right? You can't overthrow the establishment from scratch, can you?'

He nodded, uncertain-looking, and Ella changed the subject while she was slightly ahead.

'Molly's asked if I can help out with some fundraising for a local homeless shelter. She wants to crowdfund a book of essays.'

'Yes, that's really going to stick to the man,' Dylan said, an acidic edge coming through.

He didn't like Molly. He'd never met her but he seemed to dislike her instinctively. And Ella suspected she knew why; Molly had helped her and Dylan resented that. He wanted to be the one she went to for advice, the only one. It was beneath him, she thought, but he could be jealous too.

'I've met some of the people who're submitting pieces,' she said. 'They're serious, dedicated people. She's got Martin Sinclair to write something about the monetisation of homelessness. I didn't think he'd remember me but he acted like we were old friends. It was ...' She wanted to say 'nice', but she knew how Dylan would intepret the safe little word, that he'd recognise the hint of lust she was trying to hide under it. 'I think it was promising. He's given me some good advice about my PhD too. He was very generous with his time.'

Dylan's eyes had lit up at the mention of Sinclair's name, but he shut down again, as if he didn't want to acknowledge her rising status. She wondered if he felt diminished by it and realised, with a tender pang, that he *was* diminished slightly in her eyes, measured against her new friends.

'Sounds like Molly has plenty of other people to make this book happen,' Dylan said coolly. 'She doesn't need you as well.'

'But I've said I'll do it already. If I let everyone down, they'll think I'm a lightweight. And Molly's only asking me to do the media side of things. It's manageable.'

'It wasn't five minutes ago.'

She never should have told him. Why couldn't he let her vent like a normal person?

'Tell her no,' he said, sliding his hands up the outside of her thighs, squeezing the flesh there. 'Tell her you're too busy with your PhD. She'll understand and if she doesn't, then she isn't much of a friend.'

'I can't.'

'Is she really that important to you?'

'You know what she's done for me,' Ella said softly, feeling suddenly vulnerable, sitting there naked with only the pillow covering her.

Dylan took a deep breath, lifted his hands off her. 'I know, Ella. Believe me, nobody understands better than I do.'

'She's vouched for me with people who wouldn't give me the time of day before she said it was okay. Half the women I've interviewed for my PhD brushed me off when I approached them. They weren't going to talk to a policeman's daughter in a million years. But they know Molly and she knows me, so now they'll talk. They actually *like* me now. Do you know what a big deal that is for me?'

Annoyance twisted his face and Ella didn't know if it was what she'd said or the whiny tone she was irritated to realise she was using.

She looked at her clothes scattered across the white-painted floorboards, thrown off with a hot abandon that felt more distant than it really was. Less than ninety minutes since he'd answered the door to her, holding up a hand to tell her to stay quiet while he finished a phone call. She'd smiled at him, standing close enough to recognise the voice on the other end, started to unbutton the fly of his jeans, followed him as he stepped back, giving her a warning look. She'd ignored it, worked her hand down past the waistband of his boxers and felt him harden against her palm, his voice lifting very slightly as he gave a final assurance that yes, of course, he would find out, he understood, yes, yes, he would get right on it this afternoon.

All of that pleasure and now look where they were, she thought. Eyeing one another defensively across the rumpled sheets, sad and sexless in their nudity.

'So, let me ask you something,' he said. 'How long are you going to let Molly keep directing your life?'

'That's not what I'm doing.'

'You want to keep her happy, though? You're going to take on a stupid, completely pointless project just because she wants you to. Despite the fact that you're exhausted and stressed out and have a hundred other things to worry about. How is that not Molly dominating your decision-making process?'

Sometimes Ella thought he'd made a wrong career choice, that he would have been better becoming a psychiatrist. Or some imitation of one.

'I got an interview with Carol Dearborne,' she told him, slapping down her last and strongest card. 'Through Molly.'

Dylan's brows lifted, not hiding the surprise. 'About—'

'Yes, about,' Ella said, delighted that she'd finally impressed him. 'Carol Dearborne, who never talked, who trusts almost nobody, who is still a ball of anarchic fury thirty years later, invited me into her home for the weekend and gave me fifteen hours of on-the-record information that's absolutely fresh to the market.'

'Shit.' Dylan grinned, rubbed his cheek. 'Well, your PhD just got a lot more interesting.'

'Interesting doesn't even begin to get close to what it is,' Ella said, fluffing her pillow and lying back down. 'And the off-the-record stuff...'

'Is it taped?'

'I can't use it,' Ella said, shoving him in the chest with her foot. Hard enough to make him wince. 'I'm probably committing some kind of criminal act just by knowing most of it.'

'You could pass it on to the police.' He crawled up the bed and lowered himself over her. 'If your conscience is getting twitchy.'

'Yeah, I don't think I'm going to do that.'

'You'll be an accessory if you don't.'

'Only if she gets in trouble,' Ella said, tipping up her hips as his teeth played at her ear. 'And for all I know it's just a bunch of talk, right?'

'Right,' he murmured. 'But what if it isn't talk?'

Ella smiled. 'Then I've made a very cool new friend.'

Molly

Now – 18th March

The first steels for the new building arrived this morning. Within a couple of hours the skeleton of Rise 2 was going up, men swarming all over the huge red beams, craning them into position, checking their lie with laser levels before bolting them into place, firmly, irrevocably. A twenty-four-storey building put together like a child's toy.

I watched from the balcony until I couldn't bear to watch any more.

So I went down to the Embankment with some vague idea of getting the mudlark's attention, even if it meant braving the slippery steps and meeting him on his own territory. I wanted to photograph him, but not from a distance. I wanted to take his portrait and hear his story. Spirit him away to a dim and rowdy old boozer and excavate his secrets.

But the water was sitting high when I reached the river wall and he was somewhere else, turning over different stones and finding other treasures.

Now afternoon is wearing on into evening and I don't want to go home, because I know how much higher the tower's bones will have climbed into the darkening sky and how the view I've loved for thirty years will be disrupted, taken away from me in strips. Before very long, the gaps will be filled with grey blocks and huge sheets of glass and wooden cladding, until all I'll see when I stand on my balcony is another wedge of empty rooms and the neighbours who couldn't afford to buy on the river side of the development looking back at me with disgust.

If I'm still there.

The young Polish barman with the neck tattoo comes and clears my empty glass, gestures at my cup, which is still a third full, the coffee cold and filmed over.

'I'm still working on that one.'

He takes pity on me, leaves me to my table even though I'm dead money sitting here as the bar fills up. A couple of those lingering suits stopping in after work could claim it, the small group of women drinking Prosecco. The suits are eyeing me up, weighing the ease of bullying a pensioner against the social stigma of doing so.

Fuck them, they've claimed everything else around here. If I won't leave my home for £185,000, I'm not going to move from this padded-leather banquette for free, am I?

The letter arrived this morning and I guessed what it was by the quality of the envelope, thick and slightly textured, an expensive bone white. I've seen hundreds of them now, all from the Clerkenwell legal firm that represents the developers. It's in my pocket, read once, folded in half, dismissed. I'll throw it in a bin on the way home.

Another £5,000 on the offer. Maybe because Stacey Frears is leaving and has gone cheaper than they expected, the owners feel like they can splash the cash. Maybe they think an old woman like me will be getting concerned for her safety now I'm going to be alone there with just Callum and Derek, and his Jenny bedbound.

We *are* vulnerable, but we have been since the site was sold five years ago.

This offer won't get me out.

I'll be the last to leave on principle. Even if the price has dropped by then. The money they're offering won't allow me to build a new life in London. I could have a few years of high living in a nice rented flat, then step in front of a Tube train, perhaps. It's a grimly appealing option compared to the alternative; moving out to the sticks, finding a bedsit or a place in some over-sixties facility with alarms in every room in case I fall off the toilet, surrounded by geriatrics talking about the grandkids who never visit and how everything was better back in their day.

I know there are good lives to be lived outside London, I'm not such a snob. But I just can't see me in them. Suddenly alone and having to begin again, make new friends and acquaintances, stoke them up from a dead start. The thought is excruciating. When you're young you can do that. Drink helps and drugs and sex. All of that common ground. What does a lone sixty-year-old woman do when she enters a new community? Join a book club and hope for the best? A choir? Am I supposed to bingo?

I can't do it.

I can't face the prospect of getting old like that. The terms forced on me by the state of my finances.

When I bought my flat, back in the eighties, I didn't think about the future.

I'd had a choice between Nine Elms or Islington and if I'd gone north rather than south I'd be sitting on close to half a million, thanks to the unpredictable ways of the London property market. Not that I care about the money. The real difference is I would have owned my home outright. I can still remember viewing the Islington flat, a small mews place: one bedroom, a kitchen little more than a cupboard and inter-war plumbing. I remember the estate agent smiling his cheap smile and saying 'some remodelling might be in order'.

Freehold.

I didn't stop to consider how important that one little word might become.

I had other things on my mind. Work and protests and the man I was fucking. I can still remember his name but not much else about him. If I passed him on the street now I probably wouldn't recognise him, but that afternoon in Islington I skittered along the cobbled mews, thinking about him when I should have been thinking of myself.

None of us believed we'd get old. That's been the curse of my generation. We were the first to be teenagers, the ones who tore up the rule book, did whatever and whoever we wanted. Didn't stop at thirty or forty, didn't see why we should grow up, refused to become our parents.

And that was fine for those of us who bought in Islington but not those who plumped for the spacious and well-situated ex-council flats freed up under Right to Buy in Nine Elms.

Would my life have been different if I'd stayed north of the river? Would Islington have tamed me? Maybe I'd have settled down with the bloke I was screwing back then and become the kind of woman he wanted me to be, instead of running in fear from the possibility of getting trapped in a second bad marriage less than a year after I escaped the first. Maybe we'd have kids now and grandkids and be living in a cottage in Cornwall with a lovingly restored *trullo* for wintering in Puglia, all nicely set up for a civilised retirement because on a different day I might have made a better choice.

I laugh quietly to myself and it isn't funny, because my life has been shaped by bad choices, but what happens if you don't laugh?

You weep, that's what. And who wants to be the old woman crying in the corner of a perfectly nice pub on a weekday early evening?

When I look up from the polished-mahogany tabletop I notice that the suits have left and decide I might as well haul myself off home too.

Work has ceased on-site by the time I get back; only the security team are left behind and they're in the middle of their handover as I walk past their Portakabin, one lot heading home to wherever on the margins of the city their wages allow them to live, the fresh ones coming in from the second job they probably have to do to keep a family here. They look tired, all three of them, but the sympathy I feel doesn't go very deep.

You can't have sympathy for foot soldiers, even when they seem nice enough, even when they're suffering their own privations.

Back at Greenham some of the women would talk to the troops on the other side of the wire fence – the English ones, not the

154

Americans – and I remember how Carol ordered them to stop. Told them they were like the French women who collaborated with the Nazis. And maybe it was hyperbole, but I think she was right to pick them up on it even if I didn't agree at the time.

You only get to choose your side once and those young men, likely economically conscripted, likely bullied on a daily basis, had chosen to serve their own oppressors rather than admit they were victims of the same system we were.

At the main doors I force myself to turn and look properly at the new structure.

Four floors high, two hundred feet wide. Its sudden rise, the sheer scale of it, disorientates me and I feel the ground lurch under me. I surely must have been away longer than one day for all of this new metal to have sprung up.

It's like some dark alchemy has been worked.

Tomorrow it will be twice as tall and two days after it will have doubled again. It will loom over us and I'll fear it falling but welcome it too, just as I did when the first tower went up and I'd dream of the metal buckling and twisting, hear it screaming as it sheared, the bolts popping like cannon fire. Those mornings I would wake up feeling so sure of my dreams that I wouldn't believe the building was still standing until I went out on to my balcony and saw it for myself.

One of the security guards has come out of his hut. He holds his radio to his mouth but doesn't speak. He just watches me and I wish I was dangerous enough to justify his suspicion, but I'm not. Not these days.

I go inside and walk past the lifts without pausing, still thinking about the steel skeleton and how much I don't want to look at it any more tonight.

There's no escaping it, though.

I go up to Callum's flat. He's on the other side of the building and his views are safer and even if they weren't, he always draws his curtains as soon as it begins to get dark.

When I get there I have to knock three times before he answers the door and he looks like crap, all sunken-cheeked and squinty-eyed. Behind him the flat is lit only by the light from the television, which he has turned down so low I can't hear it.

'What's up with you?' I ask, closing the door behind me, watching him return to the nest he's made on the sofa; cushions and pillows and the wash-faded peach floral duvet that might have been his mum's.

He burrows down. 'I've got the flu.'

I place my palm on his forehead and feel clammy heat there. 'Have you taken anything for it?'

'Just let me sleep.'

He closes his eyes and for a moment I look at him, this big man felled and fragile, and decide I shouldn't leave him on his own.

In the bathroom I check the cabinet over the sink for anything that might be vaguely helpful. He doesn't have much, but I've not seen him ill in the three years I've known him so I'm not surprised. There's an empty packet of ibuprofen and some paracetamol, cough mixture two years past good and, on the top shelf, a collection of medications, which I think were his father's.

The names of the drugs are long and unfamiliar to me and the dates stamped on the side of them are from the last century. I don't know if it's sentimentality or laziness that has stopped him from throwing them away, but I suspect the former.

Callum's flat is inherited from his parents and he's never troubled to redecorate it, although there are places where items are obviously missing; family photos removed because they're too painful to look at, empty shelves in the old teak unit where other people might display trophies. There will be evidence of Callum's military service somewhere, I think; parents of soldiers always create altars in readiness for the worst. I wonder how soon after his father's death Callum chose to put everything away and how differently I would feel about him if I hunted it out. Could our friendship survive me seeing him in uniform? Holding a gun? Smiling as he stands in the ruins of some torn-apart city with the rest of his men?

I close the cabinet door and meet my expression in the mirror. Who am I to judge him?

156

After what I've done.

Callum is asleep now, curled up with his back to the television, snoring and snorting like a bull.

I go into the kitchen and put the kettle on to make myself a coffee. It's been a long day and I've not eaten since breakfast. In the cupboard I find some rice pudding and have it cold from the tin, sitting in the armchair near the TV, watching a soap opera play out soundlessly.

All drama becomes comedy when you strip away the words.

I think about Callum, coming home from Iraq or Afghanistan – he's never said which war he was 'only a cook' in – and wonder if his father found him changed from when he left. If he still felt like his son. Callum has never spoken much about his parents, only said enough that I know his mother died while he was away and his father soon after he returned.

They lived here as long as me but I never met them. I didn't have much to do with any of my neighbours before the developers moved in and forced us to become the community we've been invoking to protect our homes. Maybe we lost because it was a lie. A real community might not have rolled over so easily.

My phone pings as a text message comes in. Martin Sinclair, on at me again about finding a good time for a chat. He wants an interview for his new book. He's already spoken to some of the other women from Greenham and I know Carol has turned him down, not trusting we'll get a sympathetic hearing from any man. Even him. I like Martin well enough; yes, he's a sell-out and he wants to put himself above the story, but at heart I think he genuinely believes in the power of protest. If anyone's going to write about it, he's the best of a bad lot.

The soap opera gives way to a nature documentary and I doze off in the chair for a while, wake up feeling like I've been asleep for hours but discover it's been less than forty minutes. I go into the bathroom for a pee and hear someone knock at the door.

It's probably Derek with another rat he'll need Callum's help disposing of. I'm relieved when I hear him go to answer it, knowing I'd be no use to Derek.

'What the fuck is this?' Callum growls.

I rush back to the living room in time to see DC Gull snapping a pair of handcuffs around Callum's wrists while DC Wazir finishes giving out the caution.

Callum shoots me a desperate look, tries to come towards me, but Gull pulls him back. When I start towards them Wazir tells me not to move and something in Callum's eyes stops me in a way her command wouldn't.

'Mol, I'm sorry.' His face is red and clenched the way it goes when he wakes up crying. 'I'm so sorry.'

Wazir is smiling thinly, already opening the door.

'He didn't do anything,' I say and immediately know how useless the statement is. 'What are you charging him with?'

'It isn't really any of your business, is it?' Wazir says, stepping aside to let the men through.

I follow them, feeling like a terrier nipping at the copper's heels as he walks Callum out, one big hand on his shoulder, the other holding the rigid black cuffs. It's heartbreaking to see him so completely cowed and I want to say *something* to make him feel better, let him know I'm here for him, but I can't find the right words and instead I say, 'Don't talk to them without a solicitor present. No matter what they do, insist on a solicitor.'

Callum won't look at me, keeps his eyes fixed on his feet as they shuffle across the floor, wearing a pair of old brown moccasins lined with matted fur. I wish I'd found his shoes, made him change them before they took him. I can't stand to think of him being walked into a police station in his worn-down slippers.

'You haven't done anything wrong,' I say, out in the corridor with them now, following them to the stairwell, hoping he'll turn and look at me again, but he doesn't. 'Twenty-four hours, Cal. That's all they can keep you in for.'

When Gull shoves the door open, Wazir moves to block me off.

'We'll have your toy boy with us a lot longer than twenty-four hours.'

The stairwell door slams home with bone-shaking finality.

Ella

Then – 22nd September

'Carol didn't do anything special, you know,' Molly said, as they leaned into the steep climb of Ripon Road, moving in single file because the pavement was lined with bins waiting to be taken in by residents not yet home from work. 'Did you get in touch with Brenda?'

'I'm still trying,' Ella said. 'She's a councillor, she must get loads of requests for interviews. And it's not like my PhD is that important.'

'I think she'll be happy to talk to you.' Molly stopped to let a kid on a bike whizz past them down the hill. 'She made something of herself after the strikes. That's the kind of story you want. Miner's wife turned political player. Still fighting for her people. That's impressive, right?'

Was Molly jealous of her interest in Carol's campaigning? Ella wondered. Was that why she was trying to deflect her attention away on to other targets?

Carol and Molly had been friends since the mid-eighties and on the handful of occasions Ella had seen them together she might have taken them for sisters. There was a bond there, unmistakably strong, the kind forged in adversity. And from what she already knew of the time they'd spent at Greenham Common together, she imagined they'd shared some long dark nights, couldn't have many secrets left from one another.

That kind of bond was sometimes as much hate as love.

My generation didn't invent the frenemy, she thought. We learned it from our mothers, and even a committed feminist like Molly wasn't immune, it seemed.

If Molly had been involved with Women Against Pit Closures, Ella would have gladly accepted her input. But she'd spent the miners' strike taking photographs only the left-wing press would buy, because her reputation blacklisted her everywhere else. She'd given money, but that wasn't a story.

'Make sure you tell Brenda I said to get in touch.' Molly glanced back over her shoulder. 'And make sure she knows about your run-in with the riot police. She saw enough of her friends beaten up; it'll be a good icebreaker. That's the key with interviews. You've got to establish a rapport right from the off.'

Ella sighed quietly, wondering if Molly realised how patronising she was being.

Most of the summer had been taken up with interviews. Eight weeks of establishing a rapport with women who hadn't wanted to talk to her to begin with. Who opened their doors to her already deeply suspicious.

Yes, Molly *had* got the doors to open, but the rest Ella had done for herself.

And she was proud of that.

Molly stopped outside a white stucco terrace with flaking black railings and a palm tree poking up from the yard of the garden flat, fairy lights wrapped around its scaly trunk. It was a touch of whimsy Ella struggled to accept from the hard-faced, hard-talking woman she'd met before. The sash window was up, letting out the smell of dope smoke and Patti Smith's plaintive voice, a song Ella could sing by heart.

Carol opened the door in denim shorts and a man's shirt, her dark-blonde hair piled into a rough bun.

'Get yourselves in here,' she said, smiling broadly. 'Dinner's been ready half an hour.'

Ella could smell a complex mix of spices coming from the kitchen, heavy on the ginger and cinnamon, the earthy base note of cumin, deep and vaguely animal.

Carol showed them into the living room, where a low, dark-wood coffee table had been set for three with mismatched crockery and cutlery, scatter cushions on the floor for chairs.

It was like the common room in a student house. Shambolically furnished, a battered sofa and two different armchairs, all shrouded in clashing throws and cushions. The purple walls were covered in posters for foreign films and framed press cuttings. There was no TV, but the space in the corner where it would have usually sat was filled by a bulky turntable, housed in teak, and an extensive vinyl collection.

'You've got such a lovely place, Carol.'

'It's not much, but...' She shrugged. 'I'm lucky to have it.'

Ella almost said how homely it felt, but she knew it might sound condescending, even though it was genuinely felt. Carol's house *was* homely. Immediately welcoming in a way few houses Ella had been in were. She'd hoped her studio flat might come to feel like this in time, but it kept defying her attempts at nesting. Despite the rugs she bought and the carefully chosen bedding and the washed-linen curtains she'd been delighted to find in a local charity shop one afternoon, it felt wrong in some vague way. You couldn't fake atmosphere, she realised. It was something you accrued rather than conjured.

She knew no place of hers would feel like this while she was living such an uncertain and transient life.

Molly offered to help with serving up and the pair of them went into the kitchen together, already laughing, but soon they were talking in hushed voices that Ella couldn't make out, even when she was close to the open door. She gave up and took her seat at the table, thinking how unbelievable it was that she'd made it here, into Carol's home and, hopefully, her confidence.

She was a tough woman to get close to, but maybe she was wise to be that way.

Ella thought of Dylan. She'd let him get too close, even though she knew his motives ran counter to her best interests. Soon she'd have to do something about that.

161

He was like her unhomely studio flat – frustratingly close to being right for her, but there was something lacking in him, just like there was something lacking in the flat. Both withheld part of themselves from her.

Maybe that was where Dylan's appeal lay, though, she thought. Through school and university she'd been out with the nice boys, the quiet ones – Jack, who taught her how to play backgammon and asked permission before committing each escalating act of sexual intimacy; Nicholas, who campaigned for the Green Party on the weekends and only read female authors; Christian, who left her when he found out she smoked weed. They were sweet and safe and boring.

They didn't test her like Dylan did and some part of Ella realised that their relationship was really a contest being played to undefined rules with only the scoring system agreed upon.

And she would not lose to him.

Molly came in with bottles of beer in one hand and naan breads in the other, beginning a relay as she and Carol brought in lots of small dishes: chickpeas and dhals, and two different vegetarian curries, spiced tofu and chutneys and finally a large bowl of white rice studded with split green cardamom pods and finished with crisply fried onions.

'Wow.' Ella clapped. 'This is amazing. Where did you learn to cook like this?'

'Not my mother,' Carol said, opening their beers with the handle of her fork. 'She thought chicken Bisto was dangerously exotic.'

'My mum's not much of a cook either,' Ella said. 'Wall-to-wall ready meals.'

It was a lie but a forgivable one, she thought. She wanted Carol to like her and, as she discovered in the early days of her friendship with Molly, pretending her mother was defective in some way helped build that initial bond with older women.

They ate quickly, conversation coming in snatches, talking with their mouths full, laughing and joking, Carol telling a story about some man who'd come into the Waitrose where she worked and demanded to see the manager because they didn't have English radishes even though they were in season. It amazed Ella that she worked there. Everybody had to work somewhere, of course, but she couldn't square Carol's non-curricular activities with serving Woolwich's well-heeled with quinoa and burrata every day.

An hour later they were still sitting on the floor, picking over the cold dishes, Molly and Carol opening their third beers, joints lit, Malian blues playing low on the turntable, all twang and holler.

'Did you talk to Rita?' Carol asked, dipping a scrap of bread into the remaining tarka dhal.

'Back in June, I went up to York to see her.'

Ella remembered the pebbledash semi, the smell of plug-in air fresheners and photos of her great-grandchildren on the mantelpiece. All so achingly normal until she started talking.

'She's moved, then,' Carol said. 'How's she doing?'

'Still going strong.' Ella sipped her beer. 'She's got arthritis and diabetes and high blood pressure, but she's still campaigning. Anti-fracking, now.'

'They need good people on that.'

'Have you been involved?'

Carol gave her a sly look. 'I'm being kept in the loop.'

'Wouldn't it be best to start fighting before it gets bad?' Ella asked.

Carol leaned over the table, scooped up a few chickpeas on her fork. 'Some people do the talking, others do the action.'

Ella reached into her bag and brought out her phone. 'I think we're starting to get into stuff I'm going to want to use. Do you mind?'

'No.' Carol fixed her with a hard look. 'But when I say off the record I mean it's off the fucking record. Okay?'

'Of course,' Ella said quickly. She started the recording, identified herself and Carol, gave the time and date. 'How do you think they should be approaching the fracking?'

'That's not for your PhD,' Carol said with a smile.

'No,' she conceded, with a smile of her own. 'That's just for me. I'm looking for all the good advice I can get right now.'

'About direct action?'

'Ella's doing just fine raising awareness at Castle Rise,' Molly said.

She'd gathered a few more cushions together and was lying out flat on the floor, occasionally exhaling a thin line of smoke. Ella had almost forgotten she was there.

'Raising awareness is all well and good, but it only gets you so far,' Carol said. 'Eventually you have to fully commit if you want to make positive changes. Anything else is just self-aggrandisement.'

'That's not fair.' Molly straightened up. 'Ella's doing good work. There are people who have got much better deals for their flats than they could have dreamed of because of what she's done.'

'So you think hitting the developers in the wallets counts as an attack?' Carol asked, ignoring Molly, attention fixed fully on Ella. 'Their wallets are huge.'

'Maybe we could do more,' she conceded, cowed by the force of Carol's words.

'Of course you could. Once you start making it about the money, you're playing on their pitch. It's not a protest any more, it's a negotiation! You get ten or fifteen grand more for someone and feel like that's a success. It's not. The bastards you're fighting probably spend fifteen grand on a pair of cufflinks.'

'What do you suggest, then?' Ella said.

'You need to not care about money. You'll never win that way.' Carol stabbed her fork across the table. 'You have to go further.'

'How?'

'Creative disruption,' Carol said. 'Reputation damage. It's too late now for Castle Rise. You need to look forwards.'

'I'm still there,' Molly reminded her. 'Just under half of the residents are still hanging in. We're making life very tough for those fuckers.'

'You'll be done in six months.' Carol plucked the joint from Molly's fingers. 'Sorry, love, but one bad winter...'

Ella slumped back against the sofa, drew her knees up to her chin. 'Then why bother fighting?'

'Because fighting empowers other people to do the same and maybe they do win.' Carol's face lit up. 'The miners' strike failed. But it mobilised a generation of women who'd been told they were good for nothing but getting fucked and keeping house. If Thatcher hadn't come for us, I'd still be stuck in Ollerton, being told how worthless I was on a daily basis by a man who could barely write his own name. Thatcher was a cu—'

'Carol,' Molly said in a warning tone. 'That's a word that hates women.'

She rolled her eyes. 'Well, she was one. But she radicalised working-class women in a way nobody in the feminist movement had even wanted to before then.'

Carol took a deep drag and held it in for a few seconds before she exhaled.

'That's why your PhD's important. You look at everything that's written about the miners' strike: us women are barely present. Yeah, alright, they'll talk about the food parcels and keeping the home fires burning. But we were in the thick of it.'

Ella waited, fighting the urge to prompt her, knowing she didn't need to.

'And from that we get to Greenham and Molesworth, Faslane; it all springs from a losing battle in the coalfields. Women who never thought they had any fight in them being led into action and discovering what they were made of.'

'You keep saying "they". Like you weren't there.'

'This "me" wasn't,' Carol said hotly. 'I wasn't this me until Greenham. Maybe not even then. It's been a long time, Ella. You get hardened in stages. The really tough stuff takes some working up to.'

'How tough are we talking?'

'Off the record.'

Ella hit stop, but the recorder in her pocket was still running. She'd told herself it was a back-up when she slipped it in there, but she knew, deep down that this might happen.

'I'm not giving you dates or times or locations.'

'We're off the record,' Ella reminded her, trying to ignore the twinge of guilt she felt.

'I don't care.' Carol started to roll another joint. 'Creative disruption, that's what we're talking about, right? You do it quietly; you don't go looking for headlines. You hit them in a way that they can't really tell whether it's an accident or an attack.'

'What good does that do?' Ella asked.

'It slows down their business, it damages morale. You do anything to have a destabilising effect on their operations.' Carol licked the edge of the cigarette paper. 'Think guerrilla warfare.'

Ella nodded. Just the words 'guerrilla warfare' sent a thrill through her.

'So, what we did was we made it look like an accident. Broke in to the main electrical contractor's office. Started a fire that looked like the result of faulty wiring – because you might as well have some fun. Wrecked the whole place.' Carol grinned, lit her joint and inhaled deeply. 'Records gone for good. Payroll, contracts, insurances, contact details, tax details, the whole shebang.'

She laughed, her hand on her chest, like it was the heist of the century.

Ella noticed that Molly wasn't laughing, appeared to have completely removed herself from the conversation now, staring up blank-eyed at the ceiling.

'Nothing moved on that site for two months. Bosses couldn't bring in another firm because it was a locked-down deal. Company couldn't discharge their responsibilities.'

'They must have been insured,' Ella said and immediately regretted it, as Carol scowled at her.

'That isn't the point. We hit their reputation by forcing them to miss their targets and exposing how unfit they were to conduct business. Nobody would give them another contract. Six months later they were bankrupt.'

It was traceable, Ella thought. If she wanted to, she could probably find out whether this story was true or just showing off. It would take time and expertise she wasn't sure she had, but it would be worth it to know whether Carol was the serious prospect she was claiming to be or, like Molly said, nothing special.

In her gut, Ella knew it was true. But her gut wasn't enough.

'You did all that on your own?'

'Me and my young blood,' she said, and giggled. The weed was getting to her now. She took another deep hit. 'He's got some skills, this boy.'

'Do I know him?'

Another laugh. 'Oh, Ella, hon, you and him move in very different circles. By the time someone like you knows him, he's finished.'

'You think he'd help us at Castle Rise?'

'We don't need that kind of help,' Molly said.

She was listening, after all. Ella had thought it would make Carol more talkative to have a former partner in crime there. Now she realised Molly was dangerously close to being the unwelcome voice of conscience in the room and that only made her more determined to get into Carol's inner circle. If Molly didn't want her there, then it must be a worthwhile place to reach.

'You'd like him if you met him,' Carol said to her and the regret in her tone made Ella suspect this was a continuation of an older conversation between them. 'He reminds me of you, Mol. Back in the day. He's got that same fire in his belly.'

'He's a bad influence on you,' she said.

Carol laughed, nodding. 'But it keeps me young.'

Another line of smoke was all the answer Molly gave.

'I'd like to meet him some time,' Ella said, as casually as she could.

'Quinn doesn't just play with anyone.' Carol's shoulders dropped into a conspiratorial hunch. 'He—'

She broke off to pick up a piece of spice-stained tofu from Ella's plate and put it into her mouth, chewed it for longer than necessary, eyes unblinking, fixed on a point to the left of Ella's shoulder.

'Why are you doing this?' Carol asked, cocking her head to one side so sharply that Ella heard her neck crick. 'What did Mummy and Daddy do that was so bad you had to rebel like this?'

'It's got nothing to do with them,' Ella snapped.

'Very defensive.'

'Leave her alone,' Molly said, voice a vague blur.

'No. She wants my story: I get hers.'

'Carol.' Firmer. 'Stop it.'

'Oh, it's bad, then?' Carol's eyes glinted. 'Come on, all girls together, you can tell me.'

'You walked away from your family,' Ella said fiercely. 'You didn't let them define you; why should I always be judged by what my father did?'

Carol put her hands up, ash flaking on to her forearm, but she was too focused on holding Ella's gaze to feel the burn or notice the tremble in Ella's fingers when she reached for her beer, needing a quick hit to calm her down.

'Your father's a bastard,' Carol said, grinning lopsidedly. 'They all are. But I think we're going to put you to the test, Ella. See if you're still Daddy's little princess or your own woman.'

Molly

Now – 20th March

The new building is now eight storeys high and Callum still hasn't come home.

Twenty-four hours has become two days, which means the police have information compelling enough to keep him in custody, even though he's innocent and the murderer – I see from her social media – is currently in Hackney protesting the closure of a day nursery and I, the accomplice, am here on my balcony watching the final steels going on to the roof of Rise 2.

What can they possibly have on him?

Is it just that he's a lone man of a certain age, living in a flat that he hasn't decorated since his parents died? Or that he's an ex-soldier; what would a profiler make of that? It makes him dangerous, experienced in killing; would they say he got a thirst for it that civilian life can't slake? That he snapped, that he has PTSD and can't help himself? They don't blame him: the army did it, they'll say. We understand; just tell us the truth and we can make sure you get the help you need.

Callum is the perfect scapegoat.

He has no alibi and he looks wrong. Never mind there can't be any actual evidence against him. Sometimes that's enough.

I don't know how he'll be holding up under questioning. His life is regular and ordered and I've long suspected he needs it to be that way to keep himself on an even keel. Could he be one of those men who crack in the confinement of a holding cell? Will two nights hearing the racket of other prisoners be enough to make him confess to something he didn't do?

The thought of him, sleep-deprived and vulnerable, makes my eyes sting, and I can pretend it's the wind cutting across the site but it isn't. I'm surprised by the depth of this feeling, then ashamed of myself for being surprised that I miss him, that I'm scared for him.

It's so easy to imagine some old stain on his soul being laid out in front of him and this new crime seeming like a way for him to finally atone.

I know he's wracked by guilt. I've heard him scream in his sleep on bad nights and tasted tears on his face the morning after the quietly tortuous ones. Part of him wants to confess, and God knows I understand that. Not the urge to tell the law but to tell *someone*. There have been moments when the words almost spilled out of me – 'Ella killed a man and I helped her cover it up.' The night after it happened, when he told me he heard Ella arguing outside his flat, the night he sat so pale and shaken in my kitchen with the image of the corpse he'd found filling his eyes. Almost every time we were alone together I could have said something.

And maybe I should have.

Maybe if we'd shared our darkest secrets we'd both have found a kind of peace.

If he'd shown me his demons and let me give him whatever absolution a lover can, then maybe he'd have a fighting chance of getting through this.

But what if it isn't him they suspect?

What if they're going to use him to get to me?

If I hadn't been in his flat when they came to arrest him perhaps he would already be free. There's a chance he's being pumped for information rather than confession.

I go back inside, slide the door closed behind me, blocking out some but not all of the building-site clamour, drop into the chair at my desk and run through what he knows.

Callum heard Ella arguing with a man on the night it happened.

170

He doesn't know it's the man she killed but it's hardly a wild deductive leap and even if he says nothing to Wazir, I know it will be preying on his mind.

I need to be tough about this, put my emotions aside for a moment.

Would he grass? Is he the type?

Callum isn't one of us. He doesn't share our sense of solidarity. Under pressure he won't throw his chin up and say 'no comment' to every question fired at him.

I suspect he has a strong sense of morality lurking somewhere deep down. He wouldn't be so haunted by his past if he didn't. Which means, no matter how close we are, how friendly he's always been to Ella, we can't rely on him lying to protect us.

If they ask, he tells.

Wazir and her crew probably know by now that Ella was arguing with the dead man in the corridor, which means they could feasibly start to consider her a suspect and the fourth floor the place where he was killed.

They could already be making plans to return and toss the flats up there, filing search warrants and arrest warrants in mine and Ella's names. They might already be out there looking for her.

I send her a quick text, telling her I'm feeling fluey and could she pick up some shopping for me? I add a short list of items. Say I'll pay her back.

Part of me is thinking how it will look if it's checked out later. Part is considering whether she'd actually turn up if I told her what was really happening. But we need to talk now, straighten our stories up.

Ten minutes of smoking and fingernail chewing and staring at the wall later, I get a text back to say no problem. She'll be around in about an hour and make sure I put a scarf on to keep my neck warm.

While I wait for her I decide to try and get an update on Callum. Wazir's card is in my desk drawer. I doubt I'll get anything out of her, so I call the number for the station and get caught in an options system, which eventually leads me to a phone that rings and rings. I put the call on loudspeaker as I light another cigarette and let it keep on ringing, from a sense of perverse determination, sure that someone is sitting inches away from it.

Finally it cuts out and I swear into the empty flat.

Wazir it is.

Her mobile goes straight to voicemail. I picture her switching it off before she goes into the interview room and wonder if it's Callum waiting in there for her. Another round, grind him down with repetition, the oldest, most boring trick in the world, but it works.

I think of her parting shot in the hallway the other night. 'We'll have your toy boy with us a lot longer than twenty-four hours.'

At the time I thought she was playing mind games with me, but now I realise they might actually have come for him with solid information.

I'm still thinking about it when Ella arrives, plastic carrier bags clutched in one hand, and walks straight through to the kitchen to unpack them, pausing briefly to look me over. 'Oh, you don't look very well at all, Mol.'

Is it any wonder?

I'm putting on more make-up just to bear the sight of myself in the mirror, an ever-thicker ring of kohl. Ella, by contrast, seems to be back to her old self and for a short and bitter moment I resent her youthful resilience.

'Callum's been arrested,' I tell her.

Ella stops, clutching a loaf of bread. 'Why?'

'I don't know. You talked to the police last.'

She slams the bread down. 'Why would I say anything about him?'

'Well, someone's put them on to him.'

'They'll have been interviewing everyone from the guest list,' she says slowly, as if it's just dawning on her. 'Maybe one of them mentioned the weird maintenance man and they ran with it.'

'He isn't weird,' I snap.

'I didn't mean that, Molly. But he might look that way to other people.' She glances towards the window, bites her lip. 'How well do you really know him?'

172

'Well enough.'

It's a meaningless comeback and a lie. I'm not about to share what little I know about Callum with her and I feel a flicker of sadness that I no longer trust her enough to air my fears.

'He was in the army, wasn't he?' she asks, stowing the bread in a cupboard, reaching for the marmalade she's bought. 'What did he do?'

'He was a cook,' I say firmly.

'I'm sure it's nothing to worry about. He's a grown man; he can take care of himself, right? He'll probably be home later today when they realise he didn't do anything.'

'They've had him over twenty-four hours,' I tell her. 'They obviously have some kind of evidence or they wouldn't be able to keep him in.'

She looks thoughtful. 'He found the body. Do you think maybe Callum went to check if he was definitely dead and left his fingerprints or DNA or something?'

I'm sure that's not how it happened. The man had been dead for days, no room for hope on a body that's laid for that long. And Callum isn't naïve, he'd know the difference between a corpse and someone who's only unconscious. And how would he have reached the body? Jumped down into the lift shaft or climbed up through the service hatch?

'It's human nature,' Ella says with a shrug, putting milk and butter in the fridge. 'You see a body and you reach out for it. You want to help them.'

Strange, because that isn't how she reacted when he was lying dead at her feet. She couldn't bring herself to help me move him until I shouted at her. Her recollection is changing, she's twisting it to suit some new narrative in her head. Maybe one where she wasn't involved at all. That's what good liars do, convince themselves it happened another way to make the story easier to sell.

And I'm realising that Ella is a well-practised liar, if not yet a good one.

At each turn she's tried to wriggle away from the truth. I've presented a challenge to her and she's countered. Over and again.

She didn't know him and then she did, but not well, and she didn't see him at the party, but then the photographs contradicted her and so she couldn't remember. I put her on the spot that time; she didn't have chance to formulate an excuse.

Now, she's concentrating on flattening out the empty carrier bags on the worktop, folding and smoothing them until each one is a small, neat square she can slip into the drawer next to the sink.

'Callum heard the two of you arguing before you killed him,' I say. 'I told you that already, didn't I?'

'It wasn't me.'

'What if he tells the police about it?'

'Then I'll tell them the same thing. He was mistaken.'

She sounds so sure of herself. Her voice becoming clipped and prim, how I imagine her mother talks when she's sending back something in a restaurant or telling the cleaner that her work isn't up to par and she'll have to do it again before she can go home.

I wonder if she used that voice with the police, letting them see where she comes from. Did she drop her father's name to Wazir and Gull? Did she need to?

Faint disgust crimps her nose when she looks back at me and that's something she can't straighten out as deftly as a plastic bag. The emotions I've been tamping down the last two weeks are rising in my chest. It's physically painful, facing up to what I've known but haven't wanted to admit.

I was wrong about her.

Ella isn't like me or Carol or any of the dozens and hundreds of people she's worked alongside since she came to London. She might believe in the importance of the causes she supports, but she doesn't care. Carol said Ella was a tourist, a little rich girl slumming down here to annoy her parents. That she was using the movement to build a name for herself with the ultimate aim of shifting into politics or some well-remunerated think-tank position in a couple of years' time.

And I defended her. Time and again I stood up for her, telling Carol and God knows how many other doubters that we

174

shouldn't judge Ella on her background. She was her own person, I said. She wants to make a difference, I said. And I believed all of it, every stupid lie she fed me, right from the first brief conversation we had in the A&E department at St Mary's while she sat with her arm broken and her spirit rising.

I was so gullible I could drop to my knees and die of shame on the kitchen floor.

But I can't buckle, not yet.

'Did you put the police on to Callum?'

She must be able to hear how furious I am, even though I speak in a low voice. How sad I am for losing him and losing her and already sinking into self-pity too.

'How can you ask me that?'

'People get in trouble around you, Ella. Have you noticed that? Other people suffer, but you walk away scot-free.'

'Callum is going to be fine,' she says softly, almost sing-song.

'This isn't just about Callum.'

Her eyes harden in an instant. 'Brighams? You want to bring that up now? Like we don't have enough to worry about.'

'It's all the same thing,' I say, the words rushing out of me. 'You got those blokes into it and when it all went pear-shaped, where were you? You ran off and left them to take the fall. And I fucking helped you! Like an idiot. I lied to the police for you then, just like I'm lying for you now, and I don't think you've told me the truth about any of this.'

I press my lips together, trying to hold back the tears, but they're pricking the corners of my eyes and I feel a lump in my chest, making every heartbeat reverberate like a blow.

'That isn't how it happened.' She crosses the floor, propelled by an anger that seems to scare her. She takes a step back, visibly reins herself in. 'Quinn *promised* me we were only going after the computers. That's all I agreed to. You know that, Molly. He lied to me.'

'And now he's doing five years,' I say in a strangled voice.

She throws her hands up, turns a circle in the middle of the kitchen.

175

'Quinn's out. Okay? He got released a while back.'

I blink at her. 'How?'

'How would I know? I just heard he'd got released early.' She gives me an acidic smile. 'Maybe he decided to turn informer. He knows everyone, Carol reckons; that's the kind of information the police would spring him for, isn't it?'

'It was him,' I say, before I'm fully aware of thinking it. 'You killed Quinn.'

'What? Don't be ridiculous.'

'He got early release and he came to have it out with you, didn't he?' I move in on her, feeling like I'm floating above the floor. 'Carol was here; he must have come in with her. That's who he was!'

Ella takes a deep breath but she swallows hard before she can speak. She's almost as scared as on the night it happened. She's trying to control it, but I know her too well to be sold the lie of composure she's desperately reaching for as she tosses her head and drags her satchel off the counter.

'This is stupid.' She starts out of the kitchen, stiff-legged and jerky. 'I'm going home. We can talk about this when you've calmed down.'

I follow her to the door, watch as she struggles with the tricky latch she's usually alright with, but not when her fingers are shaking. Finally she gets it open and leaves without a backwards glance.

My hands are shaking as well. The rest of me along with them. I feel spun off my axis as I close the door and replace the chain, just like on any other day, like a person whose world hasn't crashed around her. For a few more minutes I manage to keep up the facade for myself as I put away the shopping she's left on the counter in her haste to storm out of here. I make a cup of tea and light a cigarette and realise as I stub it out that I have been talking to myself this whole time, muttering under my breath, questions and answers and entreaties and denials.

All pointless.

I go to my desk and google Ryan Quinn before I think better of it and by the time I realise how it might look to the police, in the event of them searching my computer, it's too late. The screen is full of Ryan Quinns. But there's only one image of the man I want. The Brighams attack wasn't widely reported and where it was, the photos used were of the damage rather than the accused.

Until he was found guilty and then they used his police mugshot.

I was expecting an instant reaction, yes or no, but I can't tell for sure if it was Ryan Quinn whose pulse I couldn't find, whose body I carried along a semi-lit corridor and threw into a lift shaft.

This Quinn was photographed with the evidence of his crime still covering his clean-shaven face: smoke smudges and black smears and under it his skin a livid red from the heat he probably didn't expect to flare so fast and fierce. His hair is blond, oddly fascist in its cut, and singed heavily, his brows and lashes gone.

I study the image more intensely than I've ever studied one before, trying to fit this face onto the one I remember from that night, but it's impossible.

That man was thickly bearded and pale-skinned, how this man might have been before the fire, but I don't know for sure. Maybe the line of his jaw is similar and the tilt of his brow. Prison can change people beyond all recognition. It could have made Quinn softer or harder and I've no way of knowing which.

An hour passes and I keep staring at the photo and still there's a knot of fear and fury in my stomach.

Finally I do the only thing that will bring me peace or answers.

I call Carol.

Ella

Then – 5th August

Dylan was waiting for her when she got to the little, black-fronted coffee shop just off Poland Street. He had his laptop open on a zinc-topped cafe table, studious-looking in the heavy glasses he was usually too vain to wear. He was more attractive with them on, she thought, less like his real self, more like the man she'd hoped he would be. For a moment she watched him through the window, wondering if she'd give him a second glance if she didn't know him. He looked like half the men in London around his age, the same cultivated shagginess to his hair and carefully tended stubble, the slim jeans and plaid shirt. Nothing to alert any unsuspecting woman to his darker corners. His dirty secrets. The things that had drawn her to him when she should have run in the opposite direction.

She was the one who insisted on meeting here rather than at the flat, believing a public setting would be safer. He was too aware of his position to risk making a scene in a cafe, even a fairly quiet one like this.

But that was under normal circumstances and the last couple of days had not been normal.

Since she'd dropped off the face of the earth, leaving the hospital with Molly and going back to her flat in Nine Elms, his texts and voicemails had become more aggressive, switching from a decent approximation of concern to wounded entreaties for her to let him know she was okay, before finally moving to something close to an outright threat. That was when she finally conceded that they should talk.

Ella felt a thrum of nervous energy beating up her spine, throbbing at the same tempo as the medically dulled pulses of pain in her broken arm. A compound fracture, the doctor at St Mary's had told her, as he studied the X-rays.

'Very nasty.'

He didn't ask how it had happened. The police officers who had taken her into A&E did that, she guessed, reporting it to the nurse behind reception while Ella sat on a chair nearby, shaking uncontrollably, cradling her crushed arm against her thigh, biting down hard on the pain because she wouldn't cry in front of them. Wouldn't give them the satisfaction.

Dylan had rushed in a few hours later, furious and full of questions, which she'd only partially answered before a porter came to take her away for a brain scan. She'd been given the all-clear on that front, but she couldn't quite believe it. She'd hit the road so hard she'd been blinded momentarily and the headache that had started in the back of the police car reasserted itself as each dose of codeine began to wear off, feeling like small spikes pricking her eyeballs, making even the dimmest light unbearable. Nothing could hurt so much and be unimportant, she thought.

Her next dose was due in ninety minutes and already she was aware of the pain in her arm changing, becoming sharper and more localised around the break. The sensation of grit behind her eyes, shifting and scraping.

Just get through this, she told herself. Get him off your back and then you can rest.

Ella took a deep slow breath and went into the cafe, a bell sounding as she opened the door.

Dylan looked up from his laptop at the noise and Ella froze, pinned there by the ferocity in his eyes. She wanted to turn around and walk out, but knew that if she did she would only be delaying the inevitable.

A woman came up behind her, thanked her for holding the door. Ella moved to let her in and kept moving, one wobbly foot in front of the other, until she was standing at the table.

'Sit down.' An instruction, not an invitation. 'I'll get you a drink.'

She took the seat with her back to the window and watched him at the counter. She could see how wound up he was, hand braced, foot tapping, as the woman in front of him tried to work out what she could safely order with her complicated set of food allergies. He was usually better at hiding what he really was.

When he glanced over his shoulder at her, Ella smiled automatically, got a blank look in return, and cursed herself for falling into their usual pattern so quickly. Today was not usual, she reminded herself. She needed to be strong. Not let him dictate to her or manipulate her. She needed to remember that he wasn't in control of her any more, even if he thought he was.

Dylan returned with a mango and passion-fruit smoothie, full of crushed ice and garnished with a few raspberries the same colour as the fat straw sticking out of the fragrant glass of slush.

It was a drink you'd bring a child, Ella thought.

Across the table he poured a sugar into his espresso, stirred it violently, sending coffee sloshing into the saucer.

'Where have you been?' he asked.

'Staying with a friend.'

'What friend?'

'A new one.'

'The old woman I saw at the hospital?' he asked. 'The Keith Richards lookalike?'

Ella nodded, ignoring the jibe. 'She was at the protest. She's asked her solicitor to handle the police-brutality claim. He's doing it pro bono.'

'The assaulting-a-police-officer charge, you mean.'

'I'm the victim here,' Ella said, forcing herself to hold his gaze even as he glowered at her. She wouldn't make any more apologies to him, no more excuses or explanations for things she'd done right that he insisted were wrong. She would stand by her actions. 'And if you don't understand the distinction, and why it's so important, then there's no point talking to you.'

Ella could see that he was struggling to stay calm. The tables around them were empty but there were enough customers in the cafe to keep his voice low. He threw back his espresso, tapped the empty cup against the saucer a couple of times, a tiny movement that only gave away how angry he still was. Angrier than when the conversation began, she thought, because he'd already lost control of it.

'I suppose it was your new friend's idea to check you out of the hospital,' he said. 'Do you realise how dangerous that was? You have a head injury, Ella.' A thin smile tightened his face. 'Explains a lot. You'd have to be brain-damaged to do what you've just done.'

Ella scowled at him.

'It doesn't explain why you were at that fucking protest when you were supposed to be meeting me, though.'

She placed her broken arm on the table. 'I told you I was going.'

'And I told you not to get involved. There—' He stopped as a man walked past them, heading for the door. 'There were people waiting for us. You've made me look like an idiot, Ella.'

'If you'd taken me seriously that wouldn't have happened,' she said. 'I'd made it totally clear how important that demonstration was, I told you I had to be there. You don't get to dictate my life, Dylan.' She gave him the fiercest glare she could muster through the gathering pain. 'You don't have to be in my life at all.'

He laughed, low in his throat. 'So, that's it? You breaking up with me?'

Ella could feel the thin cardigan she'd borrowed from Molly sticking to her shoulders, damp under the arms with sweat.

'Look, let's go back to the flat and discuss this properly,' Dylan said.

'No, we're talking about it here.'

'Don't you trust me?'

She dropped her gaze, looked at the cloudy finish of the zinc tabletop, a spray of tiny black spots like burn marks. She brushed her thumb across them, feeling his eyes boring into the top of her skull, waiting for an answer she had already given by suggesting they meet here in the first place.

Of course she didn't trust him. In the year they'd been involved Dylan had done nothing but undermine her, bully her, try to worm his way inside her head. And she'd let it happen because she believed seeing what he was doing was the same as resisting it. She'd felt a haughty kind of amusement when he started to turn on the charm last winter, let him manipulate her in bed just the same as he did out of it. She'd stood outside herself as she panted and begged, pretending this was how she got the upper hand with him, that she'd always had a plan.

Now she realised how naïve she was.

Just a kid, after all. Playing games with a master.

Behind the counter a glass smashed and Ella flinched, looked up to find Dylan staring intently at her. When they were together he rarely looked elsewhere, didn't check out other women like most men did, didn't glaze over while she was talking. When she was with Dylan she was under a microscope. Pinned like a specimen, scrutinised by a sharp and practised eye.

'You need me, Ella.'

'And you need me to keep my mouth shut,' she said. 'If anyone found out what's been going on between us, you'd lose your job. What would happen to me? I'd finish my PhD. Get a career, get on with my life. You'd have nothing.'

'Threats now? That's nice, after everything I've done for you.' He tapped the teaspoon on her knuckles, one after another. 'You're not the only person who knows how to cause damage. And you're so much more brittle than I am. All those secrets, Ella. All those weaknesses. You're only as strong as I've made you.'

She shrank back from him, the sting of truth in his words.

'We both know what the real Ella Riordan looks like, don't we?' He nodded, seeing he'd hit her where it hurt. 'You think your new friends would like that Ella? The girl from Garton...'

'They know I started police training.'

Dylan blinked at her.

'I'm not ashamed of where I came from,' she said determinedly. 'In fact, I did an interview this morning where I talked about everything that happened there. Why I left. The investigation. All of it.'

'Ella, for Christ's sake, are you *insane?*'

'I wanted it all out in the open. After this—' She lifted her broken arm. 'I wanted to talk about where this kind of police brutality comes from, and the journalist had done his research. He asked me about Garton; I told him the truth.' Ella felt herself swell where she sat, relishing the unfamiliar sensation of having wrong-footed him. 'It's really freeing, not having to hide it any more.'

'Where's it going to run?'

'The *Guardian.*' She couldn't keep the delight out of her voice. 'Martin Sinclair interviewed me. He's an old friend of Molly's. She set the whole thing up.'

Ella smiled at the memory of sitting with him in Molly's flat, this man whose articles she'd read, whose new book she had on her bedside table. He'd batted away her praise, clearly embarrassed, but flattered too. After he left, Molly teased her about fancying him, then warned her off older men. 'They're sexual vampires, Ella. They stay young by fucking all the life out of girls like you.'

It struck her now, looking across the table at Dylan, how right Molly was.

Ella shook the thought away.

'It's going to be a significant piece, Martin says. I know you'd have told me not to do it, I thought that when Molly suggested it – "Don't make a spectacle of yourself, Ella. Right?" – but I think it's an opportunity for me to raise public awareness of a very important issue.'

'That's why you were ignoring me,' he said, almost to himself.

'I've got two more interviews lined up for tomorrow.' Ella swallowed another mouthful of her smoothie. 'So, I think going to the demonstration was actually a pretty smart idea. I'm going to be able to do so much more good with this new platform. You should see my blog stats. They've gone through the roof. I'm picking up thousands of followers. Have you seen the photo Molly took?'

'I've seen it,' he said darkly.

'She's made me famous.' Ella grinned, secretly thrilled by the attention. She'd been keeping an eye on her stats since she left the hospital and each time they rose she felt a physical thrill, something akin to the chemical rush of instant attraction; she would flush and press her fingers to her mouth to hide the smile she knew was silly and self-indulgent but couldn't stop from spreading wide across her face. Finally she was making progress and in such a crazy, unexpected style. People were calling her a hero. Others scum. She deserved a medal or locking up with the key thrown away. She was fierce. She was weak.

She was being talked about. And that, Ella realised, was what she'd always wanted.

But she couldn't let Dylan know she felt that way. If he got any inkling how much she was enjoying this new development he'd only become more determined to crush it before she really got started.

Dylan blew out a long sigh, his whole body sagging and splaying in the chair, making its joints creak. For a few seconds he stayed that way, head tipped back, eyes closed, and Ella held her breath, waiting to find out whether she'd read him right. She wouldn't believe she'd won the argument until he gave her a clear surrender. She'd been tricked too many times before.

Abruptly he straightened, all the fight gone out of his face. He hadn't wanted her to leave – all the talk about her mental state, her problems keeping up with her work, the insomnia and the anti-depressants he'd hunted down in the hiding place under her wardrobe; that was Dylan's professional side speaking.

The real him, the imperfect, unprofessional man, wanted to keep her close.

'Okay,' he said. 'What do you want me to do?'

'I just want everything to stay the same.' She reached across the table and took his hand. 'You know how much I need you.'

'Darling, I know exactly how much you need me.' He squeezed her fingers so hard she winced. 'Which means, from now on, you're going to behave yourself.'

Ella nodded, forced herself to smile.

Molly

Now – 20th March

Carol comes to mine straight from work, still wearing her forest-green Waitrose fleece under her quilted winter coat, and it prompts a moment of dislocation when I answer the door; my most radical friend's face above that symbol of gentrification. I've never seen her in her work gear before and she catches my look.

'Don't say a word.'

'It's just weird.'

'It's bloody warm,' she says, shrugging off her coat. 'I wouldn't have it on otherwise.'

'Good camouflage too.' I smile. 'Nobody would ever think a manager at Waitrose was plotting to bring down the system.'

She's brought a bottle of gin and cans of tonic, a couple of ready meals from the reduced section. If she knew why I needed to talk to her so urgently I doubt she'd have been so concerned about food.

'Have you got any weed?'

'Just some resin,' I say, pointing her towards the mother-of-pearl box on the coffee table.

Carol starts on a joint while I go into the kitchen and make us stiff gin and tonics. I pick up one of the fat lemons Ella brought earlier this afternoon. I almost put it back in the fruit bowl, feeling like it's tainted by association, then decide I'm being stupid and cut a couple of slices and drop them into our drinks.

I gulp down half of my own and top it up again before going into the living room.

'This takes me back,' Carol says, her voice constricted from holding down the smoke. She exhales. 'My guy never has it, he reckons there's no call any more.'

'Mine must have an older client base.' I hand over her drink, take a quick hit before giving her back the joint. 'Callum's been arrested.'

'The murder?'

I nod. 'Have the police talked to you yet?'

'Couple of them came to the store. Didn't go down well with management, that.' She kicks her shoes off. 'They know what I'm into but that's the first time it's got too obvious to ignore.'

'I'm sorry.'

'It's not your fault.' She curls up on the end of the sofa. 'Fuck 'em, anyway. They don't have a right to dictate what I do in my own time.'

She looks relaxed already and I wish I felt the same. I realise how infrequently we've done this during the last year, got together for drinks and food and idle chat. The only times I've seen her recently have been driven by Ella. Wanting to interview Carol, wanting to get involved with her campaigning.

Now, with my blinkers off, I can see what she was doing. Using me to ingratiate herself with Carol, because she's well connected and influential, far more so than I am. If Ella's always had long-term career goals beyond crowdfunding books and flash mobs, then Carol would be the perfect target for her tactical admiration.

Except ... that isn't what she used Carol for, is it? She used her to get to more serious players, the dedicated hardcore. Quinn.

'I'm sure your Callum'll be alright,' she says. 'He didn't actually kill that bloke, did he?'

Here's where I should come clean.

I've been trying to think of the right way to broach the subject since I called her this afternoon and she's gifting me an opening, but I can't bring myself to take it. I want to stay in this little bubble for a while longer yet, where we are still friends and allies and I have nothing to be ashamed of.

'Callum's not that sort of man.' I sip my drink, notice I'm almost through it. 'What did the police ask you? Do they think it's murder?'

She shrugs. 'The one who did all the talking didn't seem too sharp. He only asked me if I saw anything suspicious. As if I'd have told him anything.'

'Did they show you a photo of the dead man?'

'No.'

'That's weird.'

'Maybe they already know who he is,' she suggests. 'Not many people walking about without ID on them these days and if he wasn't robbed it's all there.'

'But they didn't give you a name?'

'Nope.' She rearranges herself on the sofa, puts a cushion behind her back. It's been bad for years, something with a disc her doctor can't fix. 'Didn't they ask you all this stuff too?'

'Yeah, but I talked to them days ago. I wondered if they knew anything more.'

Carol eyes me through a plume of smoke. 'You think you know who it is. Someone from the party? Is it someone I know?'

There's an unmistakable thrill in her voice and I'm surprised by it, because she isn't usually one for gossip, far too moral for that. This is murder, though, and I'm realising it brings out the ghoul in the best of us.

Now's the time. No more avoidance.

I've known this woman for half of my lifetime, we've been through things so serious neither of us have ever spoken of them, knowing that to voice them would be to let out a demon best kept bottled. But this is different. This is about Ella, who she hates, and Quinn, who she is besotted by in a strange fashion halfway between maternal fervour and girlish lust.

She's going to be furious with me.

But I need to know.

'Did you know Quinn got early release?' I ask, trying to sound casual, like this is me changing the subject away from something unpalatable.

'Yes,' she says slowly. 'I picked him up from Wandsworth myself. Why?'

'How come they let him out early?'

She's leaning forward now, elbows on her knees, a posture I know well. Eagerness and suspicion, readying for an argument.

'He did a deal. Got some information out of his cellmate and they released him.'

'He grassed?'

'The code of silence is for our allies,' she says coldly. 'It doesn't extend to scoutmasters who murder little boys and refuse to give up where the bodies are buried.'

That sits me back. 'Quinn got that out of him. How?'

'Ryan knows how people tick.' Pride in her voice and a hint of threat, I think. 'If he'd had a better education he'd have made a good barrister.'

'You need a refill.'

I snatch the empty glass out of her hand, go back into the kitchen and take my time mixing two more drinks, making hers stronger. For a moment I stand with my hands braced against the worktop, staring at my own reflection in the window. I look like a guilty person.

'Why the sudden concern for Quinn?' Carol asks when I give her the fresh G&T. 'You didn't give a shit before he got sent away.'

'Carol, we've been through this.' I lower myself on to the sofa. 'I was just protecting Ella. You'd have done the same for him.'

'He's different,' she says quietly.

'The police caught him at the scene, covered in accelerant, for Christ's sake. He was never going to walk away from that. What was the point of Ella going down as well?'

She doesn't answer and I'm relieved she doesn't have the stomach to go through this conversation again. We've each said our piece half a dozen times and I thought when she agreed to come to the party that it was a sign of maybe not forgiveness, but at least understanding.

These things happen when you take part in direct action. Some people get arrested, others are luckier and make their escape. And it isn't like he was blameless. Quinn led Ella and that boy into a situation neither of them were prepared for, changed the game with no warning and expected full and total support. Carol has always insisted they knew the score, but she's blind to Quinn's failings.

Just like I'm blind to Ella's, she'd say.

And she would have been right a few days ago.

'Would she do the same for you?' Carol asks gravely. 'Put herself on the line like that? Lie to the filth to protect you?'

I give no answer and she nods.

'That girl is no fucking good, Mol.'

'I know.' It's almost a whisper and I press my fingers to my mouth as soon as I've spoken, feeling tears welling up, all these days and sleepless nights catching up on me in a rush. I take a deep breath and then a long drink. 'Where's Quinn now?'

'Spain,' she says. 'He's gone to Barcelona to meet up with some friends.'

'When did he leave?'

Carol's brow furrows. 'What's this all about?'

'Please, Carol. When did you see him last?'

'The day he got out, I went to meet him, took him for a drink and something to eat. He was pale as a ghost – good thing he's gone abroad, he needs some sun on him.'

'When was this?' I ask, sick of dancing around the big question, wanting to just say it but still not ready.

She checks her phone. 'He got out Wednesday, March the first. He was taking the Eurostar on the Friday morning. We found him a cheap ticket while we were in the pub. Alright?'

Meaning he was in London the night of the party and planning to leave the very next morning. If he was going to repay Ella for getting him sent down, then the party would have been the perfect time to do it, leaving almost no chance for his crime to be reported before he was gone.

'Did he know you were coming to Ella's party?' I ask.

Carol stands up sharply. 'What the hell's all this about, Mol?'

189

'Please, sit down,' I say, immediately infected by her tension. 'Carol, please. This isn't easy for me to tell you but you have to promise to stay calm and hear me out.'

She stares at me, eyes wide, caught between confusion and anger. Slowly she sits again and even that small gesture feels like a success in this atmosphere.

'Have you spoken to Quinn since he got to Barcelona?'

'No.' She spreads her hands wide. 'Why?'

'Have you got a photo of him on your phone?'

For a moment she looks incredulous and then, finally, mercifully, she catches on and I don't have to say it.

'You think Quinn's the bloke they pulled out of the lift shaft?'

I hesitate.

For a second I think she's going to lash out. But she doesn't. Her hands curl into fists, knuckles white, all the energy running into them.

'Ella did that,' she says. 'Did she tell you?'

'It's not like that.'

'Did she tell you she killed him?' Carol says, each word hard and deliberate.

'Please—'

'I knew it. I knew there was more to the Brighams action than Quinn was telling me. It was Ella, wasn't it? He was going to tell everyone she was there and she had to stop him.' Carol snatches up her phone. 'She's not going to get away with it.'

'Wait.'

Carol reaches into her bag, starts rummaging through it but can't find what she wants. She turns it out on to the sofa.

'What are you doing?'

'Calling the police.'

'We don't grass,' I say desperately.

'She killed Quinn,' Carol snarls. 'This isn't grassing, it's justice.'

The room is spinning around me as I get to my feet. I grab her by the shoulders and turn her to face me. It takes all my strength.

'It was an accident.' My voice is weak, my heart is hammering. I've never seen this much hate in Carol's eyes before, but I keep babbling. 'He attacked her and she pushed him away and he fell. He just fell, Carol. It wasn't Ella's fault. It was just bad luck.'

'You *knew*?'

Her eyes are popping. She shoves me back so brutally I almost go over. I see her twitch, that instinct to help too deep to fully contain, but she stays where she is.

'Why am I surprised? Of course you've been covering for her. Christ, Molly, she isn't your kid, okay? Do you get that? She's just some little rich girl on the make. She's used all of us. You more than anyone. You need to stop protecting her.'

'I'm protecting me,' I shout.

Carol's face goes slack. She looks like another person, someone I don't know, who I've never known. Thirty years and here we are, made strangers by this moment.

'What did you do?' she asks, her voice low and toneless, and when I don't answer fast enough, she grabs my arm, squeezes hard. 'Molly?'

'I didn't know it was him. She called me and said some bloke had attacked her. She could barely string a sentence together she was that scared. She needed someone to help her.'

'And still it's all about Ella,' Carol sneers.

'I would have done the same thing for you,' I tell her. 'He was already dead, there was no saving him.'

'You could have called the police. Turned her in.'

'Is that what you'd have done?'

'Yes.'

'No, you wouldn't. Not to a friend. You never did.' I hold her furious gaze until it begins to soften. The thirty long years close around us again, all the cold nights protesting out under the stars, huddled inside tents and, when they were ripped away from us, inside the back of police vans. Always together and stronger for it. 'Carol, I'm really scared. I think Ella's going to put this all on me.'

My voice cracks.

I'm shaking, swaying on my feet. I feel like I've been standing here forever arguing with her, and before her Ella, and before that lying to Callum and the police before him. I'm all punched out, voiceless and empty.

When I open my mouth to apologise to her no sound comes.

Carol draws me into a hug, a distant and perfunctory one. Still, I feel better for having finally told someone. She steps back with a new determination on her face.

'You understand that if it is Quinn, then Ella's lied to you about it being an accident?'

'We don't know that.'

'If it was anyone else, I'd agree with you,' she says. 'But this is Ella and Quinn we're talking about. Their kind of history is a motive, right?'

Reluctantly, I nod.

'If she killed him, she did it to stop him exposing her involvement at the Brighams attack.'

Again, I nod. I don't agree but Carol is beginning to cool down and I can't risk making her flare up by challenging her right now.

'And if you think there's a way she can put it all on you, then there's going to be a way you can put it all on her.'

'No,' I say. 'That's not how it works and you know it. Her father was a high-ranking police officer. He's got decades of favours to call in. The only way I stay out of jail is if she does.'

A sour look crosses Carol's face.

'We need to find out if it was Quinn,' I tell her, knowing he's her main concern and that her position will change if it isn't him. 'Have you got a photo of him? The only one I could find online was his mugshot.'

'Quinn's always scrupulous about not being photographed. And obviously we don't take each other's photos,' Carol says. 'Come on, this is basic. If I get arrested and his photo's on my phone then the filth know we know each other.'

He is good, I realise. To be his age now and do what he does, without creating any kind of easily searchable online footprint. That takes guile and dedication far beyond the norm.

'Can you get in touch with him?' I ask.

'If he's still alive, you mean.' She rubs her temple. 'He's gone dark for a few weeks. No mobile or anything. He messaged the people he was going to meet on my phone before he left London. I can contact them and see if he's arrived. Assuming they'll tell me.'

'Why wouldn't they tell you?'

'They're an anarchist collective, Mol. They don't trust anyone.' She points a finger at me. 'You could learn from them.'

As she taps out the text, I stand at my photo wall, looking at the image of Ella laid out in the road with a police baton poised to strike her. I think of how far she's come since that afternoon and wonder how much of her progress is accident and how much she's achieved by design. What, ultimately, does she want? To be an agent of progress or the kind of loud and persistent agitator who eventually gets drawn into the establishment because she's too troublesome to be left outside it?

I wonder how far she's prepared to go to get what she wants and to keep herself safe. Who she'd sacrifice. Who she'd silence. Whether there's a line in the sand she thinks she'll never cross or if she's already gone over it.

I wonder if Quinn is the only enemy she's made.

Ella

Then – 5th August

It was 79°F degrees according to Ella's phone, but that was the air temperature when she was standing up. Down on the ground, on the sun-baked tarmac, surrounded by a crush of seated and sprawled bodies, suffering from heatstroke and dehydration, she was sure it was closer to ninety. She'd dressed for an English summer in jeans and a T-shirt and a light-weight parka that she'd shed within minutes of arriving at the demonstration.

At first, she'd seen a lot of half-familiar faces; other students she recognised from around campus and the reading rooms and the roads nearby where most of them lived in shared houses just like hers. A few lecturers, mostly junior ones who would feel the force of the new zero-hours contracts sooner than their senior peers, and who probably felt they had so little to lose already that the fight was worth taking to the streets.

When Ella asked around, she discovered that the older men and women were mostly from the unions, while a few others were dismissed as professional agitators. The kind who turned up anywhere there was a possibility of clashing with the police or taking a small chunk out of whichever branch of the establishment was available that month.

The man who told her that was a lecturer in the politics depart-ment. A young fogey in a cream linen jacket who seemed to loathe anything vaguely left wing. Until he needed them to turn out and protect his employment rights.

He went on talking, while Ella scanned the crowd for some-one she knew and could join, complaining about the recent no-platforming of an Israeli historian. Ella had been at that event too, remembered discussing it with Dylan afterwards, feel-ing a mounting sense of frustration as he dismissed her concerns. The man was passionate about the upsurge of anti-Semitism in academia, rattling off the names of splinter groups she was surprised he knew. He warned her about getting involved with them.

'Unless you're planning on taking your PhD to Al Jazeera.' He laughed and reached into his bag for a bottle of water. 'In all seriousness, though, you should be careful which causes you support. You're young, you don't want to get blacklisted.'

He pointed towards the police cordon, where fifty riot officers sweated inside their gear. A woman in civvies, large sunglasses and a wide-brimmed hat shading her face was standing near them.

'See the woman with the video camera? Intelligence gather-ing. They identify troublemakers and sell access to the lists to employers.'

'Aren't you worried about being on it?' Ella had asked, shocked by his coolness.

'I'm in it for the love, not the money,' he said, with an enig-matic smile.

A couple of hours after she arrived, she thought she caught sight of Dylan crossing the street on the other side of the cordon. But when he drew closer she realised it was just someone who looked like him, a touch heavier, and slightly younger.

Another text vibrated her phone and she looked at them stacked up on the screen.

I'm at the flat, where are you?

I'm at yours. Has something happened?

The meeting's in fifteen minutes! Where the fuck are you?

The meeting had been and gone and Ella imagined him making excuses for her, unable to hide his annoyance from the rest of them. People just as exasperated as he was, thinking that her failure to show only served to prove Dylan's fears about her state of mind were well founded.

It had been coming for months. She'd tried to hide it from him, kept working to maintain the image of someone fully in control, making progress, juggling her PhD and everything else she had going on. But Dylan saw through the facade. He started calling more often, at odd times of day and night, checking in on her, always catching her at the wrong moment. It was like being under surveillance. Then he found the pills, a prescription in her mother's name, stolen from her bathroom cabinet during Ella's last visit, and they had The Talk.

After that there was no question what happened next.

She was to go home for a while. She needed to recuperate. A month, he suggested, maybe two. And just like that, it was agreed.

But Ella knew once she stepped on that train there'd be no getting back here. Her father would have his say, her mother would find out everything and between them they'd make sure this new life she'd built for herself would be over for good.

Sitting on the road, a white line burning hot under her calf, the distant prickle of a broken light casing digging into her palm – not unpleasantly – she surveyed the scene around her. More people were sitting than standing now, which gave her a clear view across the tops of all those heads to the police cordon.

It had started as a march but the police were ready for them and they'd been corralled quickly on to a side road, allowing the Saturday-morning traffic on Camden High Street to keep flowing. Then the cordons started moving in, riot shields up, faces hidden behind helmets. Not as aggressive as Ella had expected, but they walked with determination, never gave ground, never slowed, just kept compressing the loose crowd of two hundred protestors into the smallest space they legally could.

It was smaller than Ella was comfortable with, but she'd managed to keep her claustrophobia at bay by talking to people. If she focused on their faces she could block out the clammy crush of bodies around her and the fact that she couldn't just get up and walk away.

Now, with the sun at its height, burning her skin, making the roots of her hair sweat, she was beginning to feel the familiar climb in her heart rate, the telltale constriction around her lungs.

'Have you got anything to drink?' she asked the girl next to her.

'Just Coke.' The girl offered her the bottle.

'Thanks.' Ella drank a mouthful of flat, hot liquid.

The police in their riot gear were breaking away at regular intervals to remove their helmets and pour water over their heads, other officers filling in the gaps they left in the unbroachable wall. They were getting impatient, she realised. Overheated and irritated.

When a young man went up to the shield wall to try and get out, he was barked at, told to sit his arse down. It wasn't meant to be like that; when you wanted out they were supposed to let you out, Ella thought.

But she remembered Garton, the men and women she'd trained alongside, and how single-minded they could be. Unable or unwilling to accept nuance in any situation. Some of them could be behind those masks, she realised. The bigger, dumber ones who were never going to make it to plainclothes and who were too aggressive to be satisfied with the day-to-day tedium of walking a beat. One man sprang immediately to mind, but he'd left Garton when she did, talking about joining the army, where the real action was.

The girl next to Ella let out a low groan.

'Are you alright?'

'Bloody period pains,' she said. 'I didn't think we'd get trapped like this. I don't suppose you've got any ibuprofen or anything on you?'

'Sorry, no. Have you asked about?'

'A few people, yeah. Nobody else was organised either.' She wrapped her arms around her abdomen and let out another muted wail. 'It's bad enough with pills. I don't think I can stay here.'

There was a film of sweat on the girl's brow, pain etched in every angle of her body. Ella felt her own midsection tense up in sympathy and knew she had to do something.

'Let's get you out of here.'

Ella stood up and helped her to her feet. They picked their way across legs and around bags, up to the cordon, Ella trying to find the most sympathetic-looking face behind the steamed-up visors. They all looked the same, though.

'Please, my friend's in a lot of pain,' she said to the man. 'She needs to get out and take her medication.'

'Back into the middle.'

'She's going to pass out,' Ella said. 'Look at her, can't you see what a state she's in?'

'Should have stayed at home then.' His tone was flat and disinterested. 'Back into the middle.'

The girl gripped Ella's arm. 'It's fine, I'll ask some more people. Someone's bound to have brought a first-aid kit with them.'

She drifted away and Ella stood for a few seconds longer, trying to find the face through the visor, convinced in that moment that it was someone she knew behind there and that was why he was being such an arsehole. He was the right age, no older than her. Barely more than a boy once you stripped away the uniform and the borrowed power it gave him.

'Move,' he barked.

Ella's phone rang and she answered it without thinking, eyes still fixed on the man's face. She almost ended the call when she heard Dylan's voice.

'You're at that fucking demo, aren't you?'

'I'm kettled,' she said, smiling at the irony of this ring of police protecting her while they thought they were imprisoning her. 'I'm not going anywhere.'

'Too fucking right, you're not,' the man said, his mates laughing behind their shields.

A door slammed at Dylan's end. 'Ella, we talked about this, you agreed to take a break.'

'No, you said I had to. I never agreed to anything.'

The copper nudged his mate. 'Feminist.'

More laughter.

'Your parents are expecting you to be on that train.'

'I'm not going,' she said. 'You can't make me.'

She turned her back to the shields and the comments and the sniggers, seeing that the people in front of her were listening as well, could tell from their studiously averted eyes and the tilt of their heads. She didn't care.

'Don't be such a child,' Dylan snapped. 'This is why you've got to go home. You're burnt out, for God's sake. It happens all the time. Just accept it.'

'What if I refuse?'

'You don't get to refuse,' he said. 'This isn't your decision to make.'

Because he'd found pills with her mother's name on and he wouldn't believe she hadn't taken any. Which meant she was potentially unstable and a liar and because prescription drugs could lead to recreational drugs and her issues with them were already a matter of record. Even though it had only been a few months and she had stopped cold.

'I'm staying here.'

'Aww, listen to her,' the man said. 'Stamping her little feet.'

Ella rounded on him.

'Fuck you!'

'Who are you talking to?' Dylan asked.

The copper grinned at her through his visor.

'Fuck me?' he asked. 'Probably do you some good, girl. You look like you've not been well fucked in months.'

Ella stepped up close to his shield and he bounced it lightly off her chest, still smiling. The man next to him said something under his breath, too low for her to hear, but it sounded like a warning and it wasn't aimed at her.

A ripple went through the crowd, the ones who'd seen it telling the ones who hadn't.

'Big man, yeah?'

'Oh, yeah.'

'Hiding behind a bit of fucking plastic.'

At her back people were stirring. She heard the scrape and rustle as they started getting to their feet, a murmur of rising voices. Of dissent. They'd seen enough, scented the coming trouble. Somebody grabbed her elbow and told her to walk away, but she shrugged them off. Someone else told the copper he couldn't touch them.

When she glanced over her shoulder she saw that they were being recorded by several people.

'Ella?'

Dylan in her ear, distant now. Unimportant. She knew what she was going to do.

The lecturer with the immaculate cream jacket was by her side, face so close to her ear she could smell the staleness of his breath. 'Don't give them the satisfaction.'

'Listen to your boyfriend,' the copper said. 'Walk away before you get yourself in trouble.'

She bared her teeth at him, held her ground.

The crowd was gathering. Not unified yet, but there was a tremor of anger running through them, shouts and sneers, jostling for a position closer to the cordon.

'Ella, don't make me come and fetch you.' Dylan's voice was wavering and she knew that he was worried. She ended the call, slipped her phone into her pocket.

Someone shoved into her back and she stumbled towards the riot shield. The man ducked down and braced for impact, lifting it at the last moment and slamming it into her shoulder.

Pain shot down her arm, up into her neck. Around her the crowd noise fell away and she took a deep breath, flashed a grim smile at the riot officer, their eyes locked.

Then she was moving. Quicker than she'd moved in her life. Thinking with her body. She grabbed the top of the shield, jammed her foot against it at thigh height. Her muscles screamed as she levered herself up, one hand on a plastic helmet, one foot on a padded shoulder, springing up and over the cordon.

She landed heavily in the open road, rolled on to her side but regained her footing fast. Blood rushed in her ears, blocking out the crowd noise, the traffic noise, the shout she only saw on the man's face as he broke away from the line to come after her.

His baton swung through the air in a low arc, whipping her legs out from under her. Ella screamed, falling, and her head slammed into the tarmac. White light flashed across her pupils then a black blur came at her. She threw her arm up instinctively and heard herself cry out as the bone shattered.

Molly

Now – 23rd March

Everything is falling apart.

Derek knocked on my door in the early hours this morning, white-faced in his PJs, and told me he thought his Jenny was dead. I followed him to their flat, numb from lack of sleep and the last of the bourbon I finished in a cup of hot milk. When I got to Jenny I was shaking, unable to face another crisis, and not happening to someone as good as her.

But she was breathing still and I found the pulse that Derek had been too panicked to feel, beating weakly in her frail wrist. I told him to call an ambulance and we waited together for it to come, both watching her, as if the intensity of our vigil would be enough to keep her going until help arrived.

Now, I'm at her bedside again. In the acute ward at Charing Cross.

Derek isn't in much better health than she is and I sent him home for a rest, told him to bring some clean clothes for her and the pictures of her boys. He didn't want to leave her but she's going to need him to be strong and at his age one long night on a hard chair, in a draughty waiting area, can soon turn to pneumonia.

Jenny is sleeping; she looks peaceful, oblivious to the hustle and noise in the surrounding bays. Every hour a nurse comes and checks her pulse and temperature, pricks her finger to test the levels of her blood, speaking in a bright voice, heavily accented. Jenny barely stirs. I don't think she realises I'm here.

The nurse asks if I'd like a cup of tea.

She looks at me with the same level of compassion as she lays on Jenny and I tell her I'm fine, thanks. The next time she comes around I ask where she's from and we talk for a few minutes about Athens, where her husband and children still live, in a house they share with his parents and sister and her two daughters, and how she hopes things will get better there one day.

In the other beds are women working through their own problems, the surprised ones in hospital gowns, the regulars in their own nightdresses. Jenny, despite her stroke last year and whatever happened last night, looks healthier than all of them.

The visitors come and go and I try to block out their talk. When a pair of brothers begin fighting across their mother's bed I take myself outside for a smoke, check my phone, find no messages from Carol, who is still waiting for Quinn's friends to get back to her.

After three days we both know it won't happen. She's beginning to talk about hopping a cheap flight down there herself, as if her radical radar will magically guide her to the paranoid anarchist group he was supposed to be squatting with.

Ella hasn't called me either. I don't want to talk to her but I don't want this silence to continue.

First thing this morning I went to Kennington station to try and find out why they were still holding Callum, what he was being charged with. When I arrived, the desk sergeant refused to speak to me because I wasn't a relation. I asked to see Wazir or Gull and neither could be reached. Finally, I realised Callum might not even be at that station and when I checked, the woman confirmed that he had been but he was released days ago.

Which means something has stopped him coming home.

'You got a light?'

A young man, tan and rounded with dark shadows like bruises under his eyes, holds up his Superking at me. I cup my hand around the lighter flame and he nods his thanks before walking off.

Where else could Callum possibly have gone?

Knowing he was in police custody was bad enough. At least he was safe there. Now he could be anywhere, sleeping rough or squatting. For all I know this has tipped him over the edge and he's killed himself.

I take a breath, pull back from the idea.

He has no reason to do that, does he?

Does he?

What the hell do I know about him to make such an assumption?

Still, something has changed while the police had him, and all I can think is that he's been given information that has turned him against me and that's why he hasn't come home. It would have to be serious, though, and if it was serious then I wouldn't be standing out here smoking, I'd be arrested already.

Nothing makes sense any more.

There's a cafe in the reception area and I buy a flat white and a small packet of biscuits, take them back with me along the warren of pastel corridors to the acute ward. Twice I get lost and have to retrace my steps, past doors protected by keypads and wards in mothballs because of staff shortages.

When I reach the right bay I find Jenny's bed empty.

'She's just gone for a scan, love,' the woman across the aisle tells me.

'Thanks.'

I sit down with my back to her, not wanting to get dragged into a conversation about her ailments. I've already heard it all, told to the nurse and the junior doctor who did his rounds an hour ago.

Joylessly, I eat the biscuits, trying to remember if Callum ever mentioned other family in the city. Or anywhere, for that matter. Our relationship has not been a talkative one, I now realise. We'd drink together and sleep together, watch a film or whatever was on TV, and sometimes we'd talk about that, but otherwise it was always the evictions and the fight to stay.

We don't really know each other.

His parents came down to London from Inverness, that much I remember. But it was after he left home and signed up for the army. When he mentioned it, in a dark and drunken mood, I decided not to press him on the details, sensing they wouldn't be good.

Somehow I doubt he's gone back up there, anyway. He never talked about the place, didn't seem to miss it. I'm sure he's still in London.

When I get back to the flat I'll start calling the homeless shelters where I know people, ask them to keep an eye out for him. Maybe I should be calling the hospitals too, in case he's had an accident, but in my gut I know it's not that which is keeping him away.

It's me.

There are things I've done that would make him hate me. He knows more about my past than I know about his, but not everything. There are things the police might have thrown out to make him turn on me. Activities a soldier wouldn't approve of.

What would he make of my police file? Not just the convictions but the suspicions too. That's how they'd damn me.

I rub the scar on the inside of my left ring finger, remembering the sting as the cut fence tore it open, the split second of numbness before the blood welled and the night air chilled the wound. Callum could have been on the other side of that fence. Politically he is. That's why we never talk about the news. I only mentioned being at Greenham Common once and saw the expression on his face, the disapproval and the way his jaw hardened as he resolved not to say whatever he was thinking. Do soldiers ever stop believing what they've had drummed into them?

How ironic would it be if I overlooked his history only for him to judge mine?

A cheery porter wheels Jenny back on to the ward and brings her over to the bed. She's listless and slumped in the chair and he has to lift her out of it, careful as he lowers her on to the mattress. Discreetly he arranges her right arm and leg, which have been immobile since her stroke last year, and pulls the blue waffle cover over them. She looks woozily at him, doesn't notice me, and as soon as her head is on the pillow she closes her eyes.

'It's best she sleeps now,' he tells me. 'MRIs always take it out of you.'

I smile and nod. 'I'll just wait until her husband comes back.'

He wheels the chair over to another bed and helps the woman there into it, laughing when she makes a flirty comment.

For a while I manage to tune the ward noise out. I drink my coffee, but the caffeine isn't strong enough to overcome the bone-deep tiredness I've been dogged by since this started. My limbs are heavy, my spine hollow-feeling. I'm numb. All of me. Just existing from moment to moment; walk here, lift this, say that. Say the wrong thing, mostly, because I'm not thinking straight.

I feel like I haven't made a single correct decision since that night when I stood at the window with Ella and the dead man behind me, and convinced myself that the only way out was to hide his body.

How do criminals live with this?

How come I can't? It isn't like this is the first illegal thing I've done in my life. It might not even be the worst, depending on your moral framework.

I suppose the difference is, I could justify those acts as part of the greater good and so I barely paused to consider what would happen to the other people involved, or to me if I was caught.

When the food comes around the smell of it makes my stomach flip and I go outside for another cigarette. There's a police car parked in the unloading zone; nobody in it, but the driver's-side rear window is smeared with blood, a distinct handprint on the white paintwork around it.

A female officer comes out with a cloth and wipes the blood off the car, shaking her head as she does it and muttering under her breath. For a brief moment I imagine going and telling her what I've done, giving her Ella's name and address and letting this whole problem be handled by somebody else. But I'm too scared. I've been in prison before and never want to go back. Especially not now I'm older and more vulnerable.

And Ella would cope even worse than me. She thinks she's slumming in that thousand-pound-per-month flat in Camden that her daddy's paying for.

If it's Quinn she killed, will I tell the police? If it's out-and-out murder she dragged me into?

I watch the policewoman drop the bloodied cloth into a bin and pause to study her hands to check for traces left on her skin. She looks up sharply, straight at me, and I look away, feeling like she's read the guilt on me and the fleeting urge to confess.

When I finally lift my gaze from the toes of my biker boots the policewoman is gone and Derek is walking towards me, stooped inside his bright-orange anorak, the hood up against the cold, carrying a floral overnight bag with Jenny's things in.

'How is she?' he asks.

'Sleeping. She's just been down for an MRI.'

'You heading back now?'

'I'll come over in the morning,' I say. 'If they don't release her this evening.'

'They won't.' He shifts the bag from one hand to the other, winces; his arthritis must be playing up. 'Thanks for sitting with her. She'll have appreciated that.'

I give his arm a quick squeeze before he walks away and go to find a taxi. It's a luxury, I shouldn't be squandering money, but I'm too tired to wait for a bus.

The driver refuses to pull on to the site when we arrive at Castle Rise, stopping at the mouth of the gateway instead and sourly regarding the sprawling development, before leaning across the wheel to look up at the sparkling monolith of Rise 1.

'Wouldn't live up there if you paid me,' he says. 'Mate of mine's a builder, reckons they'll be crumbling inside of ten years. Right waste of money.'

'I don't live up there,' I tell him, as I pass a twenty through the slot. 'I'm in the block they're pulling down.'

'Oh, right. Sorry.' He takes the note and hands back my change, doesn't ask if I need a receipt because why would I, somebody living in a condemned building, need that? He says, 'You going to get back to your door alright, love?'

'I'll be fine, thanks.'

'It's not very well lit. You sure you'll be alright?'

'There's plenty of security about,' I tell him and wish him a good night and step out on to the pavement, wondering how he sees the place, whether it really looks so dangerous that he isn't entirely happy to let a stranger head into it alone.

I walk up the centre of the road, boots scuffing in spilt sand and dust from the demolition, which somehow remains weeks after the debris itself was cleared away. An entire block of flats, sixty homes, all of those lives, reduced to tiny specks that stubbornly cling to the dimpled tarmac. Breezeblocks and plasterboard and wallpaper and doorframes where children's heights were once marked, climbing year on year, all of it indistinguishable now, so insubstantial it barely crunches under my feet.

Ella

Then – 2nd April

It felt illicit, sneaking around to Dylan's flat like this. Even more so than the occasions when he'd arranged to meet her in hotels. Then he'd text her an address and a room number and she'd find a way out of whatever she was doing, go to him with her head full of conversations, the things she wanted to tell him, the advice she needed him to give her. The only problem with those last-minute, snatched meetings was that she didn't have the chance to dress for him and Ella had discovered that she enjoyed the process of putting together an outfit he would enjoy taking apart.

The boys she'd been with before him weren't interested in how she dressed. As long as she was prepared to take it all off they were happy.

With Dylan there was a whole new layer of pleasure to be taken. She picked up on the small cues he gave without realising he was giving them. He preferred her to be understated and covered up, button-down-collar shirts and simple knitted dresses, slouchy boots and leggings and oversize tees big enough for both of them to crawl inside.

He told her not to wear too much make-up; she didn't need it and it didn't suit her. She was a PhD student now, remember? She wasn't up north any more.

The old Ella Riordan was wiped away and replaced with someone more London-appropriate. The kind of girl who didn't stand out for what she was wearing but for the force of her ideas.

She turned on to Murray Street and almost sprinted up the front steps, rang the doorbell already smiling to herself.

A man she'd never seen before answered and for a moment she thought she'd got the wrong address. She'd only been here a couple of times before and all the townhouses on this row were similar under the streetlights.

'Is Dylan home?' she asked.

'Upstairs.'

The man let her in, eyed her head to toe as he did it. No insinuation in the movement, only curiosity, she thought. The same as she felt about him. He was kind of rough around the edges, gym-toned and bearded, smelling freshly showered but with a trace of cigarettes too. He slid a heavy security chain on and double-locked the door. It wasn't a rough area but Dylan had explained before that it was always best to be careful.

'Not seen you here before,' he said.

'You don't live here?' she asked.

'Just dropped in for a couple of days.'

'Dylan's Airbnb?'

He smiled, crow's feet cinching. 'Warmest welcome in town.'

Ella knew what he was, supposed she wasn't fooling him either.

'You're a bit young, aren't you?' he asked, heading into the living room.

Ella stopped in the doorway, saw another man waiting for him at a small, round dining table where a card game was in progress, just the two of them playing. The other man was younger, shaven-headed, dressed in boxers and a varsity T-shirt.

'Is she joining us?'

'She's here for Dylan.' There was the insinuation. 'One of his "students".'

He threw the quote marks around the word with his fingers and the men shared knowing smiles, which made her feel suddenly uncomfortable.

She went up to the attic, the men's voices falling away behind her. The door to the attic flat was ajar, music playing low, something minimal and instrumental. It wasn't what she expected him to like and it was different from what he played when they were together; it made her feel like she'd seen a part of him he usually kept hidden and she wondered what it meant.

He opened the door wide, kissed her quickly on the cheek. 'I thought I heard you. Are you coming in?'

'Might as well.' She smiled. 'Since I'm here.'

He hadn't done anything more to the place since she was last there six weeks ago, despite the fact that they'd discussed him warming it up a bit, making it a little more homely. The walls were still bare, the sofa still didn't have any cushions, and Ella would bet that when she looked in the fridge he'd have nothing but beer and jam and cartons of orange juice.

She dropped her satchel on to the table, near his laptop, where the music was coming from, slightly tinny-sounding and distorted now she was close to it. He took her parka and hung it up on the coat hook on the door, making a point of looking at the small enamel badge she'd pinned to the collar.

'Boycotting Israel now?' he asked. 'Is that what the cool kids on campus are into?'

'I went to a couple of meetings,' Ella said. 'They got quite heated, actually. There's a group of students who want to block visits from Israeli scholars. They're talking about picketing more events, bookshops, galleries, that sort of thing.'

She started to tell him about the various factions, which lecturers were involved, who was stirring up trouble for the sake of it and who seemed more ideologically driven, but he didn't appear to be listening. He seemed more concerned with changing the music on his laptop and tidying away some paperwork into his bag.

'There were some pretty scary individuals involved,' she said, hoping that might pique his interest. 'Incomers, you know? Not actually students.'

'That's common enough at unis these days. Lots of soft brains ready and willing to be manipulated.' He smiled. 'Coffee?'

'Have you got any beers in?'

'I think there's a couple left.'

He fetched two bottles of Peroni from the fridge and Ella saw, across his shoulder, how empty the shelves were. He snapped the tops off, passed her one. 'I shouldn't be encouraging this, should I?'

'It's okay,' Ella said. 'I'm a big girl, I can handle one beer.'

'Do you need it?' he asked, going over to the sofa.

He had an unerring way of knowing when she was down, Ella had noticed. She'd come in here full of talk, but he'd seen through the excitement in a moment. It made her feel better about his apparent disinterest in what was happening on campus, knowing he cared about that, but he just cared about her more.

'I didn't think it'd be like this,' she said, dropping down next to him.

She curled up then changed her mind, kicked off her boots and stretched her legs out over his thighs.

'How did you think it would be?'

'Just ... different, I suppose.'

'More exciting?'

'Maybe.' Ella took a drink of her beer. 'I didn't think it would take this long to settle in. I've been here almost a year and I've done nothing. I hardly know anyone.'

Dylan frowned, absent-mindedly rubbing her knee. 'You're making an effort, though, putting yourself out?'

'I'm trying,' she said, thinking of the people in her shared house she just hadn't clicked with, the people she'd swapped numbers with who never called, all the groups she'd signed up to and meetings she'd attended, looking for a circle she could make her own. Somehow it had all come to nothing. 'Do you think it's my background?'

'Being a northerner?' he asked, and smiled. 'There are plenty of you lot in London, Ella.'

'You know what I mean.' He was going to make her say it. 'Garton.'

'I seriously doubt anyone you're running into knows you started police training,' Dylan said. 'How would they?'

'There are records, right?'

212

'Records of why you left, yeah. And anyone who's weird enough to background-check you will see what happened and realise how meaningless it is.'

Ella wanted to believe him but couldn't. Something was holding her back and she was sure it wasn't anything she was doing.

'It's like, I've got this list of people I need to talk to for my PhD,' she said. 'Two dozen women, all involved with the miners' strike, all active and easily accessible, very vocal women who take every opportunity they can get to keep the story alive. So, I reach out to them and almost every single one has ignored my emails. You tell me why that is?'

He threw his hand up, half shrugged.

This wasn't what she expected from him. Dylan was supposed to be the wise, older head. Have all the answers, give the perfect advice at the perfect moment.

'It takes time to settle into a new place,' he said weakly.

'I've given it time!'

'You're putting too much pressure on yourself. You've not even finished your first year, for Christ's sake.' He gestured at her with his beer bottle. 'You're a perfectionist and a control freak and you need to learn to let go. People can find that very intimidating.'

'Nobody gets this far in life without being … ambitious and careful about their work, do they?' She heard how snotty she sounded, tried to dial it down. 'If I wasn't, I'd be back in Durham working in some shitty office, staring at spreadsheets all day and looking forward to my one night out a week with the girls.'

'Or you'd be walking a beat in Durham, picking up the girls when they fell down drunk in the street on their weekly night out.' Dylan grinned at her and she felt her mood lighten, slightly.

'I so wouldn't be a uniform,' she said, playing along. 'Not a control freak like me.'

'No, course not. You'd be a detective inspector by now.'

She laughed at the idea, imagining a boring, navy trouser suit and polyester blouse with sweat patches under the arms. Saw herself, so stupidly young and even younger-looking, walking into a crime scene, squatting down to peer at a dead body she would vow to get justice for.

That was almost her life. The one her father wanted for her and the one she'd thought she wanted too. But it was always his dream and, within days of beginning her training, she realised just how badly he'd misled her about the profession. Deliberately or innocently, she'd never know, but the Garton he waxed lyrical about was not the one she found herself in. Not just the physical space, which had been redeveloped and renamed, although the old name still stuck, but the culture. The bad old days were over, he promised her. No more racism, no more homophobia or sexism; this was the modern police force she was entering.

He failed to appreciate that modern sensibilities and attitudes hadn't changed everywhere at the same pace and that only made it worse when you walked into a pocket of resistance.

Dylan squeezed her leg. 'It's going to be fine, Ella. Trust me. You just need to be a little more patient and a lot more proactive.'

She finished the rest of the beer, washing away the defence she wanted to mount. He knew how patient she'd been, exactly how hard she was trying. That was the unfairest advice he'd given her yet. But, if he thought that was the way to go, she'd do it. She would stun him with how wildly, dangerously proactive she could be.

Molly

Now – 27th March

The police are here again.

Lots of uniforms, forensics vans. It's a search party. They're looking for the place where he was murdered. Died. Whichever turns out to be true. Ella's version or the one Carol believes? I'm still debating which I believe.

Another day with no firm word from Quinn. A week since Carol first tried to make contact with his friends.

It's beginning to look inevitable that he's the man I helped dispose of. That Ella has tied me up in a long string of untruths in order to protect herself.

Not a stranger, not an attacker, not an accident.

Sitting at my desk, scanning the internet for news reports, which all say nothing, and non-existent speculation on social media, I can hear the search team moving about around me. Heavy feet on the floor below, locked doors being smashed in with a battering ram, distant voices calling to one another as they move methodically through long-abandoned rooms, picking around in the dusty remnants of lives that have shifted to new suburbs and cities. I wonder if they can feel the loss that lingers in the furniture left behind, the half-stripped cupboards and the desiccated limbs of dead house plants.

The building has been almost empty for so long that its bones complain at all of this fresh body weight disturbing its equilibrium. Without music or the television to mask the sounds I can hear every creak and crack, the stairwell doors opening and closing under heavy hands, curtains being shoved back on lengths of plastic tracking to let the sunlight in.

They're drawing nearer to me.

Nearer to flat 402.

If they don't get that far today they'll be back tomorrow and all I can do is hope they'll be so bored of opening doors on to so many similar scenes by then that 402 receives only the briefest of searches.

It doesn't look like a murder site.

I made sure of that. Scrubbed the hearth where he bled out. Wiped away every trace of violence I could see. Luckily there wasn't much blood. It's the scalp lacerations that make a mess, that much I do know from experience. Those wounds gush.

Whatever killed him it was internal, the blows softened by his hair and the hat he was wearing when he fell.

Thinking back, I'm not even sure where the blood I cleaned up came from...

Maybe it was Ella's.

The thought is a twinge, an old injury playing up.

His blood only gives them a murder scene. *Her* blood gives them a witness or a suspect. Eventually it gives them me too.

I need to stop these thought spirals.

The blood is gone. The flat will be one of the last they check in. The all-too-human desire to clock off and go to some bar or get home to the family will save us.

Along the hall the stairwell door opens.

If they go into 402 with Luminal we're in trouble, though. I don't think they will, but who's to say? It's been years since I had such up-close and personal contact with a police investigation and I don't know how they operate now, only what I've seen in the crime shows I've watched with Callum. He likes the American ones, flashy and fake programmes, which I'd lie there scoffing at, thinking all the smart science was propaganda, designed to make any wannabe murderers in their audience too scared to actually commit a crime.

In reality, I hope it's going to be nothing more sensitive than the human eye sweeping over the worn and faded carpet and the green-veined tiles.

I start as someone knocks on my door.

It's Derek, standing with a handful of mail.

'Yours, love.' He shoves the envelopes at me with an uncharacteristic roughness that makes me think there's something from the developers among them, says, 'Thought I'd best bring it up since...'

'Since Callum's not around to do it.'

He nods, looks down at his trainers. 'Sorry.'

'He'll find his way home when he's ready,' I say, and it doesn't come out as lightly as I'd intended. It sounds just as sad and wounded as I feel. 'I miss him.'

Derek clears his throat, shuffles his feet.

'He's a good lad, Callum. Probably he just needs a bit of time to clear his head. Getting taken in by the coppers like that.' He waves a hand as if it actually completes the thought, but all it does is give physical form to the illogic of what's happening. 'See they're back again. Good, innit? Couldn't get the bastards out here when we was overrun with junkies and every thieving little shit in a five-mile radius, could we?'

'They only bother with people like us when they think they can make an arrest,' I say, and try to smile, because nothing that comes out of my mouth sounds right just now and I need him to know it was a joke.

'Tell you what, that dead bloke must be someone important for all this palaver,' Derek says. 'You see them putting these hours in if some poor homeless lad fell down the lift?'

My stomach plunges. He's right and I hadn't even considered that. All these man-hours mean somebody, somewhere up in the police hierarchy, cares that this victim is avenged.

'How's Jenny doing?' I ask.

'Bit better. It was another stroke. Only a small one, the doctor says. She's talking again.' He smiles, relieved. 'Should have made the most of the quiet while I had it, shouldn't I?'

217

Derek leaves and for a moment I stand in the corridor listening to the feet coming up the stairs as he goes down them. I slam the door shut and toss the mail aside.

The police must have identified him. They haven't released the name to the press yet but there are plenty of reasons not to do that immediately. Family to inform. Suspects they don't want to spook into running before they can find enough evidence to arrest them.

Quinn is a convicted arsonist and a political activist. The kind of man the police shouldn't care about. One less piece of shit off the streets, they'd say.

Except, if he's been killed by one of his own and they can get that person for it, then it's two pieces of shit off the streets. A potential provocateur removed from action, a whole movement cut off.

Do they have their sights set on somebody at the party? If not Ella yet, then one of the other loose band of protestors it attracted? Carol knew him well, but I'm not sure the police know that. It depends if either of them were under surveillance. She picked him up from prison so there's a chance she's a suspect.

For a moment I consider sharing this with her but decide against it. She's already frantic about him and I'm not sure she'll hold her silence for much longer, even without that added provocation.

I go to my picture wall and look at the image of Ella with the riot officer standing over her.

That girl shouldn't have got anywhere near someone like Ryan Quinn. She was a student protestor with no criminal record, no contacts beyond a few other people at her low level, the kind who went along to demonstrations so they'd have something different to post online, an interesting blog entry. The ones who called themselves activists but only at parties when they were trying to get laid.

Quinn was – is – hardcore.

Ella never explained how she talked him into taking her along on the Brighams incursion. I know Carol was involved, that it all started at that dinner we shared at her house, when Ella was working so hard to ingratiate herself.

It was only when Ella arrived here, scared and breathless, hair and clothes reeking of smoke, that I realised how serious she was about stepping up. Quinn gave her the opportunity to prove herself and Ella, stupidly, took it. She narrowly avoided being caught at the scene. Begged me for an alibi I had no option but to give her. And that wouldn't have kept her out of prison if it wasn't for the other man involved taking a shine to her, swearing to the police and the court that it was just him and Quinn in the estate agent's when it went up in flames. No matter what Quinn claimed.

That boy protected her just like I'm doing.

And now Quinn is missing and Ella is hiding from me and that boy is still locked up, for all I know, staring down the barrel of however many more years inside.

Did it start as she lay on the hot tarmac, howling in pain, her arm broken, her head banged up? The good girl, the copper's daughter, seeing what it felt like to be on the wrong side of her daddy's tribe?

Because something changed her.

The moment after I took the photograph I ran over to her, saw the tears streaming down her face, the splintered bone sticking through her sunburned skin. I asked her name but she couldn't speak. A policewoman pushed me back as a couple of her mates – including the big bastard who'd hit Ella – got her to her feet and hustled her into the back of a patrol car.

I don't know why I got involved.

I'd seen worse in my life and remained detached. I took my photos, sold them, saved my fighting for the people I knew and cared about, the trusted ones who would do the same for me.

But I made Ella my fight.

I grabbed a taxi without pausing to think what I was doing, and followed the patrol car as it passed three hospitals, obviously hoping to get her treated at some distance from the scene of the crime. Still, she had to wait in A&E along with all the other walking wounded and that was when I approached her, exploiting one copper's need for nicotine and the other's attraction to the man on reception.

I remember the relief on her face when she realised I was going to help her. How small and alone she looked, sitting there, how impossibly vulnerable she was. When I asked if there was someone I could call for her – boyfriend, parents – she sobbed. It reminded me of my own first arrest, in with a dozen other women who kept me strong, told me what to expect and how to stay safe, and I felt an overwhelming urge to protect her just like they'd protected me.

She was processed and treated, given a caution for assaulting a police officer, which they said could become a charge if she wasn't very careful. Blackmail, I explained, when she told me about it, sitting in the back of a taxi bringing us here to my flat.

By then she'd been identified online. The photograph I took was already circulating, hitting the media because it was the summer silly season and they were reporting anything to fill their pages, even a student protest. Ella was finding out fast what it meant to put your head above the parapet and she wasn't prepared. I saw that the process would flatten her if she had to endure it alone.

I told her she could keep her head down and the police would leave her alone. But she wanted the man who hit her to be punished.

'I'm done walking away from fights,' she said, sitting on my sofa, wrapped in one of my old cardigans, her tear-stained face hardening. 'And I'm done being pushed around by men like him.'

He wasn't punished, though. Not even a reprimand. He did his job, she was cast as the aggressor, the serial protestor who had spent the first year of her PhD attending one demonstration after another, neglecting her education, more concerned with causing trouble than cracking books.

Maybe that was when she changed.

When she realised you couldn't make things better with sit-ins and peaceful protests.

Now I can see a logical progression from there to here. From having her arm broken by a man in uniform to walking into an estate agent's with Ryan Quinn and letting the place burn.

If I'd never met her would she still be another fair-weather anarchist?

Those first couple of days out of the hospital, while she was staying with me, we talked a lot and I realise now that it was mostly me talking. I was lecturing her, I suppose, laying out my philosophy of dissent because I believed her version was too soft and therefore doomed to continual failure and frustration. I thought I was helping her, giving her survival skills. But did she take my lessons to heart? Did I turn her into what she's become?

Could it be my fault she's a killer? That Quinn's dead?

The thought is unbearable but inescapable now. We can endure far more than we can bear, though; we keep going, chest aching, head spinning, guilt pounding us flat.

There's no easy escape.

I eye my phone, willing Carol to call and tell me Quinn's okay. I need that one slim consolation. I want Ella to be the sad and scared girl in A&E again, the one who needed taking under my wing. I can live with her being the teary, terrified one who called me from 402 with a dead man at her feet. Just as long as that dead man is someone who deserved what he got. Some stranger who attacked her.

My phone rings.

An unknown number on the display.

'Hello?'

'Mol?' His voice is thicker and gruffer, but I let out a small sob of relief.

'Callum! I've been trying to find you.'

I can hear other men in the background, barracking, an aggressive edge to the laughter. Every sound echoing and hollow. A hostel, probably.

'Have you got your post?' he asks. 'I sent you something. Should be with you by now.'

'Fuck the mail,' I snap. 'Where have you been? Are you alright? I've been off my head worrying about you.'

'Please, hen. Just … find the letter.' I imagine him pinching the bridge of his nose, trying to keep his cool in the way I've seen him do so many times before.

221

We can argue later, I guess. Once I have him safely home.

The mail is where I tossed it on the sofa, mostly junk designed not to look like it. But only one is addressed to me rather than 'the occupier'. I put down my phone to open the envelope and see the letterhead from HMP Addiewell. It's a visiting order.

'You're in prison. Where is this? Is this Scotland?'

'Mol, please, don't make me do this over the phone.'

'Why are you in Scotland?'

'Please,' he lowers his voice. 'Just come up. I need to tell you this face to face.'

Callum ends the call and I'm left holding the visiting order.

Ella

Then – March 2016

The bruises were taking longer to fade than she'd expected. Almost a month on they were still faintly visible across her ribs, a slight yellowing in some places, brownish smears in others, and still painful when she touched them or stretched too far this way or that. Her mother insisted it was because she hadn't been taking proper care of herself while she was away at uni.

Healthy bodies healed quickly; unhealthy ones didn't have the internal resources.

So, she'd made chicken soup and fruit smoothies packed with protein powder, hearty puddings, heavy on the cream, because she'd heard that fat wasn't bad for you any more and did Ella know that in Italian hospitals patients were fed double cream and prosciutto to speed up their recovery?

It wasn't working, but Ella dutifully ate every meal that was put in front of her, then went to walk them off. She took the footpath that bordered the bottom of her parents' garden, following it in a five-mile loop around the village, passing the primary school she'd hated and the churchyard where she'd had her first sip of alcohol. Passed fields full of early wheat and paddocks where old friends stabled their horses and the farmhouse, white and very distant beyond the edge of the village, where her last serious boyfriend still lived and now worked, so she'd heard, as an unpaid hand doing the heavy lifting his father could no longer manage.

Coming home was not part of the plan, but she had dutifully done that too.

The last few weeks it felt like somebody else was making all of her decisions for her. Where she slept, what she ate, who she spoke to and precisely what she was allowed to say to them. One last decision, freely made by her – the wrong one, apparently – and then everything changed. She was no longer in control of her own life.

Maybe some people would enjoy this, she thought, as she let her jumper fall back down over her abdomen, sick of the sight of her bruised skin and the memory of how it happened. Some people would love to have the burden of responsibility lifted off their shoulders, but Ella was not that kind of person.

She was desperate to be in control again.

In her bedroom, tomorrow's outfit was laid out ready for her. Had been laid out by her mother, an act she hadn't performed since Ella was a little girl, about to start primary school. She almost felt like that child now, remembered how monumental the first day seemed and how she'd cried the night before.

She felt the same sense of apprehension about tomorrow morning, but this fear was more like stage fright. Half nerves, half excitement.

It would be easier to get through if she thought of it as a performance and this her costume. Her mother had taken her shopping, into the grand old department store where they used to go for afternoon tea on her birthday, and Ella let her make the decisions, content to accept that this was one thing her mother knew better than her: the art of looking respectable.

They'd come away with a knee-length tweed skirt in shades of brown and a white shirt her mother decided would be best worn under a simple camel jumper. Thick tights and low-heeled boots were tucked under the cheval mirror, where her outfit was hanging to keep it free of creases. On the dressing table her mother had laid out the gold crucifix Ella hadn't worn for years and a pair of small pearl studs, which were a family heirloom.

'I thought the first time you borrowed these would be on your wedding day,' her mother had said, smiling sadly as she closed the lightly worn shagreen box.

Ella had long since given up on being the kind of daughter her mother wanted, but she couldn't quite shake off the sense of failure bound up in those words. Not her failure, but her mother's. How sad it was that she couldn't see any bigger achievement than marriage, that she truly believed Ella was a lost cause already at twenty-four years old. Maybe it would be different if she understood what was really happening here.

But Ella doubted it. Knew she'd never be truly proud of her until she presented a fiancé and then a grandchild.

Her father, who knew everything – almost – wasn't proud. At first he was furious with her. Told her not to complain, work it out for herself, she was a big girl, she was smart, if she couldn't deal with something like this then what hope did she have of standing up against hardened criminals once she was qualified?

Then she showed him the bruises on her ribs. It made her wonder how she would have convinced him without the physical evidence. If she'd been attacked another way – if she'd been drugged and raped – would he have believed her?

The question kept gnawing at Ella and she found herself looking differently at her father, wondering just how well he'd done his job all those years; if he truly was, as her mother always said, 'a good man'. Because if he doubted his own daughter's word then how would he have reacted to a stranger making a similar complaint?

He apologised the next morning. Confessed that he knew it was always a danger of her joining up, that his name would make her a target for people who would believe she was getting an easy ride and try to knock her down a peg or two. He'd seen it happen before, he should have warned her, but he thought times had changed.

Then Ella told him the rest and he got furious all over again.

Four days later, he still hadn't calmed down. Had barely talked to her since he'd delivered a long and rambling screed about her poor decision-making and her lack of experience and why she shouldn't have done anything without talking it through with him and her mother first.

He thought she was throwing her life away.

He didn't realise she was simply embracing an opportunity to make her life much more fulfilling than the one he'd mapped out for her.

From the bedroom window she could see him exorcising his temper on the garden, hacking away at the clogged heart of an ancient crab-apple tree, which should have been pruned in the winter rather than now, when it was putting on new shoots and birds were building their nests in its highest branches.

If they were going to make up before she left, Ella knew she would have to be the one to take the first step.

She went down into the kitchen and brewed a pot of the Guatemalan coffee her father liked, found his special mug and added sugar and a splash of cream. He wasn't supposed to have the stuff since his GP had put him on medication for a slight heart problem, but she knew he preferred his coffee made that way and would sneak one when her mother wasn't there to watch him.

Outside the sawing had stopped and he was pulling the cut branches free, tossing them on to the immaculately mowed lawn, swearing as he did it.

'Made you a cuppa, Dad,' she called, as she crossed the grass.

He climbed out of the tree more nimbly than a man his age had any right to be doing, on to the stepladder, which didn't look too firm, and down to meet her.

'I was just about to come in for one,' he said, taking the cup from her. 'Thank you.'

Ella tucked her hands into the back pockets of her jeans. 'The garden's looking good.'

'I've had a think about your predicament,' he said, as if she hadn't spoken. 'I'm not happy with what you're doing. I think this is the biggest waste of potential I've ever seen and that you will live to regret your decision.'

There was a but coming.

'But I'm going to help you as best I can.' He started towards the house. 'Come on, then, before I regain my senses.'

They went upstairs to his study and he told her to sit down as he lifted a sheet of paper from the tray of the printer on his desk.

'Read this.'

Ella scanned it quickly, not quite believing what she was holding in her hand: an outline of the hearing she was going to face tomorrow. There were too many specifics in there for it not to be the real thing.

'How did you get this?'

He waved the question away. 'Never mind that now. What we need to do is get you properly prepared so they can't trip you up. Because that's what they're going to try and do. If they can undermine your version of events or smear your reputation, they will.'

'I told you what happened,' Ella said, resenting the suggestion. 'Don't you believe me?'

'Of course I do.' He sipped his coffee and placed it carefully on the coaster. 'But you have to appreciate that this process isn't about establishing the truth. It's about your credibility versus his. And, since you've decided on this course of action, you have to consider the implications. Once all of this is down on record it's there for ever and for anyone determined enough to look it out to read. You might be walking away from Garton but it will always be there in the public domain. Do you understand?'

She nodded.

'Good.' He nudged the mouse on his desk and his computer screen blinked into life. 'So, while your mother's out, you and I are going to construct a solid, unexploitable narrative.'

'Is that ... it doesn't seem right.'

He peered at her over his reading glasses. 'Do you want to win, Ella?'

They spent an hour thrashing out a first draft, Ella telling her version and then her father finessing it, pumping up elements, toning down others. He asked her questions that weren't in the briefing, tougher ones, telling her she needed to be prepared for blindsides. He stood up for those, looming over her, hardening his stance.

227

This was the version of him that had risen through the ranks so quickly. The man who had a fearsome reputation within his own force and beyond. A man you did not want to cross.

She would never be like him, she realised. No matter how well she was schooled or how long she spent learning on the job, she would never have acquired the right instincts to be a detective. As he blasted and cajoled her, forcing her to repeat her story again and again, his version of it now, Ella became even more convinced that she'd made the right decision.

'Isn't it true that you provoked Mr Pearce?'

'No.'

'Several people have reported that you threatened him,' her father said, staring down at her, radiating impatience and disbelief. 'And I quote – "If you touch me again, I'll fucking drop you."'

'I'm the victim here,' Ella said.

He sighed, took off his glasses and pinched his nose. 'More emotion, Ellie. You sound like the woman who does the speaking clock.'

'You use the speaking clock?'

'Concentrate.' He snapped the piece of paper at her. 'Come on, again. Remember how you felt when it happened. Tap into that.'

She remembered the stunned faces watching in silence, the dirty carpet pressed against her cheek, the smell and texture and how she knew she wasn't the first person to bleed on it. She remembered the look in his eye, a sick mix of lust and fury.

And then the sensation of becoming splintered.

'I'm the victim here.'

'Better,' her father said. 'But don't be afraid to go bigger. They want you to appear detached and unaffected. That's what a good copper does in this situation. If you play it that way you'll lose. You need to be unpredictable, unhinged even. Hysterical.'

'Okay.' She took a deep breath, trying to blow out the tremors that had crept up on her, remembering how she'd struggled to get away, crawling over the filthy carpet, blinded by tears and pain.

'I know this is an intimidating process,' her father said, putting aside his glasses and the paper, wheeling his captain's chair over to her. 'It's designed to be intimidating because it wheedles out false accusations that way.'

Ella glared at him but he didn't seem to see the anger.

'I'll be right there with you.' He patted her hand. 'Try not to worry. We'll get you through this, poppet.'

Molly

Now – 31st March

I get to Euston fifteen minutes before the Caledonian Sleeper leaves. The other passengers look set for clean and bracing weekends out in the country. There are groups of middle-aged men with bikes kitted out in unforgiving Lycra, couples with camping gear strapped to their backs and a dozen Chinese students who I hope are going to Edinburgh for a hardcore drinking session rather than anything as tedious as fresh air and open spaces. They break my heart, kids now, shunning vices for fear of ruining their appearance or job prospects.

When I reach my berth I find a woman about my age has already claimed the bottom bunk and spread her things across the floor, bag and coat and walking poles with vicious spikes on them. She's removed her shoes and is massaging some camphor-smelling ointment into her red and gnarled feet. It seems like something she could have done at home.

She looks up at me, small black eyes in an apple face beginning to turn in on itself.

'I thought I'd have the cabin to myself,' she says.

'Don't worry, I'll be sleeping.'

I scramble up on to the top bunk and tuck my bag against the wall, turn my back on her and pretend to drop off. Even on a better night I wouldn't want to make conversation with her.

She noisily unfolds a map and begins to murmur and mutter to herself, repeating directions over and again as if she's trying to memorise them, while the paper crinkles and rustles.

I tune it all out, preoccupied by the uncertainty of my own path once we arrive.

As soon as Callum put the phone down on me I googled him and everything fell into place. His nightmares, the way he's isolated himself, that dangerous edge I'd put down to him being a soldier rather than a cook. Turns out he wasn't a combatant. That, at least, was the truth. I didn't misread his capacity for violence, though.

At first I wasn't going to do this. Didn't think he deserved the opportunity to explain himself, especially when the details appear so clear-cut. I screwed up the visiting order and tossed it in the bin, got on with my day, trying to push him out of my head.

But he wouldn't go easy.

I kept thinking about all the time we'd spent together, the small acts of kindness he'd shown me and other people, how he would help out Derek and Jenny no matter what they needed. I thought of the unexpected friendship we'd forged and how that had become deeper so fast that it had to mean something. Because I'm not a kid any more. I don't just fall for a man because he makes me come reliably. There was something else between us. And it was more important to me than I'm entirely comfortable admitting.

I miss him.

I want to see him again.

So, the visiting order came out of the bin and he'll get a chance to tell me whatever it is he has to say that's too delicate to be shared over the phone. It'll be an excuse for what he did, I guess. Everyone who's committed a crime of that magnitude has one. Even me. I have dozens of excuses I keep rehearsing in my head but none of them ring true.

I hope I'll have a good one in time for the hard questions, which are well overdue.

The police completed their search of the building without finding anything of interest. After they left, long after, once it was dark, I went up to 402 and found the door smashed in. The curtains were still closed, as I left them, no sign of disturbance anywhere. If they lifted the rug I placed near the hearth, they put it back very carefully.

That kind of good luck has to be balanced out.

Something bad is on the way.

Probably Quinn.

He would have called by now if he was okay. Carol knows that. I know that. We've spoken about it, brief conversations, loaded with reproach, and it feels like her patience is running low. She says she'll report him missing first thing Monday morning. Make it official.

She won't turn us in but she's going to lead the police to Ella.

Another betrayal from someone I thought I could trust to the end of the earth. Another punch to my already pummelled old heart.

At Waverley I have a couple of hours to kill and spend them drinking coffee and chain-smoking outside an early-opening cafe, until it's time to catch the Glasgow train, which is packed but thankfully quiet. I watch the countryside go by, remembering the last time I was up here, heading for the Faslane peace camp with Carol. It seems much longer than eighteen months ago. All the other times we went there during the last twenty years now blurring together in my memory.

When I get off at Addiewell I realise that most of the other people on the platform are heading for the prison too. There are a dozen women, who seem to know one another, little kids in tow acting like it's just a fun day out, the older, more astute ones dragging their feet. There are a few men among the group. Disappointed fathers, I think, sympathetic brothers.

I follow them up to the gates, to a building that looks like the centrepiece of a middling business park designed in the early nineties. Threatening in its sheer banality.

Ahead of me the visitors let themselves be processed with bovine calm and I try to behave the same way when it's my turn, but the attitude of the staff during the search rankles me and I resent having to give them my fingerprints.

'You'll be through quicker next time,' one of the disappointed fathers tells me. 'First time's a bother.'

It hadn't occurred to me that there might be a next time. I can't see this becoming a regular feature of my existence, once a month for the next ten years to life, coming to sit with Callum and struggle to make conversation. I can't imagine that far ahead.

The visiting room isn't what I expected: light and airy, high-ceilinged and white-painted, clusters of softly padded chairs arranged around low tables. There are thirty or so tables, half with men in the same prison-issue T-shirts already seated, waiting for their visitors. Nothing looks bolted down, but the room is heavily staffed and the mood of relaxed congeniality could flip in an instant.

I hang back, waiting for the rest of the group to find their people, make their greetings, clear my path to Callum, who's sitting under one of the long, high windows full of flinty sky, at a table slightly distant from the others, a cordon of empty ones around it.

We make eye contact and he stands, seeming not to know what to do with his hands as I walk towards him. He looks different here, broader, harder. He holds himself with an air of menace I recognise as survival instinct. His hair has grown in a little longer, furring his head black and grey, and he wears a beard already shaggy and threaded with coppery strands.

It seems impossible that he's changed so much in a fortnight.

Or maybe this is who he always was. His old identity reasserting itself.

He mumbles something that sounds like a thank you and gestures for me to sit down, as if I'm his visiting solicitor or some charitable drop-by.

I didn't expect us to fall weeping into each other's arms, but this coldness is disconcerting. Painful, even.

I sit down, legs crossed, feeling as defensive as I must look.

Callum hunches over, elbows on his knees. I see that his knuckles are bruised and wonder which of these men he's been fighting with already, whether he was the victim defending himself or the instigator making his mark, warning off the others.

Knowing his history now, I suspect the latter.

'I didnae want ye tae find out like this,' he says, his accent so thick it's as if a stranger is speaking through his face at me.

'Because you had a better way you were going to break it to me?' I'm angrier than I thought I was. The hours travelling, convincing myself I can handle this, are immediately revealed as a lie. 'Come on then, tell me why he deserved it.'

The nearest prison officer turns towards us, alerted by my raised voice. He comes closer. Folds his arms and waits.

Callum brushes his hand over the top of his head, kneads the muscles across the back of his neck for a few seconds before he finally looks up at me.

'He didnae deserve it. I wis drunk and I didnae like the way he looked at us. If he'd huv stayed down I'd huv left him be, but he was after a fight. I wisnae going tae back down.'

It was the same story the local press told at the time. Two stupid young men, both drunk, getting into a fight at a taxi rank outside a nightclub. Twelve years ago now. Callum would have been twenty-six, the boy he killed barely old enough to get served a drink. I doubt it was a fair fight but will never know. The press told one story, Callum will tell another, and the truth will be somewhere between the two.

All I know for sure is that he skipped bail a few days before sentencing. Going AWOL at the same time because he was home on leave from the army when it happened, up in Inverness visiting family. Two cousins who'd been given suspended sentences for their involvement in the attack. They might come and visit him, anyway.

'Why did you do a runner?'

'Wouldn't you if you wis looking at ten years inside?' he asks incredulously. Then frowns. 'No, you wouldnae, hen. You've no' run, huv you?'

I don't answer the question. I can't. Not here.

'How did it take them so long to catch up with you?' I ask. 'You went to your parents'; it's the first place they'd have looked, surely?'

'I wis on the streets for two, three years,' he says, punching his fist into his palm. 'When Ma died and I wis too scared tae go see her off. But Dad needed me, he wis on his knees. Whatever time I got with him, it'd be worth it. But naebody come.'

'What about when your dad died?'

He shrugs. 'Different country, different polis. Stuff gets lost in the cracks.'

'And then you found the body.'

'Aye.' Callum sucks air through his teeth. 'Should never huv opened that lift up. Thought it wis a rats' nest stinking. Derek saw the lad. Mebbe I wouldnae huv reported it if I wis on my own. He wis calling the polis before I could stop him.'

I remember that night: Callum sitting stunned at his kitchen table, trying to act normal and failing. And, selfishly, I thought it was about me, that he knew Ella and I were involved and was worried what would happen. But it was knowing they'd want to talk to him. That the minute his name was put into the system a big red flag would pop up.

'Why didn't you leave before they got to you?' I lean forwards in my chair, closing the space between us. 'You knew what was going to happen.'

'Where was I going tae go? I've got nothing. I'm too old to go back on the streets.' He shakes his head and I notice he's sounding more like the Callum I know again, as if I've coaxed that man out of his hiding place. 'I've had a lot of time tae think on what I did, Mol. I belong here.'

Without thinking I reach out and grab his hand. His fist opens and he takes my hand inside his, lifts it to his face and kisses my fingers, once, quickly and drops it again.

He looks around to check if anyone has seen. It's a weakness, caring about someone; it can be used against him. Callum belongs in here but I'm not sure he's built to survive it, big as he is and strong as he is. Emotionally, he's too soft.

'Have they questioned you yet?' he asks.

'Not properly.'

'What about Ella?'

This isn't the conversation I came for. I've had enough of talking about Ella and thinking about Ella. I want to get up and walk away but, surrounded by so many happy visitors, it's going to look wrong for me to leave now. At the very least it's going to arouse interest. And when a new prisoner has a public bust-up with his visitor, that tends to get noted, followed up on. Especially a prisoner who's been recaptured during a murder investigation.

'I heard them arguing,' he says, dropping his voice. 'I knew it was her. I've known the whole time. For Chrissakes, Mol, d'you think I'm simple?'

I shake my head.

'And you helped her, aye?' he says. 'Stands tae reason. She wouldnae have moved him on her own. No' a lad that size. No' with those wee arms of hers.'

I glance towards the nearby prison officer but see only a stretch of wall where he was standing.

'Callum, this isn't the time.'

'It's the only time we're going tae get, Mol.' He looks sadly around the room, at the other men with their wives and girlfriends and kids, and I feel him retreat from me and the possibility of the other visits I'd decided upon the moment he kissed my hand.

'Were you there when she did it?'

Part of me doesn't want to answer. I think of Quinn, getting an early release for informing on his cellmate, and wonder if Callum has been made a similar offer. A reduction on his sentence in return for information. Would he do that to me?

Now I retreat from him. Unwillingly and instinctively.

We've been close but we're not a couple. We have no history beyond eighteen months of casual sex and shared dinners and bad films watched on my sofa. It was enough for me to grow to care about him, but who's to say whether he feels the same? Was I just handy? Easy-going company and sex on tap.

'Did she tell you it was an accident?' he asks.

He's too earnest, he *needs* an answer. He's physically straining towards me to get one. And that scares me.

'Because it wasnae an accident.' This time he reaches across the space for my hands. 'I saw the post-mortem photos, Mol. They were shoving them intae my face, shouting at me. They said I grabbed the lad's head and kept smashing it intae the hearth until he was dead.'

'They're lying,' I whisper.

'No, I saw his head. There wis three, mebbe four, breaks on his skull.'

I think back to that night, try to recapture the scene, but it's all scrambled up in my memory and coloured by the fear I'd felt the second I walked into the flat and the sense of desperation to get us both away as cleanly as possible. It didn't look like a violent crime. It looked like an accident.

But, really, how can I know? I didn't pull off his hat and check his skull. When I was close to him, searching for the pulse that refused to come, then when I was carrying him to the lift, I was focused on Ella, trying to keep her calm, keep her moving.

Callum has no reason to lie, does he? Not now.

Unless he's trying to make a deal, negotiate down his sentence in return for handing the pair of us in. I can't believe he'd do that, though. Despite the lie he's been living for years and the crime he committed, I just don't believe he'd do that to me.

'She told you it was an accident,' he says, nodding to himself.

'Who was he?' I ask.

'I don't know.'

'They must have told you.'

'They were asking me who he was,' Callum says. 'Mebbe they've found out now, but they didnae know when they wis questioning me.' He flicks a quick look around to see if any officers are nearby. 'You not know who he is?'

I shake my head, thinking, Quinn. Because even though I don't know for sure, it's coming to feel like the inevitable explanation.

'Hasn't Ella told you?' he asks.

'We've not talked for a while.'

He frowns at me. 'You've done that for her and she's no' talking to you?'

'It's complicated.'

'Hen, it's no' complicated.' His eyes widen fearfully. 'She's a fucking murderer and you're the only witness to what she's done. You need to watch out for yourself now.'

237

Ella

Then – February 2016

One of the spotlights was emitting a high-pitch buzz, which rose and fell and for a few seconds would stop, making Ella think she was imagining it, before it started again, the intensity rising, sounding like a hornet was trapped inside the flush chrome casing, battering itself to death against the burning bulb.

It was the light in the corner, set above the low sofa and the modular armchairs, which looked like leather and probably were, because this was the office of someone important enough to demand the best and get it. He hadn't managed to get maintenance in to fix that bulb, though.

Ella had been directed towards the sofa, told to make herself comfortable, but she'd taken a seat facing the desk. She lowered herself into it gingerly, biting down on the pain in her ribs, holding her palm flat against them as if that would contain the damage done. She wanted to be upright when he came back, show that she wasn't defeated, that she had stood up to one bully and she would stand up to him as well.

Because she knew how it was going to go.

She'd been here before and had her complaints disregarded. It was 'part of the training exercise' or 'the normal cut and thrust of role playing'.

But there was no excusing what had happened. Not this time.

No passing it off as good-natured joshing or banter. With the CCTV footage there was no chance of denial, even if the other people present decided they'd seen nothing.

Finally, she had the bastard.

And yet, she didn't feel triumphant. She thought she would, eventually, when she was calmer and when the pain was gone, but now she felt sick and edgy, even through the sedative she'd been given by the doctor who checked her out and assured her there was no internal bleeding and that the rib fractures were hairline, nothing to be done but rest them.

She wondered if her doctor could be convinced to give her a couple more days' worth of Valium and then dismissed the idea. It would be too easy to hide from this rather than push through it. And too easy to go seeking a medicated escape next time she felt life rushing away from her.

It was tempting, though, as she sat in the office with the sound of the fizzing light and vacuum cleaners along the hall.

Just take a pill and let it smother the unbearable stress Garton induced. The pressure to perform, to succeed, to come out top every time. That's how it had always been with her, ever since she could remember, right through school and university. She was always top of the class and she had no intention of letting any of her fellow recruits beat her.

She realised that was what had led her to this point, sitting battered and disorientated in her course leader's office. She'd wanted to be the best and that had made her a target for people who never would be.

The office door opened and ex-DCI Gould came in carrying two cups, placed one in front of her before he went around to his side of the desk.

He looked less troubled than when he'd walked out of the office ten minutes previously to fetch some tea. Calls had been made, she guessed, the first line of enquiry checked out to see if this was another meeting he could bring to a quick close with a promise to speak to the parties involved and keep an eye on them, a suggestion that she 'rise above it'.

'Shouldn't I have a rep in here?' Ella asked.

'You're a trainee,' Gould said. 'You don't get access to a union rep.'

'So, who's looking out for my best interests?'

'I am.'

Ella snorted and the colour rose instantly in Gould's lightly pockmarked face, red right to the roots of his wetly gelled hair. She could see how much he wanted to shout at her, be the DCI again, throw his weight around. But he was a teacher now, to all intents and purposes, and she was a student with a legitimate complaint he had to pretend to be concerned about.

'This is a delicate situation,' he said. 'I'm sure you can appreciate that.'

'I was attacked and I want to press charges,' Ella told him, relieved that she sounded firm even though inside every part of her was churning furiously. 'It's not a delicate situation, it's a very simple one. You have ignored numerous incidents in the run-up to me being attacked today – don't worry, though, I kept my own records – and you've failed to give me even the most basic protection I should be able to expect as a student here.

'You, and the rest of the faculty, have failed to provide a safe studying environment. Your continued refusal to intervene in a campaign of bullying against me is not something I'm going to accept quietly.'

Gould's gaze flicked away to the door as it opened and an immediate look of relief spread across his face. He stood quickly, smoothed his hand down over his tie and nodded to the woman who'd come in. She was tall and slim, with steel-grey hair cut into a soft bob and a weathered tan that suggested she wasn't as comfortable in her severely tailored suit and heels as she would be in walking shoes and waterproofs.

'Peggy, I'll leave this to you now.'

She didn't reply, only stood aside to allow him to bolt from the office. Then she turned to Ella and smiled, warmly, the skin around her eyes crinkling.

'You've been in the wars, pet.'

'It's been a long and hard-fought campaign,' Ella said, watching her carefully as the smile deepened and she shook her head. 'Who are you?'

240

'You can call me Peggy. No need for us to be formal.'

'But who are you?'

She didn't answer.

In the corner of the office the light was still buzzing and Ella tried to ignore it and focus on this woman. Peggy walked around Gould's desk, stood with her hands thrust into the pockets of her suit jacket as she looked over his family photographs, then lifted the lid on a small glass jar containing jelly beans.

'He ever offered you one of these?' Peggy asked.

'No.'

'Not his favourite student?' She picked the jar up and rattled it at Ella, who didn't take one. 'Don't blame you. Bet these have been in here since he took the job.'

'Do you know what happened to me?' Ella asked impatiently. 'That is why you're here, isn't it?'

'I know.' Peggy sat down in Gould's cream leather chair, leaned back, perfectly relaxed. 'And I know what you gave out back.'

'I've got two broken ribs,' she snapped.

'And Mr Pearce lost a couple of teeth.'

'His response was disproportionate,' Ella said firmly. She knew what this was; bring another woman in, play on female solidarity, get her to back away from bringing charges. Like she was stupid. 'Don't you even care how it reflects on the force? What he's done. Do you think that's good PR?'

Peggy folded her arms on the desk. Ella noticed the discreet watch she wore, leather and gold with a few small stones around the bezel, the wedding ring and a band of platinum and diamonds on her middle finger. Everything expensive but unostentatious.

'I don't care about PR,' she said. 'I'm just a regular old copper.'

She took a sip of the tea Gould had brought in, pulled a face.

'Bloody water down this way's rank.' She pushed the cup to the edge of the desk. 'You had a decent cuppa since you been down here?'

This woman was going to talk about nothing until she was ready to get to the point, and Ella realised she had to let her do that. Whoever she was and whatever she was here for, she'd get to it eventually. She started going on about the hard water and the Victorian pipes and how she'd had a softener put in at home, spent a small fortune on the thing, but it still wasn't like a proper cup of tea made with good Northumberland tap water.

'So, why did you move down here, then?' Ella asked.

'Same reason you did, pet.' Peggy smiled again, spread her hands wide. 'It's where the action is.'

'I wasn't looking for "action",' Ella said, so fiercely that the pain flared in her ribs again. 'I wanted to help people. I thought that was why everyone joined up. But it's not that, is it? Some of them are just thugs who want a uniform to hide behind.'

'"Them"?' Peggy asked. 'Are you not one of us any more?'

'I can't be part of a force that allows this kind of bullying and violence to go on.' She knew she was going to say it, but they'd got here faster than she expected and she felt tears welling as the future she'd always planned fell away around her. She willed down the emotion, told herself to be strong. 'If Pearce's done this to me – a fellow recruit – what the hell do you think he's going to do once he's serving? He's an animal.'

Peggy nodded, leaned back in the chair, regarding Ella thoughtfully.

'There are plenty like him, yes.'

'Because you don't stamp on them early.'

'We need them,' Peggy said. 'That's the simple truth. For every smart, conscientious officer like you, we need a couple of dozen unthinking idiots like Pearce.'

Ella let out a humourless laugh. 'So you look the other way?'

'Do you want to be the one stopping and searching lads with knives as long as your arm on the street at one in the morning?' Peggy asked. 'No, because you're educated and it'd be a waste of your talents. But someone's got to do the dirty work.'

'He's going to kill someone,' Ella told her, thinking of the look in his eye as he loomed over her, his hand at her throat. 'You all want me to suck it up and keep quiet. Gould has been blaming this on me for weeks. And I'm not having it any more! I will shout this from the rooftops if I have to, but I'm going to make sure nobody else has to tolerate this kind of aggression while they're trying to train for the most important job anyone can do.'

'Sounds like you don't really want to leave us at all,' Peggy said.

'I don't. But it's the only way.' Pressure swelled her chest, pushing against her damaged ribs, as she tried not to cry.

Without ceremony the life she'd committed herself to before she was even old enough to consider alternatives was being taken away from her. So quickly she could barely comprehend how it was happening.

At least you didn't fail, Ella thought, and that scant comfort only made her feel the loss more acutely. She'd done everything right and yet here she was.

'There are other options.' Peggy got up and came out from behind Gould's desk, perched on the edge. 'We really don't like to lose students with your grades and your potential.'

Ella felt her face harden. The sadness in her beginning to curdle into something altogether darker and angrier.

'But I have to keep my mouth shut?' she sneered.

'Pearce is gone.' Peggy put her hands up in a gesture of surrender. 'Or he soon will be.'

'You'll let him quietly drop out of training, you mean?'

'No, there's going to be an investigation and he'll be charged. Adam Pearce will never wear a police uniform.' She cocked her head, smiled. 'Well, not unless his next job's stripping for hen parties.'

'What about Gould?' Ella asked. 'He let it go on. There's a culture of bullying being perpetuated because he allows it. He's just as guilty.'

Peggy tucked her hands into her pockets. 'Gould's a first-rate teacher and he's very well liked. He's not going anywhere. Pick your battles, Ella.'

So, that was why Gould was so relieved to see her enter the office. Whoever this woman was, she clearly held sway high up in the management. She'd been brought in with the ultimate aim of keeping Gould employed, safeguarding his job and the pension he could only be a couple of years off claiming.

They would sacrifice Pearce. Naturally, there were hundreds more where he came from, but not that many Goulds.

Ella thought of how dismissive he'd been, treating her like a whiny brat running to the teacher because her toys had been stolen, rather than a grown adult in fear for her safety. Making her feel like she was inviting the aggression somehow, forcing her to monitor her behaviour and moderate it, to no avail. All rather than simply doing his job and disciplining Pearce.

Pearce was a piece of shit but Gould was his enabler. He saw Pearce as perfect officer material and that made him the dangerous one. The one she needed to expose.

But she couldn't do that without appearing to give this Peggy-whoever-she-was the right reply. Once the investigation was open, Ella would point the finger at Gould, and if he kept his job then at least she would have shown what a complete and utter disgrace he was and her conscience would be clear.

'Okay,' Ella said. 'I understand.'

'Good girl.'

Peggy held out her hand. 'Let's get you up.'

Ella fought the urge to bat it away and took the help, held her breath as she was brought to her feet, seeing Peggy wince in sympathy with her.

'Think I'd best drive you home,' she said. 'Don't want you on the bus with those injuries. And we can talk about what you might want to do next on the way.'

They went out past the empty offices and the cleaners working in the corridors, down to the car park where Peggy led her to a black Audi sitting in a visitors' bay, asking if she thought she could manage a little bit of dinner, line her stomach for the painkillers. Ella played along, said she thought she could, thank you, that's very kind of you. Thinking how scared they must be to launch this kind of charm offensive and how pathetic it was that they believed she would buy it.

She was out.

She'd seen the force for what it really was, beyond the talk of transparency and cultural sensitivity and noble service. She'd been lied to, ever since she was a little girl admiring the crisp lines and shining buttons on her father's dress uniform, thinking that one day she would have her own. For every good man like him there were two dozen Pearces, with the Goulds and Peggys defending them.

And she would not become one of them.

Molly

Now – 31st March

The journey back to London is a blur. Six hours lost to a fruitless search for memories I don't have and certainties I desperately need. I keep replaying the conversation with Callum, looking for some hint I missed, some nuance that would let me believe he was lying. But I know he wasn't.

I've been in such deep denial this last couple of weeks. I was convinced everything would turn out right. I backed off from Ella when I should have pressed her harder, because, I suppose, on some level I knew that pushing her would have brought us to a truth so terrible I wouldn't be able to ignore it.

And, maybe, it was partly because I know how much of this is my own fault.

There was that moment, standing in 402, looking out across the city before I snatched the curtains shut, when I made a decision there was no going back from. I was drunk and stoned and yet I fervently believed it was the wisest course of action. A few more minutes' breathing space and perhaps I'd have made the right decision instead of the easy one, told Ella to call the police, explain that she was only defending herself, promised I'd back her to the hilt.

She wouldn't have done it, of course, because she knew what the most basic investigation would uncover and how quickly her claim it was an accident would be undermined.

But when she refused, I would have learned she was lying and I could have walked away. I wouldn't have been entirely innocent, but innocent enough to keep from being a proven accessory after the fact.

Except … would I have walked out of there and left her to defend herself?

No.

In my heart I know I wouldn't have.

I've always gone too far for the sake of my friends. It's the curse of us without proper families to overinvest in people who don't deserve it. We know we'll be wrong many times, end up giving and giving to someone who only takes, but we think it's worth it to find the one person in a hundred who turns out to be something more than family.

Carol was one of them. We crossed lines for each other, made sacrifices without being asked or thanked, without even pausing to consider the outcome. Because that's what you do for the rare individual who feels like your sister/mother/daughter combined. Losing Carol is going to hurt more than losing Ella.

I'm starting to think I might actually hate Ella.

It's been creeping up on me since I exposed that first, seemingly unimportant lie of hers, when she told me she'd never seen him before and I unearthed the photo of them together. Lying is a form of violence. It's an act of contempt. She lied to me because she didn't trust me with the truth and because she was so confident of my continued support that she had no fear of me abandoning her if I found out.

And I didn't.

Not after that first lie, or the second or the third or however many she racked up before we got to the big one. Not an accident but murder.

A brutal murder. Because if what Callum said was right – if what the police told him during questioning is right – then Ella must have knocked that man down and sat astride his chest, her hands full of his hair as she repeatedly smashed his head into the tiled fireplace.

She's dangerous.

I never saw that coming.

A normal person pushed to violence recoils after they've struck the first blow. They see themselves from the outside, rendered strange and ugly by the act, and they hate and fear what they've just done. They drop the weapon. They stumble away.

They don't make sure to finish the job.

The train pulls into King's Cross and I wait for the other passengers in the carriage to gather their things and leave before I get up, stretching the long journey out of my legs, flexing my numb toes.

Outside the same people are smoking under the canopy to avoid the rain or rushing towards the Tube trains they'll probably miss or the long queue for taxis. I want to walk, I need to move again, but the rain forces me on to a bus that's so busy I find myself standing.

By the time it empties enough for me to get a seat, we're in Camden and I'm stepping off again into rain that is thinner now and more invasive, stinging my face and plastering my hair to my skull within a minute. Other people caught out by it rush past me, heads down, and I feel a moment of kinship with each and every one of them. We are life's gamblers, too devil-may-care to pack an umbrella in our bags at the start of the day.

I thumb the buzzer at Ella's shared house and the same boy opens up as last time I was there, still glued to his phone, and he lets me in without question.

Upstairs I knock on Ella's door, softly at first, then harder when she doesn't answer, and harder still, now shouting at her to let me in.

The door of the neighbouring flat opens and a girl looks at me with a flash of annoyance. She's in her dressing gown, getting ready to go out, with her black hair teased into an elaborate rockabilly do but her make-up unfinished; only one false eyelash on, giving her a faintly menacing *Clockwork Orange* vibe.

'She's not there,' the girl says. 'It doesn't matter how hard you knock.'

'Are you a friend?' I ask.

'Yes. Who are you? Her mum?'

I lie. 'Yes, she was supposed to meet me here.'

'Oh.' The girl's annoyance gives way to discomfort, she bites her lip. 'Look, I don't want to get Ella in trouble or anything, but you should probably know, she's been arrested.'

The hallway tips and turns around me and I reach for the wall to steady myself. The girl takes half a step towards me but doesn't seem to know what to do next.

'When was this?' I manage to ask.

'This morning. First thing. A whole load of them came and dragged her out.' She presses her hand nervously to the back of her lacquered hair, a gesture from the wrong generation. 'I mean, it's probably nothing. You know what she's like, always demonstrating against something. It's just what happens, isn't it? The police pull people like her in all the time.'

I nod.

'I'm sure she's fine,' she says quickly.

I must look terrified because the girl pats my arm and makes a consoling face rendered comic by her one big eye and her one small one. I feel a manic laugh rising up from my chest and swallow it down.

This is it. The police have finally come for her and there's no way she'll talk herself free. Because if they've taken this long to work it out they probably have a ton of evidence to back up their suspicions. She's already linked with Quinn in the police database, I guess. She's a known associate at least, a potential accessory to a crime he went down for and she didn't, meaning even the slowest copper would see a ready-made motive.

Or am I giving them too much credit?

Maybe this is Carol's doing. Has she gone back on her promise to wait until Monday?

The girl glances towards her flat, wanting to get on with her evening.

I thank her and walk away, shakily, make it halfway down the stairs before I begin to feel woozy. For a moment I sit on the striped runner, one hand curled around the barley-twist spindle, which has been repainted so many times it's beginning to lose its form.

Where do I go now?

Home doesn't feel safe, because what if Ella has talked, spilled everything and pleaded remorse? The police could be waiting for me already.

Then again, I have nowhere else to go and delaying the inevitable won't change it.

I let myself out and hail a passing black cab. To hell with the expense. Arrest and charge will at least put an end to the tedious frugality I've been living with for the last few years. No need for savings when you're banged up.

The driver is having his own crisis, talking in a hushed voice on his phone to someone I think might be his son, getting angrier as he reminds him how long it's been since he visited his mother, how he promised he would make more effort.

As we head down Euston Road, I realise I should probably call Milton. Try to set up a meeting before I'm actually arrested. It's always best to unburden yourself to your solicitor before the police get involved, formulate your plan in private. I've never trusted them not to be listening to what's said in the interview rooms between solicitors and clients.

When I take out my phone I realise it's been switched off since HMP Addiewell. I turn it on again and see I have four missed calls from Carol, all within the last couple of hours, but no messages. She doesn't like to leave any more of a trail than necessary.

For a few minutes I watch the streets go by, wondering if she'll be apologetic or self-righteous. If I'd done to her what she's done to me I'd cut all contact just to preserve my sanity. How can you expect to chat to someone you've just betrayed?

The driver has ended his call but is muttering to himself, shaking his head, saying all the things he wanted to but couldn't or didn't think of at the time. I can see how tightly he clutches the wheel and on any other day I would probably ask if he's okay. I hope he is and that his son visits his mother and that they make peace.

The world is too cold and hostile to give up on people.

I call Carol.

'I've been ringing you all afternoon,' she says, slightly breathless. 'Don't you ever charge that phone?'

'Ella's been arrested,' I tell her. 'Did you know about that?'

'What? No. Shit.'

'Yeah. It is. And you know what happens next,' I say.

Her old whistling kettle sings a wonky note in the background and I close my eyes, thinking of the endless cups of coffee she made us from it, the hundreds of hours spent in that poky room with its little table and the view across the garden she never bothered with, planning how we would change the world.

It stops singing as she takes it off the heat. 'Sorry. Look, Mol, you knew they were going to arrest her at some point. It's probably routine questioning anyway. It's inevitable when it was her party he died at, right? Just try to chill out.'

Now I know why she's so chipper.

'You've got in touch with Quinn, haven't you?'

'He was out hiking in the wilds with some girl,' she says, her voice rising with delight. 'They only just got back this morning.'

Her relief is infectious and for a few seconds I enjoy the feeling, smile and sigh and let my body relax in the seat. I'm happy for her, genuinely. Quinn means a lot to her and I'm happy she hasn't lost him.

But my problem is still in front of me and in a perverse way it's just become even more confounding. Because if Ella had murdered Quinn it would be terrible but at least there would be some twisted logic to it. They had history, after all.

I desperately need to talk this through with Carol. Everything that's happened with Callum, what the police told him and what that means. Who the hell Ella has murdered if it wasn't Quinn. I need my old friend's wise counsel, but she isn't my friend any more, even though she's chatting away still, like nothing's changed – like she wasn't preparing to turn me in to the police – about the group Quinn is with and how she's considering going over there for a couple of weeks in the summer, see if she can help them out, meet this girl he's fallen for.

She's mid-sentence when I end the call and I know that's the last time I will ever speak to her.

I am absolutely alone now.

251

Ella

Then – February 2016

Ella didn't want to go to the pub but somehow she'd been dragged along to a down-at-heel place a few streets away from the Garton campus, not the sort of establishment she was used to from back home or the kind she'd gone to while she was away at Cambridge. Not what she'd had in mind for her time in London either. This was a relic of the London of last century, filthy patterned carpet she'd bet had every blood type in existence ground into it. Photos of darts players and winning greyhounds on hunter-green painted walls. A big-screen TV, of course, half a dozen fruit machines and a full-size pool table where a couple of other recruits were already playing, going up against a pair of men she clocked right off as potential trouble. Late thirties, all slouch and swagger, a bit too much gold on them and a lot too much laughter, which was as fake as the leather covering the banquette her friends noisily filled while she went to the bar.

Somehow she was getting the first round in. Because they'd all pegged her for money within the first few days and, no matter how much she tried to convince them she was in the same boat they were, it was obviously a lie. Wrong accent, wrong university. What was a girl from Durham doing training alongside graduates from Aberystwyth and Sunderland? Why wasn't she at law school, if she was so smart and dedicated to the pursuit of justice?

The barman came over and chucked his chin up at her.

'What'll it be, love?'

'Four Beck's,' she said. 'Bottles, please.'

He nodded, took his time getting down to the fridge, having to steady himself with his fist pressed to the bare concrete floor back there. He was old and overweight, had the look of an ex-copper about him, Ella thought. Maybe that was why he'd bought the place near Garton, always full of raw recruits. A nostalgia trip.

She paid for the drinks and took them over to her friends, irritated that she had to sit with her back to the pool table on an uneven three-legged stool.

Paola and Kat were huddled over on their phones, swiping and laughing, totally lost in whatever they were looking at. Laurel was watching the game unfolding, her eyes on Aaron as he cued up a shot and sent one of the striped balls riffling into a corner pocket. They'd been going out for a couple of weeks, screwing noisily in her room at the house Ella shared with Laurel and two other girls. He never stayed the night and Ella wondered if he was going on to another girl after he was done with Laurel. It was his style, she thought.

No wonder him and Pearce had buddied up. Aaron had the looks, Pearce had the mouth and the aggro to get his mate out of trouble when he stepped over the line with some other bloke's girlfriend.

Ella had seen the pair of them at work, on evenings when Laurel hadn't come along and during classes she didn't attend. She'd seen Aaron flirt with female instructors and the women who worked in the canteen, years older than him some of them, but it didn't seem to matter. All while Pearce stood back, watching and waiting, and it occurred to Ella that Aaron's performance was perhaps more for Pearce's benefit than the women he was charming.

When Aaron popped the eight ball into the same pocket, Laurel jumped up and cheered, earning her sneers of derision from the blokes they were playing.

'Double or nothing?' one asked.

'Not going to take any more cash off you, bro,' Pearce said. 'Don't look like you can afford to lose it.'

The man laughed, gestured at his friend who was already rechalking his cue. 'Boy here's questioning my means.'

'And your skills,' his mate said. 'Be fair, though, I was sinking everything on our side. Should be me and him double or nothing.'

'Nah.' The man took out his wallet, slapped a twenty on the table. 'Me and you, blondie, rack up.'

Pearce shrugged. 'Can't say I never warned you.'

It was a blatant hustle and Ella wondered where Pearce had been before he got to Garton to not see what was happening. All that attitude with no experience to back it up. Maybe that was why there *was* so much attitude. Plain old inadequacy.

Almost six weeks in and he'd not made a move on any of the girls. There was some gossip that he was gay, but Ella knew better; she'd felt his hard-on digging into her side when he took her down during a personal-defence class. He held her pinned to the mat for longer than necessary, smiled at her like an invitation, his knee between her legs. The instructor was barking at someone at the other end of the room and Pearce didn't move.

'You feel that?' he'd asked. 'That's chemistry.'

Ella drove her knee up into his balls and he rolled screaming on to his back, red-faced, tears streaming down his cheeks.

That was when she got her first warning. Dragged into Gould's office and told that violent conduct would not be tolerated under any circumstances. 'You do not hit a man in his tackle, Riordan!' Never mind that Pearce started it. She couldn't prove what he did to her, while his injury was all too obvious.

The next class they were put together again. The instructor telling her, with a smile, to play nice. Ella had been suspicious right away, but she wasn't going to back down and ask to be moved. Pearce might be bigger than her and stronger, but he was unschooled and too arrogant to protect his vulnerable points. He didn't even seem to realise where most of them were.

Wrist, she'd thought. The arch of his foot and back of his knee. Three strikes, maximum damage inflicted without it looking too aggressive. Just like her father had taught her.

But she hadn't got the chance.

First move, Pearce made a blocking motion he later claimed to have misjudged, and hit her in the throat.

Four days ago now but still it hurt every time she swallowed and a hoarse note remained in her voice. Gould bought Pearce's story, backed up by the instructor, and she was supposed to think about whether she was really equipped to deal with the physical intensity of a life in the police force. Whether she had the correct temperament for it.

As if *she* was the one acting out of line.

Across the table Laurel was talking about Aaron, some club he wanted to take her to at the weekend, some hipster place, she said, her eyes widening like it was an exotic suggestion. She was from Taunton, so maybe it was.

'You should come,' she said, fizzing with enthusiasm. 'It could be like a double date.'

'Who with?' Ella asked, already knowing she meant Pearce, but surprised she was stupid enough to suggest it.

'Come on, you know how much he likes you.' Laurel gave her a teasing grin. 'Aaron says he's always talking about you. He's just too shy to ask you out. He thinks you'll shoot him down.'

'I'd shoot him in the face if I could.'

Laurel tutted, but lightly, because she thought it was a joke rather than something Ella found herself fantasising about more and more often.

'Give him a chance, he's actually really good company. I mean, he's hilarious. And look at him, Ella. That body!'

Behind her the sound of balls striking and Pearce swore as he missed his shot. She could feel his presence moving around the table, allowing the other man space to take his turn. She heard his soft but heavy footfalls stopping very close by and noticed Laurel flick a glance towards him before she lowered her voice, leaning in.

'Just come out with us,' she said. 'One date, see if you click.'

Ella leaned in too, felt her bruised windpipe protest. 'He punched me in the throat. You think we're going to click after that?'

'It was an accident,' Laurel said pityingly. 'He's totally gutted about hurting you. I saw him when it happened, he was mortified. Seriously. And he apologised straight away, didn't he?'

'Of course he did; an apology's the most effective way of doing whatever the hell you want to people with no repercussions,' Ella told her. 'If they're stupid enough to buy it.'

Laurel's face hardened but she still looked like a naïve little country girl, Ella thought, all big blue eyes and freckles on her cheeks. She wasn't tough enough for this job. Or smart enough. If she couldn't see Pearce for what he was, she would be eaten up and spat out by the criminals she'd eventually find herself squaring up to.

'He's prepared to forgive you for kneeing him in the balls – don't you think you owe him the same chance?'

Another mis-strike behind her and Pearce moved away. Once again Laurel's gaze strayed towards him for a second.

'It's not like you're going to get a better offer, Ella.' She mugged a concerned frown. 'I mean, no offence, but he's way out of your league.'

'If you fancy him so much why don't you go out with him?' Ella snapped, louder than she meant to. 'I bet him and Aaron would love to go twos on you. I bet they talk about that all the time, too. Who gets the good end and who has to look at your face.'

'You sad bitch,' Laurel said, trying to be cool but she was angry now and Ella was too, shaking with rage that had crept up on her, this conversation tipping her beyond the point of self-control. She dug her fingertips into the edge of the padded stool.

'Me? I'm not the— fuck!'

Her hand went to her spine. The pain immediate and intense, on the point of the bone. She saw a striped red ball land by her foot. Saw Pearce smiling, straightening up from the shot he'd just chipped at her.

'My bad, Ellie.' He gave a big, open-chested shrug, palms up. 'I know you'd prefer my balls on your chin than your back.'

A gale of laughter, Pearce the loudest, but they were all against her. He fist-bumped Aaron, who repeated his joke like an idiot.

'That's a foul,' Pearce's opponent said, pointing at him across the table with his cue. 'And you should buy the lady a drink to apologise.'

Ella heard their debate as if at a distance, blood rushing in her ears, heart rate climbing. Every movement she made felt heavy and deliberate and slowed to half speed; she reached to retrieve the ball from the floor, feeling how snugly it fitted in her palm. She stood, fully focused on Pearce, who was coming towards her with his hand out.

'Need my ball back, if you can stand to part with it.'

Four metres away. The pool table separating them.

She smiled and it felt manic on her face, but he didn't see it. He didn't care about what women wanted enough to bother reading their reactions or studying them for nuance. Another vulnerability that would get him in trouble.

Three metres and they were drawing together at the corner of the table.

Ella's fingers flexed around the ball and then loosened as she let it roll from her palm into the curve of her knuckles.

She saw Pearce's mouth open, didn't hear what he said. Felt more laughter ripple the air around her. She told herself to keep breathing.

Pearce turned towards Aaron, showing her his exposed cheek.

Ella whipped her arm over and threw the ball at his head, expecting to miss, intending it as a warning. But it connected with a sickening crack and he bent double, blood rushing out of his mouth as he looked up at her, his eyes full of adrenaline-fuelled rage.

She couldn't move.

She saw it coming but her legs were frozen, knees locked in place, and she didn't even manage to get her hands up to defend herself before he launched himself at her. He caught her around the midsection, driving the wind out of her lungs, and slammed her down on to the floor. Ella threw her hands over her face, felt his full weight press down on her torso but only for a moment as he snapped back to his feet and then his big boot came down on her ribs.

A scream broke out of her. She turned on to her side and tried to crawl away, but his foot crashed down on her again. It was as if he was trying to stamp right through her body and grind his heel into the carpet she could taste now, on her lips, feel its coarseness and greasy slick against her cheek. She could hear shouting, a man snarling his name, girls screaming.

She was going to die. Here. Like this. After everything. All the hard work. All the sacrifice. She was going to be killed by a man who should have been her comrade, his big boot stamping her ribs to splinters.

No.

No.

She rolled on to her back. Her vision was blurred but she could see him. The smudge of his legs coming towards her again. She kicked out and connected with air, the action sending bolts of pain ricocheting around her ribcage.

He leaned over her and she managed to strike at his face. Too slow. He caught her hand, placed it gently on the floor and held it there, moved in closer, inches away from her face, before she could see him clearly enough to realise it wasn't Pearce but the landlord.

'You're alright, girl, don't move. Ambulance is on the way.'

THIS IS HOW IT ENDS

Ella

Now – 31st March

'You should have a solicitor,' DC Wazir says.

'I don't need one. I haven't done anything.'

Wazir doesn't like it and Ella knows her boss won't either. The solicitor isn't really for you, it's for them, especially when you take whoever's on the duty roster, some stranger who doesn't know you and doesn't care about your fate. They won't do any more than the bare minimum. But their presence serves the investigating officer because it guarantees that everything has been done properly.

Without a solicitor she could claim coercion later. Or worse.

She won't do that. Her escape route is nothing so common as playing the victim, but she feels sure she won't need it. Not this time, anyway. This is a fishing expedition and as long as she stays cool, stays composed, then she'll learn more from them than they'll learn from her.

Because the problem with detectives, especially the ones like Wazir, who's probably been underestimated her whole life, is the desperate need to display the intelligence people can't believe they have. Show them disrespect, scratch that raw nerve, and they'll overwhelm you with the evidence of their superiority.

Another life lesson from her dad and Ella doubts he ever thought she'd use it in this context. It was advice to help her climb the greasy pole once she was on the graduate fast track. He'd wanted her to understand how the officers above her worked so she could ultimately take their jobs. He has a Machiavellian streak he's tried to pass on to her and not much of it has stuck, but she's grateful for it in moments like this when she can summon his steady voice in her head and have him talk her through an awkward situation.

Wazir sighs, theatrically, and goes to get her boss.

Ella holds herself straight in the hard, plastic chair, resists the almost overwhelming urge to let out the nervous sigh that is fluttering in her chest. The camera is on, high in the corner, watching over her, and she knows the DI in charge of the case will have the feed playing onscreen in his office, studying her body language, waiting for her to give some small sign that she's weakened and ready to say more than she should.

She tries to look how the Ella Riordan they think she is should look at this moment. Defiant but unconcerned. This isn't her first interview room and, given her activism, she doesn't expect it to be her last. Just the price of making your voice heard, standing up for others, taking the establishment's heat.

Inside, the Ella Riordan they don't know she is feels very different.

But she can't let them see the fear churning in her stomach, the sick feeling that has somehow spread to her bones and skin and the fluid inside her spine, every atom of her spinning dangerously close to losing control.

She wants a drink of the water Wazir brought in but doesn't trust herself to lift the bottle steadily. She's dehydrated from being hauled out of bed two hours ago and given nothing since. With a deliberate movement that she hopes looks like boredom, she drags the bottle off the table and uncaps it in her lap, glad she hid the motion when she sees how badly she's trembling. She takes a sip to wet her tongue but no more, knows that if she drinks it all down she'll only feel worse.

They want her to do that. Drink too much, need to pee. Because people will say anything when they feel some urgent physical pressure.

Or, they want her to not drink because dehydration knocks points off your IQ, slows your responses and dulls your recognition.

It's a no-win situation.

She tells herself to stop second-guessing them and focus on what she does know and what she can control.

Ella stares at the wall opposite her. White-painted and pristine, so recently redone she detects a hint of chemicals in the air still, along with the taint of her own body. She's rank from not showering for two days and from living in these joggers and jumper, sweating in them, pacing in them. Forty-eight fitful hours trying to decide whether to call her father and tell him everything.

If she walks out of here today she'll ring him.

Take this as a warning and do the right thing. He's going to be tough on her. She can already picture the depth of disappointment creasing his face and dropping his shoulders. Then she sees him grimace and gasp and clutch his chest.

Shit.

No.

She can't tell him. Not the whole, unfiltered truth. She'll have to decide upon a different truth for him, but she'll have three hours on the train to do that and she's tested several versions out on Molly already, so she knows what doesn't work.

Without thinking she clasps her hands on the tabletop, every muscle from her hips to her skull tensing up at once.

Molly.

This must have come from her. After all her big talk about never grassing and protecting your brothers and sisters, Molly has betrayed her. She should have known. People who are that clingy are always the ones who turn on you the hardest when the time comes. They invest too much in you because it distracts them from the holes in their lives and then, when you don't live up to the idealised version that only exists in their heads, it's all your fault.

But it is her own fault, Ella realises.

Right from the start of this mess she handled Molly badly.

The woman craved emotional connection, to have someone who would stand firm with her in her beliefs and causes. If she'd come clean with Molly as they stood over his body in flat 402, she would have shielded her from the police, because the truth – or the ninety per cent of it Ella could give her – chimed perfectly with Molly's world-view and personal history. It would have bonded them stronger than a thousand hours of sit-ins and marches.

She'd almost done it, too.

As she'd sat there alone, watching the life go out of his eyes, she'd calculated how much she could afford to reveal and what would have to stay secret. She'd tried to predict Molly's reaction based on the direction of her various loyalties and their relevant potency, and decided, finally, regretfully, that they weren't close enough yet for her to be relied upon.

Yes, Molly had covered for her in the past but always with a slight reluctance. She'd seen it the night of the Brighams arson, a split second of fear that made Molly look all of her years suddenly.

Instead, scared and muddled, Ella had settled on an ugly half measure – manoeuvre Molly into helping her get rid of his body and provide her with a credible story for how he died. And then, just when she needed to bind Molly closer to her, she ignored all of her instincts and did the exact opposite: pulled away, dropped out of contact, piled lie upon lie. Giving in to the childlike urge to run and hide and pretend none of it had happened, just stay quiet and wait for the adults to come and tidy up after her.

No wonder Molly turned on her. It's all she deserved.

The interview-room door opens and Wazir comes in, trailed by an improbably tall, middle-aged guy, so pale and insubstantial Ella feels she can see straight through him. He folds himself into the seat opposite her and says nothing as Wazir performs the formalities in her brisk fashion. But he keeps watching Ella. His long fingers twitch on the frame of the tablet he's brought with him, as if he can't wait to show her what the device contains.

Ella meets his gaze, sees the hunger in his eyes, despite the stony expression.

Her stomach gurgles and she resists the urge to apologise, states her name for the record at Wazir's prompt.

He does the same. DCI Sean Naysmith. London accent, or Estuary at least.

'Before we begin, I would urge you to reconsider continuing without legal counsel present,' he says.

'I don't need a solicitor,' Ella replies. 'I haven't done anything wrong.'

Naysmith's eyebrows lift very slightly and he touches the knot of his tie, straightening it needlessly. 'If you change your mind at any point, make sure you speak up, Ms Riordan.'

Suddenly she wants to speak up, so urgently she has to press her lips tight together. Say the magic words and make all of this stop, but it's too soon. There's still a chance she can get out from under what she's done. Who she's killed.

Wait, she tells herself. You might be okay.

'Can you identify this man for us, please?' Naysmith asks, pushing the tablet across the table to her.

The face onscreen is several days dead, the skin discoloured, marbled with veins full of blood gone bad, bloated beyond recognition for a casual acquaintance.

But Ella knew him better than that. Would have recognised him by the line of his lower lip or the way the tip of his nose turned up and narrowed almost to a point, an oddly feminine quirk for such a masculine man.

This will not be okay.

'Um...' She forces herself to keep looking at the screen, feeling revulsion, which she hopes they read as a reaction to the shocking sight in front of her. She presses her knuckles to her mouth. 'I'm sorry, this is – I think you could have warned me.'

'You must have seen this sort of thing during your police training,' Naysmith says coolly.

'She didn't get that far,' Wazir chips in. 'How long did you last, Ella? Six weeks, was it?'

Ella doesn't answer, keeps staring at the image onscreen, remembering how close that snub nose had been to her own, how hot his breath bloomed across her face as he shouted at her, his hand clamped around the back of her neck, rough-skinned and stronger even than she thought he was. She remembers the rage boiling off him, the sharpness of his sweat and how she knew he would kill her. If she didn't stop him.

But they wouldn't care about that.

Better the innocent dead victim than the live one whose guilt is up for debate. So much messier to be guilty and innocent at the same time.

'Are you going to pretend you don't know him?' Naysmith asks, propping one icepick-thin elbow on the table.

'I don't recognise this man,' Ella says.

Naysmith reaches over and swipes the screen. 'How about now?'

The same upturned nose and full bottom lip stretched into a broad grin.

'Name eluding you?' Wazir asks. 'Funny that, considering how many times you used it to register complaints against him.'

She has a few sheets of paper stapled together and she makes a show of looking through them.

'This is a good one – from the statement you made on April the seventh 2015, after he put you in hospital with two broken ribs. "Adam Pearce is not fit to wear the uniform of Her Majesty's Constabulary. He represents everything that was wrong with previous generations of police officers and, if you want to move forward into greater diversity and cooperation with the general public, you cannot allow a man as dangerous as Adam Pearce to represent you, out there, on the streets."'

Ella listens to the words her father had written for her, the ones she'd spoken in that dreary wood-panelled room, which wasn't a court but still laid down sentences and doled out punishment. They were part of another life, had been spoken by another Ella Riordan, and now they were returning to haunt her.

Just like Pearce had.

He was at the back of the party crowd when she spotted him from her milk-crate stage, the only person not clapping as she finished her speech, his face lit by one of the paper lanterns swinging in the breeze.

266

'You got him put out of training,' Wazir says, relishing every word and the implications behind them. 'Adam had wanted to be a copper since he was four years old. Did you know that? His mum told us all about it. Her dad was a copper, too. Adam idolised him.'

Ella thinks of him taking another drink from his bottle of beer, the contempt he managed to project across the roof at her. So potent she took an involuntary step back off the crates and would have fallen if Molly hadn't caught her. Everyone thought it was the drink. But she was completely sober. The alcohol neutralised by fear and adrenaline.

Wazir is still talking, Naysmith apparently happy to let her take the lead. A good copper, some old part of Ella's brain thinks admiringly, letting his subordinate finish the job she started, enjoy the glory of nailing the murderer.

'It's quite clear from your complaint here, and the numerous ones brought before he attacked you, that Pearce was a violent individual.' Wazir changes tone. 'Do you want to tell us what happened, Ella?'

She doesn't.

'You were suffering from PTSD for some time after he attacked you,' she says, more paperwork in her hand. Medical-looking. 'I understand it's quite common for people with PTSD to act in unpredictable ways when they're faced with triggers. Like seeing their attacker again.'

Seeing him, she thinks. Being dragged down a set of stairs by him, along a hallway, trying to reason with him, find out what he wanted so she could give it to him and go back to her new and better life. Naively assuming that he was someone who could be negotiated with.

'You must have been terrified,' Wazir says softly.

Terrified was good. Terrified dredged up an offer that cut through his rage and slackened his hold on her arm.

'People will understand, Ella.'

Meaning a jury. Not all people. Just the twelve who could convict her and put her away for a very long time.

'Was it self-defence?'

Ella looks at Wazir, sees the desperation masquerading as concern, and knows she's put this together herself, is staking her future on being right because, if she isn't and she's harassed ex-ACC Alec Riordan's daughter without being able to prove her case, it'll be the end. A few phone calls between old pals and an indelible black mark will be stamped on Wazir's record.

Ella knows the look because she's that young woman too.

If things had played out differently after the hearing maybe they would have ended up working together. They would have hated each other, of course. Too similar, she thinks, and too ambitious. The kind of colleagues who were smart enough to give the appearance of full and complete cooperation while they sharpened special blades for one another's ribs.

Yes, Wazir's scared but Naysmith isn't. Which means this isn't a punt. His experience is showing and Ella trusts it.

'It would be better for you to own up now,' he says. 'A full confession, Ella. I think you acted in self-defence and then you panicked and hid his body. Which is entirely understandable given the circumstances. And, in all honesty, I feel a great deal of sympathy for you and I'd like to help you. But, I can't do that unless you tell us what happened.'

Lies.

Obviously.

Ella knows what she's done and that the post-mortem will have given them a very good idea of how the murder unfolded, too. Even the most expensive barrister would struggle to spin that into self-defence.

The first blow; maybe she could pass that off as an accident. He'd come at her, but after last time she was expecting it. And she was not that girl any more, the one who froze. She was stronger and faster and better drilled. So when he charged towards her she spun away and used his own momentum to turn him towards the fireplace, sticking out a foot, which upended him and sent him head first into the tiled hearth with a sickening crack.

That was somewhere between an accident and self-defence.

'It wasn't an accident, though, was it?' Wazir asks.

Ella wonders how long they've been sitting here in silence. She glances towards the clock and sees that almost an hour has passed since the interview began and yet it feels like minutes. She's losing perspective. Losing control.

'One blow – that's accidental. Self-defence? Okay.' Wazir taps her inky-painted fingernails against the file. 'But it wasn't one blow, Ella. It was three. At least.'

She'd lost control then, too.

Four blows. The first an accident. Almost. The rest – with her hands gripping his ears through his knitted beanie, which slipped as she slammed his skull against the hearth – they were the actions of a person she didn't recognise. Not New Ella. The one who gave interviews to the *Guardian* and hosted literary evenings at Foyles, the one who sat with old ladies she barely knew, reading to them because they weren't able to since their stroke and they missed their Maeve Binchy stories.

Not even Old Ella did things like that.

When *she* was attacked, she froze and let the boot strikes rain down on her.

Whoever killed Pearce was someone else altogether. The version of her most capable of escaping from this filthy mess.

Ella looks between them; triumph on Wazir's face, curiosity on Naysmith's. She licks her lips, tastes copper where the thin skin has split and bled.

'I want to speak to DCI Joe Dylan. I won't speak to anyone else. You need to bring Dylan here, right now.'

Molly

Now – 31st March

From my balcony I watch the Frears packing their belongings into a rented van. Derek is helping them because visiting hours are over and he doesn't want to be in the flat alone, I guess. I wonder who'll help him when the time comes, because I doubt I'll be here to do it and he's not a man with a lot of family or friends. All of that fell by the wayside when he married Jenny. He's dedicated to her in a way I can't help but envy.

And it makes me miss Callum all over again.

Tomorrow morning it'll just be me and Derek left in the building.

For the first time since we started this fight I feel vulnerable. As long as there were half a dozen of us scattered around the place it felt occupied, no matter what state the other flats were in, or if the roof was leaking here and there and some of the windows had been smashed and boarded over.

It's the least of my worries, really, but I can't shake the discomfort.

I light another cigarette and look out across the water, my view partially but ruinously obscured by the metal framework of the Rise 2 tower. No matter where on the balcony I stand, whether I stoop or stretch tall, there is always a strip of grey blocking my sightline. Censoring the view.

Another thing I shouldn't care about.

It's displacement activity. I know that. But what else am I going to do?

I phoned Milton when I got back from Ella's flat but she hadn't called his office for legal representation. Either because she didn't think she needed a solicitor or because she knew she needed a better one. Milton's a pro but he's not going to get anyone off a murder charge.

No mention of an arrest on the local evening news. No mention of the case at all.

For a few minutes I allow myself the indulgence of planning an escape. I could gather together some cash, pack a small bag, and call a taxi to take me to St Pancras, follow the same route Quinn did. Down through France and further south to Barcelona. Join the group he's with or one like it. There are plenty of communes squatting in half-finished tower blocks abandoned by the developers. I speak a little Spanish, I wouldn't mind the heat or the sun or the liberal measures they pour in the bars. Disappearing always appeals to me.

But I won't.

Because I'm not young enough to do that any more. At twenty you can find odd jobs or odd people to keep you until you've adapted to your new situation. At sixty, who's going to help me?

I've used up all my fight.

Ella has drained it out of me. Along with my faith in other people and the previously unshakeable trust in my instincts.

A black cab pulls up in front of the building, its headlights flooding the inside of the removal van, showing up how shabby the contents are and how little the Frears have deemed worthy of continuing into the next stage of their lives.

Martin Sinclair climbs out of the taxi, pauses for a minute to speak to Derek, before he heads inside.

Shit. I'd forgotten about this. The interview he wants to do for his 'definitive history of dissent in the twentieth century'. Questions about Greenham and Molesworth. A look at my portfolio to see if there are any shots he can use. I should never have agreed, but he caught me at a bad time and I said yes just to get him off the phone.

He's brandishing a bottle of good bourbon when I open the door, smiling like this is a social call, which, under different circumstances, it almost would be. I like Sinclair, he's interesting company and he's been a rare high-profile voice of support for the last fifteen years. He's also done a lot more behind the scenes than anyone would give him credit for. More revolutionary than hack once you start scratching the surface.

We air-kiss and I point him to the sofa, where he settles himself while I fetch a couple of glasses. He thinks the drink will loosen my tongue, but I've been locked down hard for weeks and have no intention of saying anything I shouldn't. Not about the past or what's happening now.

Because he'll know. He's too good not to be curious.

'How's the book going?' I ask, pouring generous measures in the mismatched tumblers, handing him the one with the wider base and the larger capacity.

'You're my last interviewee.' He raises his drink in a toast, winks. 'Got you.'

I curl up on the opposite sofa, thinking he doesn't look quite himself this evening. He's always cultivated a dishevelled, down-to-earth vibe, but this is something else. There are bags under his eyes and his usual stubble is now a beard. When he finally shrugs out of his coat, passing his drink from one hand to the other rather than putting it down, I see that his jumper is crumpled and marked at the cuff with what appears to be coffee.

'Have you spoken to Ella recently?' he asks.

'I went to see her earlier,' I say carefully. 'She wasn't home.'

'She's been arrested.' He drains his glass in one mouthful. 'Dawn raid, they pulled her in, stripped her flat. The works.'

I try to look like it's a surprise but realise he's not interested in my reaction. He reaches for the bottle and pours himself another drink, leaves the cap off.

'Did she do it?' he asks. 'You were here that night, you must know.'

'You seriously think Ella's capable of something like that?'

'She's your protégé.'

272

I glare at him but he's impervious. 'What's that supposed to mean?'

'PC Gareth Kelman,' he says. 'Or Chief Constable Kelman now.'

A name I never want to hear again as long as I live and I thought Sinclair was better than this. Throwing it in my face, knowing what memories it would dredge up; the freezing holding cell in the dank basement of that Victorian cop shop. Shit smeared up the walls from the previous occupant, left because they thought it would get to me. My food overturned on the floor when it was delivered. Spittle flying in my face during questioning; threats and slaps and fat fingers tangled in my hair as my head was shoved down hard at the tabletop but stopped just before striking it. And all the while, the bloodstained hammer right there in front of me.

'I spoke to Joy Prior,' Sinclair says. 'She gave me the whole story.'

'Joy's got Alzheimer's,' I tell him, even though he knows that. 'You must have noticed when you were at her nursing home.'

'Yeah, she does. She can't remember her kids' names or whether she's had breakfast, but she's got a perfect recollection of that night. You coming back to the peace camp with blood on your face. Boiling up water on a Primus stove to wash it off before you burned your clothes.'

'That wasn't me,' I say slowly. 'I don't know why, in her sadly muddled brain, she's made it into me, but it wasn't.'

Sinclair snorts. 'It's nothing to be ashamed of, Molly. The bastard had it coming.'

'Too fucking right, he did. And if I'd have done it he wouldn't have got off with a concussion. I'd have smashed his skull flat.' The remembered rage, so long burned away, shocks me with its sudden reignition. 'Is this what you wanted to know about, Martin? Not all the good we did. Not all the shit we suffered and what we managed to grow out of that protest. You want to know about some piece of filth, rapist copper, who got smacked in the head coming out of a fucking bookies?' I slam my glass down on the table. 'Whose side are you on, mate? Because it doesn't feel like you're on ours right now.'

'I'm sorry.' He puts his hands up in surrender, his glass almost empty again. 'This isn't for publication. I'm not recording any of this. I just wanted to know for myself.'

For a few minutes we sit in an uncomfortable silence, not looking at one another, while the building creaks and heaves around us, the sound of a blind fluttering and clattering against a freshly broken window in the neighbouring flat as the wind sucks at its aluminium slats.

Part of me is still there, smelling the metal and the blood, seeing every hair stuck to the hammer head. Part of me stayed there, I think. Something soft and vital. Was it the piece of me that would have called the police rather than colluding with Ella in covering up her crime? Because until then I'd still had a modicum of respect for the law.

When I look at Sinclair again he's staring into his glass and I realise he's scared. Maybe he's concerned about what the police will find when they crack Ella's phone and laptop. Maybe there's incriminating stuff about him on there, friends he's put her in touch with, other groups still operating under the radar who are now in danger of exposure. I know they were close, that he's made as many introductions for her as I have and his contacts would be far more interesting to the police and the services above them.

Perhaps I'm being unfair to him and it's a personal concern that's twisting him up and sending his hand back to the bottle once again. The way he tossed the accusation out there ... was that professional curiosity or hurt speaking?

I think Ella actually liked him; then again, I thought she and I were close too.

'She didn't manage to throw him down that lift shaft on her own,' Sinclair says, shaking the bottle at me.

I hold out my glass and notice how unsteadily he splashes in a double measure.

'How do you know he didn't fall in there?'

'I've got my sources.' He stays hunched forward on the edge of the sofa. 'But I think you know what went on better than any of them.'

'Looking for a scoop, are you?'

'I just want to know what happened.'

'Why?'

'She's my fucking friend, Molly.' He almost shouts it and there's a hint of confession in his tone that makes me suspect they were more than friends. He presses his balled fist over his mouth, taps it a couple of times, working up to something, and I wish I'd never let him in here because I can see my own doubts and fears playing across his face and I don't want to shepherd him through a process I'm still struggling with. The realisation he's been duped by her.

'Okay, let me tell you something I know that I think you probably won't.'

The multiple head wounds, I'm thinking. The impossibility of it being an accident.

'They've identified him,' Sinclair says and I fight the urge to prompt him as he pauses. 'It was a couple of days ago I got this and I don't know why they've not released his name to the press, but I have one theory and it isn't good.'

'Who is it?' I ask, out of patience.

'A guy called Adam Pearce.'

I know the name but I don't know why.

'Ella was at Garton with him,' Sinclair says. 'She must have told you about this – the bloke who attacked her. He got thrown out of training, she left in a blaze of whistle-blowing glory. It's what changed her entire world-view, how the hierarchy there tried to cover up the culture of bullying and the—'

'Yes, I was here when you interviewed her after the demo.'

And I've heard the fuller version from her since and I know that bastard had it coming just as surely as PC Gareth Kelman did.

Why didn't she tell me it was Pearce right from the off? I can already see how it would have played out: he wants revenge because she ruined his career; he tracks her down and attacks her. I understand. I'm not judging her.

That fierce protective drive returns in an unbearable rush and I throw down my drink, thinking of how hard I've been on her, the growing hate I've been nurturing in my breast, and I'm so ashamed of myself for doubting her I could weep.

No wonder she reacted with such violence. She must have been terrified. Alone with him, isolated from the party upstairs, already knowing exactly what he was capable of when others were watching.

My poor Ella.

I snap back to Sinclair.

'Hold on, why do you think the police have delayed identifying him?' I ask. 'Maybe they're just trying to track down his family.'

'His family know already. His mum ID'd his body.'

'Maybe they don't want the bad press,' I suggest. 'Naming him dredges everything up again.'

'He's the victim,' Sinclair says. 'No bad PR in that.'

'So?'

Sinclair knits his fingers together, twists them painfully. 'I think Pearce was an undercover cop. And I think Ella was one of his informants. Unwittingly, maybe. But—'

'No.' I stand up sharply. 'Don't be stupid. Ella might be a lot of things, but she's no fucking grass.'

But even as the words are leaving my mouth I'm thinking of Quinn and Lewis, going down for the Brighams firebombing while she miraculously walked away.

Quinn saying she was there should have been enough to damn her. Even though Lewis denied she was involved. Wasn't it strange that the police took his word as gospel? That she alone out of the three of them didn't leave any forensic evidence at the scene. That I was considered a sound alibi.

It's just how grasses are protected. The focus is shifted away from them. They aren't considered innocent, but there's no appetite to prove their guilt. People around them get caught. They get lucky.

276

I swear into my hands.

'The alibi you gave her for the estate agent's,' Sinclair says, as if he can read my thoughts. 'That was fake, right?'

I stay silent and he nods.

'You still don't trust me. Okay. But the ringleader – Ryan Quinn – he called me from prison a few months back wanting to sell a story about Ella. He said she was a police informant. He gave me a whole list of people who she'd been sniffing around who found themselves suddenly under surveillance. These were people totally unknown to the police beforehand.'

'How did they know they were under surveillance?'

He rolls his eyes at me. 'Come on, Molly. You know.'

He was right.

'When I raised the subject with Ella she fobbed me off with some rubbish about Quinn resenting her success and wanting to cut her down to size because he thought she was just in it for the attention.' A queasy look crosses Sinclair's face and he pinches his ear. 'Four hours after that conversation she suddenly decided I was somebody she found completely irresistible and dragged me into a toilet for a quickie.'

The confession makes him sag where he sits and he looks an older man, his usual boyish confidence cut out from under him. She's toyed with both of us, played on our weaknesses; Sinclair's to be needed physically, mine to be needed emotionally. And we're not people easily fooled, I think. This isn't about our gullibility, is it? It's the scale of Ella's guile.

Sinclair is pouring another drink and I resist the urge to stay his hand over the glass.

'Ella did fancy you,' I tell him. 'I could see it the second she met you. Whatever reason she might have had ... professionally.' That word sticks in my throat, bloated with connotations. 'She wasn't faking the attraction.'

'That's good to know,' he says bitterly. 'But it doesn't change anything. Think about it, Molly: what's she been doing? She makes all these contacts, but she's never really been active. She's not *done* anything. Ella has positioned herself to gather information and feed it out to someone without ever compromising herself or acting illegally.'

'Breaking in to Brighams was highly illegal.'

I'm *still* defending her. I can't seem to stop myself.

'Quinn said he forced her hand. He told her she was acting like a copper and that was what finally made her get on board. If she didn't do the Brighams attack, it would be an admission of guilt.'

I shake my head. 'That's a huge leap, Martin. You can't lay an accusation like that on her with no evidence.'

'But you agree it's possible?'

'Anything's possible,' I say, throwing my hands up. 'I know people who think you're managed opposition run by MI5.'

His phone rings – a distinctive and discordant tone – and I expect him to ignore it, but he says, 'My guy at the station,' before he's even got his mobile out of his pocket.

The conversation is short, barely twenty seconds, and Sinclair rings off with a promise of 'the same as usual'. Meaning some kind of bribe, I guess.

He places his phone on the table, a pained look creasing his brows.

'They've released her without charge,' he says and I feel a moment of elation, my shoulders rising, the tension leaving my muscles. 'Some DCI came and took her away. They were told to give him a copy of the case file. Everything they've got on her.'

I sit before I fall.

Sinclair's face is ashen. 'She's not the informant.'

'No,' I say. 'She's the fucking undercover.'

Ella

Now – 31st March

Dylan hustles her out of the police station the back way. He says nothing as he unlocks a black Range Rover with tinted windows and gets behind the wheel, expecting her to follow without question. Ella climbs in next to him, snaps on her seatbelt and asks where they're going, but gets no reply beyond a shake of the head. He digs a pair of sunglasses out of the door pocket and slips them on before he pulls on to the road.

The vehicle seems wrong for him, she thinks – too brash and muscular – but then, what does she know about him really? Beyond their occasional meetings, she doesn't know what he does with the rest of his time, where he lives, even. If there's a girlfriend somewhere, kids. The thought of him having a family makes her feel sick with guilt.

As they cross the bridge into Westminster, she realises she's been treating this like a game. Savouring the bubble of unreality the pair of them exist in, playing at being the Ella he needs her to be, testing his rules and boundaries and delivering her smartest moves for his approval.

But she doesn't know him and maybe she shouldn't trust him.

Not now she's failed so catastrophically.

'I'm sorry,' she says. 'I thought I—'

'We're way past the point where your apologies count for anything.'

They drive through the centre of the city, the traffic slowing them down and making the painful silence even more acute.

Ella keeps glancing at him, hoping he'll feel her eyes on him and turn, give her something, a small sign of forgiveness or support, but he keeps his head straight, hands rigid on the wheel, as if gripping it is the only thing stopping him from throttling her.

Around them the Saturday-afternoon shoppers are mingling with the Saturday-night revellers, the early starters heading for pre-theatre meals and drinks, late kick-offs and cinema showings to act as a primer for whatever entertainment comes next.

Her night is a terrifying void.

Dylan's got her out of Kennington station but she's still in police custody and this is a far more unpredictable kind. Off-grid, no protection, no cameras and solicitors, nothing on record.

She curls her hand around the armrest, noticing that the doors are unlocked. Nothing to stop her jumping out and bolting.

Except that Dylan has sprung her, which means he owns her now. Running will mean the withdrawal of his support, the reinstatement of her guilt and inevitable imprisonment. Stay, and she might just be able to find her way through this.

Once he's calmed down enough to stand the sight of her and the sound of her voice. Ella hopes being back at the safe house on Murray Street might help. That the memory of all the hours they've spent there together might draw some softer feelings out of him.

But they're not going to Camden, she realises. He heads into Islington and quickly they are on a tree-lined residential street of Victorian houses that have long since passed the seven-figure mark. Lit windows where the inevitable wooden blinds haven't yet been closed, showing well-proportioned and impeccably decorated drawing rooms, happy-looking families inside.

Dylan pulls into a space at the end of the road, tells her to get out of the car.

They walk to a house in the centre of the row and he shoves her up the steps ahead of him, grips her arm as he speaks to the camera on the intercom.

'It's us.'

A few seconds later the front door opens and Peggy Armstrong lets them into her home.

Ella hasn't seen Armstrong since she was been deployed into the field almost two years ago, but her boss looks no different. There are a few more very fine lines around her eyes perhaps, a bit more white in her grey bob. But she's as formidable as ever, even standing barefoot on the wide wooden floorboards, dressed in black yoga pants and a cashmere hoodie, like they've pulled her away from an afternoon ashtanga class. She has a tattoo on the side of her left foot, Ella notices, Sailor Jerry style. A souvenir from her own time undercover, maybe.

'What are we going to do with you, pet?' she says, giving Ella a look of such crushing disappointment that she feels like she might cry.

'It was self-defence.'

Behind her Dylan snorts, mutters something under his breath.

Armstrong's face softens slightly and she squeezes Ella's arm. 'I wouldn't have expected it to be anything else. But it's all the same now, isn't it? A mess is a mess and how it got there doesn't change that it wants cleaning up.'

'I tried—'

'You covered it up,' Dylan snaps. 'Badly. Using an unreliable accomplice.'

'Molly isn't unreliable, she's covered for me this long.'

'Ella's right.' Armstrong turns to Dylan, who's standing near the front door still, like he's working up to walking away from all this. 'If there's one thing we know for sure about Molly Fader, it's that she'll not grass Ella up.'

'Oh, yeah, I forgot; Ella's her surrogate daughter, right?' He smiles, incredulously. 'People turn their *actual* kids in all the time.'

Ella moves to get between Dylan and Armstrong, wanting to be in her eye line.

'This isn't as bad as it looks,' she says, trying to sound calm and reasoned and in control, play-acting like she's been doing for the last two years. But it's different now because these people are her teachers and they'll see through all the tricks they've taught her. 'Once Molly knows who he is she's—'

'You didn't tell her?' Armstrong asks.

'No.'

'Why not?'

'I thought it was best if she thought he was just some nobody.'

'You must have realised he'd be identified eventually.'

'I panicked,' Ella admits, face flushing with shame. 'Then once it was out there, I had to run with it. But, you have to understand, Molly won't care once she knows it's Pearce. She's not going to turn me in. This isn't as bad as it looks. Really.'

'She's completely fucking deluded,' Dylan says, striding past her into an unlit living room done out in copper and teal, like he owns the place.

Armstrong watches him, her jaw hardening.

'Ella, go and get yourself something to eat,' she says, pointing along the hallway. 'I'll call you when we're ready for your input.'

Reluctantly, she goes, hearing the living-room door close softly as she walks into the large kitchen extension at the back of the house. It's a searing white box with a glass rear wall, lined with glossy black cupboards and marble counters, a horseshoe of a low long sofa at the other end of the room. She won't go and sit on it, no matter how inviting it looks and how much her body aches. Instead, she takes a smoothie from the fridge and settles herself on a high stool at the breakfast bar where the Saturday papers have been read and piled up again, pastry crumbs and coffee stains on the headlines. A pair of glasses too big for Armstrong left there alongside a puncture-repair kit.

She wonders where Mr Peggy is and how often she allows her work to intrude on her home life.

He was out the only other time Ella had visited the house, brought around for dinner and a chat about her future. She'd assumed Armstrong was going to try and bribe her into silence and she had, dangling a very tempting opportunity in front of her nose, one that punished Pearce and kicked her career into a far more interesting direction than she ever could have hoped.

And now she's destroyed all of that.

He'd destroyed it for her. Crawling out of the woodwork, challenging her somewhere public so that she only had one option how to respond. If he'd been less impulsive she might have been able to involve Dylan, let him find some way to take Pearce out of play.

But Pearce never gave her a chance to do that, and once he was dead, calling Dylan wasn't an option. She'd sat there in the long minutes after it happened with Dylan's number on her phone screen and convinced herself that if he knew about this he would instantly pull the plug and all her hard work would be wasted.

She'd told herself the work was too important to be stopped. It wasn't about her or Pearce or Dylan; they were all secondary to the job at hand.

Deep down it was shame and self-loathing that stopped her, though. She couldn't bear the idea that he'd been waiting for her to fail and this would confirm every doubt he'd ever had about her. She'd been the same ever since she was small, tearing up her less-than-perfect drawings and hiding every B she scored in a test. Then, older, driving herself into the ground to avoid the ignominy of a 2:1 even as her friends were praying they'd achieve one.

It was a disease, this perfectionism. She'd realised that some time ago but it didn't help to stop the symptoms. Her inability to control the symptoms – the anxiety and stress and bouts of ragged depression – just became another thing to loathe herself for. Another way in which she wasn't quite up to scratch.

That was why she'd called Molly instead of Dylan. Because she knew Molly wouldn't judge her.

Ella rubs her face, tries to concentrate on the here and now.

She can hear them talking through the closed door. Dylan saying more than Armstrong, but that's his way and probably why she's the boss. Ella can't make out the words, only the tone, and it sounds bad.

But Dylan isn't the person she needs.

If she can assure Armstrong of Molly's support, it will change everything. And all she needs to do is tell Molly who they dropped down that lift shaft. Not Quinn, but Adam Pearce, who she doesn't know, has no loyalty to, couldn't possibly care about.

Ella slams her hands down on the marble counter. If only she hadn't panicked in the interview room. If she'd kept Dylan and Armstrong out of this, how much easier would it be to protect herself?

The door opens and Dylan shouts.

'Ella – in here, now.'

Armstrong stands by the fireplace, a large mirror reflecting the room, and Ella catches sight of herself in it, small and cowed, already defeated. She draws herself up, plants her hands on her hips.

'Can I say my piece now?'

'No,' Dylan tells her. 'We're pulling you out.'

She turns to Armstrong.

'Sorry, pet. We can stop you being prosecuted but once that's done you're going to be keeping your head down for a good long while.' Armstrong carefully realigns a set of tealight holders on the mantel, while Ella watches, too stunned to speak. 'It'll be a managed withdrawal, standard practice; you'll start telling people you're depressed, that you can't handle the level of harassment you're suffering. You'll close your social-media accounts with a big song and dance. Go up to stay with your parents for a few weeks and … you never come back to London.'

'And then what?' Ella demands, but she already knows.

A desk job, if she's very lucky, in some out-of-the-way station, reduced to the status of a jumped-up secretary while other, far less capable officers do the important work. More likely, she'll be out of the police altogether, and where will her CV take her? Which version will she be allowed to use? The one with undercover cop on it or the one where she's a burnt-out political activist?

They're dumping her.

From so high up it feels as if the fall is calculated to be fatal.

'There'll be people to help you decompress,' Armstrong says. 'It was always going to happen; everyone comes out eventually. And then you get on with your life.'

284

'This *is* my life!'

Panic seizes her, thinking of all the people she won't be allowed to contact again. Friends lost, just like that, because Armstrong rules it. Genuine friendships, the kind she'd never managed to build at school or university, ones she can't bear to give up even if they're built on lies. What on earth are they going to think of her? What are people going to say?

'I told you, boss,' Dylan says. 'She's been slipping for months. I should have been stricter with her, but I thought she had it under control.'

Ella glares at him. 'I'm fully under control.'

'You've gone native.' He speaks slowly, enunciating each word. 'It happens to everyone, you're not special. Although you've gone off the rails quicker than most.'

'That's not what this is.' Ella looks between them, settles on Armstrong. 'I am under no delusions about the people you sent me to infiltrate. They are not my friends; they are not my comrades. They're the enemy and they're very dangerous.'

'Everyone tries that line when it's time to quit.' Dylan sits down on the teal sofa near the window like he's settling in for a show. 'You think it's what we want to hear but we've heard it before. We've *said* it. You get addicted to the excitement and the freedom of behaving like a criminal without the guilt or the potential legal fallout.' He smirks. 'You can't lie to me, Ella. You're enjoying the life.'

'No, I'm enjoying knowing that I'm doing something worthwhile *with* my life.' Ella presses her hands together. 'This is important work. You know that. Look at what I've given you.'

She spiels out the persons of interest she's identified, most being monitored now, a couple already charged. One woman, she knows for sure, has turned informer against a grassroots hard-left group Armstrong has high on her shitlist as the next general election approaches.

'You can't stop me now. Not when I'm finally getting to the heart of this thing.'

'You murdered a man,' Armstrong says, quietly. 'You're no longer reliable.'

'It was self-defence.'

'I've seen the file, Ella. It was murder.'

'What if I confess?'

Dylan jumps to his feet. Armstrong pushes away from the fire-place, comes quickly across the room with her finger stabbing at Ella's face.

'Don't you dare try and bluff me, lady.'

'I'm not bluffing. I confess, say it was self-defence and take my chances with a jury.'

'You've fucking cracked,' Dylan says, laughing raggedly.

Ella snarls at him, 'Stop trying to undermine me.'

He grabs her arm, steps up close to her face. 'When you're prepared to risk prison to stay in position, it's time to get out.'

Ella shakes herself free of him and goes to sit down in one of the velvet armchairs.

He's right and it's insanity, but it's better than the alternative. With Pearce's record a jury will sympathise with her. Her parents will spring for the best representation and she knows money can buy verdicts. If anything, it might enhance her reputation.

Dylan is squatting in front of her, his hands on her knees, talking in a low and serious voice, but she's not listening, only watching the shapes his mouth makes and how infrequently he blinks.

She hears the slap before she feels it, stinging her left cheek.

'Joe, that's out of order,' Armstrong says, shoving him away.

He apologises to Armstrong, not Ella, as she slowly touches her hand to her face.

'He's right, though, Ella.' Armstrong perches on the low coffee table. 'We should have taken better care of you. This is on us. We didn't realise how deep in you were. But we're going to get you sorted out now. Get you home and all fixed up; there's nothing that can't be sorted with rest and talking things through.'

She smiles and it's supposed to be reassuring, but Ella can see the fear in her eyes.

'With respect, ma'am, you're not looking at the big picture.' Armstrong's smile fade as she catches on. 'If it comes out that I'm an undercover police officer it will take you years to get anyone else in as deep as I am. In all likelihood, you'll never manage it.'

Armstrong sighes. Dylan swears, softly.

But she keeps going.

'I couldn't get in right away, remember?' Ella gestures at Dylan, because he knows, he remembers how frustrated she'd been in the beginning. 'Nobody trusted me. Not until I got attacked by that riot officer. That sealed my reputation.' Ella tries not to look smug. 'You'll never be able to make that happen again. Not after everyone knows about me. And what'll happen in the meantime, while you've got no human intelligence coming out? Nobody's using their phones any more, nobody trusts email or apps, they know their data's stored and accessible within seconds any time you want to look at it. Everyone's going old-school. Word of mouth. Trust you can't earn any way but putting the time in and having contacts that are near impossible to make in the first place. You think you'll get anybody as close to Martin Sinclair as I've got?' She feels a swell of pride, straightening her spine and lifting her chin, thinking how much she's achieved and how quickly, with no help from either of them once she was in the field. 'I'm totally irreplaceable. We all know that.'

Armstrong glances at Dylan, as if he can help. It's all the signal Ella needs.

'I'm not leaving,' she says, rising to her feet, standing impervious. 'And if you pull me out, I'm going to go straight to the press. You said this department had cleaned its act up; let's see if the people agree once I tell them how you used me. How you put me in with a handler who sexually exploited me.'

Armstrong shoots a sharp look at Dylan. 'You fucking idiot.'

'Yeah,' Ella nods. 'Good story, right?'

'You need to shut your trap,' Armstrong says, as she backs away. 'One more word and I'm going to hit you myself. You are *out*. As of this minute. You are going to drop off the edge of the fucking earth, young lady.'

Blood rushes in Ella's ears.

'I want to speak to your boss,' she says.

Armstrong laughs.

'I want to speak to Kelman,' Ella tells her, stepping up closer. 'And he'll want to hear what I have to say.'

'Going to tell him what a cow I've been to you?' Armstrong asks. 'Think he cares what happens to any one little cog in his machine? Don't be soft. You've got nothing to say he'll want to hear.'

Ella smiles, trying to look certain as she makes her last wild play. 'I know who attacked him. Back in eighty-four, coming out of the bookies. Not only do I know, but I can get her to admit it.'

'Molly Fader?' Dylan says.

'Assuming he gave a shit, what makes you think she'll tell you?' Armstrong asks. 'Word is she took days of interrogation that bordered on torture during the original investigation and she gave them nothing. She didn't do it.'

'She did,' Ella says, hoping she's right, that Sinclair's hunch was built on solid journalistic instincts. 'She's as good as told me already, she only needs a push.'

Something wordless passes between Dylan and Armstrong and Ella sees the years of partnership they've shared in that moment. She wonders how it had been when Armstrong was Dylan's handler. If he'd made her proud. How Armstrong had conducted herself in the field. The sheer vexation they're exhibiting now makes her suspect neither ever made a move as audacious as this one.

They go into the hallway, hold a conversation so low Ella can't make out a single word of it as she counts the seconds until Armstrong comes back into the living room.

She shoves her mobile at Ella, looking like she's just been kicked in the stomach.

'He wants to speak to you.'

Molly

Now – 31st March

I offer Sinclair my sofa for the night, but he says he needs to get home, drink a lot of coffee and fire up his laptop. So I call him a taxi and, from my balcony, I watch him drunkenly try and fail to open the door twice before he falls into the back of the waiting vehicle. The bottle he brought is empty now, and I'm not sober but not drunk either. I'm in that odd halfway place where you achieve a specific kind of clarity you wouldn't find anywhere else but in the mix of neat spirits and a sudden and complete removal of certainties.

It's almost midnight.

Tomorrow, Sinclair is going to run a story about police infiltration of the anti-gentrification movement. No names, just 'sources close to x' and 'sources within the police say'. He'll mention a murder suspect being whisked away from the interrogation room of a south London station in a blacked-out Range Rover and a family who are already finding their fight for justice stymied by back-room deals.

Because the Pearce family know something is amiss; they're a police family, one generation removed, and their unthinking trust in the force is fast being eroded. They're ready to talk to every media outlet that will listen, about their dead boy who they know in their hearts was murdered but who the police are now suggesting might have died 'by misadventure'.

Sinclair's source called again with that fresh detail while we were staring at each other across the table and trying to find a reason for Ella's get-out-of-jail-free card that doesn't rely on her being an undercover officer.

We couldn't think of one and once we knew the narrative was being changed, there was no more space for hope or denial.

Ella Riordan, who I trusted and admired and, yes, loved like my own blood – *my* Ella, is an undercover police officer.

And now I know, I wonder how I ever trusted her.

The assistant chief constable's daughter. Durham, Trinity, Garton. The girl who dropped out of training because she'd been attacked by a fellow recruit and couldn't stand the culture of bullying and the system that had tried to silence her when she reported it.

How perfect was that cover?

Maybe that's why Pearce came after her. Because a decision was made to sacrifice his career to establish her legend. It's not a new tactic. In fact, it's so old school that I thought they'd moved on to more high-tech approaches. Hacking us, monitoring our phones. Why did the police need Ella when ninety-nine per cent of the people she made contact with shared everything they were doing on social media anyway?

For the other one per cent, I suppose.

The Quinns of the movement and the Carols. And me, maybe.

I'm the one she got closest to; that had to mean something. Am I their target? Do the police think I've been a naughty girl? Naughtier than I really have? They're about ten years too late. As much as it pains me to admit it. I've not taken part in any serious direct action since I learned my lesson at Greenham Common.

The first bona fide crime I've committed in years was helping Ella dump a murdered man's body. Which, I guess, given her job, means I'm the victim of entrapment.

And Sinclair the victim of a honey trap.

He's arguably the biggest scalp of all. I can imagine Ella's paymasters salivating at the prospect of placing her close to him and his Europe-wide circle of contacts. A whole network of activists and intellectuals opens up to them through Sinclair, from boys throwing Molotov cocktails at the police on the streets of

Athens to Whitehall's twenty-first-century Kim Philbys leaking information to the press rather than foreign governments.

Perhaps it was always about Sinclair. When I think back to their first meeting and how quickly she fixed on him, it makes sense.

Ella should have known better. Her handlers should have taught her better.

Never cross a hack.

The silly girl. If she wasn't so young and inexperienced she might have known that. A man like Sinclair will be as loyal as a dog, until you give him reason not to be; then he'll turn around and tear your throat out.

I'm glad he's going to do it.

I don't know if I have revenge in me. Even though every bone and sinew and muscle in my body is screaming out for it. I want to slap her, pull her hair and choke her. I want to drop her down the lift shaft and listen to her body break at the bottom, leave her there to rot. But it wouldn't come close to matching the pain she's put me through.

The last few weeks have been torture, but now, sitting here staring at the empty glasses on the table, I realise that pain was merely a warning rumble, a twinge, in comparison to how I feel, knowing the absolute depth of Ella's betrayal. It feels like everything has been scooped out of me, my body scraped away from skull to womb, leaving me an empty, nothing person.

If I smashed one of those glasses and cut myself I'm not even sure I'd bleed.

I know I wouldn't feel the cut. I can't feel anything.

And I hope this never goes away because I'm scared what the return of full sensation will bring with it. How much fury will ride in on that wave?

I'm not a calm or forgiving person. I know I can be dangerous.

I've hurt people badly for less than what Ella has done to me.

She's used me.

She's insinuated her way into my life, playing on my sympathy, exploiting my beliefs. The things that have driven my life for longer than she's been alive, my version of religion and family and vocation. She burrowed in like a tick and drained me for useful information.

Now I'm thinking of every protest and demonstration we went to and the friends who were arrested. Did she do that? Did she provide lists of agitators beforehand, brief someone with photographs and extensive details on their alliances and weaknesses and pet projects? Was that why some quiet people were nicked and some loud ones left behind? Because Ella said so?

Nobody's safe any more.

Tomorrow, when Sinclair's piece runs, they'll know that.

And they're going to hate me for bringing this poison into our group. Throwing my thirty years' standing behind someone I trusted too easily.

I'll be cast out just as surely as Ella will. Except there's no real life for me to return to. No back-up or safety net. Not even Callum any more, who might have been a fresh start away from all this if he hadn't been hiding too.

A tentative knock at my door and I know it's her before I hear her voice.

I open up to find her staring at the floor, her hair sticking greasily to her head, her clothes ripe with body odour and not warm enough for her to have come across London in them, not even on public transport.

She wasn't on public transport, I realise, as I step back to let her in. If she's been released from custody then her handler will have taken over and there's a high probability that he brought her here. The fact that she came without washing or changing first makes me think she's scared.

But can I take any of this at face value? None of her is real or true and I need to stay mindful of that.

'Are you OK?' she asks, sitting down on the sofa and noticing the glasses. 'You've had company.'

'Just Derek.' I gather the bottle and glasses and dump them in the kitchen. 'He was worried about Jenny, so I got him drunk. He'll sleep at least, the poor old bugger. Do you want coffee?'

'No, I've had quite a lot today already.'

Which might be why she's so jittery or it might be a lie to excuse those jitters.

'Please, will you just sit down and let me say this?'

I stand over her for a moment, enjoying her discomfort. 'Are you finally going to come clean?'

Ella blinks rapidly and I take a seat before she reads too much into the question. She's still coiled and volatile-looking, sitting with the cuffs of her jumper drawn down over her knuckles.

'I do need to come clean with you. I should have been honest with you right from the start, but...' A helpless look flashes across her face. 'I don't know, I thought the more you knew, the more trouble you'd be in if it all came out.'

She's looking to me for a cue and I have to give her it.

'Was it Quinn?'

'No, of course it wasn't,' she says, grinding her fists together. 'Adam Pearce – I told you about him. We were at Garton together. He was the reason I left.'

'The bloke who beat you up.'

She nods, swallows so hard it looks like it hurts. This pain might be genuine. It might be the only moment of honesty I'll see from Ella tonight and I feel for her, despite myself. An old impulse, I remind myself, is rooted in lies.

'At first I thought he was here because he wanted to have a go at me. He got chucked out of training – my fault, right? I shat all over his dreams of becoming a detective.' She sniffs. 'I thought he was going to beat the crap out of me. Worse. I was terrified when I saw him waiting for me in the stairwell. But I couldn't run.' A slow blink as she shakes her head. 'It was just like last time: I froze. He dragged me into the flat and I thought, this is it, I'm dead. But he was smiling, like genuinely happy. And he goes, "Bet you didn't expect to see me again."'

Some of this must be lies and some of it true, but I don't know where the line is and I'm not even sure it matters. Because these are just details. I know what she is and what she did and I'm not even sure why I'm playing along, except out of a sick sense of fascination and the thrill of having the upper hand over her, finally.

Now I'm the one with the secret.

'Molly, he tried to recruit me.'

'For what?'

'He never left training,' she says incredulously. 'Can you believe that? They told me they'd booted him off the force, but he just went off to some other facility and got trained up as an undercover officer. He'd been on drug gangs but they brought him out to start looking into us because they thought we were dangerous.'

I laugh at her performance, but she thinks it's at the idea of our inflated status and I'm happy to have this moment's relief.

She's got it all worked out.

If I hadn't spoken to Sinclair I might have believed her. She understands me enough to formulate a story I'd buy, under usual circumstances, and that makes me wonder how many other times she's done this. Am I going to spend the rest of my life endlessly unpicking half-remembered conversations, trying to decide what was true and what were lies?

'The weird thing is, he never tried to talk me around. I thought they were supposed to charm you.' The irony makes my head pound. 'But Pearce just went straight to the threats. He said he had information about Brighams that could induce the CPS to look at the attack again and maybe they'd decide to prosecute me.'

'That wasn't much to threaten you with,' I say. 'The case hadn't changed. They wouldn't have had enough evidence to reopen it.'

'Quinn spilled,' she says, her nostrils flaring. 'He'd been keeping back records of our conversations so he could strike a deal if he ever needed to. That's how he got released early. He grassed on me and God knows who else.'

I almost want to applaud.

Stand up and give her the ovation this performance deserves.

'Pearce said I'd have to pass full information back to him. He was talking about building up a complete network of players in the anti-gentrification movement.' She brushes her hair out of her eyes. 'I told him to go fuck himself. Obviously.'

'That was brave.'

'I was drunk.' She smiles, sadly. 'Then he said I wouldn't be the only one going away for Brighams. You gave me a false alibi, so you'd be looking at a stretch too. He said he'd make sure they put you somewhere rough.'

Ella shakes her head and are those the beginnings of tears in her eyes?

'I couldn't have lived with myself if that happened,' she says. 'Me? Okay. I made a stupid, egotistical decision. But you were only trying to help keep me safe.'

Now I'm supposed to look grateful. I reach across the table and hold her hand for a few seconds, squeezing her fingers before I settle back.

'Were you tempted?' I ask.

'No. I was furious.' She twists into a new and more defensive shape on the sofa. 'Shit. Maybe I should have just done what he wanted. I could have controlled him, couldn't I? Fed him rubbish.'

'You wouldn't have got away with that,' I tell her. 'Undercovers cost money; they have to take results back to their bosses or they get moved on.'

Ella purses her lips and I wonder if I've hit close to home.

'It would have got him off my back, anyway,' she says. 'He'd still be alive and none of this would – have – happened—'

The tears come freely and loud; she grips the back of the sofa, white-knuckle tight. Reluctantly, I go over to her again, because that's what I would do, and I stroke her shoulders and brush her hair behind her ears when it sticks to her wet face. This is real. These tears. But they're not for this moment.

She must be terrified. The police have caught up with her and maybe the department that runs her doesn't have enough clout to make a murder charge go away. Not for somebody as inconsequential as her. It isn't like she's stopping terror attacks or telling them where hundreds of millions of pounds of cocaine's coming into the country.

She's small fry.

And I bet she hates that.

'I can't live with this, Molly,' she sobs, finding my hand and gripping it tight. 'I hate myself so much. I keep thinking about it. I'm never not thinking about it.'

'But it was an accident, right?'

Ella springs off the sofa and walks a few steps away, arms folded. 'No. It wasn't. I'm sorry. I lied about that too. I wanted him dead. I knew exactly what kind of man he was and I couldn't stand the idea of him having power over me. He was going to abuse that power. He made that perfectly clear.'

She's standing in front of the photo wall now. Blocking out the image of herself hanging there.

'I know I was right,' she says wildly. 'But I can't live like this any more.'

'It gets easier,' I tell her.

Something glimmers in her shining wet eyes. Something sly and out of place.

'You don't know that,' she says. 'You're just trying to make me feel better.'

'I do know.'

There it is again. Hope.

'No, you feel guilty about helping me,' she says. 'But you don't have his death on your conscience. I nearly ended it today. I had the pills lined up on the table but I couldn't do it. My mum called and we talked for about half an hour and she didn't suspect a thing. Can you believe it? I was sitting there listening to her and I was crying but she didn't ask. I don't even think she noticed. How can that be right? A mother not realising?'

'Not all women have a maternal instinct.'

'You're right, she was never any better. You've been more of a mother to me than she has.'

The feeling of a slim blade cutting into my heart; actual, physical pain. I'd wanted to hear those words for so long, and some small part of me, the weakest, most needy part, almost believes them even though the rest of me knows better.

I need to stay hard.

She's lying. She spent the day in police custody. She hasn't spoken to her mother. She hasn't sat in front of a line of pills.

Ella has manoeuvred us to this point. She wants something, but I don't know what.

If I wait, maybe she'll show me. I can see the desperation on her, how she flexes her toes inside her trainers and chews the inside of her cheek.

Is she just trying to ingratiate herself again?

Does she honestly believe this situation is recoverable?

Or is it me? Does she want to take me down with her?

It can't be the murder because this has been one long confession on her part.

She turns her back on me, peers at the photograph hanging next to her own; Greenham Common, three police officers carrying a woman away, her small child torn from her grasp and dumped on the ground, left crying for her.

'I always wonder where this kid is now,' Ella says, glancing over her shoulder. 'Do you know what happened to her?'

Ella

Now

'Him, not her,' Molly says, rising from the sofa and coming over to the gallery wall. 'No, I don't know what happened to him. Oona – his mother – dropped off the scene after that. She wouldn't even come back to the camp to collect him. I took him to her parents' house and she picked him up from there.'

Ella's heart is hammering. They're so close, Kelman there on the wall in front of them, holding the woman's shoulders as she's hauled off towards the waiting van. Less than a week later he was the one being lifted from the ground by uniformed men, bleeding and unconscious, not expected to survive the journey or the night.

Ella wets her lips, tries to sound casual. 'Why did she stop protesting?'

'Because she was assaulted,' Molly says, tapping the photo. 'By that bastard. PC Gareth Kelman. It happened while she was in a holding cell. He told her not to bother reporting it because she was just some stupid dyke and nobody'd believe her.'

'Did she report it?' Ella asks.

'No.'

'Why?'

'Because back then the police had all the power.' Molly turns away, but Ella catches a hint of satisfaction crinkling her heavily painted eyes. 'Nobody would have believed her. We were hated, Ella. You've got no idea. We were seen as disrupting the natural order because we were out protesting rather than playing the dutiful wifeys and girlfriends.'

Molly's drifting off-track into one of her speeches about patriarchy and how they'd dealt it a heavy blow, just by refusing to be called home when it was time to make dinner. Ella needs to bring her back to Kelman.

'So, he got away with it?' Ella asks. 'Like Pearce did with me.'

'Neither of them got away with it.'

Across the room Molly is searching down the back of the sofa, an unlit cigarette hanging from her bottom lip. She plunges her hands between the cushions, comes up with loose change and a hair clip and stops when she brings out a small wooden-handled pocket knife.

Callum's, Ella guesses, but she doesn't ask, because that would only drag them further away from where she needs to be. She pretends she hasn't noticed and watches out of the corner of her eye as Molly puts it back where she found it.

'What happened to Kelman, then?'

'Hmm?' Molly starts going through her desk drawers, rattling the contents. 'What about what now?'

'Kelman?' Ella asks, sure she's given something away by the inflection she put on the first syllable. 'Did he do it to someone else? Did they report him?'

'He'd done it to others before Oona. Three that we knew of for sure, maybe others. A lot of women came and went, only stayed for a few weeks, and lots left after being arrested, so...'

She lets out a triumphant growl when she finally finds a lighter under the cushion on her leatherette office chair, but after four strikes without a flame, she tosses it into the bin and resumes her search, heading into the kitchen.

Ella closes her eyes for a moment, feels the nervous griping in her stomach and the sensation of fear, like a heavy hand, wrapped around the back of her neck. This is it, her one chance, make or break. She takes a deep breath, hearing Molly swearing in the kitchen, exhales slowly.

'But surely if several of the women could corroborate each other's statements somebody would have had to listen to them,' she says.

'Who'd listen?' Molly asks, stalking out of the kitchen. 'The press? They weren't any better.'

There's a strange energy sparking around her. She's moving differently, almost prowling, the way Ella has seen her behave on demonstrations, like she can drop thirty years off her body at will, and revert to that wild and lethal young woman she'd once been. The one in the book Martin Sinclair showed her.

This is who attacked Kelman and, seeing the transformation happening in close quarters, constrained by the dimensions of the flat, Ella can believe she did the deed.

She hadn't believed it before. Not entirely.

When she'd struck her deal with Kelman three hours ago, in the living room of Peggy Armstrong's Islington townhouse, she was just hoping for the best. Now, Molly's back there in her memory and her movements are giving her away.

'I don't understand,' Ella says. 'How do you mean, "neither of them got away with it"? Do you mean, like, karma caught up with him?'

Molly hauls the sliding door open on to the balcony.

'Oh, Ella, kitten. Not karma. Karma's a lie the system sells people so they don't fight back. More "the meek shall inherit the earth" bollocks. You have to be the *agent* of karma if you want to see it take someone down.'

She goes out on to the balcony and a moment later Ella hears a lighter strike and sees a small red point burning through the reflection of the room laid across the glass door.

When Molly doesn't come back inside, Ella goes out to her, finds her leaning on the wall, looking across the river.

'Kelman was attacked,' Molly says. 'Hit in the head with a hammer.'

'Did he die?'

'No.'

'Shame.'

'Yeah. If I had my time again I'd have hung around and finished the job. Or maybe I'd have used a bigger hammer.' She turns to Ella and smiles. 'You know what's funny, though? Someone saw me. Some guy out walking his dog. He clocked Kelman's uniform and he just nods at me, and goes, "Nice one, girl." He could have identified me in a flash, but he hated the police so much he never went to them with what he saw.'

Ella grins at Molly, who reads it as amusement rather than the relief it really is and starts to laugh, keeps laughing so hard that her eyes began to water. When she finally stops, she wipes her face dry, smearing her kohl liner across her temples, like warpaint.

It doesn't feel how Ella expected.

There's no elation but no guilt either. She guesses this numbness is a defence mechanism her body has triggered to keep her going until she's away from Molly. She knows that later she'll be a mess, because despite everything, she and Molly have been close. Molly *has* been like a mother to her in some ways. It's not a lie. She'll miss her when she's locked up.

And that's going to happen. The deal she's struck depends on it.

Kelman gets his closure and in return he lets her stay out in the field.

Initially there was some resistance over the feasibility of her plan but Ella had the angles all worked out. This recording she's making, via a pin-sized microphone inside her collar, will never go into evidence. Molly can never be charged with Kelman's attempted murder because that would compromise Ella's position.

But the Pearce family need closure too: a trial and a guilty party, and that will be Molly. While Ella's samples will become corrupted in a private forensics lab with a notoriously bad track record, Molly's will be found to match DNA on his body. The distinctive red fibres from the coat she wore to the party recovered from his clothing and hair.

And Molly will take the fall because the alternative is both of them being sent down, and she won't let that happen. Molly won't grass or cut a deal to get her own sentence reduced. It's not in her nature. She wants to save people. Do the right thing by her friends, even if it means throwing herself to the wolves.

301

Ella watches her struggling to get another cigarette lit in the swirling wind blowing up off the site and reaches out to cup her hands around the flame.

Prison won't be too hard on Molly, she thinks. She's used to being among other women; she prefers their company, especially the damaged sort she'll find in there. It will be the family Ella's sure she's always craved, the unconventional kind, thrown together in adversity and bonded in defiance.

And she'll make sure Molly is as comfortable as possible. Visit her whenever she can, take in books and magazines, give her money so she can buy whatever perks are on offer inside. It might even be better for her than what's coming on the outside: losing her home, being forced out of the city into some dreary suburb far beyond the M25. Molly has told her often enough that she'd rather be dead than leave London and Ella believes her.

Molly is looking at her, squinting through the heat rising off her cigarette as she inhales.

'Kelman's in charge of Special Operations now, isn't he?'

A sensation like plunging into icy water.

'That's what Sinclair told me, anyway.' Molly turns to face her full on, wearing a smile of grim satisfaction. 'Which would make him your boss, right?'

She can't speak.

'Are you recording this conversation?' Molly asks, moving in close, bringing her mouth towards Ella's collar. 'Is he listening right now?'

'This is mad,' Ella forces the words out, hearing how weak they sound. 'Molly, I know you've been under a lot of stress the last few weeks but this is pure insanity.'

'I thought so too. But Sinclair worked the whole thing out. You should never, *ever*, fuck with a hack, Ella. They have vindictive natures and the best sources. He knew you were an undercover copper way back, but he's been biding his time, gathering the evidence.'

Molly jabs her fingers in Ella's face and she recoils from the tip of the cigarette.

'It's all going to come out and there's no lie big enough or smart enough to get you out from under this.'

Ella can't stay standing much longer. She wants to drop into a protective crouch, curl up and hide. But Molly keeps coming towards her, one determined step after another.

'I trusted you.'

It's over.

'I vouched for you.'

She's lost.

'I helped cover up a *murder* to keep you safe.'

The wind is rising, battering her face. She thinks of Dylan, listening to this, and wonders if he's happy that she's failed or if he feels sorry for her. Did he ever feel anything for her? Armstrong's going to be furious. Kelman even more so. They've given her a chance none of them thought she deserved and she's blown it.

She isn't the best. No more top of the class. No more sharp operator.

Adam Pearce has got his revenge on her, finally. Dead as he is, he's won.

'Was it always about this?' Molly asks, swollen with fury, taller and more menacing than Ella has ever seen her. 'Did Kelman put you in the field to get close to me so I'd confess?'

There are no more moves left.

'After all these fucking years, he still wanted to get me.'

Maybe one.

One last desperate play.

Ella cocks her head, leans towards Molly. 'You really do have an overinflated opinion of yourself, don't you?'

Molly bares her teeth, like an animal.

'We were never interested in you. You're a nobody, a hanger-on.' Ella sees the hurt begin to shrivel her. 'We wanted Carol. She was my target right from the start. You were just somebody who could get me to her.'

'Then you failed,' Molly snaps. 'Because she never trusted you.'

303

They're toe to toe, breathing in each other's exhalations and the smell of fear coming off one another's bodies. Ella shifts her weight, plants her feet firmly, trying to ignore the weakness in her knees.

'Maybe not, but you trusted me, Mol.' She shakes her head. 'How the hell did you last so long being such a sucker?'

Molly lashes out and Ella grabs her as the slap connects with her cheek, not painful enough to break her momentum. She slams Molly into the waist-high wall and hears all the air rush out of her lungs. She buckles, groaning. Her full weight falls against Ella and she grits her teeth as she shoves Molly against the wall again. Molly tries to brace herself. She knows what's coming.

'Are you going to kill me, Ella?' Desperation in her voice.

Ella ignores her, keeps shoving and hoisting, trying to find the extra power she needs to send her over the edge. Molly's boots scrape frantically against the brickwork. She kicks out but Ella holds on to her.

'Getting rid of me changes nothing,' Molly says, her hands closing around Ella's wrists, nails digging in, rings grinding against bone. 'You won't be able to live with it. I know you. You will never have a moment's peace again if you do this.'

She's babbling. But she's right. There's no coming back from this. No stopping the inevitable reckoning. Sinclair's article will still run. The truth will still be revealed.

Ella loosens her grip a fraction, thinking of her parents and how crushed they'll be by this. Then Molly strikes out at her. Snarling, she grabs Ella under the arms and lifts her off her feet with a terrible and furious force.

The sky fills Ella's vision, pink and starless as Molly shoves her over the parapet. She feels the solidness of the wall under her hips and air under her shoulders. Nothing between the back of her head and the ground three storeys below. She throws her arm around Molly's neck, trying to anchor herself.

'You don't get to walk away from this.' Molly's face is tight with rage and contempt. 'You don't get to wreck people's lives and just restart yours like nothing happened.'

Ella twists and wriggles but Molly has her solidly pinned across the wall. The bricks are cutting through her jumper, sawing at her skin as she tries to get free.

'Just think, your copper mates can hear all this but they've not come to help you,' Molly says. 'They're letting this play out, hoping I make their problem go away. That's how important you are to them.'

Ella tries to claw at her face but can't reach. The fight is draining out of her.

This is it.

'You picked the wrong side, sweetheart.'

Molly leans over her, so close that Ella can see every feather mark in her kohl liner and every fleck of gold in her dark-brown eyes. She reaches up and twists her fingers into Molly's hair, turns and knots it around her fist, and she sees the realisation slacken Molly's mouth and feels her stiffen a split second too late.

And they're falling.

Molly

I can't feel anything.

That's a bad sign, right?

I hear the shouts coming along the road and the heavy feet and I can hear Ella still, somehow, breathing next to me, a wheeze on the inhale that tells me one of her ribs has punctured one of her lungs.

Oh.

No.

That's me.

That's me wheezing.

I'm going to drown in my own blood.

Soon, I guess.

A three-storey drop shouldn't be enough to kill you, but from down here on the concrete, my flat looks a long, long, long way away. I never thought she had that in her. Strangely proud, I am. Her mother never taught her that trick; she's learned something from me and I shouldn't be proud because look at what she is. Look at what I let in.

My peroxide changeling. A little blue cuckoo.

The voices are shouting and the feet are skidding to a stop and when I turn my head it's like a boulder falling, so weighty and solid, but I see them crowding around her. A man and a woman and I don't think it's her parents, but that woman is old and I know her from somewhere and I've seen him before too, the one who's got her blood on his hands now, kissing her forehead as he reaches around under her badly mashed skull and comes up with a blacker red on his fingers.

He's from the hospital. I never forget a face.

The boyfriend, is he?

No.

No, a boyfriend wouldn't be here now.

He's her handler. Him or the woman but both cops, because I can smell it on them. That happens when your ribs have cut through your lungs, your other senses become heightened. Yeah, I know what you are, son.

I see you.

Should have smelled it on him way back when I saw him coming from her hospital bed. All that swagger and the furtiveness of a criminal without the jagged edges.

'She'll be fine,' the woman lies.

Neither of us will be fine again.

And that's okay.

I want Ella to die here with me. I hope the ambulance gets stuck in traffic. She doesn't deserve another chance, she doesn't deserve to leave this place she used for her own ends and where she killed Pearce and killed me.

There's blood coming out the back of her head.

He didn't bleed that much and he died.

The man is talking to her. He keeps saying her name like it can bring her to life again. And he keeps apologising, like she didn't do this to herself. But he doesn't know that. They think I did it and I'm happy to let them. Not the legacy I would have chosen, but the right way to round out my stupid existence. Balance my account with the universal.

Kelman I wanted dead, but he survived, and Ella died even though...

The man is crying. Quietly. Crouched next to her.

Callum.

He'd cry for me if he was here, right? He'd hold his hand on my heart and hold his breath as he waited for each new slow beat, hoping it wouldn't be the last. Like this man is doing. Like he loved her.

Like I did.

Like a daughter.

ACKNOWLEDGEMENTS

First and foremost thanks to my brilliant editor Alison Hennessey for encouraging me to write this book when it was nothing but a fire burning in my belly. It takes a very special editor to allow writers to follow their convictions and I'm eternally grateful to Alison for her belief in me, as well as for her unstinting support, guidance and wisdom.

Gushing thanks as well to the whole team at Bloomsbury for the warm welcome and all the hard work they've done to take *This Is How It Ends* from manuscript to book. Special mentions to Ros, Janet, Marigold and Callum. And to Emma Ewbank for creating the perfect jacket for the book to wear as it entered the world. I couldn't have asked for a lovelier lot to work with.

To my indefatigable agent, Phil Patterson, who, among his other virtues, has the admirable knack of always finding a decent boozer in the middle of the day, thanks for everything.

Thanks, as always, to Jay Stringer, Luca Veste and Nick Quantrill, for distraction, advice and an excellent punchline rate.

Special thanks to the wonderful Karen Sullivan of Orenda Books for being a great champion and the most fun on the festival circuit.

The writing life is largely spent in isolation, so the chance to let rip at events is incredibly important and I owe a big thank you to the organisers of the Theakston Old Peculier Crime Festival, Bloody Scotland, Edinburgh International Book Festival, Noirwich, Granite Noir, Newcastle Noir and Hull Noir, for letting me back in their midsts. These events are so important as an author and a book lover and have provided some of the most memorable and pleasurable nights of the year.

As is often said, the crime scene is unfailingly generous and supportive and contains too many fabulous people to thank by name, but the writing life would be much tougher without that special group of deviants who can always be relied upon for support and filthy laughs.

Thanks to all of the marvellous bloggers who have got behind my work and helped bring the books to a wider audience with their thoughtful and perceptive reviews. You do an amazing job. (And cost me a fortune with all your recommendations.)

Finally, to my family, who are there from the earliest germ of an idea to the final, frazzled read-through, with good advice and ideas so stupid they often turn out to be bona fide genius, long lunches and afternoon teas and emergency bottles of dark rum; I could not have done any of this without you and I thank you from the bottom of my heart. You totally rule.

A NOTE ON THE AUTHOR

Eva Dolan was shortlisted for the CWA Dagger for unpublished authors when only a teenager. The four novels in her Zigic and Ferreira series have been published to widespread critical acclaim: *Tell No Tales* and *After You Die* were shortlisted for the Theakston's Crime Novel of the Year Award and *After You Die* was also longlisted for the CWA Gold Dagger. She lives in Cambridge.

@eva_dolan

A NOTE ON THE TYPE

The text of this book is set in Linotype Sabon, a typeface named after the type founder, Jacques Sabon. It was designed by Jan Tschichold and jointly developed by Linotype, Monotype and Stempel in response to a need for a typeface to be available in identical form for mechanical hot metal composition and hand composition using foundry type.

Tschichold based his design for Sabon roman on a font engraved by Garamond, and Sabon italic on a font by Granjon. It was first used in 1966 and has proved an enduring modern classic.